The Regency *Season*

GENTLEMAN ROGUES

MARGARET McPHEE

MILLS & BOON

Published in Great Britain 2017
By Mills & Boon, an imprint of HarperCollins*Publishers*
1 London Bridge Street, London, SE1 9GF

THE REGENCY SEASON: GENTLEMAN ROGUES © 2017
Harlequin Books S.A.

The Gentleman Rogue © 2014 Margaret McPhee
The Lost Gentleman © 2013 Margaret McPhee

ISBN: 978-0-263-93150-1

52-1217

THE
GENTLEMAN
ROGUE

The Regency Season

DANGEROUS DUKES
Carole MORTIMER
August 2017

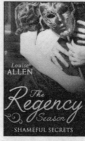
SHAMEFUL SECRETS
Louise ALLEN
September 2017

BLACKMAILED BRIDES
Sarah MALLORY
October 2017

RUINED REPUTATIONS
Mary BRENDAN
November 2017

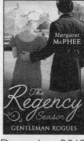
GENTLEMAN ROGUES
Margaret McPHEE
December 2017

PASSIONATE PROMISES
Ann LETHBRIDGE
January 2018

SCANDALOUS AWAKENING
Elizabeth BEACON
February 2018

CONVENIENT MARRIAGES
Sophia JAMES
March 2018

WICKED RAKES
Bronwyn SCOTT
April 2018

HIDDEN DESIRES
Anne HERRIES
May 2018

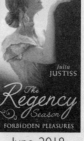
FORBIDDEN PLEASURES
Julia JUSTISS
June 2018

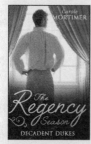
DECADENT DUKES
Carole MORTIMER
July 2018

For Gran & Grandad
and for Agnes & John
With love

Margaret McPhee loves to use her imagination – an essential requirement for a scientist. However, when she realised that her imagination was inspired more by the historical romances she loves to read rather than by her experiments, she decided to put the stories down on paper. She has since left her scientific life behind and enjoys cycling in the Scottish countryside, tea and cakes.

Chapter One

London—August 1811

Emma de Lisle watched the man covertly from the corner of her eye. He was sitting at his usual table, over at the other side of the room, his back to the wall, a clear view of the door. On the table before him sat his pint of porter, his almost-finished plate of lamb chops and, beside it, his faded leather hat.

He moved the small ivory disc over the back of his hand, just as he always did, the trick making the disc look like it was magically tumbling one way over his fingers and then all the way back, forward and back, forward and back in that slow easy rhythm. He sipped from the tankard and seemed comfortable just sitting there on his own, eating, drinking, watching—a part of the bustle of the taproom of the Red Lion Chop-House, and yet not a part.

'All right?' A short brown-toothed man muttered as he passed, giving a sullen nod of his head in the man's direction.

The man gave a nod in return and the little disc disappeared from his fingers into his jacket. Emma had noticed him before. Just as she noticed him now. Because of the way he ran the small ivory circle over his fingers. Because a slice of one dark-blond eyebrow was missing, a tiny scar cutting in a straight line clear through it, and because the eyes beneath those brows were the colour of a clear summer sky. But most of all, she noticed him because he intrigued her.

The faded brown-leather jacket he wore was cracked with age. Beneath the table she knew he wore scuffed boots that matched the jacket. His hat was leather, too, worn smooth, smoky-brown, dark beside his hair. Clothes that had lasted a lifetime, ageing with the man that wore them. Yet beneath his jacket was a shirt that, in contrast to most others she saw in here, was good quality, white and freshly laundered, and his fingernails were clean and trimmed. He kept to himself and was always on his own. And there was something about him, something of self-containment and strength, of intelligence and power. But all of it understated, quiet, kept beneath the surface. He did not seem to care what others thought of him. Unlike the other men in Whitechapel he did not make any effort to either intimidate or impress. Never tried to make conversation, just kept his thoughts to himself. He was clean-shaven, handsome too in a rugged sort of way, although handsome men should have been the last thing on Emma's mind.

'Three mixed-grill platters!' Tom, the cook, yelled, jolting her from her speculation.

'Coming, Tom.' Emma dragged her eyes away from the man, her moment of respite gone. She hurried up to the kitchen hatch, and, using the cloth dangling from the belt around her waist, quickly shifted the scalding plates on to her large wooden tray. In a much-practised move, she hefted the whole tray up to balance it on her shoulder, before bustling across the room to make her delivery.

'Here we are, gentlemen. Three of our very best mixed-grills.' She presented each of the three men round the table with an enormous platter.

On the way back to the bar she cleared two tables, took two orders for more beers, and noticed a new party of men arriving to be fed.

'I'll see to the new boys, Em,' Paulette, the Red Lion's other serving wench, said as she passed Emma.

'Four pints of ale ready over here, Emma!' Nancy, the landlady, called, setting the last of the pints down on the bar with a thud that sent the froth of their heads cascading in a creamy waterfall down the outsides of the pewter tankards.

Emma bustled over. Collected all four on to her tray and went to deliver them to the table nearest to the front door.

'Thanks, darlin'.' The big black-haired man leered down the cleavage that her low-cut chemise and tight-laced bodice of her scarlet work dress exposed. She disliked this dress and how much it revealed. And she disliked men like him. He grinned, revealing teeth that matched his hair as his hand slid against her hip.

She slapped his fingers away, kept her tone frosty. 'Keep your hands to yourself.' Wondered if she would ever get used to this aspect of the job.

He laughed. 'You're a feisty one and no mistake. But I like a challenge.' His hand returned, more insistent this time, grabbing her buttock and squeezing as he hauled her close. 'Just as much as I like that fancy rich accent of yours. Makes you sound like a real lady it does. And I've never had a lady. Come on, darlin', I'll make it worth your while.' The stench of ale and rotten teeth was overpowering. His friends around the table cheered and sniggered.

Emma fixed him with a cynical and steely stare. 'Hard though it is to believe, I must decline. Now unhand me and let me get on with my work or you will have a bar full of thirsty, hungry men waiting to be served to contend with.'

Black-Hair's grin broadened. He pulled her to him, wrenching the tray from her hand, and dropping it to clatter on the floor. 'The other wench can see to them. You can see to me, darlin'.'

Oh, Lord! She realised with a sinking heart and impending dread that he was not going to release her with nothing worse than a slap to the bottom. He was one of those that would pull her down on his lap and start fondling her. Or worse.

'I will see to nothing. Release me before Nancy sees your game and bars you.'

She was only dimly aware of the shadow of the figure passing at close quarters. She was too busy trying to deal with the black-haired man and extricate herself from his grip. So when the deluge of beer tipped like an almighty cascade of brown rain over the lout's head she was as shocked as he.

Black-Hair's grin was wiped. Emma was forgotten in an instant. He released her, giving an almighty roar of a curse.

Emma didn't need an invitation. Making the most of her opportunity, she grabbed her tray and backed clear of the danger.

Black-Hair was spluttering and wiping beer from screwed-up eyes with great rough tattooed hands. His hair was sodden and glistening with beer. It ran in rivulets down his cheeks and over his chin to drip its tea-coloured stain on to the grubby white of the shirt that covered his barrel chest. The shoulders of his shabby brown-woollen jacket were dark as rain-soaked earth. Even the front of his grey trousers was dark with it. He stank like a brewery.

His small bloodshot eyes swivelled to the perpetrator.

The hubbub of chatter and laughter and clank of glasses had ceased. There was curiosity and a whispered hush as everyone watched.

Emma shifted her gaze to follow that of the black-haired lout and saw the subject of her earlier covert study standing there. Tall, still, calm.

'Sorry about that. Slip of the hand.' The words might have offered apology, but the way the man said them suggested otherwise. His voice was the same East End accent as theirs, but low in tone, clear in volume, quietly menacing in its delivery.

'Oh, you'll be damn sorry all right!' Black-Hair's chair legs scraped loud against the wooden floorboards as he got to his feet. 'You'll be pissing yourself, mate, by the time I've finished with you.'

The man let his gaze drop pointedly to the dark sodden front of Black-Hair's trousers, then rose again to meet his eyes. There was a glimmer of hard amusement in them. He raised the eyebrow with the scar running through it, the one that Emma thought made him look like a handsome rogue. 'Looks like you got there first.'

The crowd sniggered at that.

Black-Hair's face flushed puce. His little piggy eyes narrowed on the man like an enraged bull. He cracked his knuckles as he made a fist.

By some unspoken command Black-Hair's four friends got to their feet, making their involvement clear. Any trace of curiosity and amusement fled the room's atmosphere. It was suddenly sharp-edged with threat.

The hush spread. Every man in the chop-house was riveted on what was unfolding before Emma.

The nape of her neck prickled.

'Settle down, boys,' said Nancy. 'There's no harm done. Sit down and drink your pints before they get warm.'

But not one of the men moved. They all stayed put, stood where they were, eyeing each other like dogs with their hackles raised.

'We don't want no trouble in here. You got a disagreement, you take it outside.' Nancy tried to come closer, but two men stepped into her path to stop her progress, murmuring advice—two regulars intent on keeping her safe.

No one heeded her anyway. Not the black-haired villain and his cronies. And not the man.

In the background Paulette's face, like every other, was lit with excited and wary anticipation.

The man's expression was implacable. He looked almost amused.

'I'm going to kill you,' said Black-Hair.

'And there was me thinking you were offering to buy me a replacement porter,' said the man.

'You ain't gonna be able to hold a pint of porter, let alone drink one, I swear.'

Emma's blood ran cold. She knew what men like this in Whitechapel did to one another. This was not the first fight she had seen and the prospect of what was coming made her feel queasy.

The man smiled again, a smile that went nowhere near those cool blue eyes. 'You really want to do this?' he asked with a hint of disbelief and perplexity.

'Too late to start grovelling now,' said Black-Hair.

'That's a shame.'

There was not one sound in the whole of the chop-house. The silence hissed. No one moved. All eyes were on the man, Emma's included. Staring with fascinated horror. Five ruffians against one man. The outcome was certain.

The black-haired man stepped closer to the man, squaring up to him, violent intent spilling from every pore.

She swallowed. Felt a shiver chase over her skin.

The man did not seem to feel the same. He smiled. It was a cold, hard smile. His eyes showed nothing of softness, not one hint of fear. Indeed, he looked as if he welcomed what would come. The blood. The violence. Five men against one. Maybe he really did have a death wish after all.

'Someone stop them. Please,' she said, but it was a plea that had no hope of being answered.

An old man pulled her back. 'Ain't no one going to stop them now, girl.'

He was right. She knew it and so did every single person in that taproom.

The black-haired brute cracked his knuckles and stretched his massive bull neck, ready to dispense punishment.

Emma held her breath. Her fingers were balled, her nails cutting into her palms.

The man's movement was so fast and unexpected. One minute he was standing there. The next, he had landed a head butt against the lout's nose. There was a sickening crunch. And blood. A lot of blood. Black-Hair doubled over as if bending in to meet the man's knee that hit his face. The speed and suddenness of it shocked her. It shocked the men in there, too. She could tell by the look on their faces as they watched the black-haired giant go down. The ruffian was blinking and gasping with the shock of it as he lay there.

Emma watched in disbelief. Every muscle in her body tensed with shock. She held her breath for what would happen next.

'Too late to start grovelling,' the man said.

Leaning one hand on the floor, Black-Hair spat a bloody globule to land on the toe of the man's boot and reached for a nearby chair.

'But if you insist…' The man stepped closer to Black-Hair, his bloodied boot treading on the giant's splayed fingers, his hand catching hold of the villain's out-stretched hand as if he meant to help him to his feet. But it was not help he offered. He gave the wrist a short sharp twist, the resulting crack of which made Emma and the rest of the audience wince.

Black-Hair's face went ashen. He made not one sound, just fainted into a crumpled heap and did not move.

In the stunned amazement that followed no one else moved either. There was not a sound.

'He might need a little help in holding his porter,' said the man to Black-Hair's friends.

'You bastard!' One of them spat the curse.

The man smiled again. And this time Emma was pre-pared.

The tough charged with fists at the ready.

The man's forehead shattered the villain's cheekbone while his foot hooked around his ankle and felled him. When the rat tried to get up the man kicked his feet from under him. This time Black-Hair's friend stayed where he was.

The other three men exchanged shifty glances amongst

themselves, then began to advance. One slipped a long wicked blade that winked in the candlelight.

'Really?' asked the man.

The sly-faced man came in, feigned attack, drew back. Came in close again, circling the man.

'Too scared?' asked the man.

A curl of lip and a slash of the blade was his opponent's only response.

But the man kicked him between the legs and there was an ear-piercing scream. Emma had never heard a man scream before. It made the blood in her veins turn to ice. She watched the knife clatter to the floor forgotten while the sly-faced villain dropped like a stone, clutching himself and gasping.

The man looked at the two remaining thugs.

For a tiny moment they gaped at him. Then they turned tail and ran, pelting out of the chop-house like hares before a hound.

The man stood there and watched them go.

But Emma was not looking at the fleeing villains. Rather, she was looking at the man. She could not take her eyes off him. There was what looked like the beginning of a bruise on his forehead. The snow-white of his shirt was speckled scarlet with blood from Black-Hair's nose. His dark neckcloth was askew. He was not even out of breath. He just stood there calm and cool and unperturbed.

The slamming of the front door echoed in the silence.

No one spoke. No one moved. No one save the man.

He smoothed the dishevelment from his hair, straightened his neckcloth and walked through the pathway that cleared through the crowd before him.

They watched him with respect. They watched him with awe. Soft murmured voices.

Fists and feet were what gained a man respect round here. Standing up for himself and what he believed in. Physicality ruled. The strongest, the toughest, the most dangerous. And the man had just proved himself all three.

Some regulars from the crowd half dragged, half carried the injured away.

The man returned to his table, but he did not sit down. He finished the porter in one gulp and left more coins beside the empty tankard than were needed for payment. He lifted his hat and then his eyes finally met Emma's across the taproom.

Within her chest her heart was still banging hard against her ribs. Through her veins her blood was still rushing with a shocked fury.

He gave her a nod of acknowledgement and then turned away and walked out of the place, oblivious to the entire crowd of customers standing there slack-jawed and staring at him.

Emma stared just as much as all the others, watching him leave. And even when the door had closed behind him she still stood there looking, as if she could see right through it to follow him. Six months in Whitechapel and she had never seen a man as strong, as ruthless or as invincible.

'Don't think he'll be having any trouble for a while,' said Nancy, who was standing, hands on hips, bar cloth in hand, watching.

'Who is he?' Emma asked in soft-voiced amazement.

'Goes by the name of Ned Stratham. Or so he says.'

Emma opened her mouth to ask more, but Nancy had already turned her attention away, raising her voice loud and harsh as she called out to the taproom audience, 'Show's over, folks. Get back to your tables before your chops grow cold and your ale grows warm.'

Emma's gaze returned to linger on the front door and her thoughts to the man who had just exited through it.

Ned Stratham.

A fight seemingly over a pint of spilled porter. And yet Emma was not fooled, even if all the others were.

Ned Stratham did not know anything about her other than she served him his dinner and porter. He was a man who had barely seemed to notice her in the months he had been coming here. A man who kept to himself and quietly watched what unfolded around him without getting involved. Until tonight.

It had not been fighting in any sense that a gentleman would recognise, it had been raw and shocking and, if she were honest, much more effective. It followed no rules. It had not been polite or genteel, nor, on the surface of it, honourable or chivalric.

'Backlog of chops in the kitchen, Emma,' Nancy's voice interrupted.

Emma nodded. 'I am just coming.'

Seemingly a taproom brawl over a clumsy accident and yet... In her mind she saw again that blue gaze on hers, so piercing and perceptive.

'Emma!' Nancy yelled again. 'You want it in writing?'

Lifting her tray, Emma headed for the kitchen. Ned Stratham's table had been nowhere near Black-Hair's and any man who could tumble a disc over his knuckles had no problems with balance.

And she knew that, despite his method, what Ned Stratham had just done was chivalric in every sense of the word. She knew that what he had just done was save her from Black-Hair.

Ned Stratham saw the woman again a week later on his visit to the Red Lion. His meal had been delivered by the other serving wench, but it was Emma who came to collect his cleared plate and empty tankard.

Her dark hair was clean and pinned up, her pale olive skin clear and smooth, unmarked by pox scars. Her teeth were white and straight. She was too beautiful for White-chapel. Too well-spoken, too. It made her stand out. It made her a target for men like the dark-haired chancer last week. He already knew that she wore no wedding band upon her finger. No husband. Unprotected in an area of London where it was dangerous for any woman, let alone one like her, to be so.

'Do you wish another pint of porter, sir?' Her voice was clear, her accent refined and out of place on this side of town.

'Thank you.' He watched in silence as she shifted his plate, cutlery and tankard to sit on her empty wooden tray. But once the table was cleared she did not hurry off as usual. Instead she hesitated, lingering there with the tray in her hands.

'I did not get a chance to thank you, last week.' Her eyes were a dark-brown velvet. Warm eyes, he thought as he looked into them. Beautiful eyes.

'For what?' he asked.

'Spilling your drink.'

'A clumsy accident.'

'Of course it was.' She smiled in a way that told him that she understood exactly what he had done. The hint of a dimple showed in the corner of her mouth.

It made him smile, too.

She was always polite and professional, and friendly with it, as if she genuinely liked people. But unlike most other serving wenches he had never seen her flirt with any man, even though that would have earned her more tips. She did her job with a capable efficiency and sense of purpose that he liked.

He turned his gaze to focus on the tumble of the small pale-ivory token across his knuckles. No matter how beautiful she was, there was a part of him that wanted her to just walk away as she had done all the other times, to attend to other punters on other tables. There were things on his mind more important than beautiful women. Things he had spent a lifetime chasing. Things upon which he had to stay focused to bring to fruition. He did not want distractions, not of any kind.

And the truth was he had not wanted to intervene last week, but he could not have just sat there and turned a blind eye while a woman was forced against her will, whatever the level of it. He had known men like the black-haired tough all his life. What started out as 'fun' soon escalated to something else.

He watched the rhythmic smooth tumble of the token over the fingers of his right hand. It was a movement so long practised as to no longer be a trick but a reflex, a part of himself.

'I will fetch your porter.' He didn't look up at her but he knew she was still smiling. He could hear it in her voice.

Ned said nothing more. Just kept his focus on the token, effectively dismissing her.

He heard her turn and walk away. Shifted his eyes momentarily to her retreating figure, to the soft sway of her hips. The smallest of glances; no risk to the ripple of his fingers that was as instinctive and easy to him as breathing. And yet, in that moment, for the first time in years, he fluffed the move like a novice. The token tipped from his hand, straight off the table, landing edge up on the floorboards to roll away with speed.

His heart skipped a beat. He was already on his feet and following, but the token was way in front and heading for the crowded bar. But Emma, as he'd heard her called, reached a foot forward and, with the toe of her boot, gently stopped it, balanced the tray on her hip and retrieved it from the floor.

Ned watched as she rubbed the token against the bodice of her dress, dusting off the dirt that marred its smooth pale surface. Her gaze moved over the worn ivory, studying it.

She turned to him as he reached her.

Their eyes held for a tiny second before she passed the token to him.

'Thank you,' he said.

'For what? I trust the inadvertent and clumsy tread of my boot did your property no harm.' Her eyes held his.

He couldn't help himself. He smiled.

And so did she.

Her eyes watched the token as he slipped it safely inside his jacket. 'What is it?'

'My lucky charm.'

'Does it work?'

'Without fail.'

Her eyebrows rose ever so slightly, but she softened the cynicism with a smile that did things to him that no other woman's smile ever had. It kept him standing here, talking, when he should have walked away.

'You don't believe me.'

'A lucky charm that works without fail…?' She raised her eyebrows again, teasingly this time. 'Perhaps I should ask to borrow it.'

'Are you in need of good luck?'

'Is not everyone?'

'Emma!' Nancy shouted from the bar. 'Six pints of porter here!'

'Ned Stratham.' He did not smile, but offered his hand for a handshake.

'Emma de Lisle.'

Her fingers were feminine and slender within his own. Her skin cool and smooth, even within the warmth of the taproom. The touch of their bare hands sparked physical awareness between them. He knew she felt it, too, from the slight blush on her cheeks and the way she released his hand.

'Emma!' Nancy, the landlady, screeched like a banshee. 'Get over here, girl!'

Emma glanced over her shoulder at the bar. 'Coming, Nancy!

'No rest for the wicked,' she said, and with a smile she was gone.

Ned resumed his seat, but his eyes watched her cross the room. The deep red of the tavern dress complimented the darkness of her hair and was laced tight to her body so that he could see the narrowness of her waist and the flare of her hips and the way the material sat against her buttocks. There was a vitality about her, an intelligence, a level of confidence in herself not normally seen round here.

He watched her collect the tankards from the bar and distribute them to various tables, taking her time en route to him. His was the last tankard on the tray.

'What's a woman like you doing in a place like this?' he asked as she set the porter down before him.

Her eyes met his again. And in them was that same smile. 'Working,' she said.

This time she didn't linger. Just moved on, to clear tables and take new orders and fetch more platters of chops.

He leaned back against the wooden panelling on the wall and slowly drank his porter. The drift of pipe smoke was in the air. He breathed it in along with the smell of char-grilled chops and hoppy ale. Soaking up the atmosphere of the place, the familiarity and the ease, he watched Emma de Lisle.

He had the feeling she wouldn't be working here in the Red Lion for too long. She was a woman who was going places, or had been to them. Anyone who met her knew it. He wondered again, as he had wondered many times before, what her story was.

He watched how efficiently she worked, with that air of purpose and energy; the way she could share a smile or a joke with the punters without it delaying her work—only for him had she done that. The punters liked her and he could see why.

She didn't look at him again, not in all the time it took him to sup his drink.

The bells of St Olave's in the distance chimed eleven. Nancy called last orders.

Ned's time here for tonight was over. He drained the tankard. Left enough coins on the table to pay for his meal and a generous tip for Emma de Lisle, before lifting his hat and making his way across the room to the front door.

His focus flicked one last time to where Emma was delivering meat-laden platters to a table of four.

She glanced over at him, her eyes meeting his for a tiny shared moment, and flashed her wonderful smile at him, before getting on with the job in hand.

He placed his hat on his head and walked out of the Red Lion Chop-House into the darkness of the alleyway.

I trust the inadvertent and clumsy tread of my boot did your property no harm. He smiled. Emma de Lisle was certainly one hell of a woman. A man might almost be tempted to stay here for a woman like her. Almost.

He smiled one last time, then set off through the maze of streets he knew so well. As he crossed the town, moving from one parish to the next, he shifted his mind to what lay ahead for tomorrow, focusing, running through the details.

The night air was cool and his face grim as he struck a steady pace all the way home to Mayfair.

Chapter Two

'Is that you, Emma?' her father called at the sound of her key scraping in the lock. She could hear the wariness in his voice.

She unlocked the door and let herself into the two small rooms that they rented.

'I brought you a special supper—pork chops.'

'Pork?' He raised his eyebrows in surprise. 'Not usual for there to be any pork left.'

There had not been. Pork was expensive and the choicest chop they offered. It was also her father's favourite, which was why Emma had paid for them out of her own pocket, largely with the generous tip Ned Stratham had left, the rest covered by Nancy's discount. 'Happy Birthday, Papa.' She dropped a kiss to his cheek as he drew her close and gave her a hug.

'It is my birthday? I lose track of time these days.' He sat down in one of the spindly chairs at the bare table in the corner of the room.

'That is what happens with age,' Emma teased him. But she knew it was not age that made him forget, but the fact that all the days merged together when one just worked all the time.

She hung her cloak on the back of the door, then set a place at the little table, unwrapped the lidded plate from its cloth and finally produced an earthenware bottle. 'And as a treat, one of the finest of the Red Lion's porters.'

'You spoil me, Emma,' he chided, but he smiled. 'You are not having anything?'

'I ate earlier, in the Red Lion. And you know I cannot abide the taste of beer.'

'For which I am profoundly thankful. Bad enough my daughter chooses to work in a common tavern, but that she would start drinking the wares...' He gave an exaggerated shudder.

'It is a chop-house, not a tavern as I have told you a hundred times.' She smiled. Although the distinction made little difference in reality, it made her father feel better. But he would not feel better were he to see the Red Lion's clientele and her best customers. She wondered what he would make of a man like Ned Stratham. Or what he would say had he witnessed the manner in which Ned had bested five men to defend her.

Her father smiled, too. 'And I suppose I should be heartily grateful for that.'

'You know the tips from the chop-house pay very well indeed, much better than for any milliner or shop girl. And it will not be for ever.'

'Perhaps not,' he said thoughtfully.

'No perhaps about it, Papa,' she said sternly. 'Our savings begin to grow. And I have made an application for a position in Clerkenwell. It is not Mayfair, but it is heading in the right direction.'

'Managing a chop-house.'

Managing a tavern, but she did not tell him that. 'One step at a time, on a journey that will eventually lead us back to our own world.'

He smiled. 'My dear girl, have I told you that you are stubborn as a mastiff?'

'Once or twice. I wonder where I might have acquired such a trait? I do not recall my dear mama having such a defect.'

He chuckled. 'Indeed, I own the blame. The apple does not fall so very far from the tree.' He gently patted her hand. 'Come, take a seat. You must be tired after working all evening.'

Emma dropped into the seat opposite. 'Not so tired at all.' And although her feet were aching it was the truth. She thought of Ned Stratham and the interaction that had passed between them earlier that evening and smiled. He was a man without an inch of softness in him. Probably more dangerous than any of the other men that came to the chop-house, and the men that came to the Red Lion were not those anyone would wish to meet alone on a dark night. Definitely more dangerous, she corrected, remembering precisely what he had done to Black-Hair and his cronies. And yet there was something about him, something that marked him as different. Pushing the thought away, she focused her attention on her father.

'How were the docks today?'

'The same as they ever are. The good news is that I managed to get an extra shift for tomorrow.'

'Again?' The fatigue in his face worried her. 'Working a double shift is too much for you.' Working a single shift in a manual job in the London Docks' warehouses was too much for a man who had been raised and lived as a gentleman all his life.

'What is sauce for the goose is sauce for the gander,' he said. 'Do not start with your scolding, please, Emma.'

She sighed and gave a small smile. It was his birthday and she wanted what was left of it to be nice for him.

There would be other days to raise the issue of his working double shifts. 'Very well.'

'Fetch your cup. I shall propose a toast.'

She did as he bid.

He poured a dribble of porter into her cup. Raised his own tankard in the air. 'God has granted me another year and I am happy and thankful for it.' But there was a shadow of sadness in his eyes and she knew what he was thinking of. 'To absent loved ones,' he said. 'Wherever Kit is. Whatever he is doing. God keep him safe and bring him home to us.'

'To absent loved ones,' she echoed and tried to suppress the complicated swirl of emotions she felt whenever Kit's name was mentioned.

They clunked the cups together and drank down the porter. Its bitterness made her shudder. Once it had been champagne in the finest of cut-crystal glasses with which he made his birthday toast and the sweetest of lemonades, extravagantly chilled with ice. Once their lives had been very different from the ones they lived here.

As if sensing her thought, he reached his hand to hers and gave it a squeeze. Her eyes met his, sombre for a moment with shared dark memories, before she locked the memories away in the place they belonged. Neither spoke of them. It was not their way. She forced a smile to her face. 'You should eat those pork chops before they grow cold.'

'With pleasure, my dear girl.' Her father smiled in return and tucked into the meal with relish.

Across town the next day, within the dining room of a mansion house in Cavendish Square, a very distinguished luncheon was taking place.

The fireplace was black marble, carved and elaborate.

The walls were red, lined with ornate paintings of places in Scotland and overseas Ned had never been. Above the table hung an enormous chandelier from which a thousand crystal drops danced and shimmered in the slight breeze from the opened window. There were two windows in the room, both large, bowed in style, both framed with long heavy red damask curtains with fringed swags and tails. Both had blinds that were cream in colour and pulled high.

Out in the street beyond, the sky was bright with the golden light of a summer's afternoon. It glinted on the silver service and crystal of the glasses on the polished mahogany table stretched out like a long banqueting table from kings of old. Enough spaces to seat eighteen. But there were only five men dining from the sumptuous feast. Seated in the position of the principal guest was the government minister for trade. On his left was the minister's secretary. Directly opposite the minister was the biggest mill owner in the north and one away was a shipping magnate whose line was chief to service the West Indies and the Americas. A powerful collection of men, and seated at their heart, in the position of host, was Ned Stratham.

He fed them the best of fine foods and rich sauces prepared by a chef who had once been employed by the Prince Regent. He ensured that his butler and footmen were well trained enough to keep the men's glasses flowing with expensive French wines. A different one suited for each dish.

Ned knew how to play the game. He knew what was necessary for success in business and influence over policy.

'I can make no promises,' said the minister.

'I'm not asking you to,' replied Ned.

'And the source of the figures you quoted?'

'Sound.'

'You really think it would work?'

Ned gave a nod.

'You would be taking as much a risk as us, maybe even more so as it is your money on the line.'

'Maximum gain comes from maximum venture.'

'If the vote were to go against us and the bill fail…'

'You would survive it.'

'But would you?' the minister asked.

'That's not your problem.' Ned held his gaze while the seconds stretched, until eventually the minister for trade nodded.

'I will set the necessary mechanisms in motion to-morrow.'

'Then, we're agreed.' Ned held out his hand for a hand-shake.

The minister swallowed. A shadow of unease shifted through his shrewd eyes. It was one thing to say the words, but another to shake on it. A handshake for men like him placed their honour on the line.

There was a silence that was awkward for them all save Ned. He took a sort of wry pleasure in such moments; using gentlemen's discomfort of him and his dubious breeding to his own ends.

The other three looked nervous, waited to see what the minister would do.

Ned kept his gaze on the other man's. Kept his hand extended. Both were steady.

The minister smiled and finally shook Ned's hand. 'You have convinced me, sir.'

'I'm glad to hear it.'

It was after six by the time the luncheon finally ended and four of the most influential men in the country left Cavendish Square.

The butler and two footmen returned to the dining room, standing with their backs against the wall. Faces straight ahead, eyes focused on some distant point. Ned marvelled that gentlemen discussed the details of confidential business before servants, as if they were not men, as if they could not see or hear what was going on. Ned knew better. He never made the same mistake.

He sat alone at the table, the wine glass still half-full in his hand. The sunlight which streamed in through the windows lit the port within a deep ruby-red and made the monogram engraved on the glass's surface sparkle— S for Stratham.

The minister had squirmed, but in the end the deal had been done. It would be good for much more than Ned. He felt a sense of grim satisfaction.

The butler cleared his throat and came to hover by his elbow. 'More port, sir?'

'No, thank you, Clarkson.' Ned wondered what Clarkson would do if he were to ask for a porter. But gentlemen in Mayfair did not drink porter. Not in any of their fancy rich establishments. Not even in their own homes. And Ned must keep up the guise of a gentleman.

But porter made him think of Whitechapel, and the Red Lion…and Emma de Lisle. With those perceptive dark eyes, and that vitality and warm, joyful confidence that emanated from her.

He glanced out of the window, at the sunlight and the carriage that trundled past, and felt the waft of cool air break through the cigar smoke that lingered like a mist within the dining room.

He had other business to attend to. But it didn't have to happen tonight.

Ned set the fine crystal goblet down upon the table. Got to his feet.

The butler appeared by his side again.

'I'm going out, Clarkson.'

'Very good, sir. Shall I arrange for the carriage?'

'No carriage.' Not for where Ned was going. 'It's a fine evening. I'll walk.'

Ned went to change into his old leather jacket and boots.

The heat from the kitchen mixed with that that had built up in the taproom through the summer's day to make the air of the Red Lion stifling. The chop-house's windows and doors were all open, but it made little difference.

Nancy had taken advantage of the heatwave and had her staff carry some tables out on to the street, so that the chop-house's customers could sit out there in the cool shade and drink their beer.

'Three pitchers of ale!' Nancy yelled and Emma hurried to answer.

Emma could feel the sweat dripping down her back and between her breasts. Never had a shift seemed so long. Her legs were aching and her feet felt like they were on fire. She lifted the tray, tried to blow a hair away from where it had escaped her pins to dangle in her eye and made her way across the taproom, hurrying out of the doorway, just as Ned Stratham was coming in.

She collided with him, almost dropping the tray. It was Ned who steadied it, stopping the slide of the pitchers and the ensuing disaster.

'Ned Stratham,' she said, and inside her stomach felt like a flock of starlings taking off from the fields as one to swoop across a sunset sky. 'Two nights on the trot? This is a first.' Sometimes weeks passed between his visits.

Those blue, blue eyes met hers and held for a second too long. 'You've been counting.'

'As if I would have time to be counting.'

She saw the hint of amusement in his eyes as he moved aside and let her pass through.

Emma did not look back. Just got on with serving the tableloads of customers that were outside in the alley. But all the while she was conscious that he was inside. Too conscious. She smiled wryly to herself and got on with clearing the outside tables before returning to the taproom.

There was not a seat to be had inside. Ned was leaning against the bar, comfortable, already sipping a porter. He looked unconcerned by the crowd, by the heat, by not having a chair or table.

'Six porters, two small beers and a stout, Emma!' Paulette shouted and thumped the last of the tankards down on the wooden counter beside Ned.

Emma continued her quick pace to the bar and, while unloading her tray, slid a glance in Ned Stratham's direction.

'Busy in here tonight,' he observed.

'There's a schooner in at the docks. We've had the full crew in since lunchtime.'

'Good business.'

'But bad timing. Tom did not come in today. Nancy is in the kitchen, cooking in his place.' She started loading up the fresh porters while she spoke.

'Bet that's made her all sweetness and light.'

'You know her so well.'

With impeccable timing, Nancy's face, beet-red with heat and running with sweat, appeared at the hatch as she thumped three plates down. 'Three mixed grills!' She flicked a crabbed gaze in Emma's direction.

'Where's me bleedin' platter?' someone shouted from the other side of the room.

'Any more of your lip and it'll be up your bleedin' backside,' Nancy snapped in reply and riveted the man with a look that would have blistered paint on a door.

Emma's and Ned's eyes met in shared silent amusement. 'Enjoy your porter,' she said and then she was off, collecting the platters on her way to deliver the porters.

'Come on, wench! My stomach thinks my throat's been cut! How long's a fellow got to wait in this place for a drink?' a punter shouted from the table in the middle of the floor.

'We're working as fast as we can!' screeched a flustered Paulette from behind the bar, her face scarlet and sweaty.

'Five porters, gentlemen.' Emma's voice, although quiet in comparison to the rowdy conversation, shouts and laughter in the place, stood out because she sounded like a lady. She worked quickly and efficiently, setting a tankard on the table before each man before moving on to deliver the rest of the drinks from her tray.

Ned watched her bustle across the room to the big table in the corner where the crew of the schooner looked three sheets past a sail. He felt himself stiffen as one of them copped a sly grope as she leaned across the table with a drink.

Her movement was subtle and slight, but very effective. The contents of the tankard ended up in the worm's lap.

The sailor gave a yelp, followed by a curse, staggering to his feet and staring down at the sodden stain rapidly spreading over his trousers. 'Look what the hell you've done!'

His crewmates were all laughing.

'I am so sorry,' she said without the slightest bit of sincerity. 'I will fetch you another porter. Let us just hope it does not go the same way as the first one.' And there was the steely hint of warning in her eye as she said it.

Grumbling, the man sat down.

'I wonder where you got that idea,' Ned Stratham said when she returned to the bar. He kept his focus on the token tumbling over his fingers.

'I wonder,' she said.

He moved his gaze to her. The strands of her hair had escaped its pins to coil like damp ebony ivy against the golden skin of her neck. The swell of her breasts looked in danger of escaping the red bodice. He could see the rise and fall of it with her every breath. Her cheeks were flushed with the heat and her eyes, sparkling black as cut jet, held his. They shared a smile before she hurried off across the room again. She was so vivid and vital and alive that the desire he normally held in check surged through him.

Ned wasn't the only one, judging by the way the sailors were looking at her. After months away at sea most men had two things on their mind—drink and women. They were tanked up on the first and were now seeking the second.

'What you doing later, darlin'? Me and you, we could step out for a little drink.'

'Hands off, Wrighty, she's coming home with me, ain't that right, Emma darling?' another said.

'Neither is possible, I'm afraid, gentlemen. I'm meeting my betrothed,' she said without missing a beat while clearing empties from their table.

'Shame.'

The other looked less than convinced. His gaze meandered with greed and lust over the length of her body as she returned to the bar. He wasn't alone. A man would have had to have water in his veins not to want her. And what was flowing in the veins of the sailors was far from water.

One drink, Ned had told himself. And yet he couldn't walk away now. Not even had he wanted to. He ordered another porter from Paulette.

It was an hour before the bustle waned and another two before Paulette rang the bell for last orders.

Half an hour later and what remained of the Red Lion's clientele had emptied into the alleyway outside.

Emma leaned against the edge of a table, taking the weight off her feet, while fastening her cloak in place. The taproom was empty. The tables had been wiped down, the stools upturned on the tabletops. The floor had been swept ready to be mopped the next day. Ned Stratham had gone some time while she had been in the kitchen helping Nancy scrape the grills clean. Gone without saying goodbye, she thought, and then realised how stupid that thought was. He was just a customer like all the rest. And if she had any sense in her head she should be glad of it.

'Ned Stratham's got his eye on you, Em,' Paulette teased with a sly face.

'Nonsense.' Emma concentrated on fastening her cloak and hoped the dimness of the candlelight hid her blush.

'I saw the way he was watching you. Asking questions, too.'

'Too much time on his hands,' said Emma dismissively.

Paulette smirked. 'Don't think so.'

'What a night!' Nancy swept in from the kitchen. 'Tom better show tomorrow or there'll be trouble.'

Nancy unlocked the front door to let Emma and Paulette leave. 'Watch yourself, girls, we got a few stragglers.'

Emma gave a nod as she and Paulette stepped out into the alleyway.

The last of the evening light had long since faded to an inky dark blue. The day's heat had cooled. Behind them the kitchen door closed with a slam. A lone sailor stood waiting before them.

Emma met Paulette's eyes.

'It's all right, Em. George said he'd wait for me. He's the boatswain off the ship that's in,' explained Paulette.

Emma lowered her voice. 'Paulette—'

'I know what I'm doing, honest, Em. I'll be all right,' Paulette whispered and walked off down the alleyway with the boatswain.

Behind her Emma heard Nancy slide the big bolts into place across the door, locking her out into the night. The only light in the darkness was that from the high-up kitchen window.

Emma turned to head home, in the opposite direction to the one that Paulette and her beau had taken, just as two men stepped into the mouth of the alley ahead.

Chapter Three

'Emma, darlin', you've been telling us porkies.' Through the flicker of the kitchen lamps she recognised the sailor who had asked her to step out with him for a drink. He was unshaven and the stench of beer from him reached across the distance between them. His gaze was not on her face, but lower, leering at the pale skin of her exposed *décolletage*. Her heart began to thud. Fear snaked through her blood, but she showed nothing of it. Instead, she eyed the men with disdain and pulled her cloak tighter around herself.

'Good job we came back for you, since there's no sign of your "betrothed." Maybe now we can get to know each other a bit better.'

'I do not think so, gentlemen.'

'Oh, she don't think so, Wrighty. Let us convince you, darlin'.' They gave a laugh and started to walk towards her.

Emma's hand slid into the pocket of her cloak, just as Ned Stratham stepped out of the shadows by her side.

She smothered the gasp.

His face was expressionless, but his eyes were cold and dangerous as sharp steel. He looked at the men. Just a look. But it was enough to stop them in their tracks.

The sailor who had done the talking stared, and swallowed, then held up his hands in submission. 'Sorry, mate. Didn't realise…'

'You do now,' said Ned in a voice that for all its quiet volume was filled with threat, and never shifting his hard gaze for an instant.

'All right, no offence intended.' The sailors backed away. 'Thought she was spinning a line about the betrothed thing. She's yours. We're already gone.'

Ned watched them until they disappeared and their footsteps faded into the distance out on to St Catherine's Lane. Only then did he look at Emma.

In the faint flickering light from the kitchen window, his eyes looked almost as dark as hers, turned from sky-blue to midnight. He had a face that was daunted by nothing. It would have been tough on any other man. On him it was handsome. Firm determined lips. A strong masculine nose with a tiny bump upon its ridge. His rogue eyebrow enough to take a woman's breath away. Her heart rate kicked faster as her gaze lingered momentarily on it before returning to his eyes.

'What are you doing here, Ned?' she asked in wary softness.

'Taking the air.'

They looked at one another.

She's yours. The echo of the sailor's words seemed to whisper between them, making her cheeks warm.

'I didn't think you'd be fool enough to walk home alone in the dark through these streets.'

'Normally I do not. Tom lives in the next street up from mine. He usually sees me home safe.'

'Tom's not here.'

'Which is why I borrowed one of Nancy's knives.' She

slid the knife from her pocket and held it between them so that the blade glinted in the moonlight.

'It wouldn't have stopped them.'

'Maybe not. But it would have done a very great deal of damage, I assure you.'

The silence hissed between them.

'You want to take your chances with the knife? Or you could accept my offer to see you home safe.'

She swallowed, knowing what he was offering and feeling her stomach turn tumbles within. 'As long as you understand that it is just seeing me safely home.' She met his gaze, held it with mock confidence.

'Are you suggesting that I'm not a gentleman?' His voice was all stony seriousness, but he raised the rogue eyebrow.

'On the contrary, I am sure you are the perfect gentleman.'

'Maybe not perfect.'

She smiled at that, relaxing a little now that the shock of seeing him there had subsided, and returned the knife blade to its dishcloth scabbard within the pocket of her cloak.

'We should get going,' he said. And together they began to walk down the alleyway.

Their footsteps were soft and harmonious, the slower, heavier thud of his boots in time with the lighter step of her own.

They walked on, out on to St Catherine's Lane. Walked along in silence.

'You knew those sailors would be waiting for me, didn't you?'

'Did I?'

'You do not fool me, Ned Stratham.'

'It's not my intention to fool anyone.'

She scrutinised him, before asking the question that she'd been longing to ask since the first night he had walked into the Red Lion. 'Who are you?'

'Just a man from Whitechapel.'

'And yet…the shirt beneath your jacket looks like it came from Mayfair. And is tailored to fit you perfectly. Most unusual on a man from Whitechapel.' He was probably a crook. A gang boss. A tough. How else did a man like him get the money for such a shirt? Asking him now, when they were alone, in the dark of the night, was probably not the wisest thing she had ever done, but the question was out before she could think better of it. Besides, if she did not ask him now, she doubted she would get another chance. She ignored the faster patter of her heart and held his eyes, daring him to tell her something of the truth.

'You've been eyeing up my shirt.'

She gave a laugh and shook her head. 'I could not miss it. Nor could half the chop-house. You have had your jacket off all evening.'

'But half the chop-house would not have recognised a Mayfair shirt.' Half in jest, half serious.

Her heart skipped a beat, but she held his gaze boldly, as if he were not treading so close to forbidden ground, brazening it out. 'So you admit it is from Mayfair?'

'From Greaves and Worcester.'

'How does a Whitechapel man come to be wearing a shirt from one of the most expensive shirt-makers in London?'

'How is a woman from a Whitechapel chop-house familiar with the said wares and prices?'

She smiled, but said nothing, on the back foot now that he was the one asking questions she did not want to answer.

'What's your story, Emma?'

'Long and uninteresting.'

'For a woman like you, in a place like this?' He arched the rogue eyebrow with scepticism.

She held her silence, wanting to know more of him, but not at the cost of revealing too much of herself.

'Playing your cards close to your chest?' he asked.

'It is the best way, I have found.'

He smiled at that. 'A woman after my own heart.'

They kept on walking, their footsteps loud in the silence.

He met her eyes. 'I heard tell you once worked in Mayfair.' It was the story she had put about.

'Cards and chest, even for unspoken questions,' she said.

Ned laughed.

And she smiled.

'I worked as a lady's maid.' She kept her eyes front facing. If he had not already heard it from the others in the Red Lion, he soon would. It was the only reasonable way to explain away her voice and manners; many ladies' maids aped their mistresses. And it was not, strictly speaking, a lie, she told herself for the hundredth time. She had learned and worked in the job of a lady's maid, just as she had shadow-studied the role of every female servant from scullery maid to housekeeper; one had to have an understanding of how a household worked from the bottom up to properly run it.

'That explains much. What happened?'

'You ask a lot of questions, Ned Stratham.'

'You keep a lot of secrets, Emma de Lisle.'

Their gazes held for a moment too long, in challenge, and something else, too. Until he smiled his submission and looked ahead once more.

She breathed her relief.

A group of men were staggering along the other side of the Minories Road, making their way home from the King's Head. Their voices were loud and boisterous, their gait uneven. They shouted insults and belched at one another. One of them stopped to relieve his bladder against a lamp post.

She averted her eyes from them, met Ned's gaze and knew he was thinking about the knife and how it would have fared against six men.

'It would still have given them pause for thought,' she said in her defence.

Ned said nothing.

But for all of her assertions and the weight of the kitchen knife within her cloak right at this moment in time she was very glad of Ned Stratham's company.

The men did not shout the bawdy comments they would have had it been Tom by her side. They said nothing, just quietly watched them pass and stayed on their own side of the road.

Neither of them spoke. Just walking together at the same steady pace up Minories. Until the drunkards were long in the distance. Until they turned right into the dismal narrow street in which she and her father lodged. There were no street lamps, only the low silvery light of the moon to guide their steps over the potholed surface.

Halfway along the street she slowed and came to a halt outside the doorway of a shabby boarding house.

'This is it. My home.'

He glanced at the building, then returned his eyes to her.

They looked at one another through the darkness.

'Thank you for walking me home, Ned.'

'It was the least I could do for my betrothed,' he said

with his usual straight expression, but there was the hint of a smile in his eyes.

She smiled and shook her head, aware he was teasing her, but her cheeks blushing at what she had let the sailors in the alleyway think. 'I should have set them straight.'

'And end our betrothal so suddenly?'

'Would it break your heart?'

'Most certainly.'

The teasing faded away. And with it something of the safety barrier between them.

His eyes locked hers, so that she could not look away even if she had wanted to. A sensual tension whispered between them. Attraction. Desire. Forbidden liaisons. She could feel the flutter of butterflies in her stomach, feel a heat in her thighs. In the silence of the surrounding night the thud of her heart sounded too loud in her ears. Her skin tingled with nervous anticipation.

She glanced up to the window on the second floor where the light of a single candle showed faintly through the thin curtain. 'My father waits up for me. I should go.'

'You should.'

But she made no move to leave. And neither did he.

He looked at her in a way that made every sensible thought flee her head. He looked at her in a way that made her feel almost breathless.

Ned stepped towards her, closed the distance between them until they were standing toe to toe, until she could feel the brush of his thighs against hers.

'I thought you said you were the perfect gentleman?'

'You said that, not me.' His eyes traced her face, lingering over her lips, so that she knew he meant to kiss her. And God knew what living this life in Whitechapel had done to her because in that moment she wanted him to. Very much.

Desire vibrated between them. Where his thighs touched to hers the skin scalded. In the moonlight his eyes looked dark, smouldering, intense. She knew that he wanted her. Had been around Whitechapel long enough to know the games men and women played.

Emma's breath sounded too loud and ragged.

Their gazes held locked.

The tension stretched until she did not think she could bear it a second longer.

He slid his strong arms around her waist, moving slowly, giving her every chance to step away or tell him nay. But she did neither. Only placed her palms to rest tentatively against the leather breast of his jacket.

He lowered his face towards her.

She tilted her mouth to meet his.

And then his lips took hers and he kissed her.

He kissed her and his kiss was gentle and persuasive. His kiss was tender and passionate. He was the strongest, fiercest man she knew and yet he did not force or plunder. He was not rough or grabbing. It seemed to her he gave rather than took. Courting her lips, teasing them, making her feel things she had never felt before. Making her want him never to stop.

By its own volition one hand moved up over his broad shoulder to hold against the nape of his neck. Anchoring herself to his solidity, to his strength and warmth.

He pulled her closer, their bodies melding together as the kiss intensified. Tasting, touching, sharing. His tongue stroked against hers, inviting hers to a dance she did not know and Emma followed where he led.

He kissed her and she forgot about Whitechapel and poverty and hardship.

He kissed her and she forgot about the darkness of the past and all her worries over the future.

He kissed her and there was nothing else in the world but this man and this moment of magic and madness, and the force of passion that was exploding between them.

And when Ned stopped and drew back to look into her face, her heart was thudding as hard as a blacksmith hitting his anvil and her blood was rushing so fast that she felt dizzy from it.

'You should go up now, before I change my mind about being the perfect gentleman.' He brushed the back of his fingers gently against her cheek.

With trembling legs she walked to the front door of the boarding house and let herself in. She did not look round, but she knew Ned Stratham still stood there watching her. Her heart was skipping in a fast, frenzied thud. Her blood was rushing. Every nerve in her body seemed alive. She closed the door quietly so as not to wake the neighbours. Rested her spine against its peeling paint while she drew a deep breath, calming the tremor in her body and the wild rush of her blood, before climbing the stairwell that led to her father and their rented rooms.

'It is only me, Papa,' she called softly.

But her father was sound asleep in the old armchair.

She moved to the window and twitched the curtain aside to look down on to the street.

Ned Stratham tipped his hat to her. And only then, when he knew she was home safe, did he walk away.

Emma blew out the candle to save what was left. Stood there and watched him until the tall broad-shouldered figure disappeared into the darkness, before turning to her father.

Even in sleep his face was etched with exhaustion.

'Papa,' she whispered and brushed a butterfly kiss against the deep lines of his forehead.

'Jane?' Her mother's name.

'It is Emma.'

'Emma. You are home safe, my girl?'

'I am home safe,' she confirmed and thought again of the man who had ensured it. 'Let me help you to bed.'

'I can manage, my dearest.' He got to his feet with a great deal of stiffness and shuffled through to the smaller of the two rooms.

The door closed with a quiet click, leaving Emma standing there alone.

She touched her fingers to her kiss-swollen lips and knew she should not have kissed Ned Stratham.

He was a Whitechapel man, a man from a different world than her own, a customer who drank in the Red Lion's taproom. And he was fierce and dangerous, and darkly mysterious. And she had no future here. And much more besides. She knew all of that. And knew, too, her mother would be turning in her grave.

But as she moved behind the partitioning screen and changed into her nightdress, in her nose was not the usual sweet mildew, but the lingering scent of soap and leather and something that was just the man himself. And as she pulled back the threadbare covers and climbed into the narrow makeshift bed, in her blood was a warmth.

Emma lay there, staring into the darkness. They said when the devil tempted he offered a heart's desire. Someone tall and dangerous and handsome. She closed her eyes, but she could still see those piercing blue eyes and her lips still tingled and throbbed from the passion of his kiss.

When exhaustion finally claimed her and she sank into the blissful comfort of sleep she dreamed of a tall, dangerous, handsome man tempting her to forbidden lusts, tempting her to give up her struggle to leave Whitechapel and stay here with him. And in the dream she yielded to her heart's desire and was lost beyond all redemption.

Tom did not come to the Red Lion the next night, but Ned Stratham did.

Their gazes held across the taproom, the echoes of last night rippling like an incoming tide, before she turned away to serve a table. Butterflies were dancing in her stomach, but she knew that after what had happened between them, she had to rectify the matter. She emptied her tray, then made her way to where he sat alone.

Those blue eyes met hers.

She felt her heart trip faster and quelled the reaction with an iron hand. Faced him calmly and spoke quietly, but firmly enough that only he would hear.

'Last night, we should not have, *I* should not have… It was a mistake, Ned.'

He said nothing.

'I'm not that sort of a woman.'

'You're assuming I'm that kind of a man.'

'Lest you had forgotten, this is a chop-house not so far from the docks. All the men in here are that kind of a man.'

He smiled at that. A hard smile. 'Not gentlemen, but scoundrels.'

'I did not say that.'

'It's what you meant.'

He glanced across the room to where Paulette was working behind the bar before returning his gaze to hers.

Nancy's curses sounded from the kitchen.

And she knew he knew that Tom had not come in again, that there was no one to see her home.

Ned looked at her with eyes that made no pretence as to the man he was, with eyes that made her resolutions weaken.

'Emma!' Nancy's voice bellowed.

'It is not your duty to see me home.'

'It is not,' he agreed.

As their gazes held in a strange contest of wills, they both knew it was already decided. Ned Stratham was not going to let her take her chances with a kitchen knife through the Whitechapel streets tonight.

'Get yourself over here, Emma!' Nancy sounded as if she were losing what little patience she possessed.

Ned did walk her home. And he did kiss her. And she gave up pretending to herself that she did not want it or him.

He came to the Red Lion every night after that, even when Tom had returned. And every night he walked her home. And every night he kissed her.

Ned tumbled the token over his fingers and leaned his spine back against the old lichen-stained stone seat. St Olave's church clock chimed ten. Down the hill at the London Docks the early shift had started five hours ago.

The sky was a cloudless blue. The worn stone was warm beneath his thighs. His hat sat on the bench by his side and he could feel a breeze stir through his hair. His usual perch. His usual view.

His thoughts drifted to the previous night and Emma de Lisle. Two weeks of walking with her and he could not get her out of his head. Not those dark eyes or that sharp mind. She could hold her own with him. She had her secrets as much as he. A lady's maid who had no wish to discuss her dismissal or her background. She was proud and determined and resourceful. There weren't many women in Whitechapel like her. There weren't *any* women like her. Not that he had known across a lifetime and he had seen about as much of Whitechapel as it was possible to see.

Life had not worn her down or sapped her energy. She had a confidence and a bearing about her comparable with those who came from a lifetime of wealth. She had learnt well from her mistress. A woman like Emma de Lisle would be an asset to any man in any walk of life; it was a thought that grew stronger with the passing days.

And he wanted her. Ned, who did not give in to wants and desires. He wanted her with a passion. And he was spending his nights and too many of his days imagining what it would be like to unlace that tight red dress from her body, to bare her and lay her down on his bed. Ned suppressed the thoughts. He was focused. He was disciplined. He kept to the plan. It was what had brought him this far.

The plan had never involved a woman like her. The plan had been for someone quite different. But she was as refreshing as a cool breeze on a clammy day. She was Whitechapel, the same as him, but with vision that encompassed a bigger view. She had tasted the world on the other side of London. He had a feeling she would understand what it was he was doing, an instinct that she would feel the same about it as he did. And part of being successful was knowing when to be stubborn and stick to the letter of the plan and when to be flexible.

His gaze shifted.

The old vinegar manufactory across the road lay derelict. Pigeons and seagulls vied for supremacy on the hole-ridden roof. Weeds grew from the crumbling walls.

Tower Hill lay at his back. And above his head the canopy of green splayed beech leaves provided a dapple shelter. He could hear the breeze brush through the leaves, a whisper beside the noises that carried up the hill from the London Docks; the rhythmic strike of hammers, the creak and thud of crates being moved and dropped, the squeak of hoists and clatter of chains, the clopping of work horses and rumbling of carts.

A man might live a lifetime and never meet a woman like Emma de Lisle.

Ned's fingers toyed with the ivory token as he watched the men moving about in the dockyard below, men he had known all of his life, men who were friends, or at least had been not so very long ago, unloading the docked ship.

Footsteps drew his attention. He glanced up the street and recognised the woman immediately, despite the fact she was not wearing the figure-hugging red dress, but a respectable sprig muslin and green shawl, and a faded straw bonnet with a green ribbon hid her hair and most of her face. Emma de Lisle; as if summoned by the vision in his head. She faltered when she saw him as if contemplating turning back and walking away.

He slipped the token into his waistcoat pocket and got to his feet.

She resumed her progress. Paused just before she reached him, keeping a respectable distance between them.

'Ned.'

Last night's passion whispered and wound between them.

He gave a nod of acknowledgement.

Once, many years ago, he had seen a honeycomb dripping rich and sweet with golden honey. In this clear, pure daylight her eyes were the same colour, not dark and mysterious as in the Red Lion.

Their gazes held for a moment, the echoes of last night rippling like a returning tide.

'It seems that destiny has set you in my path again, Ned Stratham. Or I, in yours.'

'And who are we to argue with destiny?'

They looked at one another for the first time in daylight.

The road she was walking led from only one place. 'You have come from the dockyard.'

'My father works there. I was delivering him some bread and cheese.'

'He has a considerate daughter.'

'Not really. He worked late last night and started early this morning.'

But she had worked late last night, too, and no doubt started early this morning. A shadow that moved across her eyes and a little line of worry etched between them. 'Delivering his breakfast is the least I can do. He has a quarter-hour break at—'

'Half past nine,' he finished.

She lifted her eyebrows in unspoken question.

'I used to work on the docks.'

'And now?'

'And now, I do not. Cards and chest,' he said.

She laughed and the relaxed fascination he felt for her grew stronger.

'Five o'clock start. Your father will be done by four.'

'If only.' She frowned again at the mention of her father. Twice in five minutes; Ned had never seen her look worried, even on the night when she had thought herself alone facing the two sailors in the alleyway. 'He is on a double shift in the warehouse.'

'Good money, but tiring.'

'Very tiring.' She glanced down the hill at the dockyard with sombre eyes. 'It is hard work for a man of his age who is not used to manual labour.'

'What did he do before manual labour?'

She gave no obvious sign or reaction, only stood still as a statue, but her stillness betrayed that she had not meant to let the fact slip.

Her gaze remained on the dockyard. 'Not manual labour,' she said in a parody of his answer to her earlier question. She glanced round at him then, still and calm, but in her eyes were both defence and challenge. Her smile was sudden and warm, deflecting almost. 'I worry over my father, that is all. The work is hard and he is not a young man.'

'I still know a few folk in the dockyard. I could have a word. See if there are any easier jobs going.'

The silence was like the quiet rustle of silk in the air.

'You would do that?'

'There might be nothing, but I'll ask.' But there would be something. He would make sure of it. 'If you wish.'

He could see what she was thinking.

'No strings attached,' he clarified.

Emma's eyes studied his. Looking at him, really looking at him, like no woman had ever looked before. As if she could see through his skin to his heart, to his very soul, to everything that he was. 'I wish it very much,' she said.

He gave a nod.

There was a pause before she said, 'My father is an educated man. He can read and write and is proficient with arithmetic and mathematics, indeed, anything to do with numbers.'

'A man with book learning.'

She nodded. 'Although I'm not sure if that would be of any use in a dockyard.'

'You would be surprised.'

They stood in silence, both watching the dockworkers unloading the ship, yet her attention was as much on him as his was on her.

'Whatever you do for a living, Ned, whatever illicit activity you might be involved in…if you can help my father…'

'You think I'm a rogue…' He raised his brow. 'Do I look a rogue?'

Her gaze dropped pointedly to the front of his shirt before coming back up to his face. It lingered on his scarred eyebrow before finally moving to his eyes.

'Yes,' she said simply.

'My Mayfair shirt.'

'And the eyebrow,' she added.

'What's wrong with the eyebrow?'

'It does give you a certain roguish appearance.'

He smiled at that.

And she did, too.

'And if I am a rogue?'

She glanced away, gave a tiny shrug of her shoulders. 'It would not affect how I judge you.'

'How do you judge me, Emma?'

She slid a sideways glance at him. 'Cards and chest, Ned.'

He laughed.

'I should go and leave you to your contemplation.'

They looked at one another, the smile still in her sunlit eyes.

'Join me,' he said, yielding for once in his life to impulse. His eyes dared hers to accept.

He saw her gaze move to his scarred eyebrow again, almost caressingly.

He crooked it in a deliberate wicked gesture.

She smiled. 'Very well, but for a few moments only.' She smoothed her skirt to take a seat on the bench.

He sat down by her side.

A bee droned. From the branches overhead a blackbird sang.

Emma's eyes moved from the dockyards to the derelict factory, then over the worn and pitted surface of the road mosaicked with flattened manure, and all the way along to the midden heap at its far end.

'Why here?' she asked.

'I grew up here. It reminds me of my childhood.'

'A tough neighbourhood.'

'Not for the faint of heart,' he said. 'Children are not children for long round here.'

'Indeed, they are not.'

There was a small silence while they both mused on that. And then let it go, eased by the peace of the morning and the place.

'It is a beautiful view,' she said.

Ned glanced round at her, wondering whether she was being ironic. 'Men in gainful employment are always a beautiful sight,' he said gravely.

'I was not thinking in those terms.' She smiled. 'It reminds me of a Canaletto painting.' Her eyes moved to the old manufactory. 'It has the same ruined glory as some of his buildings. The same shade of stone.'

'I wouldn't know. I've never seen a Canaletto painting.'

'I think you would like them.'

'I think maybe I would.'

Her gaze still lingered on the derelict building as she spoke. 'A ruined glory. There are pigeons nesting in what is left of the roof. Rats with wings, my father used to call them,' she said.

'Plenty good eating in a rat.'

She laughed as if he were joking. He did not. He

thought of all the times in his life when rat meat had meant the difference between starvation and survival.

'One day it will be something else,' he said. 'Not a ruined glory, but rebuilt.'

'But then there will be no more violets growing from the walls.'

'Weeds.'

'Not weeds, but the sweetest of all flowers. They used to grow in an old garden wall I knew very well.' The expression on her face was as if she were remembering and the memory both pained and pleased her.

Emma looked round at Ned then and there was something in her eyes, as if he were glimpsing through the layers she presented to the world to see the woman beneath.

'I will remember that, Emma de Lisle,' he said, studying her and everything that she was. A man might live a lifetime and never meet a woman like Emma de Lisle, the thought whispered again in his ear.

Their eyes held, sharing a raw exposed honesty.

Everything seemed to still and fade around them.

He lowered his face to hers and kissed her in the bright glory of the sunshine.

She tasted of all that was sweet and good. She smelled of sunshine and summer, and beneath it the scent of soap and woman.

He kissed her gently, this beautiful woman, felt her meet his kiss, felt her passion and her heart. Felt the desire that was between them surge and flare hot. He intensified the kiss, slid his arms around her and instinctively their bodies moulded together, as their mouths explored. He was hard for her, felt her thigh brush against his arousal, felt the soft press of her breasts against his chest, the slide of her hand beneath his jacket to stroke against his shirt, against his heart.

And then her palm flattened, pressed against his chest to stay him.

Their lips parted.

'It is broad daylight, Ned Stratham!' Her cheeks were flushed. Her eyes were dark with passion and shock. 'Anyone might see us.'

He twitched his scarred eyebrow.

She shook her head as if she were chiding him, but she smiled as she got to her feet.

He stood, too.

A whistling sounded and a man's figure appeared from the corner, trundling his barrow of fish along the road— Ernie Briggins, one of the Red Lion's best customers. 'Morning, Ned.'

Ned gave a nod.

Ernie's eyes moved to Emma with speculation and a barely suppressed smile. 'Morning, Emma.'

'Morning, Ernie.' Emma's cheeks glowed pink.

Ernie didn't stop, just carried on his way, leaving behind him the lingering scent of cod and oysters and the faint trill of his reedy whistle.

Emma said nothing, just raised her brows and looked at Ned with a 'told you so' expression.

'I better get you safely home, before any more rogues accost you.'

'I think I will manage more safely alone, thank you. Stay and enjoy your view.' Her eyes held to his. 'I insist.' She backed away. Smiled. Turned to leave.

'Emma.'

She stopped. Glanced round.

'I'm going out of town for the next week or so. I have some business to attend to. But I'll be back.'

'Developed a compulsion for the porter, have you?'

'A compulsion for something else, it would seem,' he said quietly. 'We need to talk when I return, Emma.'

'That sounds serious.'

'It is.' He paused, then asked, 'Will you wait for me?'

There was a silence as her eyes studied his. 'I am not going anywhere, Ned Stratham.'

Their eyes held, serious and intent, for a second longer. 'I will wait,' she said softly.

They shared a smile before she turned and went on her way.

He watched her walk off into the sunlight until she disappeared out of sight.

A man might live a lifetime and never meet a woman like Emma de Lisle. But not Ned.

A fancy new dress and Emma wouldn't be out of place in Mayfair. Ned smiled to himself and, lifting his hat, began the long walk back across town.

The letter came the very next morning.

Emma stood in the rented room in the bright golden sunshine with the folded and sealed paper between her fingers, and the smile that had been on her face since the previous day vanished.

It had taken a shilling of their precious savings to pay the post boy, but it was a willing sacrifice. She would have sold the shoes from her feet, sold the dress from her back to accept the letter and all that it might contain.

Her heart began to canter. She felt hope battle dread.

The paper was quality and white, her father's name written on the front in a fine hand with deep-black ink. There was no sender name, no clue impressed within the red-wax seal.

She swallowed, took a deep breath, stilled the churn in her stomach. It might not be the letter for which her father and she had both prayed and dreaded all of these two years past.

The one o'clock bell tolled in the distance.

She placed the letter down on the scrubbed wooden table. Stared at it, knowing that her father would not finish his shift before she left for the Red Lion, knowing, too, that he would probably be asleep by the time she returned. She was very aware that the answer to what had sent her mother to an early grave and turned her father grey with worry might lie within its folds.

Kit. She closed her eyes at the thought of her younger brother and knew that she could not get through the rest of this day without knowing if the letter contained news of him. Nor would her father. He would want to know, just the same as Emma. Whether the news was good... or even if it was bad.

She pulled her shawl around her shoulders, fastened her bonnet on her head and, with the letter clutched tight within her hand, headed for the London Docks.

Chapter Four

Emma knew little of the warehouse in which her father worked. He had spoken nothing of it, so this was her first insight into the place that had become his world as much as the Red Lion had become hers.

All around the walls were great racks of enormous shelving stacked with boxes and bales. The windows in the roof were open, but with the heat of the day and the heavy work many of the men were working without shirts. She blushed with the shock of seeing their naked chests and rapidly averted her gaze, as she followed the foreman through the warehouse. Eventually through the maze of shelving corridors they came to another group of shirtless men who were carrying boxes up ladders to stack on high shelves.

'Bill de Lisle,' the foreman called. 'Someone here to see you.'

One of the men stepped forward and she was horrified to see it was her father.

'Papa?' She forgot herself in the shock of seeing his gaunt old body, all stringy from hard labour.

'Emma?' She heard her shock echoed in his voice. In a matter of seconds he had reclaimed his shirt and pulled it over his head. 'What has happened? What is wrong to bring you here?'

'A letter. Addressed to you. I thought it might contain news of...' She bit her lip, did not finish the sentence.

'If you will excuse me for a few moments, gentlemen,' her father said to the men behind him. 'And Mr Sears,' to the foreman who had brought her to him.

Her father guided her a little away from the group. 'Bill?'

'It is what they call me here.'

She gave a small smile. The smile faded as she passed the letter to him. 'Maybe I should not have brought it here, but I thought...' She stopped as her father scrutinised the address penned upon it. 'The writing is not of Kit's hand, but even so... Someone might have seen him. Someone might know his whereabouts.'

Her father said nothing, but she saw the slight tremble in his fingers as he broke the red-wax seal and opened the letter. He held it at arm's length to read it since his spectacles were long gone.

She swallowed, her throat suddenly dry with anticipation. Rubbed her clammy palms together and waited. Waited until she could wait no more.

'Is it good news?'

Her father finished reading and looked up at her. 'It is the best of news, Emma...'

The breath she had been holding escaped in a gasp. Her heart leapt. The terrible tight tension that held her rigid relaxed.

'...but it does not concern your brother.'

The warm happiness flowing through her turned cold. She glanced up at her father. 'I do not understand.'

'The letter is from Mrs Tadcaster, who was second cousin to your mama. She writes to say that the Dowager Lady Lamerton's companion has run off with one of the footmen.'

'Why is that good news?'

'Because, my dear—' he smiled '—the dowager is in need of a new companion, a woman of gentle breeding who would understand what was required of her and might start in the position with immediate effect.'

The penny dropped. Emma suddenly realised why her mother's cousin had written to impart such trivial gossip. She knew where this was leading. And she should have been glad. Indeed, had it been only a few weeks ago she would have been. But much had happened in those weeks and the feeling in the pit of her stomach was not one of gladness.

'Mrs Tadcaster had spoken to her ladyship of you and Lady Lamerton has agreed to take you on as her companion.'

Emma could not say a word.

'Such sudden and surprising news after all this time. Little wonder you are shocked.'

She was shocked, but not for the reasons her father thought.

We need to talk when I return.

That sounds serious.

It is. Will you wait for me?

Ned's words and all they might mean had not left her mind since yesterday. Her stomach felt hollow.

'I cannot go.'

'Why ever not?' He stared at her

How could she tell him about Ned? Not a gentleman, but a Whitechapel man. A man who was tougher and more dangerous than all he had warned her against. A man who could best five men in a tavern fight and who had worked on these same docks. A man who made magic somersault in her stomach and passion beat through her blood. Whose kiss she wanted to last for ever...and who had implied he wanted a future with her.

'I could not possibly contemplate leaving you here alone.'

'Nonsense. It would be a weight off my mind to know that you were living a safe, respectable life with the Dowager Lady Lamerton. Do you not think I have enough to worry over with Kit?'

'I understand that, but you need not worry over me.'

'You are a serving wench in a tavern.'

'It is a chop-house, Papa,' she corrected him out of force of habit.

'Emma, chop-house or tavern, it makes no difference. Do you think I do not know the manner of men with whom you must deal? Do you think there is a night goes by I am not sick with worry until Tom sees you safely home and I hear you coming through that front door?'

She felt guilt turn in her stomach at the thought of him worrying so much while she enjoyed being with Ned.

'Were you with Lady Lamerton, I could find lodgings closer to the docks. There are always fellows looking for someone to share the rent on a single room. It would be easier for me. Cheaper. More convenient. And they are a good enough bunch in here. Tease me a bit, but that is the extent of it.'

'Lady Lamerton will see this as an opportunity to glean every last detail of our scandal from me. You know she is chief amongst the gossipmongers and has a nose like a bloodhound.'

'Clarissa Lamerton likes to be queen of the *ton*'s gossip, not its subject. She will grill you herself, but protect you from all others. What is this sudden change of heart, Emma? This argument is usually the other way around. You have always been so strong and committed to returning to society and tracing Kit.'

Emma glanced away.

'Lady Lamerton's ability to discover information is all the more reason to accept the position. You would be well placed, in one of the best households in London, to hear news of Kit. Lady Lamerton's son has an association with Whitehall. Rest assured young Lamerton will hear if there is anything to be heard and thus, too, his mother. You have to take this opportunity, Emma, for Kit's sake and mine, as well as for your own. You know that without me telling you.'

She did. That was the problem. She understood too well what he was saying and the truth in it.

'If you stay here, you are lost. It is only a matter of time before one of these men makes you his own. Indeed, it is a miracle that it has not already happened.'

She glanced down at the floor beneath their feet so that he would not see the truth in her eyes.

But he reached over and tilted her face up to his. 'You are a beautiful young woman, the very image of your mother when I met and married her. I want a better life for you than that which a husband from round here could offer you.'

She wanted to tell him so much, of Ned and all that was between them, but she could not. Not now, not when her duty was so pressing.

'As if I would have a husband from round here.' Her forced smile felt like a grimace.

Will you wait for me? In her mind she could see that soul-searching look in Ned's eyes.

And hear her own reply. *I am not going anywhere, Ned Stratham...I will wait.*

'I am glad you have not forgotten your vow to your mother, Emma.'

'How could I ever forget?' She never would, never could. Family was family. A vow was just that, even if it was at the expense of her own happiness. She felt like her heart was torn between her family and the man she loved.

She told herself that Ned might not love her, that she might have misunderstood what it was he wanted to talk to her of. After all, he had made no promises or declarations, and despite all those late-night conversations and all their passion, they knew so little of each other. But in her heart, she knew.

She knew, but it did not change what she had to do.

'You know you have to take this chance, Emma.' Her father's eyes scanned hers.

'Yes.' One small word to deny the enormity of what was in her heart.

'I will go past the mail-receiving office on the way home, pay for paper and some ink and write to Mrs Tadcaster.'

She gave a nod.

'Let me escort you from this place.'

Emma placed her hand on his arm and walked with him, without noticing the shirtless men who stopped working to watch her pass with silent appreciation.

She was thinking of all the days and nights she had worked so hard to escape Whitechapel, of all the times she had prayed for just such an opportunity. And now that her prayer had finally been answered she did not want to leave.

She was thinking of a man whose hair the sun had

lightened to the colour of corn-ripened fields and whose eyes matched the cloudless summer sky outside; a man who had captured her heart, and to whom there would be no chance to explain.

On the afternoon of Ned's return from Portsmouth, he went straight to a meeting in White's Club. But now the meeting was concluded, the necessary introductions made and ideas discussed. He shook hands with the Earl of Misbourne, Viscount Linwood, the Marquis of Razeby and Mr Knight.

'If you will excuse me, gentlemen?' A nod of the head and he and his friend and steward, Rob Finchley, were out of the room and walking down the corridor.

Further down the corridor, he saw the small group of men who knew his secret. Men who were bursting with longing to take him down, to expose his real identity, but could not. They knew what would happen if they did. He met each of their gazes in turn across the distance, held them so that they would remember why they could not tell what itched upon their tongues to be out. And in return they glowered with all their haughty disdain.

Rob cursed beneath his breath. 'They look at you as if you're a gutter rat in their midst.'

Ned smiled at the group of arrogant young noblemen. It had the desired effect, twisting the knife a little deeper. 'But remember what it costs them to stand there and suffer my presence.'

Rob grinned. 'I feel better already.'

They were still smiling as they crossed St James's Street and climbed into the waiting gig. It was a top-of-the-range model, sleek, glossy black exterior, cream leather seats; a small white circle enclosing a red diamond shape adorned the front plate. Ned did not look back. Just took up the reins and drove off.

'I think you hooked Misbourne.'

'Let's hope.' The wheels sped along. Ned kept his eyes forward concentrating on the traffic. 'I can't make Dawson's ball tonight.'

'Not like you to miss a big event like Dawson's.'

'I have a commitment elsewhere.' His face was closed and impassive, his usual expression when it came to dealing with friend and foe alike.

'All the bigwigs are going to be there.'

'I know.'

There was a small silence before Rob said, 'Must be important, this other commitment.'

'It is.' Ned slid a glance at his friend, let his eyes linger for a moment, in that quiet confrontational way, and smiled.

Rob smiled, too. 'All right, mate. I get the hint. I'll stop fishing about your mystery woman.'

A few hours later, Ned walked alone into the Red Lion Chop-House. Some heads nodded at him, recognising him from the weeks before. Ned felt the usual comfort and ease that sat about the place, felt it as soon as he crossed the parish boundary that divided the East End from the rest of London. The taproom was busy as usual, the tables and rowdy noise of the place spilling out into the alleyway in front. His eyes scanned for Emma, but did not find her.

The first suspicion stroked when he saw that it was Paulette who came to serve him.

'Your usual, is it?'

He gave a nod. 'Emma not in tonight?'

'Thought you might ask that.' She smiled a saucy

knowing look. 'Emma's gone. Landed herself some fancy job as a lady's maid again. An offer she couldn't refuse apparently, lucky mare. She left a message for you, though. Said to tell you goodbye. That she was real sorry she couldn't tell you in person. Said she hoped you would understand.'

He dropped a coin into her hand for passing on the message. 'Forget the lamb and the porter.' He didn't wait.

There were other chop-houses in Whitechapel. Other serving wenches. But Ned didn't go to them. Instead he made his way up along Rosemary Lane to Tower Hill and the ancient stone bench beneath the beech trees. And he sat there alone and watched the day shift finish in the docks and the night shift begin. Watched the ships that docked and the ships that sailed. Watched until the sun set in a glorious blaze of fire over the Thames and the daylight faded to dusk and dusk to darkness.

Had she waited just one week…a single week and how different both their lives would have been.

Loss and betrayal nagged in his gut. He breathed in the scent of night with the underlying essence of vinegar that always lingered in this place. And he thought of the scent of soap and grilled chops and warm woman.

He thought of the teasing intelligence in her eyes and the warmth of her smile.

He thought of the passion between them and the sense that she made his world seem a better place.

He thought of what might have been, then he let the thoughts go and he crushed the feelings. Emma de Lisle had not waited. And that was that.

Ned was not a man who allowed himself to be influenced by emotion. He had his destiny. And maybe it was better this way. No distractions, after all.

He heard the cry of the watch in the distance. Only then did he make his way back across town to the mansion house in Cavendish Square.

Along the Westminster Bridge Road in Lambeth, the evening was fine and warm as Emma and the Dowager Lady Lamerton approached Astley's Amphitheatre.

'I say, this is really rather exciting,' her new employer said as they abandoned the carriage to the traffic jam in which it was caught and walked the remaining small distance to the amphitheatre's entrance.

'It is, indeed.' It was only Emma's third day returned to life in London's high society, albeit at a somewhat lesser level to that she had known, and already she was aware that there was a part of her that had settled so smoothly it was as if she had never been away—and a part that remained in Whitechapel, with her father...and another man.

She wondered again how her father was managing in his new lodging. Wondered if he was eating. Wondered if Ned Stratham had returned to the Red Lion yet and if Paulette had passed on her message.

'In all of my seventy-five years I have yet to see a woman balancing on one leg upon the back of a speeding horse,' said Lady Lamerton. Her walking stick tapped regular and imperious against the pavement as they walked.

Emma hid her private thoughts away and concentrated on the dowager and the evening ahead. 'I hope you shall not find it too shocking.' She tucked her arm into the dowager's, helping to stabilise her through the crowd.

'But, my dear, I shall be thoroughly disappointed if it is not. This latest show is quite the talk of the *ton*. Everyone who is anyone is here to see it.'

Emma laughed. 'Well, in that case we had best go in and find our box.'

As being seen there was more important than actually watching the show, Lady Lamerton and Emma had a splendid vantage point. There was the buzz of voices and bustle of bodies as the rest of the audience found their seats.

'Do look at that dreadful monstrosity that Eliza Frenshaw has upon her head. That, my dear, is what lack of breeding does for you, but then her father was little better than a grocer, you know,' Lady Lamerton said with the same tone as if she had just revealed that Mrs Frenshaw's father had been a mass murderer. Then had the audacity to nod an acknowledgement to the woman in question and bestow a beatific smile.

Emma drew Lady Lamerton a look.

'What?' Lady Lamerton's expression was the hurt innocence that Emma had already learned was her forte. 'Am I not telling the truth?'

'You are never anything other than truthful,' said Emma with a knowing expression.

The two women chuckled together before Lady Lamerton returned to scrutinising the rest of the audience with equally acerbic observations.

Emma let her eyes sweep over the scene in the auditorium before them.

There was not an empty seat to be seen. The place was packed with the best of the *ton* that had either remained in London for the summer or returned early. Ladies in silk evening dresses, a myriad of colours from the rich opulence of the matrons to the blinding white of the debutantes, and every shade in between. All wearing long white-silk evening gloves that fastened at the top of their arms. Their hair dressed in glossy ringlets and fixed with sprays of fresh flowers or enormous feathers that obscured the view of those in the seats behind. Some matrons had forgone the feathers in favour of dark-coloured silk turbans. There was the sparkle of jewels that gleamed around their pale necks or on their gloved fingers that held opera glasses. Like birds of paradise preening and parading. Only two years ago and Emma had been a part of it as much as the rest of them. Now, beautiful as it was, she could not help but be uncomfortably aware that the cost of a single one of those dresses was more than families in Whitechapel had to survive on for a year.

There were many nodded acknowledgments to Lady Lamerton and even some to Emma. Emma nodded in return, glad that, for the most part, people accepted her return without much censure.

Her eyes moved from the stalls, up to the encircling boxes and their inhabitants. To the Duke of Hawick and a party of actresses. To Lord Linwood and his wife, the celebrated Miss Venetia Fox. To the Earl of Hollingsworth, and his family and guest.

Lady Hollingsworth did not nod. The woman's eyes were cool, her nose held high in disdain. Emma met her gaze boldly. Refused to be embarrassed. Smiled with amusement, then moved her gaze along to Hollingsworth's daughter, Lady Persephone, with her pale golden-blonde hair and her perfect pout, and the way she was flirting with the gentleman by her side, no doubt the suitor Hollingsworth was hoping to land for her. The gas lighting dimmed just as Emma's gaze shifted to the man, but for one glimmer of a second she saw him. Or thought she saw him. And what she saw made her heart miss a beat and her stomach turn a somersault.

The music started. The ringmaster, red-coated and

waxen-moustached, the ultimate showman, appeared, his booming voice carrying promises of what lay ahead that drew gasps of astonishment from the audience. The performance was starting, but Emma did not look at the ring. Her focus was still on Lady Persephone's suitor. On the fine dark tailored tailcoat, on the gleam of white evening wear that showed beneath. On the fair hair and face that was so like another, a world away in Whitechapel, that they might have been twins. And yet it could not be him. It was not possible.

Her eyes strained all the harder, her heart thudding faster. But in the dimmed light and across the distance she could not be sure.

As if sensing her stare his eyes shifted to hers and held for a second. She moved her gaze to the stage, embarrassed to have been caught staring.

Six white horses galloped with speed around the ring while the scantily clad women on their backs rose in unison to balance on one leg.

There were gasps and applause.

'Heaven's above,' muttered the dowager, but she applauded.

Emma clapped, too, but she was barely seeing the horses or the women on their backs.

It could not be him, she told herself again and again. But every time she stole another glance in his direction the man was watching her and her heart missed a beat at the uncanny familiarity. She stopped looking, aware that she was giving a strange man altogether the wrong impression. The lights would come up at the interval and she would see she was imagining things.

Ned was too much on her mind. The touch of his kiss. The feel of his strong arms around her. The promise in those last words between them. *But I'll be back... We need to talk when I return, Emma.*

I am not going anywhere, Ned Stratham. I will wait.

Guilt squeezed at her heart. She wondered what he had said when he discovered her gone, wondered if his heart ached like hers. Had she stayed he would have bedded her. Had she stayed he might have married her. She closed her eyes at that. Reined her emotions under control. Was careful not to look at Lady Persephone's beau again.

The interval arrived at long last.

The lights came up.

'Tolerably interesting, I suppose,' pronounced Lady Lamerton with a sniff. 'Would you not say?'

Emma smiled. 'I would agree wholeheartedly.'

Then, as Lady Lamerton's footman arrived to take her drinks order, Emma's eyes moved to the Hollingsworths' box.

Both the earl and the suitor were gone, leaving only Lady Hollingsworth and Lady Persephone surveying with smug arrogance. Emma's heart dipped in disappointment.

What if he did not return before the lights dimmed once more?

It was not him. It could not be him. It was ridiculous to even think such a thing.

The moments stretched with an unbearable slowness. She focused all her attention on the dowager. Only when the bell sounded for the end of the interval, only when she knew the dowager's gaze engaged once more on the melee of bodies returning to their seats, did she look again at the Hollingsworths' box.

The man was there, looking directly at her. But this time she did not avert her gaze.

She could not move, just sat there and blatantly stared.

Her heart was hammering fit to burst, her breath was caught in her throat. Something constricted around her chest and squeezed tight at her heart. She felt as though all the world had rolled away to leave nothing in its wake, save Emma and the man at whom she stared.

Only Emma and Ned Stratham.

Chapter Five

In those tiny seconds that stretched between them to an eternity Ned knew that fate was playing tricks with him. He saw a reflection of his own shock in Emma's face. And with it was hurt exposed raw and vulnerable, there for a heartbeat, and then replaced with accusation and angry disbelief. Her eyes flicked momentarily to Lady Persephone by his side before coming back to his.

Ned's gaze lingered on Emma even after she had turned her face away.

'Is everything all right, Mr Stratham? You seem a little preoccupied.'

'Forgive me, Lady Persephone.' He forced his attention to her rather than Emma.

He could feel his blood pumping harder than in any fight, feel the shock snaking through his blood.

'Such a pleasure that you agreed to accompany us tonight, sir.' Lady Persephone smiled and struck a pose to show her face off to its best. She was pampered, self-obsessed and with the same disdainful arrogance that ran through most women of her class. Her figure was plump and curvaceous from a lifetime of good living. Pale golden-blonde ringlets had been arranged artfully to cascade from her where her hair was pinned high. Her dress was some kind of expensive white silk edged with pale-pink ribbon. Her shawl was white, threaded through with gold threads that complemented her hair. A fortune's worth. Little wonder that Hollingsworth needed an alliance.

'The pleasure is all mine.' He made the glib reply with a smile that did not touch his eyes.

She fluttered her eyelashes, but as the lights went down, his eyes were not on the earl's daughter or the sleek black stallion that had galloped into the amphitheatre ring, but on the woman who sat by the Dowager Lady Lamerton's side. A woman he had last seen walking down a deserted sunlit road in Whitechapel on a morning not so long ago.

He watched her too often during the remaining performance, but she did not look at him again, not once, her attention as fixed with determination upon the ring below as the smile on her face.

The performance was long. Very long. He bided his time.

The end came eventually. He escorted Lady Persephone and her family out.

Across the crowd in the foyer he could see Emma and Lady Lamerton making their way towards the staircase.

Emma glanced up, met his gaze with icy accusation before she turned and was carried away with Lady Lamerton and the crowd.

'If you will excuse me,' he said smoothly to the Hollingsworths.

'But, Mr Stratham!' He heard the shock and petulance in Lady Persephone's voice.

'Well, I never—' Hollingsworth was beginning to say,

but Ned did not stay to hear the rest. He was already weaving his way through the crowd towards the staircase down which Emma had disappeared.

He caught up with her in the crowd on the ground floor, came up close behind.

'Emma,' he said her name quietly enough that only she would hear as he caught a hold of her arm, unnoticed in the crush that surrounded them, and steered her into a nearby alcove.

She tried to snatch her hand free of his grip, but he held her firm. 'Do not "Emma" me!'

Her spine was flush against the wall. He stood in close to protect her from the sight of passing eyes. So close he could smell the familiar enticing scent of her, so close that his thighs brushed against hers.

Anger was a tangible thing between them, flushing her cheeks, making her dark eyes glitter.

'Not a Whitechapel man after all, Ned Stratham.'

'Always a Whitechapel man,' he said with unshakeable steadfastness. 'Not a lady's maid after all, Emma de Lisle.'

She ignored the jibe, held his gaze with a quiet fury. 'Tell me, upon your return to Whitechapel, was it of your courtship with an earl's daughter that we were to have "talked"?'

'Had you waited, as you said you would, you would know.'

They were standing so close he could see the indignation that flashed in her eyes and feel the tremor that vibrated through her body.

'Know that all those nights you were not walking out with me in Whitechapel you were here, in Mayfair, paying court to Lady Persephone? Know that there was more than one woman on the receiving end of your charms?

Know that you were lying through your teeth to me when you implied you had a care for me, for your care was all for another?' Her breath was ragged. 'I am glad I did not wait to hear you spin more of your lies.'

'I am not the one who lied.'

'And yet here you are in high society.'

'With good reason.'

'Oh, spare me, please!' Her breasts brushed against his chest with every breath she took.

'No,' he said in a low voice. 'You will have your explanation, Emma, and I will have mine.'

Where his hand still held hers he felt the sudden leap of her pulse.

'I do not think so, Ned. You should return to Lady Persephone. I am sure she will be wondering where her suitor has got to. Just as Lady Lamerton will be seeking me.'

The accusation rippled between them.

He pinned her with his gaze, but she did not falter, just held it with hot hard defiance.

'We will talk, Emma.' He released her and stepped aside.

She held his gaze for a moment longer. 'Hell will freeze over first, Ned Stratham.' She stepped out into the flow of the crowd just as Lady Lamerton, who had almost reached the front door, peered behind.

He stood where he was and watched until Emma had negotiated her way through the bodies to reach the older woman. Only once they had disappeared through the front door did he step out into the crowd.

'I look forward to hearing more of your news. Yours with affection...' Within the drawing room of her Grosvenor Place home the Dowager Lady Lamerton finished dictating the letter. 'Compose another one in the same vein to Georgiana Hale. Not a straight copy, you understand, in case the unthinkable happens and they see each other's correspondence.' Lady Lamerton gave a shudder at the thought.

'Of course.' Emma passed the letter to Lady Lamerton for her signature. 'And the part about Dorothy Wetherby... I believe that Mrs Hale and Mrs Wetherby are cousins.'

'Good lord, I had forgotten. You are quite right, my dear. No mention of Dorothy Wetherby's latest exploits.' She smiled what Emma had come to call her mischievous smile. 'That would certainly put the cat amongst the pigeons.' She chuckled as she signed her name and passed the paper back to Emma.

'We had quite the time of it last night, did we not?' demanded Lady Lamerton.

'Indeed.' Emma busied herself in blotting the letter dry and finding the sealing wax. She did not want to speak of last night. She did not want to think of it. Not when she had already lain awake half the night thinking of nothing else.

'I do not see what all the fuss was about. It was not as shocking as was implied.'

'Some aspects of it were very shocking,' said Emma, although those aspects had not occurred within the ring.

'Perhaps to you with your innocence and naïvety...'

She smiled at that, but it was an ironic smile. Oh, she had been naïve, all right. Naïve to trust Ned Stratham. Even after all she had learned in these past two years. Pretending he was a Whitechapel man. Pretending he was considering a future with a serving wench when he was serious only about landing himself a title. Liar!

Damnable liar! She was so angry, at him, and at her-self for believing him. When she thought what she had felt for him…what she had done with him… When she thought how close she had come to turning down the opportunity to return to society and all it might allow her to do for Kit…and all for a man who had deceived her. She wondered if anything of what he had said had been true. But then when she had thought about it dur-ing those long hours of the night, how much had he ac-tually told her of himself? Answering questions with questions. And in her efforts to protect her own secrets she had not pressed him.

'But not to a woman of my position and experience of life and the world.'

Emma gave another smile, but said nothing.

'How was it seeing so many familiar faces again, my dear?'

'Most interesting.'

She thought of Lord Hollingsworth and his family in the box at the amphitheatre, Ned sitting beside Hol-lingsworth's daughter, and felt something twist in her stomach.

'I could not help notice the appearance of some new faces amidst the old. Faces I do not know.'

'We have had a few new arrivals since you were last in society, Emma.'

'And some betrothals and weddings, no doubt.'

'Oh, indeed. And some most scandalous. The Earl of Misbourne's son, Viscount Linwood, married the ac-tress Miss Fox and was caught up in the most appalling murder scandal. And Misbourne's daughter, Lady Mari-anne, a meek and mild little thing who wouldn't say boo to a goose, was married with rather suggestive haste to a gentleman who, let us just say, was the antithesis of what one would have anticipated Misbourne to have chosen. But then there always has been something rather shady about that family.' She leaned closer, her eyes sparkling as she relived the gossip.

'Lady Persephone must have made her come out by now.' Emma hoped she was not being too obvious in what she wanted to ask.

'Indeed,' said the dowager. 'She came out this Season and took very well—very well indeed.'

Emma felt nauseous. 'She is betrothed?'

'Heavens, no! Hollingsworth has pockets to let and needs her to make an alliance to rectify the problem. All the interest in Lady Persephone was from other titles or gentlemen with insufficient funds for Hollingsworth's liking. He is angling to catch her Mr Stratham.'

Just the mention of his name made her stomach squeeze a little tighter. She swallowed.

'Mr Stratham,' she said lightly as if the name meant nothing to her. 'I do not believe I have heard of that gentleman.'

'One of the *ton*'s new faces. Made his money from trade overseas amongst other things.' The dowager could not quite keep the censure from her tone. 'A self-made man, but enormously wealthy.' She paused for effect and met Emma's eyes to deliver the golden piece of information. 'Lives in a mansion in Cavendish Square.' One of the most elite addresses in London.

'He must be wealthy indeed.' Yet he had pretended to live in the Whitechapel streets the same as her. Had walked her home to the shabby boarding house in which she and her father had lodged. She closed her eyes at the memory of those nights and all they had entailed.

'But Hollingsworth is not the only one seeking Mr Stratham's money. Devonport, Longley and a number of others are, too. Stratham is in a strong position to negotiate the best deal.'

'A host of earl's daughters to pick from,' she said and hoped the dowager did not hear the bitter edge to her voice.

'Quite.' Lady Lamerton nodded. 'Although in the past month it has to be said he seems to have been rather distracted from the marriage mart. No doubt making the most of his bachelorhood before he makes his decision and commits himself.'

'No doubt,' Emma said grimly. 'And his pedigree?' She wanted to know more of this man who had duped her so badly, this man who had lied to and betrayed her.

'No one knows quite where Edward Stratham came from, although his accent betrays something of common roots.'

Whitechapel. The word whispered through Emma's mind, but she dismissed it.

'He is a member of White's Club, but according to m'son does not attend much. And other than his steward, Mr Rob Finchley, Stratham has no close friends or confidantes.'

'Even you have been able to discover nothing else of him?'

Lady Lamerton puffed herself at Emma's subtle acknowledgement of her prowess in the gleaning of information from persons of interest, as she liked to say.

'Stratham keeps his own counsel and when it comes to discussing matters he has no wish to discuss…how can I put it?' She thought for a moment and then said, 'He is not a man whom one can press.'

Emma understood very well that Ned Stratham was not the sort of man to be intimidated.

'But for all he is trade, he is a handsome devil and such eyes as to have half the ladies in London in a swoon.'

Emma felt the tiny clench of the muscle in her jaw. 'And what news of Miss Darrington? How does she fare?'

'Now there is a story and a half.' Having exhausted the available gossip on Ned Stratham, Lady Lamerton was more than happy to move on to another subject. 'There was the most dreadful scandal concerning Miss Darrington and the Marquis of Razeby.'

Emma finished sealing the letter and settled comfortably in her chair to listen.

It was later that same day, at half past two, when Emma and Lady Lamerton arrived outside the circulating library for the dowager's weekly visit. Emma waited as Lady Lamerton was helped down the carriage step by a footman. A rather saucy romantic novel hidden between two books on art, as per the dowager's instruction, was tucked under Emma's arm. Lady Lamerton deemed it perfectly acceptable to be reading erotic art books, but heaven forbid that she be seen with a racy romance.

'How did you enjoy the novel?' Emma asked.

'Absolute poppycock,' the dowager pronounced as she leaned upon her walking stick. And then added with a smile, 'But immensely enjoyable poppycock. A rather wicked story all about a devilishly handsome, if rather dangerous, gentleman.' She gave a little amused chuckle and Emma smiled.

She was still smiling as she glanced along the pavement they were about to cross to reach the library door and then the smile vanished from her face. For there, strolling towards them, was Ned Stratham.

Those blue eyes met hers.

Her heart missed a beat before racing fit to burst. She deliberately shifted her gaze, ignoring him, as if he were not there.

Please God... But her prayer went unanswered. Lady Lamerton saw him at once. 'Why, Mr Stratham. We were just talking of you.'

Emma felt her face scald.

'Only good things, I hope.'

'Is there anything bad?' enquired the dowager sweetly.

Ned smiled. 'Now, that would be telling.'

Lady Lamerton gave a laugh. 'La, sir, you are quite the rogue.'

'Indeed, I am, ma'am.' His smile painted the words of truth as those of jest.

Then his eyes moved to Emma and lingered.

She held her head high. Feigned a calmness she did not feel. Inside her heart was beating nineteen to the dozen, but she met his gaze coolly.

'I do not believe you have met m'companion, sir.'

'I have not had that pleasure,' he said. 'I would have been sure to remember.'

No insinuations that they had met before. No hints over Whitechapel.

Their eyes held.

She swallowed.

'May I introduce Miss Emma Northcote,' Lady Lamerton said.

Ned seemed to still and for the flicker of a second Emma saw something that looked like shock in his eyes. Then it was gone and he was once more his quiet assured self.

Only then did she remember that he knew her as de Lisle.

Her eyes held his, waiting for him to make some comment on her change of name. Her breath held, waiting as that tiny moment seemed to stretch. The atmosphere between them was obvious.

'I am pleased to meet you, Miss Northcote.' His voice was as cool as his gaze. He gave a curt bow.

'Likewise, Mr Stratham.' She dropped the smallest curtsy.

There was a deafening silence, which Ned made no effort to fill.

'We are for the circulating library, sir,' said Lady Lamerton. 'Are you?'

'No.' He did not elaborate.

The dowager inclined her head, dismissing him.

'Your servant, ma'am.'

His eyes moved to Emma's again.

This time there was no perfunctory smile on his lips and the look in his eyes made her shiver. 'Miss *Northcote*.' The slightest emphasis on her name.

She gave a nod and turned away to escort the dowager into the library.

There was no sound of his footsteps upon the pavement and she had the feeling that he was standing there, watching her. It made her feel nervous. It made each step feel like an eternity. But she did not yield to the urge to glance behind. Not until Lady Lamerton was through the door and Emma, too, was safe inside the library.

He was still standing there, just as she had thought. And there was something in the way he was looking at her, something focused and hard, as if he were seeing her for the first time, as if he were scrutinising her. Something of accusation that made her uncomfortably aware that she had not been entirely honest with him.

Only then did he dip his head in a final acknowledgement and turn and walk away.

* * *

Rob was waiting for him in his study when Ned got back to the mansion in Cavendish Square.

His friend and steward glanced round from where he was examining the arrangement of swords and sabres mounted upon the wall. 'I came early. Wanted to check over a few things before we left for Misbourne's.'

Ned gave a nod, and passed his cane and hat to Clarkson. Then peeled off his gloves and did the same.

The door closed with a quiet click behind the departing butler.

Ned walked straight to his desk and, ignoring the crystal decanter of brandy that sat there on the silver salver, opened the bottom drawer and took out a bottle of gin. He poured two generous measures into the matching crystal glasses. Passed one to Rob and took a deep swig from the other.

He could feel his friend's eyes on him and knew it didn't look good, but right at this minute he didn't give a damn.

'You all right, Ned?'

'I've been better.'

'You look like you've just seen a ghost.'

That was certainly one way of putting it.

'Business deal gone bad?' Rob asked.

Nothing so simple. 'Something like that.'

'Not Misbourne. Not the—'

'No.' He cut Rob off. Took another swig of the gin, relishing the raw kick of it. 'Not Misbourne.'

'That's a relief, at least.'

'Yes.'

There was a silence. Ned's mind was whirring. His blood still pumping hard as if he'd just floored ten men. He could feel a cold sweat on his upper lip, a clamminess on the palms of his hands. He took another gulp of gin to numb the tremor of shock that still ran through him.

'If you need to call off with Misbourne…'

'I don't.' Ned met his friend's gaze. 'I need Misbourne on board. And missing a lunch he's arranged will set him against me.'

'It's just a lunch.'

'Nothing with these men of the *ton* is just a lunch.'

'If he asks about any of the details…'

'Leave the details to me.'

Rob gave a nod.

Ned finished the rest of the gin and set the glass down on the desk.

'Let's walk. I could do with some fresh air.' To calm the pound of his blood and shutter the disbelief that was coursing through his body.

Rob nodded.

Ned rang the bell for his butler. There would be time to think later and there was much riding on Misbourne.

Ned was well practised at putting emotion aside. He did it now, coldly, deliberately, and got on with the task in hand.

'More tea?' Emma asked, teapot poised in hand to re-fill the dowager's delicate blue Sèvres teacup.

The afternoon sunlight filled Lady Lamerton's little parlour, making it bright and warm. Dust motes floated in the sunbeams to land on the circulating library's latest romance novel on the embroidered tablecloth of the tea table before them.

On the sideboard at the other end of the parlour, a book on antiquity and a heavyweight tedious literary novel had been discarded until they were required for next week's return visit to the library.

'Thank you, my dear.' Lady Lamerton gave a small nod. Emma poured the tea.

'So what did you make of our Mr Stratham?'

'Tolerable enough, I suppose.' Emma managed to keep her hand steady and concentrated on adding a splash of cream and three lumps of sugar to the dowager's cup, just the way she liked it.

'Tolerable?' The dowager looked at her aghast as she accepted the cup and saucer from Emma. 'With those eyes?'

'A pair of fine eyes do not make the man.'

'So you did notice,' said the dowager slyly. 'And I must say he seemed rather struck by you.'

'Hardly.' Emma took satisfaction in her calm tone as she topped up her own teacup.

'Indeed, I do not think I have seen any woman make such an impression upon him.'

Emma remembered again that expression on his face outside the library. The intense scrutiny in his eyes. The force of something that seemed to emanate from him. Something angry and accusatory that he had no right to feel. She took a sip of tea and said nothing.

'I wonder if he will be at Hawick's ball tonight,' the dowager mused.

Emma felt a shiver ripple down her spine. 'Is it likely?'

'Most likely, indeed.'

We will talk, Emma. She thought of the cool promise that had been in his eyes and the utter certainty in those quiet words. She swallowed and resolved not to leave the dowager's side for the entirety of the evening.

The Duke of Hawick's ballroom was heaving. It seemed that the entirety of the *ton* had returned early to London, and were here, turned out for the event since the rumour had got out that the Prince Regent himself might be present.

It was as warm as an evening in the Red Lion, even though there were no adjacent kitchens here that fanned the heat. No low ceiling or small deep-sunk windows, and bricks that held the heat in summer and the cold in winter. It was a huge room of wealth and opulence that would have been beyond the imagination of most of those who frequented the Red Lion Chop-House. The massive chandelier held a hundred candles whose flames made the crystals glitter and sparkle like diamonds. The windows were numerous and large, the sashes pulled up to allow a circulation of fresh air. At the back of the room were glass doors that opened out on to a long strip of town garden similar to that at the back of the mansion house in Cavendish Square. All of that open glass and air and yet still the place was too warm because of the throng of guests.

'Another fine evening,' Lord Longley said and lifted a glass of champagne from the silver salver that the footman held before him.

'Indeed.' Ned accepted a glass of champagne, too. Took a sip without betraying the slightest hint that he hated the stuff. He was all too aware of the way Longley ignored Rob's presence. 'You have met my steward, Mr Finchley.'

Longley could barely keep the curl from his upper lip as he gave the smallest of acknowledgements to Rob before returning his attention to Ned. He thought Rob beneath him. And Ned, too, but swallowed his principles for the sake of money.

'Harrow tells me you were at Tattersall's saleroom the other day looking at the cattle.' Tattersall's was the auction house where the *ton* went to buy their horses. Ned could hear the slight sneer that Longley always had in his voice when he spoke to him. Felt the edge of anger that he always felt amongst these men born to titles and wealth and privilege and who lived in a world far removed from reality.

'Browsing the wares.' Ned's eyes were cool. 'Were we not, Mr Finchley?'

'And fine wares they were, too,' said Rob.

'Matters equine take a knowledgeable eye.' *Which you do not have.* That patronising air that Longley could not quite hide no matter how hard he tried. 'And experience. I would be happy to teach you a thing or two.'

'How kind.' Ned smiled.

The sentiment behind the smile was lost on Longley. 'Where do you ride?'

'I don't.'

'I did not know that,' said Longley and tucked the tidbit away to share with his friends in White's should matters not work out between him and Ned as he was hoping. 'I suppose I should have realised, what with your not having come from—' He stopped himself just in time.

Ned held Longley's gaze.

The earl glanced away, cleared his throat and changed the subject to why he was standing here in Ned's company tonight. 'Lady Juliette is in good spirits tonight.' Lady Juliette, Longley's daughter for whom he was seeking a match with new money.

'You must be pleased for her.' From the corner of his eye he saw Rob struggle to stifle a grin.

'Do not need to tell you that she was quite the diamond of this year's Season. I am sure you are already aware of her.'

'Very aware.'

Longley smiled.

'Quite the horsewoman as I recall,' said Ned.

Longley's smile faltered as he realised the mistake he'd just made. He squirmed. 'Not so much these days.' He cleared his throat again. 'Excuse me, sir. I see Willaston and have a matter to discuss with him.'

A small bow and Longley took himself off, leaving Ned and Rob standing alone.

There was a silence before Ned spoke. 'There's something you need to know, Rob. The Dowager Lady Lamerton has a new companion.'

'You think I'm in with a shout?' Rob grinned.

Ned did not smile. His eyes held Rob's. 'Her name is Miss Emma Northcote.'

Rob's grin vanished. 'Northcote? I thought the Northcotes were long gone. Moved away to the country.'

'So did I.' Ned thought of the truth of Emma Northcote and her father's circumstance—the nights in the Red Lion Chop-House; the narrow street with its shabby lodging house; and the London Dock warehouse—and something tightened in his throat. He swallowed it down. Gave a hard smile. 'It seems we were wrong.'

'Hell.' A whispered curse so incongruous in the expensive elegance of their surroundings as the shock made Rob forget himself. 'That's going to make things awkward.'

'Why?' Ned's expression was closed.

'You know why.'

'I did nothing wrong. I've got nothing to feel awkward over.'

'Even so.'

'It isn't going to be a problem. *She* isn't going to be a problem.' Not now he knew who she was.

Both men's gazes moved across the room as one to

where Lady Lamerton sat with her cronies…and her companion.

Northcote, not de Lisle, the worst lie of them all.

He looked at the long gleaming hair coiled and caught up in a cascade of dark roped curls at the back of her head, at the sky-blue silk evening dress she was garbed in, plain and unadorned unlike the fancy dresses of the other ladies and obviously paid for by Lady Lamerton. She wore no jewellery. He knew that she would have none. The *décolletage* of her dress showed nothing other than her smooth olive skin. Long white silk evening gloves covered her arms and matching white slippers peeped from beneath the dress.

She had seen him the minute she entered the ball-room. He knew it. Just as he knew she was ignoring him.

'No,' said Rob quietly. 'Knowing you, I don't suppose she will.'

Ned's eyes shifted from Emma to Rob. 'Would you hold this for me?' He passed his glass to Rob. 'There's something I have to do.'

'You can't be serious…'

Ned smiled a hard smile.

'Tell me you're not going over there to get yourself introduced?' Rob was staring at him as if he were mad.

'I'm not going over there for an introduction. Miss Northcote and I have already had that pleasure.'

Rob looked shocked.

'But the lady and I didn't get a chance to talk.'

The music came to a halt. The dance came to an end. The figures crowded upon the floor bowed and curtsied and began to disperse.

Ned glanced across the floor to Emma once more.

'This won't take long.'

'Ned...' Rob lowered his voice and spoke with quiet insistence.

But Ned was already moving smoothly through the crowd, crossing the ballroom, his focus fixed on Emma Northcote.

Chapter Six

'Oh, my!' Emma heard Miss Chichester exclaim as she stared in the direction where Ned Stratham stood talking with Mr Finchley and Lord Longley. 'You are not going to believe this, Miss Northcote, but Mr Stratham—'

Emma resisted the urge to look round. 'I do not understand why Mr Stratham is of such fascination to the ladies of the *ton*,' she interrupted. 'He is just trade, for all his money.' It was a cruel and elitist remark, but after what he had done he deserved it.

Miss Chichester's eyes widened. Her pale cheeks flushed ruddy. She gave a soft, breathless gasp and pressed a hand to her *décolletage*.

'Indeed I am, Miss Northcote,' Ned Stratham's voice said. That same soft East End accent, that same slight edge underlying the quiet words.

Emma's heart stuttered. Her stomach turned end over end. She froze for a second before turning to look up into those too-familiar cool blue eyes.

'Mr Stratham,' she said with a controlled calm that belied the trembling inside. 'You surprise me.'

He smiled. 'Evidently.'

She held his gaze as if she were not embarrassed at

being caught out and ashamed of her words, but the seep of heat into her cheeks betrayed her. However, she offered no apology.

The silence stretched between them.

His eyes never faltered for a moment. He stood there, all quiet strength and stillness, with those eyes that knew her secrets and those lips that had seduced her own. 'I am here to ask you to dance, Miss Northcote.'

Her stomach gave a somersault.

Beside her she heard Miss Chichester give a quiet gasp.

'I thank you kindly for your magnanimous offer, sir.' Emma held his gaze with a determined strength, knowing that, in this battle of wills, to look away would be to admit defeat. 'But I am obliged to refuse. I am here as Lady Lamerton's companion, not to dance.'

His mouth made a small dangerous curve, making fear trickle into her blood at what he meant to do. Too late she remembered that one word from his mouth could destroy her. One word and her return to the *ton* and all that meant for her brother would be over. Her mouth turned dry as a desert.

He turned his attention to Lady Lamerton. Only then did Emma notice that all of the ladies around them had fallen silent and that Lady Lamerton and her friends were watching with avid interest.

'I am sure that Lady Lamerton would be able to spare you for some small time.' He looked at Lady Lamerton with that quiet confidence in his eyes. Cocked the rogue eyebrow.

All eyes turned to the dowager, like a queen with the presiding vote over a court.

'Mr Stratham has the right of it, Emma.' Lady Lamerton turned her focus to Ned. 'I trust you will return m'companion to me safely, sir.'

'Safe and sound, ma'am.' Ned smiled at Lady Lamerton.

Safe and sound. The very air around him vibrated with danger.

All of the tabbies watched in rapt amazement.

His eyes switched back to Emma, the bluest blue eyes in all the world, so cool and dangerous, and filled with the echoes of shared intimacies between them. 'Miss Northcote.' He held out his hand in invitation. 'Shall we?'

Her eyes held his for a tiny moment longer, knowing that he had manoeuvred her into a corner from which there was no escape. Then she inclined her head in acknowledgement.

He might have won the battle but it did not mean he would win the war.

She placed her hand in his, rose to her feet and let him lead her out on to the dance floor.

They joined the nearest set for a country dance that was neither progressive nor too fast for conversation.

'What game are you playing, Ned Stratham?'

'No game. We need to speak with a degree of privacy. This provides the perfect opportunity.'

She glanced around to all the pairs of eyes fixed upon them, to all the murmurs being whispered behind fans and into ears. 'You call this privacy? Our every move is under scrutiny.'

'Indeed. Apparently I am a source of fascination for the ladies of the *ton*.'

She blushed and eyed him with anger. She was very aware of the warmth of his hand around hers, of the proximity of his body. 'I have already told you I will not listen to more of your lies.'

'But I was not the one who was telling the lies, was I, Emma?'

'Given what you did, I do not think I owe you any explanation as to why I did not wait. And as for a lady's maid, I have undertaken such duties in the past. For a month.'

'A month.' He paused. 'As the daughter of the maid's master.' He looked at her.

'Strictly speaking it was not a lie.'

'Strictly speaking.'

She pressed her lips firm. Glanced away.

He leaned closer, so that she felt the brush of his breath against her cheek, felt the shiver tingle down her spine and tighten her breasts.

'And as we are speaking strictly, the little fact of your name, Miss *de Lisle*...' His blue eyes seemed to bore into hers.

'It was not a lie. De Lisle is my mother's name.'

'Your mother's name. But not yours.'

She swallowed again. Her mouth was dry with nerves. He was making it sound as if she were the one in the wrong. 'My father and I could hardly admit the truth of our background. That we were fallen from society. That we were of that privileged class so despised in Whitechapel. Do you think we would have been accepted? Do you think Nancy would have given me a job in the Red Lion?'

'No.' His eyes held hers, unmoved by the argument. 'But it does not change the fact that you lied to me, Emma Northcote.'

'Small white lies that made no difference.'

Something flashed in his eyes, something angry and passionate and hard. Something in such contrast to the cool deliberate control normally there that it sent a shiver tingling down her spine and made her heart skip a beat. 'They would have made all the difference in the world.'

The dance took them apart, leading them each to change places with the couple on their right. She took those few moments to try to compose herself before they were reunited once more and his hand closed over hers, binding her to him. And to this confrontation she had no wish to conduct upon a crowded dance floor.

'Do not seek to turn this around,' Emma said. 'You made me believe you were something you were not.'

He raised his eyebrows at that. *Just as she had made him believe she was someone she was not.*

It fuelled her anger and sense of injustice.

'All those nights, Ned... And in between them you were here, living in your mansion, dancing at some ball with the latest diamond of the *ton* hanging on your arm. Seeking to ally yourself with some earl's daughter while you played your games in Whitechapel.'

He said nothing.

'You would have bedded me and cast me aside.'

'Would I?' His voice was cold, hard, emotionless. There was something in his eyes when he said it that unnerved her.

Had she waited, she would know for sure.

Had she waited it would have been too late.

The dance played on, their feet following where it led. There was only the music and the scrape and tread of slipper soles against the smooth wood of the floorboards. Only the sound of her breath and his. Given all that was at stake, she had to know. She had to ask him.

'Are you going to tell them the truth of me? That I was a serving wench in a chop-house in Whitechapel? That my father is a dockworker? That we lodged in one of the roughest boarding houses in all London?'

'Are you going to tell them that I was a customer in the same chop-house?'

They looked at one another.

'You they would forgive. Me, you know they would not.'

'They would be a deal less forgiving of me than you anticipate.' He smiled a hard smile. 'But do not fear, Emma. Your secret is safe with me.'

She waited for the qualifier. For what he would demand for his silence.

He just smiled a cynical smile as if he knew her thoughts. Gave a tiny shake of his head.

It made her feel as though she was the one who had got this all wrong. She reminded herself of the shabby leather jacket and boots he had worn—a disguise. She reminded herself of what had passed between them in the darkness of a Whitechapel alleyway while he was living a double life here. For all his denials he was a liar who had used and made a fool of her.

'Now that matters are clear between us, there is no need to speak again. Stay away from me, Ned.'

He smiled again. A hard, bitter smile. 'You need not worry, Emma Northcote,' he taunted her over her name. 'I will stay far away from you.'

'I will be glad of it.'

He studied her eyes, as if he could see everything she was, all her secrets and lies, all her hopes and fears. Then he leaned closer, so close that she could smell the clean familiar scent of him and feel his breath warm against her cheek, so close that she shivered as he whispered the words into her ear, 'Much more than you realise.'

Her heart was thudding. Her blood was rushing. All

that had been between them in the Red Lion and the alleyway, and at the old stone bench, was suddenly there in that ballroom.

They stared at one another for a moment. Then he stepped back, once more his cool controlled self.

'Smile,' he said. 'Every eye is upon us and you wouldn't want our audience to think we were discussing anything other than the usual petty fripperies that are discussed upon a ballroom floor.'

He smiled a smile that did not touch his eyes.

And she reciprocated, smiling as she said the words, 'You are a bastard, Ned Stratham.'

'Yes, I am. Quite literally. But I deem that better than a liar.'

His words, and their truth, cut deep.

The music finally came to a halt.

The ladies on either side of her were curtsying. Emma smothered her emotions and did the same.

Ned bowed. 'Allow me to return you to Lady Lamerton.'

She held his gaze for a heartbeat and then another. And then, uncomfortably aware that every eye in the ballroom was upon them, she touched the tips of her fingers to his arm and let him lead her from the floor.

Ned and Rob were in Gentleman John Jackson's pugilistic rooms in Bond Street the next morning. At nine o'clock the hour was still too early for any other gentleman to be present. After a night of gentlemen's clubs, drinking, gaming and womanising—which were, as far as Ned could make out, the chief pursuits of most men of the gentry and nobility—gentlemen did not, in general, rise before midday. After a bout of light sparring together, Ned and Rob were working on the heavy sand-filled canvas punchbags that hung from a bar fixed along the length of one wall.

Rob sat on the floor, back against the wall, elbows on knees, catching his breath. Ned landed regular punches to the sandbag.

'What the hell was that about with Emma Northcote last night?' Rob asked.

'I wanted to speak to her.'

'About what?'

'To verify her identity.'

'And you needed to dance with her for that?'

'I had to put all those lessons with that dancing master to use at some time. I paid him good money.'

Rob raised his eyebrows. His expression was cynical. 'I take it she is who we think.'

'What gives you that impression?'

'Maybe the fact that you're knocking two tons of stuffing out of that punchbag.'

Ned raised an eyebrow, then returned to jabbing at the sandbag, right hook, then left hook. Right hook, then left. 'She doesn't change anything. We go on just as before.' He landed a left-handed blow so hard that it almost took the punchbag clear off its hook. He ducked as it swung back towards him, punched it again, and again. Kept up the training until his knuckles were sore and his arms ached and the keenness of what he felt was blunted by fatigue.

Rob threw a drying cloth up to him and got to his feet, gesturing with his eyes to the doorway with warning. 'That it, is it, Stratham?' he said, reverting to a form of formality now that they had company.

Ned caught the cloth and mopped the sweat from his face as he glanced round to see who it was that had entered.

There was only the slightest of hesitations in the Duke

of Monteith and Viscount Devlin's steps as they saw who was in the training room using the equipment.

Ned met Devlin's eyes. The viscount returned the look—cold, insolent, contemptuous—before walking with Monteith to the other end of the room.

Ned and Rob exchanged a look.

'Your favourite person,' said Rob beneath his breath.

'It just gets better and better.' Ned smiled a grim smile, as he and Rob made their way to the changing rooms.

Within the dining room of Lady Lamerton's town house a few streets away, Emma and the dowager were at breakfast.

'It is just as I suspected, Mr Stratham dancing with you at Hawick's ball is all the gossip, Emma,' Lady Lamerton said as she read the letter within her hand.

The clock on the mantel ticked a slow and sonorous rhythm.

'I cannot think why. It was only one dance.' Emma did not speak while the footman moved from Lady Lamerton's side, where he filled her cup with coffee, to Emma's and stood waiting, coffee pot in hand.

She gave a nod, watching while the steaming hot liquid poured from the pot into the pretty orange-and-gold-rimmed cup. The aroma of coffee wafted through the air. She added a spot of cream from the jug and took a sip of the coffee.

Sunlight spilled in through the dining-room window. sparkling through the crystal drops of the chandelier above their heads to cast rainbows on the walls.

Lady Lamerton set the letter down on the growing pile of opened papers and reached for the next one. She glanced up as she broke the seal. 'Because, my dear, Mr

Stratham has not previously been seen upon a dance floor. He does not dance.'

Emma took another sip of coffee and tried to smile, as if what had happened upon the dance floor last night was nothing. 'That must be somewhat of a disadvantage when he is at an Almack's ball.'

'Hardly,' said the dowager. 'If anything it is the opposite. It has created rather a stir of interest. The women see it as a challenge. The Lewis sisters have a sweepstake running as to who will be the first to tempt him upon a floor. It is considered to be an indicator of when he has made his choice of bride.'

Emma smiled again to hide the anger she felt at that thought. 'Well, last night certainly disproved that theory.'

'Indeed, it did. And will have made the Lewis sisters a deal richer.' The dowager paused and looked at the letter in her hand. 'They are all positively agog to know of what he spoke.'

If they only knew. 'Nothing of drama or excitement. I already told you the details.' Last night in the ballroom when there had been a subtle questioning which Lady Lamerton had parried with the air of a hawk, with its wings shielding its food for its own later consumption. And in the carriage on the way home the hawk had eaten…although not of the truth.

'The weather and other trivialities are hardly going to satisfy them, Emma. Especially as the pair of you appeared to be having quite the conversation.'

Emma took another sip of coffee and said nothing.

Lady Lamerton held her spectacles to her eyes and peered at the letter again. 'Apparently they are taking bets on whether he will dance again. And if it will be with you.'

Emma suppressed a sigh at the *ton*'s preoccupations.

An hour's walk away and the preoccupations and world were very different.

'Fetch my diary, Emma, and check when the next dance is to be held.'

'It is next week, on Thursday evening—the charity dance at the Foundling Hospital.' Emma knew the line of thought the dowager's mind was taking. 'And even if Mr Stratham is there, I made it quite clear to him that my duty is as your companion and not to dance.'

'Much as I admire your loyalty, my dear, you are quite at liberty to dance with him. Indeed—' she glanced with unmistakable satisfaction at the unusually large pile of letters the morning post had brought '—it would be quite churlish not to.'

'He will not ask me.' *Stay away from me, Ned.*

You need not worry, Emma Northcote. I will stay far away from you. The echo of their words rang in her head. And she remembered again, as she had remembered in the night, the look in his eyes—cool anger and other things...

Emma smiled as if it were nothing and led the conversation away from Ned Stratham. 'What are you wearing tonight for dinner at Mrs Lewis's?'

Her tactic worked. 'My purple silk and matching turban. I thought you could wear your dove-grey silk to complement me.'

'It would match well,' Emma agreed and listened as Lady Lamerton discussed a visit to the haberdashery to buy a feather for the turban.

Ned would stay away from her. And she would be glad of it.

More glad than you realise.

And a tingle ran over the skin at the nape of her neck at what those strange words might mean.

* * *

'I see Mr Stratham is here,' Lady Lamerton said *sotto voce* not five minutes after they had entered the drawing room of Mrs Lewis's Hill Street house that night.

'Is he? I had not noticed,' Emma lied. He and his steward, Rob Finchley, were over by the windows talking with Lord Linwood and another gentleman, one whom Emma vaguely recognised but could not quite place. Ned was smartly dressed in the best of tailoring, his fair hair glinting gold in the candlelight. He looked as at ease here as he had in Whitechapel. Beneath that polished surface emanated that same awareness, that same feeling of strength and danger held in control. His eyes met hers, hard, watchful and bluer than she remembered, making her heart stumble and her body shiver. She returned the look, cool and hard as his own, and curved her lips in a smile as if he bothered her not in the slightest, before returning her attention to Lady Lamerton.

Their hostess appeared, welcoming them, telling Lady Lamerton how wonderful she looked and asking which mantua maker was she using these days.

Emma saw some of the women who had been friends of hers in what now seemed a different life. Women who had attended the same ladies' educational seminary, who had made their come-outs at the same time, and against whom her competition in the marriage mart had necessitated spending a fortune on new wardrobes. They were dressed in the latest fashions, immaculately *coiffured*, safe in their little group. Emma knew how penniless ladies' companions were viewed in their circle, the whispered pity; she, after all, had once been one of the whisperers. Not out of malice, but naïvety and ignorance. But who her father had been, and who she had been amongst them, still held influence for, despite her reduced status, most smiled and gave small acknowledgements. Only a few turned their heads away.

'Lady Lamerton, how very delightful to find you here.' Mrs Faversham arrived, all smiles and politeness, but with the barely concealed expression of a gossip hound on the scent of a story. 'And Miss Northcote, too.' Her eyes sharpened and lit as she looked at Emma.

'Mrs Faversham,' cooed Lady Lamerton and smiled that smile that, contrary to its softness, indicated when it came to gossip she was top dog and would be guarding her object of interest with ferocity. Emma's father had been right.

'Such a shame I missed Hawick's ball. It seems it was quite the place to be. I heard that Mr Stratham finally took to the dance floor. But one can never be sure with such rumours.'

'I can confirm the truth of it, my dear Agatha.'

'Indeed?' Curiosity was almost bursting out of her. 'You must come to tea, dear Lady Lamerton. It has been an age since we visited together. Would tomorrow suit?'

'I am taking tea with Mrs Hilton tomorrow. My tea diary is quite booked these days. But I might be able to squeeze you in at the end of the week…if that would be agreeable to you.'

'Most agreeable.' Mrs Faversham smiled and could not help her eyes straying to Emma once more. 'And will Miss Northcote be there?'

But Emma was saved by the sound of the dinner gong.

The table was beautifully arranged with a central line of squat candelabras interspersed by pineapples. In the middle was a vast arrangement that involved the head and tail feathers of a peacock. Emma tensed, worrying that she would find herself seated beside Ned, but, for all his wealth, in the hierarchy of seating at a *ton* dinner table trade was still looked down upon and Ned and his steward were seated further down the table. A lady's companion, effectively a servant, was deemed higher because her family had once been one of them.

Lord Soames, one of her father's oldest and dearest friends, took his place by her side.

'And how is your papa fairing out in rural Hounslow, young Miss Northcote?' he bellowed on account of his deafness.

'He is well, thank you, Lord Soames.' She nodded and smiled, aware that the volume of Lord Soames's voice was loud enough to be heard all around. Loud enough for Ned to hear those few seats away.

'Glad to hear it, m'dear. You must tell him when you see him next that his presence is sorely missed.'

'I will.' She smiled again and smoothly changed the subject. 'Such uncommonly good weather we have been having.'

'What's that you are saying? Speak up, girl.'

'I was merely commenting upon the pleasant weather of late.'

Lord Soames held his ear trumpet to his ear. 'Did not catch a word of it, Miss Northcote.'

'Miss Northcote was speaking of the good weather,' a man's voice said from close behind. It was a voice that Emma recognised: aristocratic, educated, with a slight drawl of both careless sensuality and arrogance. She stiffened.

'Splendid weather indeed,' agreed Lord Soames with a nod and sat back in his chair to await his dinner.

'Good evening, Miss Northcote,' the voice drawled and its owner sat down in the vacant chair to her right.

The blood was pounding in her temple. She felt a little sick. Took a deep breath to steady herself before she looked round into the classically sculpted face of Viscount Devlin.

'I think you are mistaken in your seat, sir.' Her eyes looked pointedly at the small white place card with the name of Mr Frew written upon it.

Devlin lifted the place card and slipped it into a pocket of his dark evening tailcoat. 'I do not think so, Miss Northcote.'

Emma blinked at his audacity, met his gaze with a fierceness and flicked her focus a few seats along to where Mr Frew was sitting meekly. The gentleman had the grace to look embarrassed before rapidly averting his eyes.

She returned her gaze to Devlin, her face as much a mask as his, even if her heart was still pumping hard with anger and loathing beneath. She knew that she could not start causing a fuss, or refuse to sit beside him. Guests were already sliding sly glances their way. Everybody would be watching to see her reaction to him. Everybody remembered her mother's very public castigation of him and his friends. Everybody knew the history of him and her brother.

So she smiled, even if her eyes held all the warmth of an arctic night, and kept her voice low. 'What are you doing, Devlin?'

'Enjoying an evening out at dinner.' He smiled, too. That lazy charming smile of his she had once thought so handsome.

Across the table Lord Fallingham had taken the seat beside Mrs Morley. His eyes met hers. He gave a nod of acknowledgement before he turned to Mrs Morley and engaged her in a conversation that had no room for anyone else.

She did not glance round at Lord Soames. She could hear Mrs Hilton on his left shouting a conversation with him.

Devlin smiled again as if he had known her thoughts.

She did not smile, just held his gaze and waited.

'So how have you been, Miss Northcote?'

'Never better…' Her mouth smiled. Her eyes did not. 'Until a moment ago. And you, sir?' A parody of politeness and sincerity.

His smile was broader this time, lazier, more charming. 'All the better for seeing you.' And yet there was something in his eyes that gave lie to his words.

'I cannot think why. Given your interchange with my family before we left London, I did not think that there was very much we had left to say to one another.'

He made no reply, just leaned back in his chair, and took a sip of his champagne as he watched her. 'How did you find Hawick's ball the other evening?'

By its own volition her gaze moved to Ned further down the table. His glance shifted to hers at the very same time. She looked away. Lifted her glass with a rock-steady hand.

'It was a pleasant enough affair.'

Devlin flicked a glance towards Ned before coming back to her. 'Pleasant enough to tempt Mr Stratham on to the dance floor so I hear. A hitherto unheard-of feat.'

'I would not know, having been absent from society for so long.'

He smiled at the barb, a smile that did not touch his eyes. Took another sip of his champagne. 'It is quite the accomplishment, I assure you.'

'I will take your word for it.'

He smiled again.

'He's new money,' he said in that same disparaging tone with which all of the *ton* viewed self-made men.

'So I have heard.'

'Men like Stratham do not play by the rules of our world. Some of them do not play by any rules at all.' He paused, then added, 'Especially when it comes to women.'

'That is rather rich coming from you.' The whole of London knew that Devlin was an out-and-out rake.

'Maybe.' Devlin smiled. 'But *my* affairs are conducted with those who know the score.'

There was a silence and in it lay his unspoken insinuation over Ned. He held her gaze.

'Why are you telling me?'

'For the sake of my friendship with your brother.'

'Friendship? Is that what you called it?' She raised her brows.

'And even if it were not so, given Stratham has expressed such an…interest in you, I would not be a gentleman were I to keep quiet and say nothing.'

'One dance does not constitute an interest.'

'I think, in this case, it rather does.'

'I am sure you are well intentioned, sir.' She kept her voice quiet and light, as if they were in truth discussing nothing more than the weather or the latest summer theatre show. 'But what I do, and with whom, is not your concern.'

'Maybe not.' Devlin's gaze flicked down the table to Ned and when he looked at her again there was a strange, almost possessive expression in his eyes. 'And then again maybe it is more of my concern than you realise.'

The expression was gone so quickly that she doubted she had really seen it. She stared at him, wondering if he had just actually said those words.

He smiled again, that charming smile that had so many women fluttering their eyelashes and hoping to be the one that tamed him.

There was the clatter of dishes, the scrape of cutlery, the chink of glass and glug of wine being poured as the meal was served. Footmen were moving between them, offering dishes for their serving. All around was the hum of conversations and small laughter.

Emma felt the slink of unease in her stomach.

But when the footmen moved on, Devlin's attention was across the table. 'How was your chicken, Mrs Morley?'

'Superb as ever can be expected from…'

The conversation played on. The seconds ticked slow.

Emma's eyes moved down the table to where Ned was talking to Mr Jamison. He glanced up and met her eyes with cool speculation, before returning his focus to whatever it was Mr Jamison was saying.

Chapter Seven

The morning sky was a yawning blue. The air was fresh and perfect. Ned's gig, sprung for sport and speed, and dark and sleek as the panther rumoured to be kept by the Prince Regent in his Tower menagerie, skimmed smooth and light over the roads towards Hyde Park.

'Did you see that Devlin was seated beside Miss Northcote?' Rob spoke loud enough to be heard above the noise of both the gig's wheels and the horses' hooves.

'Devlin was not seated there. He intimidated Frew into swapping seats.' Ned kept his attention on the four matched-black horses trotting smartly before them.

'I wonder why.'

'I would guess that he wished to speak to Miss North-cote.'

'You think he's sweet on her?'

'Maybe. But she's sure as hell not sweet on him.' Whatever it was Emma felt for Devlin was more akin to dislike and anger judging by the look on her face when Devlin had first sat down. Certainly not a prearranged meeting and not one she wanted to be a part of. It shouldn't have made any difference. She was nothing to him. But it did make a difference.

'She does not like him. That's why he had to wait until she was at the dinner table before he approached. Because she would have walked away otherwise,' Ned said.

'Strange that she should dislike him so much.'

'Is it?'

He could feel the glance that Rob flicked his way. 'Maybe he didn't like you dancing with her.'

Ned smiled. 'I'm sure he didn't like me dancing with her.'

Rob chuckled.

There was the whir and rumble of the wheels, the clatter of the horses' hooves, the noise and hubbub of the traffic all around them. They stopped at the junction behind a queue of carriages and waited while a road sweeper darted out ahead, sweeping the fresh pile of steaming horse manure up into his shovel ahead of the two city gentlemen who followed and receiving a tip for his trouble.

The carriages in front moved off. Ned gave a flick of the rein and his team followed.

'You're getting too good at this carriage driving,' observed Rob with a grin. 'Lessons paid off well.'

Ned smiled.

They lapsed into silence as they sped past the buildings.

When Rob spoke again it was in a voice not to be heard by any others. 'Do you think Devlin said anything to her about…?'

'No.' Absolute. Categorical. 'Whatever Devlin feels about me, he will not drag Emma Northcote into it. It's more than his honour is worth.'

'You'll forgive me if I don't set so much store by gentlemen and their honour.'

Ned smiled a hard smile.

'Miss Northcote—she's not what I thought she'd be. Not spoiled and pampered like the rest of them.'

Ned made no comment, but he thought of her in the red tavern dress dealing with the men in the Red Lion. He thought of her in his arms in the darkened alleyway, her mouth meeting his with passion and sweetness. He thought of the warmth of her smile, of her irrepressible spirit and strength of character. And how he had wanted her in his bed, in his life…in his future. He pushed the thoughts away with a will of steel. 'Whatever she is makes no difference to us.'

Rob smiled and leaned back in his seat to enjoy the view of the fine town houses.

Ned drove the carriage onwards to Hyde Park.

Emma stood alone by the window in the dining room of the dowager's Grosvenor Place town house, watching London wake to another day.

The Fortnum and Mason cart was passing, the delivery boy perched high on the back ready to spring down and run in with the groceries ordered by housekeepers and wives. Two milkmaids were on the other side of the road, wooden yokes across their shoulders, balanced like a weighing scale with large wooden churns. There seemed a never-ending stream of coaches and carts and gentlemen on horseback taking their mounts for exercise in the park. A clamour of activity, which was the reason that Lady Lamerton had chosen the house.

The sky was blue, but mired with that slight haze that would burn off as the earliness of the morning advanced and the sun climbed high in the sky. It was going to be another hot day. Emma could feel the clammy warmth in the air already. She massaged a hand against the tightness nipping the nape of her neck.

She was thinking about last night and Devlin… and Ned.

An uneasiness still sat upon her over Devlin's veiled suggestion that he had an interest in her and over his implication about Ned and gentle-born women.

How Devlin could even think that there could be anything between them… Devlin, after all, was one of the men responsible for Kit's downfall and the financial ruin of her family. And even were he not, he was a rake, a man who lived a life devoted to empty hedonism and lavish luxury. He had no thought for anything serious or meaningful. He spent his time bedding women of the *demi-monde*, gaming and drinking. After her months in Whitechapel she could not like a man like him.

She thought of Ned seeking his pleasures on the other side of town as much as Devlin. She thought of Devlin's hints and wondered what it was Ned had done with another gentle-born woman. The thought made her chest tighten with a heavy rawness and sent a bitterness pumping again through her blood. Had he lied to her as he had lied to Emma? Had he deceived Emma as to what was between them? And over his offer to help her father? She closed her eyes at the thought of that small unnecessary cruelty.

And in her mind she saw again her father that day at the warehouse.

'Oh, Papa,' she whispered soft as a breath and that ever-present nagging sense of worry over him stole out from where it lurked in the shadows to fill her mind. And she thought, too, of what he would say if he ever discovered what she had done with Ned Stratham.

'Ah, here you are, Emma.' Lady Lamerton's voice made her start. She hid away those feelings. Took a breath and turned to face her employer.

'I did not mean to startle you, my dear.'

'The fault is all mine. I was wool-gathering and did not hear your approach.' She smiled and, moving from the window, directed the dowager's attention elsewhere. 'Cook has quite surpassed herself with the ham and eggs this morning.'

'She has a temperament that requires handling with kid gloves, but...' Lady Lamerton smiled and lowered her voice to share the confidence '...she is worth her weight in gold. Worked for the royal household for years. When she left, Amelia Hilton tried to snaffle her, but I got in first.' The dowager leaned on her walking stick and gave a very satisfied cat-that-got-the-cream smile that made Emma smile in earnest.

Emma lifted a plate from the heater and helped Lady Lamerton to a selection from the breakfast dishes before they both took their seats.

Lady Lamerton peered at the empty space before Emma. 'I trust you have eaten?'

'I have, thank you.' She knew how precious food was. How hungry a person could get. So she had eaten whether she had appetite or not.

'I see Mrs Lewis seated you beside Devlin. Hardly the most sensitive of seating arrangements given the history of your families.'

Emma made no comment.

'Did he upset you?'

'Not at all,' she lied and thought of Devlin's insinuation about Ned.

Lady Lamerton glanced across at Emma as she ate. 'And yet you have something weighing upon your mind.'

The butler appeared with a fresh pot of coffee and set it down on the table between them, sending wafts of steam and its rich roasted aroma through the air. By unspoken consent both Emma and Lady Lamerton waited until he had departed again before they resumed their conversation.

'I was thinking of my father,' Emma admitted, aware that the older woman was no fool. It was the truth, just not all of it.

'Wondering how he is faring in Hounslow without you?'

In his small comfortable cottage living a quiet but respectable life in Hounslow. So many lies. Emma met Lady Lamerton's gaze. There was a formidable kindness in it. She wondered what Lady Lamerton would do if she knew the truth? Of Whitechapel and the hardship of life there, of the dockyard warehouse and the Red Lion Chop-House. Part of her wanted so much to tell. To unburden herself. To cease the dishonesty. But Emma knew she could not. She was under no misapprehensions. Lady Lamerton had a kind heart, but she would not understand. And she certainly would not have a woman who had been a serving wench living in her house, acting as her companion. So Emma just smiled in reply.

'I am taking tea with Mrs Hilton this afternoon. There is no need for you to come. Take the day off. Travel out to Hounslow and surprise your papa with a visit.'

And discover for herself the truth of how he was coping. 'If you are certain...'

'Quite certain. I would not say it were I not. As long as you are returned before evening. Remember we have agreed to a card evening at Lady Routledge's.'

'I will be back long before evening.' No woman wanted to be walking the Whitechapel streets at night. And that made her think of the night that Ned Stratham had stepped in to save her from the two sailors. Of his walking her home...and all it had led to. She stopped the thoughts. Closed her mind to them. Thought of her purpose in being here.

'I have been meaning to ask you whether Lord Lamerton has yet had word of Kit?' she asked.

'It is early days, Emma, and m'son continues with his enquires. We must leave the matter in his capable hands.'

'I am most grateful. My father will be, too.' It would be the first thing her father would ask.

'If there is word to be had, Lamerton will be the one to have it.'

'He will.' Emma smiled, but as she sipped her coffee the question on Emma's mind was what that word would be.

It was a couple of hours later when Emma made her way across town, walking at a brisk pace. The new olive-green walking dress, cream spencer, bonnet and gloves, all part of the wardrobe Lady Lamerton had bought for her upon her arrival, allowed her to belong in Mayfair. But not so in the East End. It was only when she got into Spitalfields and then headed further east into Whitechapel that she was aware of the way people were looking at her.

Before, in her own old and shabby attire, or the serving dress lent to her by Nancy, she had fitted in, drawn no notice. Now her new and expensive clothing proclaimed her from another tribe, an intruder from another world. The further she trod into Whitechapel the more uncomfortable she became.

Streets that only a couple of weeks ago had been her home, her locale, seemed threatening. Men, lurking in doorways, eyed her with sly speculation. Women, sitting upon their steps, did not recognise her as Emma de Lisle, one of Nancy's girls from the Red Lion, but as someone who should not be here, someone who did not fit in. Only two weeks had passed, but already she had forgotten the depth of the darkness, the stench of the dirt and the cutting danger of this place.

Five miles separated Whitechapel and Mayfair. It might as well have been five thousand. They were worlds apart. Little wonder Ned changed his clothes to come here. She wished she had done the same.

But although her clothes were all wrong, she knew these people. She kept her head up, maintained her confidence and stayed true to herself.

It was with relief that she eventually reached the London Docks.

In the warehouse was the same foreman she had met before. He did not recognise her at first. Did a double take when she apologised for inconveniencing him and asked him if she might speak to her father.

'Of course, miss.' He gave a nod. 'Come right this way for Mr de Lisle.'

Not Bill this time, but Mr de Lisle. It struck her as odd, as did the fact he led her into an office at the front she had not noticed before.

Her father was not shirtless and glistening in sweat. The clothes he wore were new—a fine fitted tailcoat and matching breeches, pale shirt and stockings, dark neckcloth and waistcoat. His grey hair was cut short and tidy and combed neat. A new pair of spectacles was perched on the end of his nose. He was the very image of respectability, sitting there at a large desk in the middle of the room writing within a ledger. Like the gentleman he had once been. So many emotions welled up at the sight. Surprise and relief, pride and affection. She pressed her gloved fingers to her lips to control them.

'Emma!' He set the pen down in its wooden holder. Got to his feet, came to her and embraced her.

She heard the office door close behind the foreman.

'Oh, Papa! How on earth…?' She looked him up and down before gazing around them at the change in his environment.

'It is a miracle, is it not?' He laughed. 'The very day that you left the company deemed they had a need of someone who could manage the accounts in-house rather than farm it out to an office on the other side of town. A money-saving venture they said. They seemed to know that I had something of an education and offered me the job. Fate has dealt us both good fortune, Emma.'

'It seems that it has,' she said quietly.

'And the vast increase in wage means I can afford some very fine rooms not so far away in Burr Street, although I have not yet had a chance to write to Mrs Tadcaster so that she could inform you.'

'And you are eating?'

'Like a king. There are some splendid chop-houses in the vicinity.' There was a twinkle in his eye as he said it.

Her smile broadened. It was so good to see him like this.

'Now tell me all about how things are with you, my dear girl. I have been worrying over you.'

'I accepted the position with Lady Lamerton so that you would not worry.'

He smiled. 'Ah, it is true. But I confess that my worry is a great deal less than it used to be. And besides, it is a father's duty to worry over his daughter.'

'And a daughter's duty to worry over her father.'

They laughed and talked some more. She told him that young Lord Lamerton was making enquiries as to Kit's whereabouts. She told of her life with the Dowager Lady Lamerton, of what was the same in the *ton* and what had changed. But she made no mention of the newcomer Mr Stratham.

'You see,' said her father. 'Am I not proved right? Accepting the position was the best thing to do.'

'It was,' she said, but she did not smile.

Her last view of him as she left was of him sitting at the big wooden desk, a contented expression on his face, as he dipped his pen into the inkwell and wrote entries into the large ruled ledger open before him.

Emma left the London Docks and headed west towards Mayfair, walking with a hundred other people across roads and along pavements. All around was the hurried tread of boots and shoes, the buzz of voices, and, louder than all, the clatter of horses' shoes. But what she heard in her head as she walked were the words that Ned had spoken to her on a morning that seemed now to belong to another time and another world.

I used to work on the docks... I still know a few folk in the dockyard... I could have a word. See if there are any easier jobs going.

And she knew that it was neither fate that had rescued her father from hefting crates upon the warehouse floor, nor a miracle, but Ned Stratham.

Chapter Eight

$\mathcal{CO}$

Mrs Morley's picnic in Hyde Park took place three days after Ned and Rob's early morning drive in the same place. The weather had grown hotter and stickier. It was a select affair arranged by one of the *ton*'s *grande dames* to raise funds for her husband's regimental charity. The price of the tickets guaranteed only a select attendance; as did the limited number of places.

Ned was there, with Rob, not because he enjoyed such frivolous wastes of time, or displaying the style of his dress. Ned did not care about clothes or fashion or the style of his hair. He kept the knot in his cravat simple and had looked at his valet in disbelief when the man suggested tying rags in his hair overnight to curl it. To give the valet his due, he had not asked again. Ned was there because he knew the importance of maintaining a presence when it came to doing business with these men. And being on a level meant attending social functions like this on a regular basis. It meant dining with them and being a member of a gentlemen's club.

He nodded an acknowledgement at Lord Misbourne across the grass. Misbourne was of particular importance to him, more so than the others. But Ned had sown the seeds. Now he had to wait for Misbourne to come back to him.

'Quite the turnout,' he said, looking over to where Spencer Perceval, the prime minister, and the Prince Regent were speaking to Devlin and his cronies. Beyond them he could see Emma Northcote and Lady Lamerton.

'Old boys' club,' said Rob.

Ned gave a small smile of amusement and accepted a glass of champagne from the silver tray the footman offered.

'Such a fine day for our picnic, don't you think, Mr Stratham?' Amanda White, a pretty young widow of a certain reputation, announced her arrival. Her neckline was just a low enough cut to afford an unhindered view of her cleavage and transparent enough to more than suggest what lay beneath. She looked at him with bold, seductive eyes and a lazy, sensuous smile.

'A fine day, indeed, madam.'

'I'm positively famished and need some advice over which are the tastiest morsels on offer.' She glanced across at the feast of extravagant dishes set out on the line of tables, the tablecloths of which gleamed white in the sun. 'Whether to have the wafer-thin sliced chicken or ham. Or something bigger, more masculine and… substantial. Like steak. Such a choice as to quite confuse a lady.' She touched her teeth against her bottom lip, biting it gently. 'What do you think, sir?'

From the corner of his eye he could see Rob's gaze fixated on Amanda White's ample bosom.

'I think you need the guidance of a renowned epicure. What good fortune there is one so close at hand…' He glanced round at Rob. 'Mr Finchley…?'

'I would be delighted, ma'am,' said Rob and offered his arm.

Amanda White could not in all civility refuse. She eyed Ned for a moment, knowing full well what he had just done, but then she smiled and tucked her hand into the crook of Rob's arm.

Rob smiled, too, as he led her away towards the picnic tables.

Ned's eyes moved across the distance to where Emma Northcote and Lady Lamerton had stood, but both were gone. He located the dowager at the far edge of the party, talking intently with Mrs Hilton. His eyes were still scanning the crowd when he heard Emma's voice behind him.

'Mr Stratham.'

A tiny muscle tightened in his jaw. Other than that, not one other sign betrayed him.

'Miss Northcote.' He turned to face her. Did not smile. 'Shouldn't you be with Lady Lamerton?'

'She and Mrs Hilton are discussing something which they deem unsuitable for an unmarried lady to hear.' She gave a small ironic smile. And in that moment, standing there dressed in their finery with champagne glasses in their hands and the extravagance of pineapples upon a banqueting table, surrounded by the elite of London's *ton*, Whitechapel and all that had happened there whispered between them.

The hint of a breeze flicked lazily at the olive-green satin of her bonnet ribbons. The colour suited her dark complexion well, highlighting the velvet brown of her eyes and the glossy dark gleam of her hair.

Neither of them drank their champagne. Both stood there, glasses steady in hands, appraising the other with calm measure. She watched him with those same dark perceptive eyes as the woman he had met in the Red Lion.

'I came to thank you.' Her voice was quiet enough that only he would hear.

'I have done nothing for which you should thank me.'

A smile, there then gone. 'You helped my father.'

'Did I?'

They looked at one another across the small distance, aware of the layers of tension between them.

'You were not lying, after all.'

'No.' His eyes held hers, serious, focused, revealing nothing of the hard beat of his heart.

'But you *were* courting titles on the marriage mart.'

'Before you. And after.'

'And in between?'

'No.'

Her eyes scanned his. 'You really are from Whitechapel.'

'Born and bred.'

Their gazes still held locked. 'You needn't worry, Ned. Your secret is safe with me.' The very words he had spoken to her upon Hawick's dance floor.

He smiled a crooked smile.

And she smiled, too, that glorious warm smile of hers that revealed the small sensuous dimple.

Ned's gaze shifted to beyond Emma, to the four tall dark figures that were making a beeline for them.

'Miss Northcote,' Devlin said as he came to stand at her side. Monteith stood by Devlin. Fallingham and Bullford took her other flank. Aligning themselves around her. Aligning themselves against him. 'And... Mr Stratham.' There was a slight razor edge in the way Devlin said his name. The viscount held his gaze with disdain and contempt and a hint of threat.

Ned found the less-than-subtle attempt at intimidation amusing. He had grown up the hard way. He knew how to read people. He understood Devlin better than Devlin understood himself. And he knew exactly which buttons to press to play him.

'Lord Devlin.' He smiled. 'How nice of you all to come over.'

The remark hit the spot. Devlin stiffened, then forced a smile. 'Miss Northcote's company beckoned.' The viscount turned his attention to Emma. 'I trust you are enjoying the picnic, Miss Northcote.'

'Very much, thank you, Lord Devlin.' Her words were polite, but Ned could hear the cool tinge in them. Her smile was small, perfunctory. It did not touch her eyes. Her dimple remained hidden. Her gaze skimmed over Devlin and his friends. Her poise was calm and controlled, yet beneath it Ned could sense her discomfort.

'And you? Are you enjoying being here?' Ned asked of Devlin.

'Not as much as you, it would seem. I do not suppose they have picnics where you come from. Where was it again? I am not sure you ever did say?' Devlin sipped at his champagne as he played a dangerous game.

Emma shifted with unease.

'Such an interest in me, Lord Devlin. How flattering. I could give you my life history—where I came from... how I came to be here... All the details, if you want. We never really have had a chance to chat.'

Devlin's eyes narrowed with contempt. 'I am a busy man. My time is precious. And I have no interest in trade.'

Emma's eyes widened at the implied insult.

Ned smiled. 'And yet here you are, sharing that precious time with me.'

Devlin bristled. A muscle twitched in his jaw as he clenched his teeth. He glared at Ned for a moment before addressing Emma. 'If you will excuse me, Miss Northcote.'

She gave a tiny nod of her head.

The four young noblemen made curt bows and walked away.

Emma and Ned looked at one another.

It could have been just the two of them standing there, as it had been that day at the old stone bench. But that day was long gone and was never coming back.

His eyes traced her face.

'Goodbye, Emma.' A small bow and he walked away.

That evening was one of Lady Lamerton's rest evenings, as she called them. One of two or three evenings a week when she stayed at home. To rest and nurture her strength and vigour and to make her presence all the more appreciated at the Foundling Hospital's ball the next evening. Every night and they grew tired of one, she said. Too few evenings and they thought one out of it. The trick was in getting the balance of nights in and nights out just right. And the dowager knew a thing or two about such subtleties of the *ton*, having spent a lifetime mastering its handling.

They sat together in the little parlour playing whist.

'Apparently the picnic raised more than three thousand pounds for Colonel Morley's regimental charity.' Lady Lamerton eyed her cards.

'A very successful fundraiser. Mrs Morley must be happy.' Emma placed a card down on the pile.

The dowager gave a tut when she saw the card.

Emma smiled at her.

And the dowager smiled, too. 'Positively crowing. You know she never got over Lamerton—God rest his soul—choosing me over her. Accepted Morley as a poor second best.'

'I did not know that.'

'It was so long ago that there are few enough of us left to remember.'

'Was it a love match between you and Lord Lamerton?'

'Good heavens, no!' She gave a chuckle as if it were an absurd suggestion. 'Lamerton needed my papa's fortune.'

As too many earls needed Ned's.

'I was in love with someone else.'

The revelation was so unexpected. It allowed Emma a glimpse into the past and the young and passionate woman that Lady Lamerton must have been.

The dowager placed her card down on top of Emma's with deliberation. When she looked up to meet Emma's gaze she smiled. 'Elizabeth Morley's contribution to the picnic was paltry. Considerably more is expected of the hostess than a few seed cakes. Little wonder her face was so sour when she saw the magnificence of my peach flans.' She gave a small cackle.

'You are incorrigible.'

'I am blessed with natural ability.'

They both smiled.

'I saw you talking to Devlin and Mr Stratham. Matters between you and Devlin seem amicable.'

They were hardly amicable, but in her role as the dowager's companion Emma could not be anything other than civil to him. She gave a smile that the dowager interpreted as agreement.

'You do know that Mr Stratham contributed the pineapples.'

'Rather too extravagant,' said Emma.

'I would describe it as a clever move. When it comes to cultivating the *ton*, he knows he must make his money work for him.'

Ned was a shrewd man. She thought of the way he

had sat in the Red Lion all those months. Self-contained, serene, but with so much beneath. She thought, too, of Devlin's words about Ned and women. She hesitated just a moment, then spoke.

'And yet I heard a rumour concerning Mr Stratham.'

'A rumour, you say?' The dowager raised an eyebrow and looked interested.

'That Mr Stratham is less than discreet or honourable when it comes to women.'

'Rather a *risqué* rumour for the ears of an innocent.'

Emma smiled. 'I could not help overhearing a conversation as I was passing.'

Lady Lamerton smiled her appreciation of eavesdropping. 'It is a quite misinformed opinion, my dear. Stratham is not that manner of man at all.'

'And yet he did spend time with Mrs White at the picnic.' Emma thought of the vivacious young widow and the way her violet eyes had looked so seductively into Ned's, the way she had touched a gloved hand on more than one occasion to his arm.

'Amanda White is always angling after him, but without success.'

'That is surprising.'

'Not at all. He is focused upon his business interests and on securing himself the best marriage alliance for his money. Stratham undoubtedly attracts women, but however he conducts his affairs it is with discretion. There has been nothing untoward. And believe me, had there been, I would know. Gentlemen of trade are not exactly welcomed with open arms into the *ton*. He is under constant scrutiny.'

There was a truth in that. Emma knew very well how the *ton* viewed self-made men.

'Who was speaking of him?' the dowager wanted to know.

'I could not see. I was trying to be discreet.'

'I must teach you better.'

They exchanged a smile, then went back to their cards. With the last trick played the dowager had won again.

'You are too good at this,' said Emma.

The dowager chuckled.

As Emma shuffled the pack and dealt the cards again, her mind strayed to Ned and their conversation earlier that day.

But you were *courting titles on the marriage mart.*

Before you. And after.

And in between?

No.

He had not lied about her father. Maybe he was not lying about the rest of it.

She had the feeling that her initial reaction, natural though it was to finding Ned Stratham living the life of a gentleman in Mayfair, had been misjudged.

Ned had never hidden the fact that he kept secrets. He had not lied about his. He was right; she had been the one who had lied about hers, even if it was for the best of reasons.

But I'll be back…. We need to talk when I return… She remembered the look in his eyes, serious, intent, soul-searching. About their future, she had thought. A future together.

She wondered what would have happened had she waited for him as she said she would.

She wondered with all her heart what Ned Stratham would have said.

Within the main hall at the Foundling Hospital the next evening the ball was in full swing. The turnout was more than good. In one corner of the room a posse of musicians played Handel's music, on account of the many fundraising concerts the composer had played on behalf of the Hospital. The design inside the hall, like the rest of the building, was Palladian, yet simple and unadorned; the Hospital did not want to be open to accusations of extravagance.

Ned and Rob stood across the room from the musicians. It was a position that Ned had chosen from instinct drummed into him across the years. Always keep your back to the wall so that no one could surprise you from behind. Always have a clear view of the doorway—both to see who entered and for exiting purposes. Where they stood satisfied both criteria.

On their right was the wall lined with long rectangular windows that had no curtains or blinds, only shutters that were fixed open. On their left were the internal wall and doorway that led in from the hallway and chapel. The dying sunset outside lit the windows, casting the hall with a rosy glow. From the centre of the high ceiling hung a massive but unadorned chandelier lit with the flicker of candles. It was a glamorous event, select, fashionable, six months in the organising. Tickets had been priced at one hundred pounds and every single one had been sold. To the richest and most elite of the *ton*. Ned smiled at that thought.

Rob gave a faint gesture of his head towards the door. 'Thought that Devlin and his cronies would have been at the *demi-monde* masquerade ball in the Argyle Rooms. Wonder what they're doing here instead?'

'Supporting the Foundling Hospital.' Ned gave a wry smile.

Rob laughed. 'A nice thought that.'

'Very nice.'

'Would get right up their noses as much as you do, if they knew precisely where their money was going.'

'If things go well with Misbourne, it won't be too long before they discover it for themselves.'

Rob grinned.

But Ned suspected that there was more to Devlin's presence here than just a night out. As if on cue, Devlin glanced at Emma.

Ned didn't need to follow his gaze. He already knew that she and the Dowager Lady Lamerton were standing with a group of the *ton*'s tabbies at the other end of the room. He knew that beside her the other women seemed faded and bland and that, beneath her calm, capable, polite interchanges, Emma was as aware of him as he was of her.

Devlin scanned the rest of the crowd until his eyes finally met Ned's.

Ned curved his mouth in a smile, drew Devlin a tiny acknowledgement, at which the viscount couldn't quite hide his contempt.

'Caught looking and he doesn't seem too pleased about it if the expression on his face is anything to go by,' said Rob. 'He normally likes to pretend you're so beneath him that he doesn't even notice you.'

And yet they both knew that were there a thousand people in this room Devlin would still have noticed him.

Ned's gaze shifted to Emma Northcote one last time.

And at the very same time her eyes met his. Something rippled between them before she looked away, engaging her attention more fully on Lady Lamerton and the group of women around her.

Ned pushed the thought of her from his head. It did not matter whether she was here or not. He had business to attend to. 'Time to go and talk to Misbourne.'

Rob gave a nod.

The musicians finished their tuning and began to play the initial bars of the first dance.

Ned sat his empty glass on the tray of a passing footman before making his way with Rob across the dance floor.

Emma was standing with Lady Lamerton at the other end of the Foundling Hospital hall. Lady Lamerton's social life was such a whir of activity. It had been so long since Emma had lived amongst the *ton* that she had forgotten what it was like to have so many social engagements, to plan one's entire life around them. The Season and Little Season were possibly the most important events of the year. Wardrobes were built around them. Débutantes launched in them. Marriages forged. And money, huge amounts of money, spent on and because of them. Emma had grown up accepting it as normal, but since her return from Whitechapel she questioned it.

After six months in that other world she could see it with fresh eyes. The vast luxury of it. The wonder. The sophistication and elegance. It took her breath away at the same time as it made her feel uneasy. She wondered if this was how Ned must have felt when first he came to Mayfair; wondered if he still felt it or had grown used to it.

She glanced across the length of the hall at where he stood with his steward, Rob Finchley. The midnight-blue tailcoat served to show his strong square shoulders. Other men padded their shoulders, but Emma knew that Ned Stratham's required no padding. She remembered too well how lean and hard and strong his body was.

Her eyes moved over his white cravat and white-worked waistcoat. Dark breeches clung to those long muscular thighs that had pressed to hers. White stockings and dark slippers. Hair that was cut short and cast golden by the candlelight.

And yet all his expensive tailoring did not disguise Ned's slight edge of danger and darkness. There was something untamed about him. Like a wolf amongst a pack of sleek, pampered, pedigree dogs. She thought of what it took to survive in a place like Whitechapel. She thought of what it must have taken him to rise up out of it.

Her ears pricked up at the mention of his name. It dragged her back to the presence of Lady Lamerton and the surrounding conversation.

'I would not have thought to find Mr Stratham here,' Mrs Quigley, a tabby with the sharpest claws, was saying. Her little eyes flicked a look of superiority in his direction.

'I would be more surprised over his absence,' Lady Lamerton said in a tone that put Mrs Quigley in her place. 'Given that Mr Stratham is a patron of the Foundling Hospital.'

That was news to Emma and apparently to Mrs Quigley, too.

'I have it from m'son that Edward Stratham is the hospital's most generous single donor.'

'Garnering favour with the prospective fathers through marriage,' said Mrs Quigley.

'Tush,' said Lady Routledge. 'Any prospective fathers through marriage are likely to be up to their necks in River Tick and would be more impressed if Stratham kept the cash in his own coffers.'

'Indeed.' Lady Lamerton adjusted her walking stick. 'But who I am surprised to see here are Devlin and his friends.'

'Not their usual scene at all,' said Mrs Hilton.

'Would have thought it rather too tame for those dissolute young bucks,' said Lady Routledge. 'I hope they are not here to cause trouble.'

'They are here for something,' said Lady Lamerton. 'Take my word upon it.'

'Perhaps one of them has their eye on a respectable lady. Perhaps they have decided to give up their rakish ways and settle down. Perhaps Devlin's papa has finally had a word in his ear.' Mrs Quigley glanced across at Lady Lamerton.

'Stanborough has mentioned nothing to me.'

'That does not mean it is not true,' pointed out Mrs Morley.

The dowager drew her a look that would have felled a lesser woman.

The music started up, the rhythm of the notes thudding through Emma's head, through her blood. The first dance was announced.

Emma glanced across at Ned again and met the full force of his gaze. It made the butterflies flock in her stomach and her heart strike a tattoo just the same as it had done in the Red Lion; maybe even more so given the mess of their entanglement.

In that look was that same strength of character, that same tight rein of self-control. Calm, watchful confidence with the hint of something so resonant that it sent a shiver through her whole body.

Emma glanced away. This was not the Red Lion. He was not the same man. And even if he were, it was too late. She was here with a purpose. She could not forget her brother or the vow she had sworn to her mother. She turned away to the dowager just as Mrs Quigley exclaimed in breathy shock, 'Oh, my! I do believe he is coming to ask Miss Northcote to dance. How…unexpected.'

For a tiny moment she thought Mrs Quigley meant Ned. Emma's heart banged hard enough to escape her ribcage but when she followed the woman's wide-eyed stare it was not Ned that stood there, but Devlin.

Her stomach dropped to meet her shoes. Her palms were suddenly clammy. As those arrogant eyes met hers she felt a flit of panic at the prospect of having to dance with him.

He turned his attention to Lady Lamerton. 'Ma'am, would you permit your companion to stand up with me for this dance?'

Asking the dowager rather than Emma. Playing by the rules of society. Yet it irked Emma, making her feel every inch the paid servant that she was, rather than a woman who had a right to answer for herself.

She looked around the small circle of ladies. Every one of them was staring at Lady Lamerton, eyes goggling, waiting with bated breath. Lady Lamerton was in her element, holding them all in the palm of her hand.

'I will, sir. But only if Miss Northcote is in agreement.'

All eyes swivelled to Emma, awaiting her reaction.

There was a calculated gleam in Devlin's eyes. He knew full well the stir it would create if she dealt him the direct insult of a refusal. He smiled his usual lazy, arrogant smile, that of a man who was used to getting what he wanted.

It was almost enough to tempt her to refuse him, just to see it wiped from his face. And had there not been Lady Lamerton to consider, and all that depended on Emma's position with her, she would have done it. But there *was* Lady Lamerton. And there was Kit.

So Emma met those arrogant dark eyes and gave a cool polite smile. 'Thank you, Lord Devlin, how could I refuse?'

He held out his hand to her.

She took a breath and, placing her hand in his, let him lead her out on to the dance floor.

Ned and Rob were with Misbourne, chief amongst the Hospital's governors. Rob stood back, watching the dance floor while Ned discussed financial matters with Misbourne. Even though Ned was listening to Misbourne he was aware of what it was his friend watched so intently.

His eyes cut a glance through the crowd upon the dance floor to one couple alone. Devlin's hand upon Emma's. A light touch here. A lingering touch there. They did not speak, only danced with smooth flowing steps. Polite, formal, nothing but respectable. Emma's expression was a mask that revealed nothing.

'You really think you can drum up the investment?' Misbourne asked.

'It's already done.'

'Then what do you need me for?'

'To represent the project amongst the great and good.' They would listen to Misbourne. He was an earl. He was part of the establishment. Misbourne's sharp dark eyes narrowed as they fixed upon Ned. He stroked his beard and studied Ned as if trying to glean his measure. The earl was not devoid of prejudices and might have his own dark agendas, but Ned knew the man would do better for the Hospital than any other. And so it was to Misbourne that he made the proposition.

Misbourne gave a nod. 'Come round tomorrow at seven. We will discuss it over dinner.'

The matter was concluded.

Fallingham, Monteith and Bullford were chatting to Lady Lamerton and the rest of the tabbies. Buttering them up. Waiting. Ned had known for what as soon as they had ambled over there. Emma did not even have a chance to resume her seat after Devlin returned her from the dance floor before Fallingham had her back up. And after Fallingham, Bullford, and after Bullford, Monteith and then back to Devlin.

Misbourne's eyes missed nothing. 'Miss Northcote is quite the belle of the ball. Your dance with her the other night seems to have brought her into favour.' Nor had Emma's sudden popularity among the small group of society rakes gone unnoticed by others in the ballroom. Ned could hear the whispers. See the ripple of interest. And the speculation.

'Hasn't it just,' he said.

Emma had got through a full dance with Devlin. Danced with all the rest of his and her brother's friends with increasing discomfort. And betrayed nothing of how she felt about them. But then Devlin came again for a second dance. Pushing his luck, as ever he did.

She had managed one. She could manage two, she told herself, but when the notes of the first bar of music played she realised it was the *Volse*.

Devlin had known full well what the dance was. He smiled a knowing smile as he slid his hand around her waist.

She gritted her teeth and bore his touch.

'Why are you doing this, Devlin?'

'I thought we had put the past behind us,' he replied softly, his breath brushing against her ear.

'Given what happened, how can we ever do that?' She turned her face away from his and edged her body to maintain as big a distance as possible between them.

The music began in earnest.

It was bad enough that she had to dance with him, the

man who had corrupted her brother and turned him into
something else, but that it was this dance over all others,
this dance that allowed him to hold her, that kept them
close and almost intimate…

They danced. And whether it was the dance itself,
or his proximity, or the way those dark arrogant eyes
mocked her, she did not know. What she did know was
that it stripped away all the defences she had built around
herself. It made her feel powerless. It brought back that
terrible night two years ago, fresh and raw as if it had
been only last week. The night her brother had gone out
with Devlin and his friends and lost everything. The night
her family's lives had changed for ever. So many emotions, so long buried, that now here on this dance floor
before all of the *ton* threatened to resurface. It shocked
her. It frightened her. It made panic squirm in the pit of
her stomach.

There was a lump in her throat the size of a boulder that no amount of swallowing would shift. There
was a tightness in her chest that made it hard to breathe
and a nausea that churned in her stomach. For a terrible
moment she thought she might actually start weeping,
which was ridiculous given she had not wept through
it all. She did not understand what was happening. She
did not know how much longer she could keep herself
together. Only that every second seemed an eternity, balanced on that brink.

She forced herself to breathe deep and slow. Tried
to calm herself. Knew that they were being watched.
Knew that she had to get through this without embar-
rassing herself.

Across the dance floor she saw Ned standing by the
arch of the doorway with the Earl of Misbourne, watching.
His face was stoic, stone, revealing nothing of emotion.

Her eyes met his. *Ned.* He was the last man she should turn to for help, but in that tiny moment she did.

The dance progressed her and Devlin further away across the dance floor.

She felt Devlin's hand tighten around her waist. The panic threatened to rise up.

'Lord Devlin.' Ned's voice sounded close by, polite enough, yet with an unmistakable cold strength beneath it. 'May I?'

Chapter Nine

Ned did not wait for an answer.

While Devlin stood gaping and speechless in shock, Emma found herself smoothly wrested from his grasp and swept away by Ned.

She could not speak for a moment. Only felt the support of Ned's hand upon her waist, warm and strong. Only smelled the reassuring familiar scent of him.

The steps of the dance, fast and lively, put an ever-increasing distance between them and Devlin.

'What are you doing, Ned?' she asked when she could speak.

She did not look to the periphery of the dance floor, to where the dowager and the *ton* would surely be staring, just kept her eyes focused on his.

'I think they call it cutting in.'

'You cannot do that.'

'I just did.'

'There will be a scandal.'

'I'm trade. Such faux pas are to be expected.'

The last of her panic faded.

She took a breath to steady herself. 'You have just made an enemy of Devlin.'

'Devlin was not so enamoured of me beforehand.'

'He is a powerful man, Ned. A man used to getting what he wants. You should be careful of him.'

Ned gave an ironic smile.

'Why are you smiling? I am being serious.'

'Anyone might think you had a care for my welfare.'

She glanced away. Over at the side of the floor they had quite the audience. Already she could see the spread of the scandalised whispers and dreaded to think of the state Lady Lamerton and the ladies would be in.

Now that the panic had subsided she felt ashamed of her weakness, ashamed even more that she had turned to him. 'You really should not have intervened, Ned.'

'Shall I return you to him?'

Her eyes met his once more.

Their gazes held.

He would do it, too, she knew. If she said the word. And she should say the word, she knew that, but she could not.

'No.' She was very conscious of how close he was, of the feel of his hand upon her waist and the sensations that arose from it.

'What is between you and Devlin, Emma?'

'The past,' she said. Dangerous ground, too sensitive to tread near.

He did not smile at that.

Their eyes lingered on one another. Such a strange mixed-up strain of emotion between them.

She looked away and breathed until she had regained her composure, then steered the conversation to a safer subject. 'I saw you with Misbourne. Are you doing business with him?'

'In a manner of speaking.'

'Which means?'

'Managing the most important deal of my life.'

'Is that all?' She smiled.

And so did he.

The music slowed and came to a halt.

'Thank you, Ned,' she said quietly.

'For what?'

Her gaze held his.

His face was strong, serious, unsmiling as if they were strangers, his eyes steady and almost cool. Almost. But they had the same depth as those of the man who had spilled a drink upon a black-haired villain in the Red Lion.

She knew what he had just done.

And he knew she knew.

The knowledge sat awkwardly between them.

Neither of them said a word more.

He led her back to Lady Lamerton in silence, bowed and returned to stand by his steward.

She did not look at Devlin.

'Come, my dear, I have something of a headache. Let us return home.' And with that Lady Lamerton swept her companion from the Foundling Hospital hall out into her waiting carriage and the grilling that awaited there.

Three hours after Emma left the Foundling Hospital dance, Ned stood within the study of his mansion in Cavendish Square. The fine engraved crystal glass containing gin sat untouched on the mahogany desk behind him. He stood before the grand bow window, staring out into the night.

The summer night was warm so the hearth was bare and black. A wall sconce on either side of the mantelpiece each contained two flickering candles. Their light was warm and amber in the dimness of the room, rendering the darkening blue night through the window black and sombre by comparison. A single silver candlestick sat on the desk behind him. He could see the reflection of its tiny flame in the paned glass, framed by the dark curtains that Ned never touched. The sweet expensive scent of burnt beeswax hung heavy in the air.

'You knew what they were doing as soon as they started dancing with her,' Rob accused.

Of course he knew. Devlin had nothing of subtlety about him. 'Making Emma Northcote the belle of the ball.'

'This ain't some sort of a jest, Ned!' Rob's anxiety made his speech revert to their Whitechapel days. 'They were making it clear they don't want you anywhere near her. They must have thought your dancing with her the other night was some kind of threat.'

'They can think what they like.'

'Aren't you forgetting something?'

'I forget nothing.'

'They're dangerous, Ned.'

'I know what they are.'

'They could destroy you and everything you've worked for.'

'You think I'd let them do that?'

'I think after tonight you might have just started a war.' Rob raked a hand through his hair. 'What the hell were you thinking of, taking her from Devlin mid-dance? You might as well have taken off a glove and slapped him in the face, called him out and been done with it!' Rob shook his head. 'Why?'

He closed his eyes and saw again Emma in Devlin's arms and the way she had looked at Ned in that moment. He had understood what she was feeling, understood, too, her appeal and knew very well he should have turned away and ignored it.

'What the hell were you thinking of?'

'There is something between Emma Northcote and Devlin. She needed rescuing.'

'And you had to be the one to do it?'

'Yes,' he said simply.

'Are you deliberately trying to goad Devlin? Because if so you're doing a damn good job of it.'

Ned turned from the window to look at Rob. 'The woman I was seeing. My mystery woman as you called her. It was Emma Northcote.'

Rob stood very still, unnaturally so, as if he had suspended even his breathing for that moment.

The silence hissed loud. He heard Rob swallow even louder.

'Is this some sort of jest?'

'I wish it were.'

Rob stared at him slack-jawed, unable to comprehend the magnitude of what Ned was telling him.

The clock on the mantel punctuated the silence.

'Hell.' Rob raked a hand through his hair. 'Hell!' he said again, louder. He rubbed his fingers against his forehead as if by doing so he could wipe what Ned had just told him from his mind.

'Of all the women out there, you have to go and start messing with *Emma Northcote*…?' Rob stared at him in disbelief.

'I didn't know who she was when I met her.'

'How can that be?'

'It's complicated.'

Rob lifted his glass and emptied its contents down his throat. There was a silence before he said, 'Well, I suppose that explains things.' He looked pale even in the candlelight. His eyes shifted to Ned's. 'Are you still seeing her?'

Ned gave him a stony look.

Rob held up his hands. 'I was only asking.'

Ned refilled his friend's glass. His own remained untouched.

'What are you going to do about Devlin?'

No pause before Ned answered, 'Ignore him, as I always do.' He looked out on to the barely visible rustle that was the sway of trees in the night.

'And Emma Northcote?'

He looked through the trees, across to the other side of the Square, to where the lights illuminated the rectangles of windows. 'It's over with Emma Northcote.' His voice was uncompromising. 'There's nothing between us any more.' But in his mind he heard again their conversation upon that dance floor and felt that same draw to her, that same attraction. And although he would not act upon it, he knew that it was very far from over between him and Emma Northcote.

'The audacity of the man,' Lady Lamerton was still talking of the previous night's Foundling Hospital ball at luncheon the next day. 'Does he not know that a gentleman does not cut in on another gentleman's dance?'

Ned knew all right, despite all that he said. And she knew that he had done it to help her. She knew what the *ton* would be saying about him and felt a level of guilt.

'Any other man would be castigated. Would have curled his toes in embarrassment when it was pointed out to him what he had done. Not Mr Edward Stratham. He gets away with it, because he does not seem to care if he is castigated or not. And probably the fact that he is such a handsome rogue goes a long way to helping.'

Lady Lamerton sipped at her tea. 'Lady Routledge has quite a soft spot for him, you know.'

'I did not,' said Emma.

'But handsome rogue or not, he has danced twice with you, Emma, cutting in to secure you for one of them. A man who does not dance. It is quite the latest *on dit*.' She gestured to the mountain of letters that lay on the tea table. 'Everyone wishes to know if there is something between the two of you.'

'How could there be anything between us? I barely know the man.'

The dowager took another sip of tea, and gave Emma a shrewd look. 'Stratham is no fool. He has money. What he needs is power, influence and social acceptance.'

'That marrying into a title would bring.'

The dowager gave a smile. 'Precisely.'

Emma smiled and lifted the teapot. 'More tea?'

The dowager nodded. 'That would be delightful, my dear.' She gave a small satisfied sigh. 'And then, of course, there is Devlin and his friends.'

To Emma's credit she did not spill the tea. She finished pouring it smooth and steady, added a few drops of cream and three lumps of sugar and sat the cup and saucer before Lady Lamerton.

'I am so glad that you have managed to put the past behind you.' The same words Devlin had used.

Emma smiled. 'One has to move on with one's life.'

'One certainly does.'

She had moved on with her life after what Devlin and his friends had done to Kit. But could she so easily move on from Ned? When she had to see him every day? When she would have to watch him court and marry a title?

'I wonder if Devlin and Stratham will be there to-night. After last night, it will be very interesting to see.'

Emma glanced away. Interesting was not the word she would have chosen. 'I wonder,' she said. They both affected her, albeit in very different ways. And she had to pretend that neither did. She sipped her tea and hoped neither of them would be present that night. That was the only way it was going to get any easier.

That evening Ned and Rob sat with Misbourne and his son, Linwood, watching the first half of *Romeo and Juliet* in the Botanical Gardens down near the river.

Ned was there, not because he was interested in Shakespeare or because he wanted a night in the Botanical Gardens, but because Misbourne had asked him. The day's business had been concluded in the study of Misbourne's Leicester Square home. The deal agreed in principle on handshakes and glasses of brandy, instructions given for the contracts and plans to be drawn up by their associated men of business. And when it was done, Misbourne had suggested coming here to this Shakespeare in the Gardens.

Misbourne was on board, but Ned needed the earl committed to the alliance so, until then, he would do nothing to jeopardise their arrangement.

Across the way on the other side of the grassy stage, he could see Emma and Lady Lamerton.

The dowager had given him a little nod of acknowledgement at the start of the evening, and he replied with a bow of his head. Emma did not. Following on from their dances he knew that speculation was rife about his interest in her and Devlin's, too. Her name was upon every gossiping tongue in the *ton* and he felt a degree of regret over that.

She was wearing a dark dress and matching pelisse, the colour of which he couldn't discern in the dying light of the dusk. The light of the flambeaux around the stage and the lanterns that lit the garden's paths lent a faint orange shimmer to its silk. Her hair was pinned up in a cascade of dark curls that stirred in the breeze. She might not have acknowledged him, but her eyes met his before she returned her attention to the players upon the stage.

It was halfway through the second act when Ned's footman came with the whispered message. His eyes moved to Emma once more and held for a second too long; such a tiny moment to make such a momentous decision.

He spoke quietly for Rob's ears only. 'It's important that you keep Misbourne sweet until I get back. Don't leave him.'

Rob gave a nod.

'If you will excuse me for a few moments, sir,' Ned said to the earl.

Misbourne gave a nod. Watched him with those black eyes of his before murmuring something to Linwood and returning his focus to the stage.

Ned made his way down the lantern-lit path towards the glasshouses.

Emma watched the footman deliver the message to Ned. Watched Ned slip away with so little disruption that she doubted too many others had noticed him leave and wondered what was so important to have him abandon Misbourne mid-play. The fact that Rob Finchley remained suggested that Ned would return. She knew whatever business he had with the earl was important. The most important deal of his life, he had called it.

She turned her eyes back to the stage, to *Romeo and Juliet*, but the play could not hold her attention. She was too aware of Ned's absence. The act came to an end. The players' manager appeared to announce the interval and that footmen would be circulating with a selection of drinks. And still Ned had not returned.

There was an apprehensive feeling in her bones, a gnawing sense that all was not well.

Rob Finchley looked like he was worried, too, and that he was struggling to pacify Misbourne. The earl and his son's expressions were cool and remote. They were men that few others would risk insulting, having something rather dark and silent and sinister about them.

'I wonder where Stratham has got to,' Lady Lamerton whispered in her ear. Other people were beginning to notice, too.

Unease made the skin on the nape of Emma's neck goosepimple.

When Lady Lamerton's friends wandered over to speak to the dowager, Emma exchanged civilities with them, then sank into the background and watched Misbourne.

The earl was saying something to his son. He looked irritated and as if he were on the verge of leaving.

The most important deal of my life. Ned would not have just walked out on it. Emma knew that something was wrong. She glanced at Lady Lamerton and her friends in full gossip, then slipped away into the shadows towards the glasshouses.

The first glasshouse had been set up with screens for use as a withdrawing room for the ladies. It was while on her way towards the second that she saw the dark still shape lying between the tall hedging that led into the maze. Her stomach dropped in dread and an iciness stole through her blood because, even in the darkness, she recognised that the shape was the body of a man; a man that the moonlight showed with white shirt and cravat…and fair hair.

Chapter Ten

E mma ran the distance and fell to her knees at his side.

His eyes were closed, his bottom lip grazed as if from a fist. She touched her hand to his neck, felt the beat of his heart beneath her fingers and knew he still lived.

'Ned!' she whispered his name urgently. 'Ned!' Delivered light butterfly slaps to his cheeks. Kissed his mouth to shock some response from him.

He gave a low moan, opened his eyes, looked directly into hers for a heartbeat and then another, sharing her breath, as the confusion cleared.

'Thank God,' she breathed.

He sat up, clutching a hand to his side. 'How long have I been away?'

'About twenty minutes or so.'

'Is Misbourne still there?'

When she nodded he got to his feet, with a wince. 'I need to get back to him.' But she glanced down to see his tailcoat open and the seep of a sinister dark stain over his pale waistcoat.

'You are bleeding!' Her heart twisted in her chest. 'I will fetch help.'

'No!' He caught hold of her hand. His eyes held hers, resolute and determined.

She gave a nod, understanding what he needed.

'I'll make a pad to staunch the worst of the bleeding, if you could rip long strips from your petticoat to tie it in place.'

She did as he asked. There was nothing of false modesty in his seeing her legs. They both knew the absolute urgency of this.

He pulled up his shirt. In the moonlight the smear of blood glistened wet and dark on his pale hard-muscled belly. She could see the dark slash of a wound before he pressed his folded handkerchief to it.

'What happened?' She began to wind the strips of petticoat tight around his waist to secure the handkerchief in place as best she could.

'I received a message from you that you needed my help and asking to meet here.'

'I did not send any message.'

'I realised that when I saw the welcome party waiting for me.'

She swallowed and did not ask how many men it had taken to fell him, just concentrated on tying the strips off.

As he dropped his shirt into place she saw the long tear in the material where the knife had cut.

'It's worse than it looks. They were paid to beat me, not kill me.'

'Someone does not like you,' she said.

'Quite a few people,' he replied as she dusted down the shoulders and back of his tailcoat.

But there was one name that whispered between them.

'Devlin would not stoop so low...not over a dance.'

Ned just gave a grim smile. 'Go back now so that we are not seen to return together.' He did not need to tell her what that would do to her reputation. 'I'll finish up here and follow in a few minutes.'

She nodded. 'Good luck with Misbourne.' Reaching a hand to his face, she wiped a smear of blood from his cheek.

Their eyes held for a tiny second more before she dropped her hand and hurried back to the play.

Lady Lamerton was still talking to her circle as Emma stopped to speak to an old school friend not so far away from where Misbourne stood...as if that was what she had been doing all of the time.

The bell rang to sound the end of the interval.

Emma headed back to Lady Lamerton.

'Was that Phoebe Hunter I saw you talking to?'

'It was.'

'I thought you and she no longer spoke.'

'We did not. But if I am putting the past behind me with so many people, Phoebe should be the first of them. You know she is having renovations done at Blackloch and a new nursery built.'

'Indeed?' The dowager looked pleased with the news. The bell rang for the end of the interval and they resumed their seats once more.

The players strolled upon the stage, just as Ned slipped into his seat.

He looked just as he had done when he left—smartly and expensively dressed, his tailcoat fastened neatly in place. No one save him and Emma would ever have known what lay beneath.

Rob eyed the wound as Ned changed the dressing on his belly later that night. 'Luck of the devil, a little bit deeper and they'd have spilled your guts.'

'Not the devil,' Ned said and thought how the ivory

token tucked in the pocket of his waistcoat had deflected the blade. 'Besides, they weren't trying to kill me.'

'Doesn't look that way to me.'

'The knives only came out in retaliation for the loss of their friends.'

Rob's eyes were steady on his. 'What did you do with the bodies?'

'They were gone when I came round. They must have taken them with them.'

'And you dressed the wound yourself?'

'I had help.'

Rob looked at him in question.

'Emma Northcote.'

'You are kidding.'

Ned met Rob's gaze and raised his eyebrow.

Rob closed his eyes and pinched the bridge of his nose. 'I'm not even going to ask.'

'Better that way,' Ned said.

'What the hell was she doing with you, Ned?'

'I thought you weren't going to ask.'

'You've still got feelings for her.'

Ned pulled his shirt back down into place, and threw the brandy-soaked bloodied rags on to the fire.

There was a silence.

Ned was not a man who talked about feelings. He had quashed 'feelings' a long time ago. Feelings made one weak and open to hurt. Feelings hindered, not helped with survival. But what was between him and Emma Northcote, this thing that he felt... He said nothing and his silence was as loud as if he had shouted his agreement to Rob's statement.

Rob glanced away, uneasy and nervous. Bit at his thumbnail. 'If Devlin organised what happened in the

Botanical Gardens because you cut in on a dance with her, just think what he would do if you go after her.'

'I'm not going after her. How could I, knowing who she is? Besides, this isn't about Devlin.'

'No? If he talks, then you kiss goodbye to Misbourne. You kiss goodbye to it all.'

'You know Devlin can't talk.'

'There's something else you should know.' Rob looked away again, his manner awkward, his hand rubbing the back of his neck. 'I was asking around about her, sniffing for some gossip on her and Devlin. You said there was something between them.'

'And is there?' Ned felt his focus sharpen.

Rob gave a nod. 'Seems she blames him and his pals for leading her brother astray. Little Kit Northcote running with the big bad boys.'

Ned shook his head and gave an ironic laugh.

'I thought so, too,' said Rob. 'Just thought you should know.'

'Thank you, Rob.'

'You managed to smooth it over with Misbourne?'

Ned gave a nod.

'What did you tell him?'

'He didn't ask and I didn't tell.'

'Probably saw the bruise on your forehead and the grazes on your knuckles and guessed how you got them.'

'It was too dark to see.'

'It won't be tomorrow.'

Ned lifted the lid of the silver platter on his desk to reveal a thick slab of raw steak.

Rob grinned. 'I see you've thought of tomorrow already. Nothing stops bruising better than a raw steak compress.'

But when Rob left a few minutes later it was not

bruises or Misbourne that Ned was thinking of, but the woman who had helped him that night. Had she not come looking for him, Misbourne might have walked. But she *had* come and she had helped him, not baulking from the blood or the mess or what had to be done, although it had shaken her. It seemed he could still feel the tremble of her fingers against his face, wiping away blood he could not see, and the brush of her kiss that had brought him to his senses.

He poured himself another gin and drank it down.

You know Devlin can't talk.

Once that had been a certainty. Now, Ned was no longer so sure. Because, for all his assertions to Rob, after tonight he could no longer deny he still cared for Emma. He cared for her and if Devlin was to realise that fact then all bets were off.

It was not an eventuality Ned could afford to risk.

He took another swig of gin and stared into the flicker of the flames upon the hearth.

He had to stay well away from her. For both their sakes.

Emma could not sleep that night.

Her mind kept reliving the bloodied mess of Ned's injury and the awful shock of finding him lying there on the grass. She had thought him dead. Dead! And that stomach-dropping moment had been one of the worst in her life.

She looked down on to the quiet moonlit street, watching the trundle of the soil cart and the skulking shadow of a cat creeping behind it.

Every time she closed her eyes she saw that seeping stain so dark against the white glow of Ned's shirt, the torn linen and, beneath it, the glistening gash that gaped in the muscle of his belly. Such a thin black line to produce so much blood. His skin had been slick with it beneath her fingers. It seemed even now that she could still smell it in the air and taste its metallic tang on her tongue. Her stomach knotted at the memory. It felt like a hand had taken hold of her heart and squeezed, and would not stop squeezing.

That Devlin could have stooped so low... He was a rake, a selfish, arrogant wastrel. But despite all of that she had always thought him a gentleman. Ned himself had said he had enemies. A man from trade would always have enemies amongst the *ton*.

She shivered and pulled her shawl more tightly around her shoulders. But it was not the cold that made her shiver. She still loved him. It was not a good realisation. She closed her eyes, knowing that it was all wrong.

He was looking for the daughter of a title, everyone knew that. He might desire her, he had always desired her, but he would never marry her.

Ned was ambitious. He was an empire builder. He had his plans. And she had both her pride and her duty. A hint of scandal and her position with Lady Lamerton would be lost and with it her best hope of finding Kit. Her father was relying on her. And given what had happened between them in Whitechapel... *Fool me once and shame on you. Fool me twice and shame on me.* The old saying whispered through her head.

She loved him, but she was not a fool.

So she would wish him luck in his search for a bride and leave him to the marriage mart.

Ned was sitting alone on a wooden bench in Green Park, looking out over a view that could not have been more different than the one from another bench a few miles across the city in Whitechapel. He needed space to think outside the walls of the mansion in Cavendish Square. He needed to be alone to think. And given his schedule for meetings tonight he could not go to Whitechapel. If he were honest, it was not the only reason he was not going to Whitechapel. He had not been back since Emma had arrived in Mayfair.

The sky above was leaden, the air unnaturally still. There was barely a breath of movement. The atmosphere seemed to radiate a tension that made people uncomfortable and unsettled and all the while not knowing why. The portent of a storm to come. It kept them indoors, or hurrying along the streets to get there. It cleared the sweep of undulating green grass and its paths so that he had the place to himself, almost, save for the odd figure or two rushing away into the distance to escape that feeling and what was to come.

Ned's feeling of discomfort could not be so easily remedied. Not by returning to the house in Cavendish Square. Or by anything as simple as waiting for the storm to pass.

I'm not going after her. How could I, knowing who she is? His own words seemed to ring in his ears, taunting him.

He couldn't get Emma out of his head. Maybe because of who she was. Maybe because she was the one woman in all the world he should not want and could not have. Maybe both of those reasons or neither of them, he did not know. What he did know, what he could no longer pretend to himself otherwise, was that he wanted her as Emma Northcote every inch as much as he had wanted her as Emma de Lisle. She had not changed, between Whitechapel and Mayfair. She was the same woman. He understood why she had lied and it did not alter the facts. That he wanted her. That he had feelings for her. And the realisation complicated everything.

It brought risks he had never contemplated. To his plan, to all he had spent a lifetime working towards. To himself and the very crux of who he was and what drove him.

Ned knew what he was and had always been comfortable with it. He saw things with a clear dispassion. But this thing with Emma Northcote was different. It pushed him to a place he had not been before, a place he did not want to be. It made him question things he did not want to question. It made him question what sort of man he was.

He moved the fingers of his right hand in that old comfortable reassuring rhythm, tumbling the token backwards and forwards, backwards and forwards.

Because being who he was, if he cared for her, how could he be with her?

Unlike all the other problems he had faced in his life, blind-ended problems, problems the size of a mountain, this was a dilemma to which there could be no solution other than walking away.

He had responsibilities. He had his destiny and his duty. And regardless that he did not play by the rules of the world, he had his own moral code, his own sense of honour.

Every time he thought it through, all the arguments, all the logic told him to stay away from her. The decision was already made.

But it did not stop him thinking about her.

Emma's letter to her father had been posted. She had taken it to the Post Office herself so that no one else would see the Whitechapel direction written upon it, along with two of Lady Lamerton's letters, under the guise of a need for fresh air. The guise in itself was no lie. The air was not fresh, but still and ripe with uncomfortable promise. But since the Botanical Gardens incident she had not felt herself and she needed some time away from the dowager. She needed time alone, to walk, to clear her mind and to straighten her thinking.

Emma knew just how hard it was to live in a different world from the one you had been born to and raised within. One's roots coloured everything. To sever them and walk the other path was not easy. She thought of how much she had had to learn to survive in Whitechapel. Ned must have done, and indeed still be doing, the same here. He always seemed so confident, yet she knew that every small thing would be alien to him.

The sky was darkening, changing through shades of grey to a deep, menacing charcoal.

A storm was coming. She could feel the ominous stillness of the air. Smell the scent of promised rain, sense the slight winding of tension deep within. Knew she was still too far away from Grosvenor Place to reach Lady Lamerton's home before it hit. She cast a worried glance at the green silk of her skirt. Once a rain-ruined dress would have meant nothing more to Emma than an excuse to visit the mantua maker. Now it was different. She had walked the other path, where women had one dress to last a lifetime.

She gave a grim smile at that thought and took the short cut through Green Park.

Halfway through she saw the gentleman sitting on the wooden bench.

The image reminded her of another man sitting on a different bench, in a different place, at what seemed a lifetime ago. But within a few steps her heart began to thud harder and something trickled into her blood, making it rush, for she knew that figure with its dark-blond head and she knew that trip and magical roll of the token over his fingers. It was like the replaying of a dream in her head, except it was real and happening before her eyes.

Her heart skipped a beat. Her feet faltered and ground to a halt.

He glanced up, met her gaze, as if he had been sitting there waiting for her. The token ceased its rhythmic tumble.

Time stretched between them. A tiny moment encapsulating something too big to contemplate.

Ned got to his feet. Stood there, his eyes never leaving hers.

Emma's heart was thudding fast and hard enough to escape her chest. Swallows were diving and swooping inside her stomach. She took a breath. Resumed her walking. But she did not look away any more than he did.

She stopped before she reached him.

'Emma.' Her name was low and husky upon his lips.

'Ned.'

The ensuing silence stretched tense. She could feel the strain of so much between them.

'How are you?' he asked softly.

'Well enough, thank you,' she said slowly. 'And your wound?' She glanced down to his tailcoat and what she knew lay beneath.

'Healing well, thanks to you.' His eyes scanned hers. She saw the movement of his Adam's apple. 'You shouldn't have had to see any of that.'

'I have seen worse,' she lied. 'You forget that I worked in the Red Lion.'

'I forget nothing, Emma.' The undercurrent strengthened. Nights in darkened alleyways, passion and kisses, that last sunlit morning at the stone bench, promises and insinuations… All of it was there, whispering between them. 'You risked your safety and your reputation to help me, Emma.'

'Then we are even, Ned.'

'We will never be even.'

She did not understand his words, just saw the dark intensity in his eyes and the way he was looking at her, that made her heart race all the faster and ache for him.

She swallowed. 'I should be getting back. Lady Lamerton will be waiting for me.'

He said nothing. Just gave a tiny hint of a nod as if he agreed with her.

She gave a curtsy.

He gave a bow.

She walked on, leaving him standing there.

Only a few paces before she stopped. Touched her fingers to her forehead. Closed her eyes to stop the tears that threatened. Knew she might not get another chance to ask him, not in all of her life to come.

She turned and met his gaze.

He had not moved. He seemed tenser than normal and there were shadows in his eyes.

'May I ask you something, Ned?'

He gave a nod.

'Why did you come back to Whitechapel all those times?'

'It is my home. Where does a man go to relax but his home?'

'Cavendish Square is your home.'

'Cavendish Square is where I live.' *Not his home.*

'Can you find no relaxation here?'

'Here I must play the part of a gentleman and we both know I am nothing of that.'

'You seem to play it with ease enough.'

He smiled at that. 'I thank you for the compliment. But it took many tutors and much practice to achieve.'

She smiled, too, a sad smile. 'And the change of clothes was so that you would not draw unwanted attention.'

'Turning up at the Red Lion dressed in Weston's best...' He raised his rogue eyebrow.

She traced the scar through it with her eyes and thought of her own trip to Whitechapel. 'I can imagine.' She paused before asking, 'Have you been back recently...to the Red Lion?'

The hint of a smile vanished. 'I have been too busy.' His eyes held hers with an intensity that lent other suggestions to the reason he had not returned to the chop-house.

The tension ratcheted between them, humming with the strain. The very air seemed to crackle.

Great heavy rain droplets began to fall, hitting her cheeks and rolling like tears. Big and slow. Hitting the olive-green silk to darken it with spots, each one so big and juicy that it seeped right through the thin muslin of her spencer.

She glanced up to find the charcoal sky dimmed almost dark as night.

'I have to go.' But her words were dwarfed by an enormous crack of thunder that peeled and rolled across the heavens. The rain began to pelt with a fury that matched the roar of the emotion between them, as the storm was unleashed.

'Too late, Emma,' he said and they seemed the most ominous words in the world. Ned peeled off his tailcoat as he spoke, wrapped it around her shoulders and, taking her hand in his, they ran through the weight of the drumming rain to the nearby oak trees.

He pulled her under the cover of the low leaf-laden branches to the shelter beneath. They stood facing one another, their hands still entwined. So close that she could see the glitter of raindrops on his waistcoat and the sodden linen of his shirt, moulded transparent to the hard contours of his chest. So close that she could feel the brush of his chest against her own, the rise and fall of his breathing. So close that she could smell the scent of rain-soaked material and beneath it the scent of him, clean, familiar, tantalising.

She tilted her face up to look at him.

His hair was sodden, turned dark with the rain and slicked back against his head. And his eyes, the most amazing eyes in the world, were like a window to his soul.

The trees and driving rain were like a curtain around them, locking out all of the real world, creating a moment they would never have again.

'The last time I saw you in Whitechapel... That day on the old stone bench...when you said that when you returned we needed to talk...' The rain ran in rivulets down her face.

He stroked the drops away from her cheeks with gentle fingers. His eyes studying hers.

'Yes,' he said, answering the question she had not asked. 'I would have told you of Mayfair. I would have told you it all.' And he really would have done because he had thought her the same as him. Hard-working, smart and ambitious enough to climb from her working-class roots. A woman who would have shared his vision, who would have understood. A woman who could straddle both worlds.

'Ned...' she whispered.

She was the same woman. The same woman beneath that name and there was such a cruel irony in that.

Emma let her gaze wander from his eyes to his lips and he knew that she wanted him as much as he wanted her. He was made for loving her. She was made for loving him.

And in the heavens above was the crash of thunder as if something of the world was being torn apart. Lightning flickered, illuminating her face in its stark white light. Illuminating everything she was, everything he wanted.

'God forgive me,' he whispered with shaky breath and lowered his face to hers.

He kissed her with tenderness. He kissed her with passion. Savouring this moment that was everything they could not have.

She slid her arms around him, anchoring them together. They lost themselves in passion and emotion, and need. Lost themselves with a fury that matched that of the storm all around.

Her heart beat with his. The thunder reverberated through them, the crashing and splitting of the skies only reinforcing what was happening between them. Fate and destiny proving that they would not be denied.

He kissed her until the furore of what flowed between them calmed enough to let them breathe again. They stood there entwined, chest to chest, lip to lip, the brush of his eyelashes against hers. Two lovers, beneath the old oak trees in a busy and fashionable park in London in the middle of the day, whose reunion the heavens had conspired to hide. The thunder was quieter now, the storm moving away. The lightning no longer flashed. In the silence there was only the drum of rain, drawn like a grey screen around them.

He held her in his arms, savouring these last few moments together. He kissed her one final time. And never again.

The sky was lightening to a pale dove-grey, its dark cloak moving to the north. The rumble of carts and carriages sounded from the nearby streets as normal life resumed.

Soon the rain would cease and they would once more become visible to the world.

He closed his eyes and dug down deep, knowing what he had to say to her.

'Emma…' His voice was low and husky.

But she shook her head. 'I know,' she said. 'You need to marry a title.'

'Yes.' But it was a lie. He did not need to marry a title. He just could not marry her. 'You will make a good match, Emma.' With any man other than him.

'I will,' she said. She had her pride. Her head was high. All her defences slotted back into place. She moved out of his arms, seemingly cool and calm and removed, but he was not fooled.

'I think it would probably be wise if we stayed away from one another, Ned.'

'I think you're right. It would be for the best.'

They looked at one another for a moment longer.

For the first time in his life he was doing the right thing but, ironically, nothing had felt more wrong.

Better she think him a selfish scoundrel than learn what he really was, yet it did not make this any easier.

The rain eased around them. The curtain began to draw back.

'We should not be seen leaving here together,' she said, practical and capable as ever, no matter what she felt. And he knew she felt. He could sense it in her. He could feel it in the way his chest ached. He was doing the right thing, he told himself again and gave a nod. But he could not avert his gaze and he did not walk away.

'Goodbye, Ned.'

'Goodbye, Emma.'

It was Emma who walked away, ducking under the low-hanging branches to make her way with such dignity back to the path. He stood there and watched her until she disappeared from sight.

Even then he waited before taking a breath and following that same path.

There was a glimmer of sunlight in the sky, but it did nothing to warm the cold in Ned's bones.

He thought of Emma and of what could not be.

And he, just like Emma before him, did not notice the tall dark figure that stood watching from the shelter of a distant doorway.

Chapter Eleven

⸙

Emma's eyes were fixed upon the page of the book in her hand, but she was not reading it. Fatigue blanketed her shoulders and head, the result of a night spent with little sleep and much regret. She knew she should not have kissed Ned. It did not matter what she felt in her heart, it was what she knew in her head that counted. He was seeking a titled and powerful alliance. She had known that before she kissed him. But when she looked into his eyes, she saw a mirror of her own feelings. She saw desire and connection and care. She saw respect and admiration and tenderness. And she saw love. Or maybe she only saw what she wanted to see.

He had no serious or respectable interest in her. He had told her plainly to her face. She could not trust him. Worse than that, she could not trust herself. It was just lust on his half, just physical desire, she told herself. But she knew in her heart that was not true, that physical desire was just one part of it.

Whatever it was that existed between them, this love and desire and passion, it would ruin her. It would cast her from society for a second time. It would destroy her only chance of finding her brother and make a mockery of the vow she had sworn to her mother. It would dash all of her father's hopes. And it would destroy her own pride and self-worth.

Emma had to stay very far away from Ned Stratham.

Far enough to watch him court a title. Far enough to watch him marry another woman and feel nothing.

And she would do it. No matter what she felt in her heart. She had to do it, for her family and for herself. She had to do it, because it was the right thing to do.

'You look tired today, Emma.' The dowager interrupted her train of thoughts.

She glanced up to find her employer no longer engrossed in her romance novel, but watching her. 'Do I?' She returned her eyes to the book in her hand, placing her bookmark within its pages. 'I am quite well.'

'And yet you do not seem your usual self.'

'Perhaps I am a little tired after all,' she admitted.

'You need not worry so over your papa. I am sure he is all the more at ease for knowing you are here.'

'You are right.' More so than Lady Lamerton could ever realise. But it was not her father she was thinking of. With his new job she had less cause to worry over him. The new job made her think of Ned again.

She was saved by the knocker sounding at the front door. Lady Lamerton exchanged a look with Emma. It was her look of intrigue and curiosity. 'I wonder who that might be. I was not aware that visitors were expected.'

'They are not,' said Emma.

The butler came in and announced that the Earl of Stanborough had come to call upon Lady Lamerton.

'Show him into the drawing room and have some tea sent in, Wilcott.'

'Very good, my lady.'

'Come along, Emma. Let us see what has brought Alfred calling upon me this fine afternoon. He was a dear old friend of mine. Such a pity he married beneath him. But I suppose the March girl was dangling the heiress card and one might argue that one's papa owning a bank is not really trade. But I never believed it,' she snorted and gave a little wicked laugh.

Emma smiled. Lady Lamerton might be a terrible elitist, but she was rather endearing with it.

But the smile faded when she entered the drawing room and saw there were two gentlemen standing there waiting.

'Wilcott did not mention that you had brought your son, Devlin, with you.' Lady Lamerton smiled and flicked a gaze at the tall, handsome man who was a younger, dark-haired version of the one standing before her.

'I trust it does not inconvenience you...or Miss Northcote?' Lord Stanborough added, casting a concerned look in Emma's direction. 'But we go direct to a meeting at White's after this.'

'It is not the slightest inconvenience.' Lady Lamerton smiled again. 'Either for myself or for my companion. Is that not so, Miss Northcote?' Lady Lamerton looked at Emma.

'No inconvenience at all, Lord Stanborough.' What else could Emma say?

'I am most relieved to hear it, Miss Northcote,' Viscount Devlin said and bowed.

'Lord Devlin,' she said and sank into a polite curtsy.

'Now, Alfred, I take it you are here to discuss our little charity event?'

'Indeed, I am.'

'Excellent. I have already drafted a list of possible donors and guests.'

'Capital, capital.' Lord Stanborough followed Lady Lamerton to take the armchair opposite hers.

Emma was very aware that only left the sofa on which she and Devlin would be obliged to sit together. She walked over to stand by the window, looking out at the sunshine and blue sky.

'Such a pleasant day,' she said.

'Indeed.' Devlin came to stand beside her.

'What sort of numbers are we running to?' she heard Lord Stanborough ask Lady Lamerton in the background.

There was a shuffling of paper. The earl and Lady Lamerton leaned in closer and fell to conferring on the details in earnest.

Devlin smiled that so-charming smile of his, but there was something in the way his eyes held hers that stroked a sliver of unease down her spine, or maybe it was just the memory of their dance or the thought that he might have been behind the attack on Ned.

He looked at her. 'How have you been, Miss Northcote?'

'I have been well, thank you, Lord Devlin.' Unease stroked again. She knew with Devlin that his presence here was no chance event.

There was a small silence.

She lowered her voice, for his ears only. 'Why are you here, Devlin?'

'To enquire as to your welfare.'

She raised a cynical eyebrow.

He smiled again.

'And observe that Mr Stratham seems to have made quite the impression upon you.'

She glanced away. 'I am sure I do not know what you mean, or what business it is of yours.'

'Since we are speaking so plainly…I saw you together in Green Park yesterday…beneath the trees.'

There was a silence. In the background were the voices of Lady Lamerton and Lord Stanborough, convivial and chatty. But Emma's focus was all on Devlin and that sharp look in his eyes and the thud of her heart in her chest. She held her head up and eyed him with a calm confidence she did not feel.

'What of it?'

'I am not sure that your employer would have quite such a *laissez-faire* attitude.'

She stared at him with incredulity. 'You are here to blackmail me.'

'Blackmail is such an unpleasant term. Think of it more as a warning.'

She swallowed, glanced over to see if Lady Lamerton was listening, but the dowager was smiling and nodding over something that Devlin's father was saying. Her eyes moved back to Devlin's. His gaze was fixed and cool.

'And what is it that you want for your silence, Devlin?' She thought of the way he had sat beside her at dinner, the way he had danced with her and the probability that he had been behind the attack on Ned—because Ned had cut in on their dance. And there was a cold dread in the pit of her stomach.

A moment passed before he spoke.

'I want you to stay away from Stratham, Emma,' he said so softly that she thought at first she had misheard.

They were not the words she had expected to hear. She stared at him.

The silence hissed between them.

'Why?'

'Because he is not the man for you,' said Devlin.

'He is not the philanderer you portrayed him.'

'Maybe not, but he is not of our world, Emma. Not one of us.'

'I cannot believe your arrogance.'

'Oh, believe it,' he said quietly.

She still could not quite believe this conversation they were having.

'What is it to you what I do with Edward Stratham?'

'I have a care for you, Emma.'

The words hung awkwardly between them.

'Devlin…' she began.

'And what gentleman could stand by and watch a gently bred lady be devoured by a rat from the gutter?' he interrupted.

'Do not speak of him like that!'

'You may not like it, but it is the truth.'

She shook her head. Glanced away.

'I know I do not have to point out how well Lady Lamerton would take the news were she to discover what her latest companion has been up to.'

'You really would ruin me?' She looked into his eyes. This man who had already led her brother to his ruin. This man who professed to have a care for her but, in truth, had nothing of a care for anyone save himself.

'I will do what I have to, Emma.' The words were uttered in a soft tone, yet beneath them she could hear both the steel and the promise. Then, 'Come, Miss Northcote,' in a voice loud enough to be heard by the dowager and his father. 'Let us rejoin the party.'

She had no choice but to do as he suggested, perching at one end of the sofa when she got there.

'May I?' Devlin asked, his face a mask of polite innocence.

She gave a nod of her head.

Devlin flicked out his coat-tails and sat down by her side.

'Now look at the two of you getting along so well,' said Lady Lamerton, glancing up at them.

'Aren't we just,' Devlin said and slid a gaze to Emma. Emma said nothing.

'You and Devlin seemed to be having quite the conversation yesterday.' Lady Lamerton spoke without glancing up from her embroidery. 'What were the two of you whispering about?'

The smooth flow of the pen within Emma's hand paused upon the paper. 'The fine weather of late,' she lied.

'The most appropriate excuse.'

The words made Emma's heart stutter. She lifted the nib of the pen, but too late—the ink had already blobbed, spoiling the letter she was writing on Lady Lamerton's behalf. She took a breath before she looked up at the dowager.

'Whatever do you mean?' She asked the question lightly, forcing a quizzical smile to her face.

Lady Lamerton set her embroidery aside. 'Why, just that Devlin seems wont to seek out your company these days. He is at almost every event we attend.'

'A mere coincidence. The Little Season has barely started. There are few enough events.' But now that the dowager pointed it out she realised it was true. Devlin seemed to be there in the background too often watching her.

'Tush!' exclaimed the dowager and flared her nostrils. 'Devlin is enamoured of you, Emma.'

'You are mistaken.' But after yesterday she feared that Lady Lamerton was right.

'Why else is he everywhere you go and always appearing by your side? And accompanying his father on a visit here...' Lady Lamerton raised her eyebrows and gave a knowing smile.

Emma said nothing.

'And then there is Mr Stratham.'

Her heart stuttered and missed a beat. In her chest was the scrape of rawness. 'I do not know what you mean.'

'I am sure that you do. Stratham does not dance, but he danced with you. And I am not blind, Emma. I see the way he looks at you.'

She glanced away.

'And no doubt, so has Devlin.' Lady Lamerton smiled. 'You do know that Devlin has never liked him.'

'I had not thought Devlin to be so arrogant or prejudiced in his beliefs to dislike a man because he is self-made.'

'You sound like one of those political radicals, Emma. You will be telling me next that you think all men equal and we must do away with the class system!'

Emma averted her eyes to hide the truth in them.

'Devlin would be a very good catch for any woman, least of all one in your position, Emma. And there is nothing like a bit of competition between men to bring them to their senses when it comes to marriage.'

She could not dispute that Devlin was considered a catch. He was a viscount and one day would inherit an earldom. He was rich and powerful. His family owned a bank. But he had corrupted her brother and he was blackmailing her. She was not foolish enough to think that marriage required either affection or love. It was an arrangement between two families for their mutual good. But she could not like Devlin and the thought that he was most probably behind the attack on Ned made revulsion curl in her stomach.

I want you to stay away from Ned Stratham.

The irony was she had had no intention of going anywhere near Ned Stratham again. It just galled her that Devlin would think it was because of his insistence. And there was the added worry of what Devlin might do to Ned, given what he had witnessed in Green Park.

'I wonder if Devlin will be at Lady Misbourne's little event this evening.' Lady Lamerton slid a knowing look at Emma before lifting her tambour once more.

It was not a thought on which she wished to dwell. Emma put the spoiled letter aside and took a fresh sheet of writing paper from the drawer.

She forced the worry aside and, after dipping her pen in the inkwell, began the letter again.

The Earl of Misbourne raised a hand and a butler appeared by his elbow. 'Champagne all round,' he instructed, then returned his attention to Ned. 'Everything is signed and sealed. The project will go ahead, I give you my word.'

Ned and Misbourne shook hands.

It was done. Ned breathed a sigh of relief and satisfaction.

The butler filled four glasses and passed them round to Misbourne and Linwood, to Rob and Ned.

'To new ventures and continued success.' Ned made the toast.

And all four men toasted it, chinking their glasses in the process.

'You'll stay for a while,' Misbourne said to Ned. 'My wife is hosting a card evening. We have invited a few people round.'

'Thank you.' Ned took a sip of his champagne.

'Capital.' Misbourne clapped him on the shoulder. 'Serious gaming in the dining room. Lighter stuff in the drawing room. If you'll excuse me for a few moments...' He slipped away to speak to his son-in-law, Knight, who had just come through the front door.

Rob gestured to the dining room ahead. 'Feeling lucky?'

Ned drew him a look and instinctively touched his fingers to his tailcoat, feeling the shape of his lucky token that was secure within the waistcoat pocket beneath.

'Just as well.'

Ned glanced into the dining room.

'Devlin still in there?' Rob asked.

'They all are. We'll take a drink in the drawing room to placate Misbourne, then leave.' He did not want to run the risk of meeting Emma. Staying away from her meant precisely that.

Rob gave a nod of agreement.

But as soon as Ned walked into Misbourne's drawing room he realised his mistake.

A line of tables ran down the centre of the room, crammed with ladies and several gentlemen on either side, all intent on playing whist.

On one side of the centremost table Lady Misbourne was trying to avert a scene. A young blonde woman, with eyes that were as dark and intent as Linwood's, was being helped from the room by one of Misbourne's maids. On the other side sat Lady Lamerton and Emma.

'Ah, here comes Mr Stratham. He will step in and save us, I am sure.' Lady Misbourne glanced over to Ned and Rob's arrival.

Emma followed her gaze.

'Lady Misbourne's daughter, Lady Marianne Knight, has come over in a swoon, leaving her poor mama without a partner. And we are in the middle of a crucial match,' explained Lady Lamerton.

Ned stiffened. He made no pretence of smile or charm. For the first time since she had known him she saw something of obvious discomfort in his eyes.

'My apologies, ladies, but I do not play.' He bowed and made to leave, either uncaring or unaware of the insult he was dealing their hostess. Already Emma could see the disapproval and sneers on several faces. Already she could hear the whispers of 'trade' and 'lack of breeding.' But Devlin's warning whispered in her mind. As, too, did her own pride.

She should leave him to it. Maybe she should even be glad of it. But it was not gladness at his mistake that she felt. It was something else altogether. Something that pumped through her blood and was there in her bones, something that wrung at her heart. She looked away, trying to ignore it. Told herself that what they thought of him, what they did to him, was nothing to her. That if his slight of Lady Misbourne made her husband change his mind on whatever business deal he had with Ned, it did not matter to her. She swallowed. Gave a grim silent sigh and knew she could not sit there and let it happen.

She stood up. 'Mr Stratham is too polite. He does not wish to tread upon the sensibilities of us ladies by winning. But I assure you, sir, Lady Lamerton is a formidable player. And I am not so badly skilled myself.'

Her eyes held Ned's across the room, sending the message that this was not an invitation he could afford to refuse, willing him to put what was between them aside for his greater good. 'You must play, sir.' She said it lightly as if it were a joke, but her words were in deadly earnest. 'You would not wish our hostess to feel injured.' The subtlety of that last comment would not be lost on him and if he walked away now, he would insult both her and Lady Misbourne.

'When you put it like that, Miss Northcote...' His lips curved in the hint of a smile, but his eyes were cool and focused all on her. 'How can I refuse?'

He gallantly helped Lady Misbourne to her chair. Then, once all the ladies were seated, he sat down by their hostess's side.

She saw him glance over at his friend, Mr Finchley.

Ned smiled, but it was a smile that did not touch his eyes. For all intents and purposes he was his usual impassive self, but beneath it Emma sensed something else, something that was as tense and still and focused as the calm before a storm. Something dark and tumultuous. It was so palpable that she wondered that any of the other women did not sense it.

'Rest assured, sir, we will treat you gently,' she said to lighten the situation. The remark made all the ladies smile. Ned smiled, too, and he seemed almost as relaxed and confident as his usual self. But when his eyes met hers, she could see that it was a sham and she knew that he felt the same terrible conflict that beat in her own heart.

'You do know how to play whist, do you not, Mr Stratham?' Lady Lamerton enquired.

'I do, for my sins.'

Lady Lamerton smiled. 'Then let play begin and see if Miss Northcote and I cannot best you and Lady Misbourne.'

The dowager dealt the cards, one at a time in rotation, until the pack was exhausted. 'Ah, hearts are trumps, I see,' she said as she dealt the last card face up on the table.

Ned picked up his cards, spread them to a small fan within his hands. Across the cards his eyes met Emma's. In that moment it was as if his guard was lowered and she caught a glimpse of his soul—bared for her to see. And what she saw was such a blazing tortured intensity of emotion that it took her breath away. Their eyes clung together, as if they were the only two people in the room, as if they were the only two people in the world. As if there was nothing and no one except him and her and the force of this thing that raged between them. It shook her.

It shook him, too. She could see it in his eyes as they lingered too long on hers before lowering to his cards.

They played on. Lady Lamerton was in her element as she and Emma soon took the lead.

And then Lady Lamerton exchanged a look with her, giving a subtle gesture across the room. Emma followed Lady Lamerton's gaze to see Devlin standing there.

Devlin's eyes rested on Ned and just for a moment the expression on his face was one of utter loathing. Then he masked it and slid his gaze to Emma's. The words of his warning seemed to whisper between them.

She glanced down at her cards. Kept her face composed. Betrayed nothing. But when she glanced at him again, he was walking directly towards Ned.

She felt her stomach dip and begin to churn. Her eyes met Ned's in warning.

Ned understood. A tiny glance over his left shoulder to see where Devlin stood.

The change in his face was so small as to have been imperceptible, but Emma saw it. That slight tension and the way his hand moved to touch against the watch pocket of his waistcoat, which only she knew contained not a watch, but the small battered token that was his good-luck charm.

He played on. Lost. Again.

'Such terribly bad luck you are having today, Mr Stratham,' lamented Lady Misbourne.

Ned glanced over his other shoulder where Fallingham and Bullford now stood. 'Worse than you can imagine,' he said with a smile.

'One might almost think, sir, that you are determined to have Miss Northcote and me win,' said Lady Lamerton with a twinkle in her eye as she scooped the growing pile of winnings closer.

'As if I would,' said Ned in a teasing tone.

Devlin walked round to Emma's side of the table, came to stand close to her, close enough to have a slightly threatening possessive feel about it. For a moment she feared he meant to reveal her and Ned before them all. But then she saw the way he looked at Ned across the table. A challenging look. A look that was so obvious in its contempt that she felt her blood run cold.

As Monteith, Fallingham and Bullford crowded around Ned, the rest of the table saw only three gentlemen intent on getting a closer look at the game, swept along in the excitement and camaraderie. But Emma saw something else. She saw that the threat and danger was aimed not at herself, but at Ned.

Ned showed nothing of intimidation. He seemed relaxed enough, but Emma knew he had not been so since he had walked into the room. She could sense his tension as if it were her own.

The game dragged on, the pressure building ever higher. Every time Ned lost, Lady Misbourne scooped a trick and so they survived a little longer.

Sensing something of the atmosphere, people gathered round to watch. But closest of all were Devlin, Fallingham, Bullford and Monteith, like ravens in their black tailcoats waiting for the kill.

'All done,' said Lady Lamerton as she won the last trick.

'I must beg your forgiveness, Lady Misbourne, for having been such a poor partner,' said Ned.

'Not at all, sir. Luck was not on our side tonight, but our losses were not so bad,' Lady Misbourne replied.

Their audience began to disperse, wandering back to their own tables. But Devlin and his friends made no move. The atmosphere hummed with menace. The tension felt drawn to breaking point.

'Lady Lamerton…Miss Northcote.' Ned's eyes lingered on Emma's for a heartbeat, before he made his apologies and took his farewell of Lady Misbourne. 'If you will excuse me.' He bowed and walked out of the room.

She watched with a sick feeling in her stomach as Devlin and his friends followed him.

'We did well, Emma,' said Lady Lamerton.

'Indeed,' she managed. But there was a panic in her ready to unleash, and a dread seeping through her bones over what might happen in that hallway. 'If you would excuse me for a few moments.'

'Of course, my dear.' Lady Lamerton gave a nod.

Chapter Twelve

Ned and Devlin stood facing each other in the corridor. The look on Devlin's face was one of ice-cold fury. Standing on Ned's side was Rob Finchley. Monteith, Fallingham and Bullford were sided with Devlin.

'You can dress yourself in fine clothes, Stratham. You can feign some pretence of manners and politeness. You can attend every opera, ballet and ball that you wish. But it cannot change what you are beneath. You are no gentleman. Not all the money in the world will ever buy you that.' Devlin's voice was quiet enough, but Emma heard every word.

Ned smiled as if Devlin's rant amused him.

'Playing whist with Miss Northcote...' Devlin sneered.

'Do you wish a game? I fancy my luck would return were I to play you.'

'I would not sully myself to sit at the same table.'

'Afraid you would deal me the winning hand, Devlin?'

Devlin's nostrils flared. Emma saw the muscle tighten in his jaw, saw his eyes darken with fury, saw the barely concealed violence. The air crackled with it. Devlin's fists balled. He stepped closer to Ned. 'You have gone too far this time, Stratham. Way too far.'

Ned still seemed relaxed, but she had seen him fight and she recognised that look in his eyes and the subtle shift in his stance. She knew what was about to happen. She knew Ned would annihilate Devlin. There would be violence, and blood and a fight that would not follow gentlemen's rules, here in Misbourne's home, before his family, before all his guests. Ned would best Devlin, but there would be a cost to it more than he realised.

She stepped closer as if about to pass them, brushed against Devlin and tipped the contents of her glass of lemonade down the front of his tailcoat and breeches. 'I am so sorry, Lord Devlin. Forgive me. I am too clumsy.'

It was enough to quench the fuse that had been lit… for now.

Devlin reacted by stepping away from Ned, glancing down at his soaked clothing.

His eyes met hers. There was nothing of his usual charming or smooth self. In their place was a cold promise that frightened her. He knew exactly what she had done. 'You have made a very foolish choice, Emma,' he said softly.

She sensed the movement in Ned. Saw the tightening of the muscle in his jaw. Stepped between him and Devlin to prevent what he was about to do.

But the two men glowered at one another. Two combatants. The fight was not over. It would never be over, but only grow worse in this escalating war of which Emma was a part.

'If you will excuse me, Miss Northcote…Mr Stratham.' Devlin walked away with his friends.

She saw the flick of Ned's gaze towards the door through which Devlin had just left. Saw the hardness in his eyes.

The breath shook in her throat. She could feel a slight tremble running though her body.

'Emma...' His voice was low, husky, quiet enough for only her to hear. He was looking at her with such strained control that she could see the storm of emotion that simmered beneath. He was looking at her as if he were committing her image to memory. She felt the surreptitious brush of his fingers against hers and glanced at where Rob Finchley stood watching, before meeting Ned's gaze once more.

She knew that they did not have much time. Knew after what she had just witnessed what he would do if she told him that Devlin had blackmailed her to stay away from him and now meant to reveal her to Lady Lamerton. She could not tell him even to warn him.

'Ned,' she whispered with urgency, 'this is not Whitechapel. You must fight by different means here or be ruined.'

Their eyes held locked. They were still standing too close.

'Emma,' she heard Lady Lamerton's voice from the doorway of the drawing room and stepped away from Ned.

'If you will excuse me, Mr Stratham,' she said formally.

'Your servant, Miss Northcote.' He bowed.

She made her way back along to Lady Lamerton.

The violence she feared had not materialised, but that did not allay the worry churning in her stomach. She had the overwhelming sense that something had just happened between Ned and Devlin and herself, something from which there could be no turning back for any of them.

The Rubicon had been crossed.

* * *

Ned stood alone by the window of his bedchamber that night, staring out at the lamplit street and seeing nothing of it.

He could not stop thinking of that card game.

The choice had been between insulting Misbourne's wife in a very public way in her own home or sitting down at that table with Emma Northcote. And after all these years…after all he had striven for, on the brink of success, he had almost walked away. Almost spoiled the deal that was in the bag. And he knew why. He closed his eyes at that.

Emma had been right to stop him from walking away and delivering the insult. It was Emma who had saved the deal.

But to sit down at that table across from her… He had not thought it would affect him so. He had not realised the magnitude of his dilemma until that very moment. Now he understood it too well. He understood exactly what it was he had done two years ago.

This wasn't just about him. There were hundreds relying on him. Those who were nameless, faceless, voiceless, forgotten. How could he turn his back on them? But sitting down at that card table had not guaranteed their safety. Ned knew people and he knew the look of a man who had been pushed too far. He knew, too, how this evening must have looked to Devlin: that Ned was taunting him with a red rag, that he was rubbing his face in it. Every man had his limit and Devlin had reached his.

If Devlin knew what Ned felt for Emma, there would be nothing to stop him. He would strike. He would destroy Ned and all of his work.

What he felt for Emma.

He stared out of the window, knowing now what it was he felt for her, knowing, too, the impossibility of it.

Destiny had seen to that.

He slipped the token from his pocket and rubbed the worn surface between his fingers.

A man might gain the world and lose himself in doing so. A man's luck always ran out eventually.

Ned thought that maybe his time had come.

The weather turned cool and gloomy the next day. Within the little parlour at the back of Lady Lamerton's town house a small fire burned on the hearth to chase the chill from the room and banish the gloom. It did not banish Emma's megrim. Her head felt so thick with fatigue from a night sleepless with worry that she could not think straight.

She was on edge at every letter Lady Lamerton opened. Her stomach clenched every time the butler came into the room.

You have made a very foolish choice, Emma. Devlin's words rang in her head.

She knew what was coming and she had only herself to blame. Nor could she get Ned's expression out of her head. When he had looked at her across that card table, and afterwards, when his fingers had touched hers. Maybe she should have told him of Devlin's threat, but she had known what would have happened if she had done that. And now it was too late.

'You are wool-gathering, Emma. Have you reached the list of forthcoming events for the Little Season yet?' Lady Lamerton's voice interrupted her thoughts.

'Forgive me.' Emma forced her eyes to return to *The Lady's Journal* that lay opened on her lap. She turned the page and started to read aloud again.

It was almost a relief when Wilcott interrupted with the news that Lord Devlin had called and was waiting in the drawing room to speak to Lady Lamerton unattended.

'Very interesting,' said Lady Lamerton with a twinkle in her eye as she looked at Emma.

Emma could not smile. She knew what the dowager thought and how wrong it was. She knew what was coming and her blood was ice-cold with dread. The same dread that was pounding in her chest and tying her stomach in a knot. She should say something, utter some small warning to the dowager, it was only fair, but her mouth was too dry and the words would not form upon her tongue. By the time she opened her mouth Lady Lamerton was halfway across the room, smiling, happy as she made her way to meet Devlin.

The door closed with a click behind her, leaving Emma sitting alone.

She closed over the pages of the journal with bloodless fingers. Sat it neatly on the table and got to her feet with legs that were stiff and cold.

She thought of her father. She thought of her brother, Kit, and all that Lamerton might have achieved. She thought of Lady Lamerton's disappointment.

Only a few minutes passed before the dowager returned to the parlour and closed the door behind her. The expression on her face was unreadable.

Emma stood still as a statue. The beat of her own heart was loud in her ears as she met her employer's gaze and waited for the axe to fall.

'Devlin wishes to speak to *you*, Emma. Alone.' Lady Lamerton smiled.

Emma stared at her, shocked by this unexpected turn of events, not understanding what Devlin was doing.

'Says he has something very important to speak to you of…'

She could hear in Lady Lamerton's tone her romantic expectation, for, in the dowager's mind, why else did a gentleman call on a respectable lady at home and ask to speak to her alone?

Why else indeed?

'Well, off you go, my dear. You do not want to keep him waiting.'

'I do not.' She went to discover just what Devlin had in store for her.

Devlin was standing beside the white marble of the drawing-room hearth, with a dark look within his eye.

'Miss Northcote,' he said and then more softly, 'close the door behind you.'

She hesitated.

'Unless you have a wish for Lady Lamerton to hear our conversation…'

She closed the door with a quiet click. Came to stand before Devlin, facing him across the fireside rug. 'Does toying with me give you pleasure, Devlin? Tell her and be done with it.'

There was a silence as their eyes held.

'If I tell her, it would be the ruin of you, Emma.'

'Is that not what you want?'

'Contrary to what you think, it is not.'

'Then what do you want, Devlin?'

He smiled a strange sort of smile and glanced away.

Emma felt an uneasiness. 'Devlin?' she prompted softly.

That dark unreadable gaze met hers. He smiled again. This time his usual handsome charming smile, but it did not quite reach his eyes. 'I want you, Emma.'

All she could hear in the resounding silence was the hard thud of her heart.

She stared at him, unable to believe what he had just said. 'Is this some sort of jest?'

'I have never been more serious.' His voice was silky smooth and cold as ice. 'Marry me, Emma.'

'You cannot be in earnest, Devlin.'

The silence hissed loudly.

He stepped closer and, lifting a strand of hair away from her face, tucked it behind her ear in a gesture that was too intimate. 'You think I have no care for you?'

She stepped back out of his reach, trying not to show the horror slipping through her veins.

'And if I refuse you...?'

He stared at her as if he had not considered that as an option. Devlin was titled and rich, handsome and powerful. There could not be many women who would turn him down. Especially a woman in Emma's position.

'I think you understand the choice well enough. Marry me, or I will have to reconsider my position on speaking to Lady Lamerton.'

'You said you had a care for me. You said you did not want to ruin me.'

'Needs must,' he murmured in a voice that, for all its quietness, cut through her to make her shiver.

'More blackmail,' she said.

She thought of her father. She thought of her brother. She thought of Ned.

How could she marry a man that would think nothing of blackmailing a woman, a man who had organised that awful attack on Ned? Who despised another man simply because he had been born poor and made his own way in the world?

And how could she not, given what was riding on it?

'Do you understand what I am offering you, Emma?'

He was offering her a reprieve.

He was offering her a lifetime at his side and in his bed. She would be his to do with as he pleased. A man who had led her brother to a gaming den and sat there and let him lose her father's fortune.

She looked into his eyes, and knew she could not do it.

'I recognise the honour you do me, Devlin, but…'

'You are refusing me because of him?'

'Lady Lamerton said you have always disliked him, even before my return. Why? Simply because he is trade?' she demanded.

'Is he?' Devlin asked. 'What do you really know of Edward Stratham?'

'I know enough.'

'Do you, really? Do you know he is a Whitechapel tough, Emma, in the guise of a gentleman? A wolf in sheep's clothing and one that means to eat you up for breakfast?'

'There is nothing between me and Ned Stratham.' *Any more.* Those small important words went unspoken. 'I will not be seeing him again, I promise you.'

'Somehow I do not believe you.'

'Then you are mistaken in what you believe.'

'In the same way I was mistaken in what I saw in Green Park?'

His words echoed in the silence.

'Believe what you will. Shall I fetch Lady Lamerton that you might tell her?'

'You really will not yield.' Not a question, but a statement.

She shook her head.

His eyes scanned hers. 'You fancy yourself in love

with him,' he said slowly with the air of a man making a discovery.

'Do not be absurd!' she snapped, but felt the traitorous blush heat her cheeks. 'It is merely that, unlike you, I am not so prejudiced to judge a man on where he was born and how he came by his money.'

He laughed at that, but it was a hard, sarcastic sound. 'Such pride and principles, Emma. You really have no idea.'

'You think Whitechapel a hovel and Edward Stratham beneath a gentleman because of it.'

'No, I think Whitechapel a cesspit and Stratham the vilest of its villains.'

They stared at one another.

'He is not what you think him, Emma.'

'Whatever he is, Devlin, he is a better man than you.'

The words seemed to echo in the room between them.

'I am sorry that it has come to this, Devlin.'

'So am I, Emma.' He looked at her for a moment longer. 'So am I.'

He bowed and walked away leaving her standing there.

'Well?' Lady Lamerton was standing in the doorway, with her eyebrows raised in expectation of the news.

'He asked me to marry him.' Emma felt dazed.

'I knew it!' Lady Lamerton crowed. 'Many congratu—'

'I refused him.'

'You did *what*?'

'I refused him,' she said and sat down in the chair.

'Are you run mad, Emma?'

'Perhaps,' she said. And maybe she really was. She had refused Devlin and stoked his ire. And for all her justifications and moral high ground, she knew they were all just excuses. She knew the real reason she was jeopardising her position and risking Lamerton's assistance in locating Kit. She felt numb from what she had just done.

'Devlin is heir to an earldom. He is one of the wealthiest men in London. His mother is from a banking dynasty. And you are—' Lady Lamerton stopped herself just in time and sat down, clasping a hand to her forehead.

'A penniless companion,' Emma continued for her. 'Whose family name has been marred by scandal.'

'You are a young lady who holds too much against him, is what I was going to say.'

'Both are true,' Emma admitted. 'But given the part that Devlin played in my family's history, he and I really would not suit.'

'I think, Emma Northcote, that is a decision you will regret. And if it has anything to do with Edward Stratham then you would do well to think again. I saw you talking to him at Lady Misbourne's card party. Using him to bring Devlin to offer was one thing. But this is something else. Rest assured Stratham will have his eye on bigger fish than you, Emma, I thought you understood that. I am not unaware that young women are attracted to men who are, how shall I put it—rugged, untamed and rather dangerous. A rogue can set a lady's heart a-flutter. I was once young myself, hard to believe though it is. But trust me when I tell you that whatever else you might imagine, what Stratham wants from you is not marriage.'

Ned stood by the empty grate of his study in the mansion house in Cavendish Square. Rob sat in one of the nearby wing chairs.

'You'll have heard the whisper that Devlin proposed marriage to her and she turned him down,' Rob said.

Ned gave a nod. 'I've heard.'

'Because of you?'

'She loathes Devlin. She blames him for what happened to her brother,' Ned said, not answering the question. He let the words lapse into silence. 'I'm going to tell her. The truth. Of who I am.'

'Why?' Rob stared at him as if he had had a brainstorm. 'Have you gone mad?'

'I love her, Rob.'

His friend stared at him. Had never heard him say such a thing about anyone ever. 'I did not realise.'

'Neither did I. Until I had to sit down at that card table opposite her.'

'Hell!' Rob whispered.

'Yes,' agreed Ned. 'It was. It is.'

'If you tell her, you're risking everything.'

'Misbourne is signed in. He won't pull out.'

'And the rest of it? Everything else?' Rob shook his head. 'You could lose it all.'

'Then so be it. I am done with the charade. I cannot marry another woman. Nor can I sit back and watch her marry another man. I love her!'

'But if you tell her...you will lose her.' Rob looked in pain.

'And if I don't tell her, how can I be with her?' Ned shook his head. 'How can I ask her to wed me?' He knew what his friend was saying was right, but he knew, too, he had to do this. 'She has a right to know the truth. To make her own informed choice whatever that choice may be. I will not hoodwink her. I will not lie to her. Let the cards fall where they will.'

Rob glanced away. 'At the end of the day, she's one of them, Ned.'

'She's not what you think her. She's one of us, too.'

Rob shook his head. 'Have you thought about this? About what it will mean?'

'I have thought about nothing else for days.' He looked at his friend. 'I'll tell her tonight. There's a dance at Colonel Morley's. Lady Lamerton's name is on the guest list.'

There was a small silence during which Rob digested the enormity of what was about to happen. His face was pale.

Ned took the piece of paper from the top drawer of his desk and handed it to Rob. 'You've been a good friend to me, Rob. Whatever happens tonight…you'll be all right.'

'Thank you, Ned.' Rob slipped the cheque into his pocket.

Ned lifted the bottle of gin from where it sat ready on the drum table between them. Poured them both a drink. 'Dutch courage,' he said and sat down in the leather wing chair opposite Rob's.

Rob accepted the drink with thanks. He hesitated, then asked, 'You said that you love her. Does she love you?'

'I believe she thinks she does.'

'I'm sorry, Ned. I never imagined…'

'Neither did I.'

They lapsed into silence. Sipped their gin from the engraved cut-crystal glasses in the splendour of the mahogany-lined study.

Because they both knew that Emma Northcote would not love him once he told her the truth.

Emma heard the stifled whispers about her and Devlin the minute she walked into Mrs Morley's ballroom and knew that it had been a mistake to tell Lady Lamerton. She ignored the gossip and concentrated only on Lady Lamerton's conversation with Mrs Morley, Mrs Hilton and Lady Routledge. But the too-frequent flicker of their eyes across the ballroom warned her. She glanced across the room and saw Ned and his steward talking to Mr Dale.

The footman passed Emma the note surreptitiously as he brought the tray of lemonades across to the party of ladies. Slid it into her hand beneath the cover of tray as he offered the drinks.

She opened her mouth to ask who had sent it, but the footman was already weaving his way through the crowd. With the sudden race of her heart she thought that she already knew the answer.

Emma slipped the note straight into her pocket before anyone could notice. Her eyes found Ned's across the room. She felt the power of all that bound them together squeeze her heart, felt it twist and tug against the chains in which they were trying to confine it, felt it roar for release.

Inside her pocket the letter seemed to quiver and vibrate. She knew whatever he needed to tell her must be important for him to risk sending a note.

Their eyes held a second longer across the ballroom. His expression was intense, serious, watchful. His brows lowered. She felt her stomach tighten with worry.

She turned away, bent her head to Lady Lamerton's ear and whispered her excuse.

Lady Lamerton did not stop listening to the story Lady Routledge was relating. Barely glanced in Emma's direction. Gave a nod of her head to Emma to show that she was giving her permission.

Emma glanced at Ned again. Then she made her way from the ballroom.

Out in the hallway she stopped behind a large display cabinet and retrieved the note. The paper quivered in her hand as she opened it and skimmed her eyes over the few dark strong words written there. Her eyes widened. Her heart gave a stutter.

The note was not from Ned, but she did not even question the instruction written within it. Emma slipped it into her pocket and, with a deep breath, stopped a passing footman and asked him the way to Colonel Morley's study.

Chapter Thirteen

'The development of the site has started just as you required,' Mr Dale was saying by Ned's side.

Ned watched the footman slip Emma the note. Watched her pocket it with equal stealth. Her eyes moved to his. Held, before she turned away and whispered something in Lady Lamerton's ear. Dale's voice was still talking.

'Good. Keep me informed of its progress. If you will excuse me, sir.' Ned's eyes followed Emma as she left the ballroom.

The curtains had been drawn within the study. A single branch of candles had been lit, its soft flickering glow the only point of illumination in the darkness.

He was standing by the fireplace, staring into the blackened grate, a half-empty glass of brandy in his hand. Waiting.

'Devlin,' she said and closed the door softly behind her.

'A word, if you please.' Ned collared the footman behind the column in the corner of the ballroom, the same footman who had passed Emma the letter, and pressed a Bank of England five-pound note into the man's palm.

The footman pocketed the money. 'For that you can have any word you like, sir.'

'The name of the person who gave you the letter for Miss Northcote.'

'That would be Lord Devlin,' said the footman. 'Saw him heading for Colonel Morley's study.'

Ned pressed another banknote into the man's hand and set his untouched glass of champagne down on the footman's tray.

Ned's face was grim as he made his way from the ballroom.

Within the dimly lit study Devlin made no move. He did not so much as glance round.

Emma walked closer.

'You said you had news of Kit.'

But Devlin still stood where he was. Gave no reaction, as if he had not heard her. Not until she walked right up to him. She could see the way he was staring at that grate, with such a dark brooding look upon his face that made her dread that the news was the worst.

'Devlin?' she said softly.

He finished the rest of the brandy from the glass in a single gulp. Set the crystal down on the black-marble mantelpiece with a thump. And finally turned to face her.

'I lied,' he said.

She stared at him. 'I do not understand… Why would you send me that note saying—?' She stopped as the sinking realisation hit her.

'I see you do understand after all.' He did not smile. Just looked at her. 'That I wanted to get you here alone.'

'How despicable of you to use my brother's name to do so. Especially after your role in his downfall.'

Guilt flashed across his face. He looked away. And

when he looked at her again there was angry cynicism in his eyes. 'No one put a pistol to his head and forced him to the gaming tables.'

'Maybe not. But he was a boy and you and the others, men of the world that he looked up to, you led him astray.'

'Kit was no child, Emma. He was a foolish man, but a man nevertheless. A man who made his own choices. And one who has to face the consequences of his actions. As all men do, Emma.' There was guilt in his eyes, heart-rending and obvious before he hid it once more. 'You cannot blame others in his stead.'

'I am not a fool. I know my brother was not blame-less. He gambled the money, after all. But you and the others let him stake his last penny. You let him stake it all. You should have stopped him, Devlin. You were sup-posed to be his friends!'

'We were his friends.' He gave a cold mirthless smile. 'We still are.'

'Spare me the pretence.'

'As you insist.'

The silence pulsed between them. His eyes held hers with cool determination.

'If you will excuse me, Lord Devlin.'

'I am afraid I cannot allow you to leave.'

His words stroked a shiver of fear down her spine, but she regarded him with disdain to hide it. She calmly turned to walk away, but Devlin's hand caught her arm and held her firm.

'You should not have turned me down, Emma.'

She felt the dread slip into her blood like a single splash into a still, deep pool. She looked pointedly at where his hand held tight to her arm, then raised her eyes to meet his, feigning a calm confidence she did not feel.

'What are you doing, Devlin?'

'Whatever I have to.' His voice was soft in contrast to the hard determination in his eyes.

Fear drummed loud and insistent through her heart. She tried to pull free, but Devlin's grip was unbreakable. She ceased her struggle and conserved her energy. Faced him boldly. 'What do you mean to do, Devlin?'

'Save you from Stratham.'

She gave a cynical laugh and shook her head.

Devlin did not smile. His expression was cold, unamused, frightening.

She glanced again at where his fingers were locked around her arm. Then looked into his eyes with derision. 'And *you* lambast *him* for not being a gentleman?'

'Sometimes the end justifies the means,' he said quietly and pulled her close. So close she could see the striations in those dark eyes of his and feel his breath warm against her cheek.

Her heart was thudding so fast she felt sick. She tried to resist, but he was too strong. 'Do not do this, Devlin,' she said. 'Please.'

He swallowed, glanced away, then back again. 'Just a kiss, Emma. Nothing more, I swear. Do not be afraid.'

He slid an arm around her waist. As he shifted his grip, she managed to break free and began to run, but he grabbed her shoulder and wrenched her back to him.

'No! Do not!' She fought him, but he was too tall and powerful.

He pulled her into his arms once more, holding her there as he looked into her eyes. 'I am sorry, Emma,' he said before his mouth closed over hers.

She kicked against him, fought harder. But none of it made any difference. All she knew was his overwhelming strength and the smell of his cologne and the possession of her mouth by his and a raging fear and anger at what he was doing.

She was struggling so hard she did not hear the opening of the study door. But Devlin did. He released her so suddenly that she stumbled back against the fireplace wall. She stayed there, her spine pressed against the wall-paper. She was breathing hard, shaking with shock and panic and fight. Devlin stood where he was facing her, his eyes cool and focused upon hers. But she was not looking at Devlin, only at Ned standing there in the door frame. So silent and still and with a calmness that was a promise of something very different. He stepped across the threshold, closed the door with careful control. The quietest of clicks in the silence.

Only then did Devlin glance over his shoulder and the expression on his face changed, so that she saw it for the mask it was. Shock flitted in his eyes.

Ned's eyes held hers for a moment. She saw them drop to the neckline of her dress and only then did she realise that it had been ripped in the struggle. Something changed in Ned's eyes. Something so dark and dangerous slipped into them that it frightened even her. His gaze swivelled to Devlin. She had thought him powerful when he had fought Black-Hair in the Red Lion, and that night in the Botanical Gardens. But this was different. Every-thing of his stance. Everything of his being. The very air around him. All of it shimmered with a dark deadly promise. The quiet before the worst thunderstorm. The promise to death.

'Ned.' It came out as a whisper. Husky. Broken. Part relief, part plea. 'Stop. Wait. It is not…'

But her words died away as she realised that Ned was not listening. He did not shift his gaze from Devlin. And she knew in that moment that Devlin's fate was sealed. That Ned was going to kill him.

Devlin must have known it, too. He faced Ned. Tense. Moving ever so slightly. Ready to meet what was coming. Ready to fight for his life.

She saw the subtle gearing of Ned's body, the ripple and movement of muscles, the slight shift in balance, the honed deadly focus.

'You've crossed a line from which there's no retreat, Devlin.' Ned's voice was low and quiet. 'You may do what you wish to me. But Emma…' He shook his head.

Devlin stood his ground, a barrier between Emma and Ned. 'I will not let you have her, Stratham.'

'Step away from her.' Almost a growl.

Devlin shook his head. 'I'll see you in hell first.'

There was a moment, just the tiniest moment of silence. And then everything exploded with a speed and violence and fury as Ned ran full tilt at Devlin. The collision seemed to reverberate through the room, but Ned kept on going, the force of the momentum carrying both men across the room to land with an almighty thud on the floor. Then fists were flying, punches landing hard, feet kicking, as the two men struggled and rolled and fought. A round mahogany table was thrown over, its crystal decanter and glasses crashing in a mess of broken glass upon the hearth. One minute Ned had the upper hand, the next it passed to Devlin.

'Stop it, both of you!' Emma cried, but it was as a whisper against the roar of a hurricane. She could not even begin to get close.

Both scrabbled to their feet. The white of their shirts, cravats and waistcoats was speckled red with blood. Devlin's lip was burst. Ned's cheek was cut and the sleeve of his jacket was torn.

Devlin moved in fast, landed a blow in Ned's stomach, then, as he doubled over, Devlin let loose a series of punches to his face.

Ned staggered back.

Devlin came after him, with his fists.

Ned smiled. Caught Devlin's fist as it came again. Crushed it.

Like some kind of arm-wrestling game, the men's eyes held and their bodies strained motionless. Then Ned twisted Devlin's arm and slammed him hard face first into the wall. Devlin began to crumple, but Ned grabbed him by the neck, hauled him upright, put a hand round his throat. And squeezed.

'Ned!' Emma ran to him. 'Stop! Think what it will mean, for us both, if you kill him.' She laid her hand on Ned's arm and could feel how hard he was breathing. 'Please, Ned. Do not do this.'

He slid his eyes to Emma's and in them was such love and fierceness that it took her breath away. Their gaze held for a second longer, then he gave a nod and returned his focus to Devlin.

'If you ever touch her again, I *will* kill you. Regardless of anything else that is between us. Do you understand?'

Devlin's face was turning purple. He managed a gesture of agreement.

Ned released him and Devlin sagged, catching his breath.

'Oh, Ned,' she whispered and only then realised that she was crying.

'Emma.' Ned swept strong arms around her, moving her away from Devlin's reach.

He gathered her to him, held her. She could feel the hard beat of his heart, feel the strong pump of his blood, feel all that was between them; this warrior of a man who had saved her so many times; this man who would kill to protect her.

She tilted her face up to his, looked into his eyes, as his hand cradled the back of her head.

'I am done with pretences. Things cannot go on the way they are, Emma. We must speak in earnest.' He caressed a thumb against her face. 'But not here, not now. First things first. We need to get you tidied up and back to the ballroom before your absence is noticed.'

She nodded, knowing he was right.

But then the door opened and there was a woman's gasp and a man's guttural exclamation of shock. And she knew it was too late.

It was only when the study door opened to reveal Colonel and Mrs Morley, and Lady Lamerton, surrounded by Devlin's tight circle of friends, that Ned saw the expression on Devlin's face and understood what was *really* happening. What Devlin's intention had been. That Devlin had expected the little party's arrival, but not Ned's. He shot a hard glance across at where Devlin stood.

Emma was in Ned's arms, her face wet with tears, the shoulder of her dress ripped, her hair tumbling awry from its pins, her lips kiss-swollen. She looked like a woman who had been ravished. And even if she had not, it would not have mattered.

'Good God, Stratham!' exclaimed Colonel Morley. 'You have ruined her!'

'No,' Emma began to say. 'It was—'

Ned knew what he was going to have to do. His arm tightened around her waist, his eyes met hers in warning. He kissed the word she would have uttered from her mouth, hard and lusty, then released her and moved to stand in front of her, facing the men and shielding her from their view.

'Guilty as charged,' he said. 'If Devlin had not interrupted us…' He glanced at Devlin.

The viscount's eyes were dark and filled with loathing. But there was nothing he could do. Nothing he could say.

'Emma?' Lady Lamerton stared at her.

Ned's eyes met Emma's again, willing her to understand and say what she must.

Emma looked at Lady Lamerton and gave a nod.

'Well, sir,' proclaimed Colonel Morley, puffing himself up. He began to walk to Ned, but stopped when he saw the look on Ned's face. Morley glanced around him for support. 'Miss Northcote is a gently bred lady. There can only be one honourable outcome to this thoroughly dishonourable affair.'

'There can,' agreed Ned. It was either him or Devlin. And there was no way he could give her up to Devlin; not when he felt about Emma as he did and most definitely not after what he had just witnessed. 'I will wed her.' His face was grim.

Morley gave a nod.

There was a silence. He saw the dark expression on Devlin's face and those of Monteith, Fallingham and Bullford. Colonel Morley looked in a state of righteous indignation. Lady Lamerton looked shaken.

And Emma—she maintained a quiet dignity and poise, but he could see the relief in her eyes that it was him and not Devlin.

And something twisted in his gut, because he knew she would not be relieved if she knew the truth.

Destiny mocked him with her cold irony.

And he stood there and said nothing, to protect the woman that he loved.

* * *

'I warned you, did I not?' Lady Lamerton was in high dudgeon and Emma could not blame her. She had lost one companion. Now she was about to lose another. And Emma knew that Lady Lamerton had been good to her. Had treated her with honesty and kindness and ignored the scandal surrounding her family.

'I am sorry,' Emma said. And truly she was. For Lady Lamerton. For Ned. For her father and Kit. For all of this mess that had erupted around her.

'I knew he was no good.'

Emma swallowed. Pressed her lips firm so that she would not say the words she wanted to, to defend Ned. That it was not Ned with whom she had fought, but Devlin.

Ned looked the villain when all he was guilty of was saving her.

'Although none of us realised the depths he was capable of plumbing.' Lady Lamerton swallowed and her distaste for the words she was about to say made her purse her lips. 'To force himself upon a woman…' She shook her head. 'But I suppose that bad blood will always out. He is no gentleman, but a rogue in truth.'

Emma closed her eyes at that.

'What were you doing alone with him in the study in the first place? You told me you were for the ladies' withdrawing room.'

'I received a note,' she said slowly, hating the fact she could not tell the truth of what had happened in that study. 'It said he had information on the whereabouts of my brother.'

Lady Lamerton's face tightened to a scowl. 'A dirty trick worthy of only the lowest villain.'

'It was indeed.' Except that low villain was a viscount

and one of the *ton*'s inner circle of disreputable gentlemen, not Ned Stratham.

'Thank God that Devlin arrived! I dread to think the state you would be in had he not.'

Emma looked away, unable to bear hearing Devlin so praised and Ned so vilified.

'At least he realised he could not wriggle out of doing the honourable thing. No doubt he would have tried had not so many gentlemen been present.'

Emma could have smiled at the irony of that statement. If they only knew… If it had come to fighting, Colonel Morley, Devlin, Monteith and the rest of them would not have stood a chance. She thought of Ned's grip round Devlin's throat and knew that Ned would have killed him had she not intervened.

When she gave no response, Lady Lamerton misconstrued her silence. 'I know it is difficult, Emma, but you are going to have to marry him. You are completely ruined if you do not. And there is nothing I or anyone else can do to change that. I have asked Colonel Morley and Devlin *et al.* to remain silent on the matter.'

Emma wondered if they would. She knew how much Devlin hated Ned. But after what he had done… She shuddered at the awful memory.

'And I have told Mr Stratham in no uncertain terms he is not welcome here. Damnable cheek of him to think he could call this morning.'

Emma thought of having had to sit with Lady Lamerton in the upstairs parlour and keep on writing the dowager's letter while Wilcott informed Ned that neither Lady Lamerton nor Miss Northcote were at home to him. 'What harm would there have been in admitting him?'

'What harm indeed?' Lady Lamerton snorted.

'We will be married come Friday.'

'Let us just hope that Mr Stratham has learned enough about being a gentleman to keep the appointment.'

Ned Stratham was the most honourable man Emma had ever known. It killed a part of her to have to sit quiet and let him be so unjustly maligned. 'He would not—' she began.

'Indeed?' Lady Lamerton raised her eyebrows and looked down her nose. 'I do believe that when it comes to Mr Stratham any dishonourable thing is possible.'

Ned waited until the door closed behind his man of business before he spoke.

'It is done. All of the business and the project with Misbourne will always be taken care of.'

Rob gave a nod. 'You did good for this city, Ned Stratham.'

'It wasn't my money.'

'It was. You took an acorn and grew it to an oak whose branches stretch far beyond the petty privileged drawing rooms of Mayfair and the already-filled pockets of those that run the gaming clubs. That is where it would have ended otherwise. You can't deny that.'

'Maybe not. But it doesn't alter the truth of where the money came from.' Ned looked at the gleam of the bare mahogany desktop before him.

There was a silence.

'I didn't think he had it in him to stoop so low.' Rob sneered as he said it.

'Desperation pushes a man to his limits.'

'He went too far.'

'Way too far.' He closed his eyes at the memory of Devlin forcing himself upon Emma. It was an image that would remain branded on his brain for ever. And one that made his teeth clench and his fingers curl to fists and a cold fury of protective anger pulse through his blood.

'The irony is that Devlin only had to wait an hour. One hour more and I would have had a chance to speak to her. One hour and she would have known the truth. Of who I am, of what I am. He wouldn't have had to say one word to her, or lift so much as a finger against her.'

Rob swallowed. 'Are you going to tell her before Friday?'

'Were I to do so, do you think there would still be a wedding?' He raised an eyebrow. 'Will she willingly marry the man who destroyed her beloved brother? The man who won his fortune, and was responsible for her family's ruin?' Ned gave a tiny shake of his head. 'If I tell her now, she will not have me. And if she doesn't marry me she's ruined.'

The two men looked across the room at one another with serious eyes.

'God help you both,' said Rob.

'Amen to that, my friend,' said Ned. 'God help us both, indeed.'

Chapter Fourteen

The morning sunlight flooded into the carriage, sending silver shimmers through the silk of Emma's dove-grey dress. Outside she could hear the song of a blackbird over the rattle and roll of the carriage wheels and the clatter of horses' hooves. Inside, the silence was loud. Neither Lady Lamerton nor Mrs Tadcaster sitting opposite uttered a word. Not until the carriage came to a halt outside Ned Stratham's mansion house, in Cavendish Square.

Then Mrs Tadcaster dabbed at the tears in her eyes and said, 'Oh, Emma, I can only be glad your poor mama is not here to witness your disgrace.'

'I wish with all my heart that she were here. And as for disgrace, you blame the wrong person,' Emma said with a fierceness that made the woman look at her as if she had just been slapped.

'I wish you well, Emma,' Lady Lamerton said.

'Thank you.' Emma's eyes held the older woman's with affection. 'For everything.'

Lady Lamerton gave a nod of encouragement. 'Are you ready?'

Emma gave a single nod.

Lady Lamerton smiled sadly and only then signed to the footman through the window to open the carriage door.

There was a gentleman waiting in the hallway of the house. It was only when he glanced round that Emma recognised he was her father.

'Papa?' She hurried the rest of the distance to reach him.

He smiled a small half-smile.

'You look very well, Papa.' The gaunt hollows had gone from his cheeks and his complexion held a good healthy colour that had been missing for too many of the previous months. She glanced down at his fine expensive tailoring.

He pressed a little kiss to her cheek. 'You look beautiful, my dear.'

She felt a lump form in her throat. Felt the tears threaten in her eyes. 'I did not know if you would come.'

'To my own daughter's wedding?' He looked at her, his eyes soft and kind. 'Even if the circumstance is not that which I would have chosen.'

'They told you what happened?'

'Stratham told me. Owned all of the blame. I cannot pretend to like it, Emma.'

'It is not what you think. *He* is not what you think, Papa.' She softened her voice to a whisper that no other would hear. 'I love him.'

He gave a nod. Smiled again, a sad smile. He held out his arm to her and she placed her hand upon it. And together they walked to the open drawing-room door. They paused. Stood there and looked at the room within.

It was the wonderful scent that hit her first, sweet and beautiful as a summer day that now seemed so long ago.

She smiled as her eyes moved over the bloom of violets that decorated the room and the white-and-pink ribbon garlands that festooned the chandeliers. Violets. The significance of his choice of flower was not lost on her. The lines of chairs were filled with guests. A black-robed priest stood with his back to the fireplace. Ned, with Rob Finchley as his best man, waited patiently before him.

Ned was smartly dressed in his midnight-blue Weston tailcoat, a pristine snow-white shirt, white cravat and white-worked waistcoat. His hair was clean and shining gold as it fluttered in the slight breeze from the drawing-room window. He was tall and broad-shouldered. A man strong enough to best Devlin and every rogue in Whitechapel. Strong enough, too, to bear the villainy that belonged to another.

He had saved her from Black-Hair in the Red Lion and from two drunken sailors in the dark midnight depths of a lonely Whitechapel alley. He had saved her from Devlin's lecherous attentions. Now he stood there, saving her from ruin. Giving up his chance to marry a title and gain the acceptance and connections he could never otherwise have. She hated to think he might be doing this against his will. Stood there, frozen for a moment. Knowing that once she stepped across that threshold her life was going to change for ever.

'Emma?' her father whispered.

And just at that moment, Ned glanced round, his gaze meeting hers, and holding, so strong and true and honest that it vanquished all her doubts. She felt a surge of love for him, this man who was the other side of herself. As if it were he and she together, as one against the world. It was as if she had been destined to be his from the very first moment she had seen him.

'Emma,' her father said softly. 'Ned Stratham may be

many things of which I cannot approve. But I do believe
that he loves you and that he will care for and protect you
more than any other.'

She looked into her father's kind old eyes and saw
love and wisdom.

'I am proud of you, Emma. And your mama would
be, too.'

Tears pricked in her eyes. The lump grew bigger in her
throat. She smiled and squeezed his arm with affection.

'Thank you, Papa,' she whispered, and let him lead her
into the drawing room, to the priest and Ned Stratham.

Ned stood with his eyes facing front, aware in every
possible way of Emma standing by his side. Aware, too,
that she would not be looking at him like that if she knew
the truth of him. She would not be marrying him.

She was wearing the dove-grey silk dress that complemented the warmth of her smooth tawny skin and made
her eyes look such a soft velvet-brown and her hair shine
like a raven's wing. She was the most beautiful of women,
inside and out. She was intelligent and filled with vitality and a capacity to survive and to find happiness. Despite all that she had endured she was not embittered. Her
heart was the biggest he had ever known. And she had
given it to him. A man who had known no love in all of
his life. The man who was unwittingly responsible for
all that had hurt her.

Ned sensed her nervousness, saw the uncertainty in
those beautiful dark eyes that met his. Felt the chill of
her fingers when her father gave her hand into his and
thought he would have done anything to undo what had
happened to her, to save her from every hurt, every
hardship.

He smiled to reassure her. Closed his hand around hers

to warm it. Gave it a little squeeze that said everything was going to be all right.

She smiled at that and he saw something of her tension ease.

Then the priest started talking, reading from the small, battered, black-leather prayer book in his hand.

Ned blocked out all emotion. Got through the lines of ceremony until it came to the bit he was worried over. He tensed. Clenched his jaw. Waited for the priest's words.

'If any man can show any just cause, why they may not be lawfully joined together, let him now speak, or else hereafter for ever hold his peace.'

The silence hissed loudly.

Ned waited for it to break. Felt every muscle in his body tense and straining, ready for the interruption. Waited for the crash of the front door opening, for the sound of Devlin's voice announcing why Emma should not be allowed to wed him. And all that would follow.

But nothing happened.

He felt a measure of both relief and guilt.

The ceremony progressed and he said the words *I, Edward Stratham, take thee, Emma Northcote, to be my wedded wife*, and the rest of it and slid the heavy gold band on to her finger.

'Those whom God hath joined together, let no man put asunder...I now pronounce that they be man and wife together.'

She was his. His wife before God and the law.

He took her in his arms and he kissed her, this woman that he loved.

And it was the best moment in all his life. And it was the worst moment, too. Because he had saved Emma from penury and from scandal. He had married the woman that he loved. And in so doing he had proved himself the most despicable of all men.

The wedding breakfast was lavish. No expense had been spared. Champagne and a banquet of the finest foods, exotic and presented as if for a queen. The dining room was decorated with more violets. The tiny blooms had been woven into a garland across the mantelpiece. Every wall sconce held a tiny violet spray, and in the centre of the long dark mahogany dining table was a line of small crystal vases each containing yet more violets, interspaced with pineapples. Emma wondered how anything so lavish and thoughtful could have been arranged at such short notice.

A string quartet in the corner of the room played Vivaldi in gentle tones during the meal. There was a large white sugar creation just like those beloved by the Prince Regent, a sculpture showing a palace with sugared violets cascaded down its walls—it was both beautiful and secretly meaningful to both her and Ned.

There was the finest pork, beefsteaks and pot-roasted chicken. There were eels in wine sauce, baked soles and buttered crabs. Dishes of potatoes in garlic and cream, French beans and mushrooms. There was whipped syllabub and orange-and-almond cheesecake. And a selection of rich cakes. And on the table amidst such lavish finery, sitting like a brass farthing in a pile of gold sovereigns, a dish of lamb chops and fried potatoes.

The guest list was small but significant enough to give the illusion that the marriage was not a forced and scandalous affair: the Earl and Countess of Misbourne, Viscount and Viscountess Linwood, Mr and Lady Marianne Knight, The Marquis and Marchioness of Razeby, Lady Routledge, Mrs Hilton and a few other tabbies who were there as a favour to Lady Lamerton, as well as Lady Lamerton herself. Mrs Tadcaster and Mr Finchley. And her father, of course. But no one who had any connection to Devlin or any other of the men who had been her brother's friends. And Emma could only be glad of that.

It was a wedding arranged as if it truly was a love match, and in a way, for Emma at least, it was. She could almost pretend that nothing had occurred in Colonel Morley's library. Especially when she felt the warm clasp of Ned's hand around hers. And even more so when his eyes met hers and she felt the power of what bound them together pull and tighten and strain.

That he wanted her as a man wants a woman, she did not doubt. Even in her innocence she could feel the thrum of desire that was between them. That he loved her, she believed that, too. The way he looked at her, the way he touched her, was as if he felt all for her that she felt for him. Being here with him felt like coming home. It felt right. Like this was always meant to be. Yet she was aware that he was marrying her to save her and afraid that had not the incident with Devlin happened Ned would never have offered for her.

At last the celebration came to an end and their guests gradually drifted away to leave only Emma and Ned.

They stood alone in the dining room, the warm golden light of the late afternoon casting rainbows through the crystals of the magnificent chandelier, burnishing the darkness of her hair with a blushing halo and turning the soft brown velvet of her eyes golden. Dust motes drifted to sparkle in the air between them, making the moment seem all the more magical.

She was his wife. His *wife*. Captured through false

pretences. But right or wrong, he could not regret it. He loved her. He wanted her. He would give her the world.

He reached a hand to capture a stray curl and rub it between his fingers.

'You are beautiful.'

She smiled. 'I bet you say that to all the serving wenches.'

'No,' he said. 'Only to you, Emma Stratham.' No longer Northcote, but Stratham, and that meant much to him.

'I am very glad to hear it.' She smiled again.

And so did he.

'Thank you, Ned. For the violets and the sugar palace with its doves. For making today so special. For making them believe it is a love match.' She glanced away, but he saw her sudden discomfort. 'I know that you were forced to marry me and that—'

He touched his fingers to her chin and guided her face gently to look into his. 'Do you think me a man to be forced against my will?'

'I think you a man who cares about my honour.'

Their gazes held, warm and intimate and honest.

'Emma, I have wanted to marry you since Whitechapel. That morning by the old stone bench when I said we should talk when I returned...'

'You were going to propose marriage?' She closed her eyes but not before he saw the glitter of unshed tears in them.

'Emma,' he said softly, 'you hold my heart in your hands. You always have. You always will.' From the pocket inside his tailcoat he slipped the white velvet box and gave it to her.

She opened the box to see the gemstone violet necklace that lay inside.

'Oh, Ned!' She clasped a hand to her mouth. The petals were amethyst, the centres, diamond and the leaves, peridot and emerald.

'The sweetest of all flowers,' he said.

Her eyes met his. 'You remembered.'

He crooked his rogue eyebrow, making her smile while their eyes shared the memory of that day and all the love that had since blossomed.

'Thank you, Ned.'

He fastened the necklace around her neck, watching how the gem violet sparkled and glittered against her *décolletage*.

'I love you, Ned Stratham.'

Their mouths came together, kissing, showing with touch and taste and tongue the truth of their words. Her arms slid beneath his tailcoat to wrap around his waist. Their bodies cleaved together, ready for the union for which they had striven so long.

He scooped her up into his arms and carried her up to bed.

Ned plucked the pins from her hair, unravelled it, to let it hang long and loose down her back and over her shoulders.

'You have such beautiful hair.' He leaned in to inhale it.

Lifting a strand, he ran it between his fingers as if it were as precious as smooth polished jet. 'Like ebony silk.'

'As dark as yours is fair. We are the opposites in so many ways.'

He glanced away into the distance, a sombre look in his eyes. 'So many ways,' he echoed in a low voice.

'But opposites that were made to counterbalance each other. Together we are whole.'

His eyes returned to hers and held with such love that

it made her want to weep. 'You speak the words that are in my heart,' he said softly and brushed the back of his fingers against her cheek.

He smiled and cradled her face in his hands, kissed her with such exquisite sweetness. He was her man, her husband, her love. She wanted him, wanted this union that would seal their marriage and bind them together for ever.

He slid his hands round to the back of her bodice, unfastened the line of pearl buttons with unhurried fingers that tantalised every time they brushed against the skin beneath. The dress began to gape, slipping from her shoulders. She shrugged it off, letting the silk slide down over her legs to land at her feet. She reached to him, slid her fingers over his lapels, then opened his tailcoat, intent on easing it from his shoulders, but the fit was so perfect that she struggled.

He peeled off the tailcoat and threw it to land on a chair. His white-worked waistcoat followed.

She unfastened the knot of his cravat, unwound the length of pale silk and let it flutter to the floor, like a ribbon in the wind.

The open neck of his shirt exposed the bare skin beneath, making her blood rush all the faster. She stared at it, fascinated by the sight of him. Reached tentative fingers to pull his shirt free from where it was tucked into his breeches.

He shed the shirt, pulling it over his head and dropping it to the floor.

'Oh, my!' she whispered.

He smiled.

She reached for him, trailed her fingers light as feathers against his muscle-contoured chest, marvelling at the difference in their skin tones. Her fingers were golden olive against his paleness. She touched more boldly, exploring the unknown landscape of a man's body. She had thought him a warrior fully clothed, but half-naked, with his chest exposed like this, he was truly magnificent, all hard honed muscle, all long strong limbs, all power and strength. There was not an inch of softness in that granite sculpted frame.

The sight of him dried her mouth and sent her heart thudding in a frenzy. The feel of him made her shiver, made her thighs burn hot, sent urges and sensations and needs to throb through her body.

Her fingers trailed lower. Over the ribbed muscle that banded his stomach and abdomen. Over the thin line of scar that the tough's blade had left.

'It has healed well.'

'Thanks to you.'

The memory of that night whispered between them.

She felt the ripple and clench of muscle beneath her hand, felt how hot his skin burned beneath the chill of her fingers. She dipped a finger into his belly button and heard him catch his breath. Emma saw the blue fire burn all the hotter in Ned's eyes and realised how much she was affecting him. It was a heady feeling of power.

She laid her hand flat against his chest, covering his heart so that she could feel its beat, strong and steady as the man himself. Looked up into his eyes, the most amazing eyes in the world, that smouldered with a desire that was all for her.

He moved his hands slowly, stroked her shoulders before he untied her petticoats. The layers of linen fell away unnoticed. His gaze dropped to her lips and lower again to the swell of her breasts over the tight-boned stays, his focus so hot and hungry that she felt it as clearly as if he had touched her there. Her heart was thudding like a horse at full tilt, her blood rushing so fast to make her dizzy. Her breath was ragged with need and desperate anticipation as his eyes rose once more to hold hers.

Every second was a torture of waiting. Every second was an ecstasy of wanting.

She was desperate to feel the skim of his fingers against the exposed skin of her breasts, to feel his mouth hot and hard upon hers. But he did neither of those things. Instead, he turned her around and gently collected the lengths of her hair to bunch them over one shoulder while he unlaced her stays with firmer hands than any lady's maid had ever done. She felt them fall away, heard them tumble and land with a thud on the Turkey rug beneath their feet.

She trembled with anticipation. Wanted him to touch her. Needed him to take her. Maybe she was brave because she had her back to him, or maybe it was just her own boldness. Regardless of the reason, she slipped the straps of her shift from her shoulders and let its transparent fine silk slide down her body.

She stood there, naked save for her stockings and shoes. Stood there, waiting, until she felt the caress of his fingers against the bare skin of her back, felt their trail all the way from the top of her spine right down to its tip, sending shimmers to tingle in unexpected places. The breath escaped her in a soft gasp.

She felt his smile, felt the warmth of his breath against her shoulder blade, making her shiver, before his lips touched a kiss there.

Her breath came faster and harder.

His arm slid around her waist, pulling her closer. His palm splayed flat against her belly, anchoring her to him, her spine to his chest, her buttocks to the hard muscles of his thighs. His body was so different from her own in every way, yet it felt like they had been moulded to fit together.

She felt him caress her hair again, felt him kiss the nape of her neck, the touch of his lips to that one small place making her gasp louder.

'Oh, Ned,' she whispered as she closed her eyes and angled her neck to invite him to more.

He understood what she wanted, nuzzled kisses against her neck, her throat, did something wonderful with his tongue where her blood pulsed strongest and hardest.

His hands slid slowly up over her belly. 'You have the softest skin,' he said as he stroked higher to her stomach.

Her breathing quickened, the rise and fall of her chest only making her all the more aware of those strong manly fingers that rested so close. Of their slow teasing caress, that was making it hard to think. Of their promise to reach the destination she craved.

'Ned...' she whispered his name like a plea.

He nibbled kisses to her neck and finally moved his hands to capture both breasts.

She gasped a long low sound of pleasure and moved her arms behind, holding to him, her fingers gripping tight to the muscle of his lower back.

His weighed her breasts, stroked them, wove magical patterns upon them, but never let his fingers stray to their pebbled peaks.

She arched, driving her breasts all the harder into his hands, needing that touch, demanding it. And he finally obliged.

When he plucked her nipples for the first time her knees went weak, her fingers clung all the tighter to stop herself falling. She groaned aloud.

His strong arm snaked again around her hips, his hand

covering her sex. And then those warm long strong fingers began to move slowly, enticingly.

She groaned again, opened her legs and felt him touch her there in that most secret of places. He did not stop. One hand between her thighs, the other going between her nipples. He pleasured her without mercy. Pleasured her until she was gasping, until she was writhing, until she was begging...

Only then did he stop and still his hand over her heart as she had done to him. 'Emma.' Her name was a whisper on his breath. 'My love.'

Her fingers moved to find his, clutched his hand to her heart all the tighter. 'My love,' she echoed.

She turned in his arms and looked up into his eyes.

He swept her up and, carrying her over to the bed, laid her down upon it. He stripped off her stockings and her shoes. Stripped off the rest of his clothing.

She stared at the sight of him fully naked, at the huge wonder that made him a man, and felt a *frisson* of fear. But then he covered her body with his own, somehow taking his own weight so that he did not crush her, and she forgot the fear.

He kissed her and all she knew was her love for him and that she wanted him with all that she was.

He moved between her legs and showed her the full wonder of the love that was between them. Together they reached a place she had not known existed. A place of exploding stars and magic and ecstasy and all of it because she loved him and he loved her. A union not just of bodies but of hearts and souls. A union that could never be undone.

And in their loving she knew that they were meant to be together. That they had always been meant to be together. Destined to love. This man who was her heart and her soul and the very breath in her lungs.

His body merged with hers. And together, at last, they were as one.

Those first heady days following the wedding were the closest Ned would ever get to heaven. He wanted it to be special for her. He wanted to show her just how much he loved her. They spent every moment together; spent many of them in bed, making love. A cocoon in which only the two of them existed and there was nothing and no one else. No past. No future. Only the now, only their love.

Everything about her brought him joy. Her smile, her laughter, the sound of her voice, the way they could talk for hours and never grow weary, the passion that burned between them. He treasured each moment. Savoured it and etched it carefully on his memory so that he would never forget. As if he ever could. But even then there was a part of him that knew the transience of those moments. They were a dream. The world would not for ever stay locked outside. Reality was already knocking at the door. He did not want to let it in. But in the end he had his responsibilities, which could not be ignored. Reality knocked and Ned answered.

Chapter Fifteen

It was late by the time Ned got home from the meeting with his man of business. Emma had not eaten, but waited for him so that they could dine together. She dismissed the footmen and butler. Lifting a covered plate from the heater in the middle of the table, she brought it over to him.

'I had cook make your favourite,' she said as she lifted the lid from the plate of lamb chops and fried potatoes. 'And...' She smiled and produced a bottle of porter, unstoppered it and poured it into a new silver tankard which she set before him.

The candlelight reflected on the symbol engraved upon it, a diamond shape enclosed within a circle. He traced the outline with his finger and felt his heart expand to fill the whole of his chest and the threat of tears in his eyes.

'The symbol from your lucky token,' she said softly.

He slipped the token from his pocket and laid it down next to the tankard. 'You remembered it exactly.' His voice was low and gravelled with the strain to control all that he felt for her.

'How could I forget, when it brought us together? Do you remember the night you dropped it in the Red Lion?'

'I remember.'

She placed her hand upon his and followed the trace of the pattern. 'What does it mean?'

'It is a gaming token, Emma.' He had never told anyone in his whole life. But he told her. 'And it is the only connection I have to my mother. She slipped it into my pocket when she left me at the Foundling Hospital. It was the only gift she ever gave me.'

Her hand closed around his, holding him, supporting him. 'I am sure your mother would not have given you up lightly.'

'She didn't. I was four years old when they took me. I still remember her, and that day.'

Emma's eyes glittered with tears, but what he saw in them was not pity but compassion.

'She gave you to the best life she could. And the Foundling Hospital raised you well, Ned.'

He gave a wry smile. 'They tried, but I was a troublesome child. I ran away, time and again.'

'Why? Where to?'

'To Whitechapel and its streets.'

'To seek your mother?'

'Whitechapel was my home, not some other unknown place on the other side of town miles away from everything I knew.'

'That is why you can relax there. Because it really is your home,' she said softly.

He gave a nod. 'And despite all, I miss it. And I never want to forget. It is dirty and gritty, but it is the real world in a way that this place can never be.'

'This beau monde of wealth and luxury. But you are right, when one has seen men and women and children fight for survival and savour the smallest things in life...'

She shook her head. 'If there is nothing of substance beneath, the sparkle and glitter soon tarnishes.'

As ever, she put into words everything that he felt.

She glanced again at the token where it lay on the table. 'It must be the most precious thing in the world to you.'

'It was, Emma. But now I have something much more precious.' He raised their joined hands and kissed her fingers. 'I have you.'

'Oh, Ned,' she whispered as she leaned down to him and pressed her mouth upon his. 'Do you know how much I love you?'

He closed his eyes. Felt his chest tighten with the strength of emotions that fought and vied within him, love and guilt and shame. She loved him, but he was not the man she thought. If she knew who he was… That he was not her saviour, but her nemesis—the man who had caused all of her troubles. That he had married her under false pretences. That by loving her, by continuing to allow her to blindly love him, all the while not knowing the truth of who he was, what he was, was making a mockery of all that was between them.

It felt like the shadows of guilt were gathering, to whisper from the corners of his mind, taunting him for the charlatan he was.

It felt like the dark secret was starting to devour him from the inside.

Every night Ned loved her. And it was wild and sweet, and afterwards when they lay together in the big four-poster bed in their bedchamber her heart thumped in unison with his. And everything had a brilliance and a wonder, enough to overcome all else, so that she could only marvel at this love that was between them and think that beside it everything else was as nothing. And he stroked her hair and he looked deep into her eyes, and told her that he loved her, again and again, as if it would be the last time he would ever have the chance. Only then did that look appear in the back of his eyes; that veiled worry he thought she could not see.

She cupped a hand against his cheek. Looked deep into his eyes and tried to reassure him. 'We have each other, Ned. Nothing else matters, does it?'

He smiled and kissed her again. Kissed her until she forgot the question she had asked.

It was only later, much later, that she realised he had given no answer.

Ned stood by the window of his study looking out over the Square—the magnificence of the mansions, the neatly kept gardens whose shrubs and trees and flowers cost more than families in Whitechapel had in a year to live. Luxury and splendour and riches beyond what he once would have been able to imagine. It should have made him happy. And once it had, before he had realised the cost that went with it. Now every time he looked at it, it reminded him of the truth. Not that he needed any reminding. The knowledge was like a burr in his side, needling him, never giving him peace.

He sipped the gin from the glass in his hand, the juniper-berry smell filling his nose, the heat hitting the back of his throat and travelling all the way down to his belly. But it did not ease the weight of the burden that sat upon him, nor deaden the pain of the knowledge.

Dishonour. Deception. The accusations whispered in his ears and would not be silenced. Not now. Not ever. He had to tell her. He knew that. She had a right to know the truth. She deserved to be treated as an equal and not patronised as a simpleton or a child. But how did a man tell the woman he loved that he was not the man she thought him? How did he tell her without hurting her beyond belief?

He would lay down his life to protect her. Take every hurt upon himself to save her. How could he then plunge a knife in her heart?

They were wedded. Bound together in law. For ever. She could not just walk away from him. Move on with her life. Meet someone else. Marry. All of those options were gone.

A part of him told him to keep quiet, to shoulder the burden himself. If she never knew, she would never be hurt. And the temptation was great. So great. She had been through so much, he could not bear to hurt her. And yet, if he did not tell her, that only made him all the more despicable.

He had to tell her. For honour. For integrity. Because everything she thought him was a lie.

He had to tell her. It always came back to that. He had to tell her, because he loved her and it was the right thing to do.

Ned had spent a lifetime doing the difficult thing. He had never shied away from doing what he had to. Right or wrong. No matter how hard, no matter what it cost him. Until now.

Now, standing here, with Emma asleep in their bed upstairs, he did not know if he could do this hardest of things.

Shafts of rich autumn sunlight spilled through the window of the private sitting room that adjoined Emma's bedchamber in the mansion house in Cavendish Square. It shone warm against her back where she sat at the little bureau, writing the letter to her father. The nib was a heavyweight silver and so smooth and precise that it glided across the thick white paper without so much as a snag or a scrape. The ink flowed fine and even without a blob. She dipped the pen into the inkwell again and signed her name. She glanced over at where Ned stood by the window, staring out with a hard, distant look in his eyes.

'You have something on your mind.' She did not blot her letter, just left it to dry. Walked over to him, concerned at his preoccupation that seemed to grow only worse as the weeks passed.

'I always have something on my mind.'

'You work too hard, Ned.'

'Not hard enough,' he said and picked up the battered little oval miniature painting that sat upon the side table, the gold leaf of the frame worn smooth. Her eyes moved to the beloved miniature.

'It is a portrait of my brother, Kit, painted not six months before he was taken by Devlin and Hunter and the rest of that rakish gang to lose my family's fortune.'

'You blame Devlin for what happened that night.'

'I blame all of them. They took him to that gaming hell. They let him gamble his everything.'

'Maybe they chose the lesser evil.'

'What more could he have lost? Tell me, for I do not know.'

Ned said nothing.

'They should have stopped him. True friends would have stopped him.'

'They were not the ones who took his money.'

'Even so,' she said, unconvinced by his words.

There was a small silence.

Ned returned the miniature to its place on the table,

but his eyes lingered upon it. 'Do you ever think of the man that your brother played against?'

'Oh, I think of him,' she said with feeling. 'To win a fortune is one thing. To take the coat from a man's back, his home, his dignity, to take his all… I do not know how the villain can live with himself.'

'Maybe he can't.'

She gave a cynical laugh. 'Somehow I doubt that. I bet he could not believe his luck when he saw my brother sit down at his table. A rich young fool ripe for the fleecing.'

'Perhaps. But he could not have realised the far-reaching repercussions of his actions that night. He could not have seen the family behind the rich young fool. Or the wreckage caused to their lives. He could not have known the fool had a sister or how much she would suffer.'

'It does not excuse him,' she said.

'It does not,' he agreed. His gaze returned to the miniature. 'You do not look so very like him.'

'I have the likeness of my mother, God rest her soul, whereas Kit favours our father.'

'But there is something of a similarity in your eyes.'

She smiled at that. 'My mother always said he had mischievous eyes.'

'So do you,' he said, but he did not smile. Instead, his focus remained fixed on the portrait, the expression on his face closed and unreadable.

'Kit was a rascal of a child. Always dragging me into scrapes and adventures. Teasing me, when he grew older, in the way only a brother can do.'

'You are close to him.'

'I am,' she said. 'Although not so much in the months before he left. I could not seem to reach him then. No one could. He was…troubled over what had happened.' She glanced away at the memory of those difficult days.

'You love him very much.'

'He is my little brother. There has not been a day when I do not pray he is safe and that he will come home. I swore a vow to my mother as she lay on her death bed that I would find him. It is why I did not wait for you, Ned. Why I had to accept the position with Lady Lamerton. Her son works in Whitehall—he has connections—and is trying to trace Kit as a special favour to his mother. But as the time passes and there is still nothing… Sometimes, I fear that perhaps…it is in vain.'

She saw something tighten in Ned's jaw. 'Sometimes hope is all that keeps us going,' he said. His fingers still held Kit's portrait. His eyes stared at it with an expression that was brooding and dark. As if he were not seeing her brother's portrait, but something else all together. As if he were locked in some other world of worry and unhappiness and danger. 'My connections may be of a different class to Lamerton's, but I swear to you, Emma, I will do all that I can to find your brother.' But he did not look at her, only at the tiny painting still gripped in his hand.

She gave a nod, knowing that if any man could find Kit it was Ned. And yet, knowing, too, that things were not right with him.

She took the miniature from his fingers. Set it upon the table once more. And took his hand in hers.

Her thumb caressed his. She looked up into his face. 'What is wrong, Ned?'

He did not look at her for a moment. His gaze still lingered on the miniature. There were shadows beneath his eyes, a tight tension within his jaw.

'Ned?' she prompted softly.

His eyes met hers at last and what she saw in them was a glimpse of something tortured, something at which what she had seen in Misbourne's hallway after the card game had only hinted.

He shook his head. Looked away again.

'You are not yourself.'

'I'm not. I'm someone else all together.'

The words disturbed her, reminding her of the taunt Devlin had thrown at her— *What do you really know of Edward Stratham?* Unease whistled like a cold draught through her.

'You are frightening me, Ned.'

'I would not have you frightened for all the world.' He looked at her then. Raised their joined hands to his lips, pressed a slow kiss to her knuckles. 'You're right. Forgive me, Emma. I have too much on my mind these days.' He smiled a smile that did not quite touch his eyes.

'Ned Stratham, what am I going to do with you?' she said softly and pressed a tender kiss to his rogue's eyebrow.

He took her in his arms and held her. Where her cheek lay against his chest she could hear the beat of his heart and feel the warm protection of his arms around her.

'That is the question I ask myself, Emma,' he murmured against her hair. But there was nothing of jest or tease in his words. He pressed a tender kiss to the top of her head and he held her, just held her as if he were afraid to let her go.

Each night he loved her. Loved her as tenderly as if it were for the first time and as passionately as if it were the last. He took her with gentleness and reverence. He took her with urgency and fire. Driving into her, hard and fast as if this act purged away all of the worry she saw in his eyes. She wanted him. She needed him. And she knew, too, that he needed her.

They strove together, lost in the union of their souls and hearts and bodies. And in those blissful hours in the darkness there was nothing save each other and the power of their love.

They moved together, matching each other's rhythms, knowing each other's needs. They moved together until she was crying out his name, until she was gasping her pleasure and exploding in a thousand sunbursts of wonder. Again. And again.

And afterwards when she lay in his arms, he cradled her against him, and stroked her hair and kissed her forehead, but the worry was back in his eyes. He held her until she slept, but often she woke in the night to find the bed beside her empty and Ned standing by the window staring out at the black night sky.

There was something he was not telling her. Something that was badly wrong. She just did not know what it was or how to reach him. And she began to wonder if maybe there had been something more in the battle between Ned and Devlin than just class.

Chapter Sixteen

Ned sat at the great mahogany desk in his study. The house was still and quiet, sleeping as the rest of London did beneath the dark cover of night. But Ned could not sleep. Not tonight, or last night or the nights before that. He doubted he'd ever be able to sleep again.

He had lit no candles. The hearth was empty and black. The moon lit the room in silver shadows, gleaming against the dark polished wood of his desk enough to show the single sheet of paper that lay upon it. But Ned did not need the light to read the words that were written upon the paper. He knew each one by heart. They were etched upon his soul, words that could never be unwritten.

He heard the faint creak of the floorboard, saw the flicker of light beneath his door a second before the study door opened and Emma appeared.

She was wearing her nightgown. One hand clutched a shawl around her that was slipping from her shoulders. The other held her candlestick and the half-burned beeswax candle that flickered within it. Her hair hung long and mussed from their earlier lovemaking, dark and beautiful as ebony. She had not taken the time to find her slippers, but stood there, her bare feet a pale golden olive against the dark polish of the floorboards. There was a look of worry on her face that made his heart ache all the more with love for her.

He lifted the sheet of paper from the desk, folded it closed within his hand. Rose to his feet and moved to meet her.

'Could not sleep again?' she asked.

He shook his head.

She glanced at the paper within his hand, then back at his face. Walked to stand before him.

'Something is wrong.' She sat the candlestick down on the desk.

'Yes.' He did not deny it.

'Will you not tell me, Ned? I might be able to help.'

'You might.'

'I'm worried about you.'

The silence hissed loud and strained.

'Tell me, Ned,' she said. 'You know you have to tell me.'

'Yes,' he whispered. 'I have to tell you.'

He looked into her eyes, eyes that were dark and warm and tender, and filled with love. And he savoured that moment, all of her love and all of what she was, all of the wonder of what was between them. Love. Something he had never known throughout a lifetime. Something so glorious and powerful and strong he never could have imagined. He loved her with all that he was, and because he loved her he knew that he would do the thing he had feared and dreaded more than any other thing in his life. More than hunger and starvation. More than beatings and the icy fingers of night that stole lives from slumbering forms in doorways and alleyways. The hardest thing in the world. And the easiest.

'I love you, Emma.'

'I know you do. And I love you, too.'

He smiled at that. Took the words and the sound of her voice and the gentleness in her eyes and stored those most precious of treasures in his mind for the dark days ahead.

'I love you,' he said again. 'Always remember that. It is the truth, no matter what else you might think.'

'I would never think anything else.'

But she would. His eyes held hers, clinging to these last precious moments. He reached a hand to her face, stroked his fingers against the softness of her cheek. And she nestled her cheek against his fingers and placed her own hand upon his and held it there.

He leaned forward, breathed in the scent of her hair, placed one final kiss upon her lips.

'I am sorry, Emma. I would give everything to undo what you have suffered...everything to change what I did.'

'Ned,' she said softly, the little worry line etching between her brows. 'Tell me what it is that you have done.'

He took a breath, gave the slightest of nods.

The seconds stretched, but he felt almost relief in knowing that the time was now, that the tortuous waiting was over.

The paper was clutched tight between his fingers. He opened it out, smoothed the creases from it and offered it to her. And in so doing he pierced his heart with a dagger made of words that had destroyed a family's world.

She took the paper and held it closer to the candlelight to read the words penned upon it.

'I do not understand,' she said. 'This is Kit's vow, for our home and my father's fortune, for everything that he owned...' She shook her head, frowned. 'I do not understand, Ned,' she said again. He saw the moment that she did, the cold horror of realisation that crept across her face.

She raised her eyes to his.

'Yes,' he said in answer to the question he saw in them, the question that could not form upon her lips. 'I am the man your brother gambled against and lost. I am the man who took your family's fortune.'

She stared at him as if she could not believe it. But she did believe it. He could see it in the horror and pain and shock in her eyes. He could see it by the way the paper in her hand began to tremble.

'You?' she whispered.

'Me,' he confirmed.

'You are the man who ruined my brother… The man who destroyed my family.'

He said nothing.

'No.' She shook her head as if to deny the truth. 'No,' she whispered the word again. Scrunched her face as if in pain.

'Yes, Emma,' he said. 'I would give anything to deny it and say it was not me, but I cannot.'

'Oh, God!' she gasped and clutched a hand around her stomach. 'Oh, God, please, no!'

He reached a hand to steady her, but she pulled back from his touch as if scalded, seeing the monster he was for the first time. 'Do not touch me!' she whispered fiercely.

He held his palms up. Stepped back to give her space.

Her breath was ragged. She pulled her shawl around her. Leaned back heavy against the desk. Stared at the floor, but he knew she was seeing nothing of what was around her only the horror within her mind. 'This cannot be happening.'

Ned had said the same thing to himself a thousand times.

'How could you do it?' she asked.

He said nothing. Just swallowed.

'You knew all along who I was.'

'Not all along. Not at the start.'

'You are lying! Everything between us has been a lie!'

'I have never lied to you. I never will.'

'I do not believe you!'

He said nothing.

'You knew who I was. You tricked me. You made me love you.'

He stood there and accepted the wrath he deserved.

'How could you do it, Ned?' she asked again. This time louder, more of a cry. This time the question was not of what he had done to her, but what he had done to her brother. 'Tell me what happened that night.'

He glanced away. But she grabbed hold of his coat lapels with white-knuckled fists and stared up into his face. 'Tell me,' she said. 'I have a right to know.'

He nodded. She had every right to know.

His voice was low and empty as he relayed a very brief sketchy outline. 'A group of rich young aristocrats had taken to coming over to Whitechapel, to Old Moll's gaming den in Half Moon Alley. They liked the play there. It amused them to come amongst us and see how the other half lived. To dice with living on the edge. Devlin, Hunter, Bullford, Fallingham and your brother. They were drinking deep and playing deeper.

'I did not set out to fleece him, Emma. He...' Ned thought back to that night. To Kit Northcote. And the truth of what had happened. He looked into Emma's eyes, eyes that had something of that foolish young arrogant man who was her brother. The brother whom she loved. The brother whom she had cherished. And he thought he would do anything to save her, to take her pain upon himself. 'He was neither skilled nor lucky with cards,' he finished.

'He was young and foolish!'

'Yes.'

'He was out of his depth in such a place.'

'Way out.' She had no idea.

'And yet you took everything from him.'

'I took all he had staked upon the table.'

'You did not have to do that.'

'Yes, I did, Emma,' he said quietly.

But she did not understand. And she never would if he could help it. She shook her head.

'Because you wanted to be a gentleman?'

He said nothing.

'Because five thousand pounds were not enough that you must have even more?'

Silence.

Her fingers loosened their grip upon his lapels. She pushed him away. Hard. With disdain. 'You bastard!'

He made no defence. Because he was a bastard in every sense of the word.

She moved away, perched on the edge of the winged chair before the dark empty hearth, the small distance like miles between them. A gulf that would never be breached.

The silence seemed to echo and hiss in the room around her. She wanted to strike out at him, to hit him, to yell and scream and cry and weep. But Emma did none of those things.

She sat in that armchair and her mind was reeling. Part of her unable to believe what Ned was telling her, part knowing that it was the truth she should always have guessed. So many thoughts tumbled through her mind, terrible possibilities making themselves known, although beside the magnitude of what he had just told her she did not know why they should be so very terrible at all. She felt as if he had taken a knife and cut her heart from her chest.

'You should have told me,' she said.

'I tried.'

'Not hard enough.'

'No.'

She placed her knuckles against her lips, pressed hard to control the words, to control everything that was whirring with such fury and shock within her.

'Or maybe I was just part of your plan.'

'With you there was no plan.'

'No?' She felt flayed and betrayed, raw and weeping. She could not think straight, could only feel a gaping hurt and a roaring anger and endless uncertainty.

'What were you really doing in Whitechapel, Ned? Those nights you came to the Red Lion to eat when you lived here, in a mansion in Mayfair, with the finest of chefs to cook for you?'

'I've already told you the answer to that question.'

'And if I do not believe you?'

He said nothing, just held her gaze, strong and silent, but she saw the tension that clenched in his jaw.

'Your steward, Rob Finchley, does he know the truth? Of who you are? Of who I am?'

'He was in the crowd at Old Moll's that night.'

'How you must have laughed together at my naïvety.'

'We did not laugh.'

'He did not accompany you on your trips to Whitechapel.'

'No.'

'And you just happened to find me the Red Lion?'

'I just happened to find you, Emma.'

'Why there?'

'Because it was far enough away from my old haunts that I would not be known.'

'You expect me to believe that your being in the same chop-house, in which I worked, was just coincidence?'

'I don't expect anything.'

There was an ache in her chest, a churning in her stomach, a bitterness in her throat. All of her fears rose up, vile and goading her to the worst of imaginings.

'You took everything my family owned. Why not me? Was I just the final prize to be added to your winnings? That you could have everything from my brother: his money, his home, his position in society. That you could have even me, my heart, my body, my life? The ultimate revenge against a people you hated. Because we were rich and you were not. Because you wanted to taunt him. Because—'

A lightning of emotion flickered in his eyes. He moved then. Fast. Closed the distance between them in a breath. Grabbed her by the top of her arms. Pulled her up from the chair and stared down into her face.

'Never!' he said and the whispered word shook with the force of controlled emotion. 'I did not know who you were, not until Lady Lamerton introduced us. And, yes, I should have walked away from you then, once I knew, and God knows I tried. Hate me all you will, Emma. Despise me. Loathe me. But never ever think that I would use you so poorly. I may have nothing of honour. I may not be a gentleman. I may have been a thief and a beggar and a rogue in my life. But never doubt that one thing.' He held her eyes with a fierceness that belied the quietness of his voice.

She could feel the press of his fingers around her arms.

She could hear the tremor in his breath and feel the extent of the control he was exerting over himself.

There was a pain and rawness in his expression that shocked her almost as much as his revelation had done. And an utter sincerity.

Their gazes held, locked in a torture. The seconds stretched in agony. Until he suddenly released her. Backed away. Sat down in the winged chair opposite and stared at the empty hearth.

She was shaking so much that she dropped down into the chair beneath her.

Only the clock punctuated the silence between them.

She did not know what to say.

She did not know what to do.

Her whole world felt like it had exploded around her. Love, hope, trust, a future—all gone in one fell swoop. She did not know who he was. She did not even know who *she* was any more. And the thought that thrummed through her head constantly, insistently, was that it had been Ned there that night in the gaming hell with Kit. The enormity of it obliterated all else.

'You promised to find him, when all along it was you who drove him away,' she said almost to herself.

She got to her feet.

He glanced up at her, the look in his eyes touching the rent in her soul.

She bled. The pain was piercing. It engulfed everything, everything, so that she could not think, only feel and what she felt was agony. An agony that was tearing her apart. An agony she could not bear. She needed to be alone.

'I cannot be with you, Ned Stratham.' Not right now. She could not look at him. Could not speak another word to him. Only shook her head and turned and walked away.

* * *

Ned sat in the study for the rest of the night. This was a beating like none he had ever taken. A wound that would never heal. But he did not allow himself the luxury of self-pity.

He locked his emotions away. Thought through the steps of what must be done. The only things he could do. Nothing would make this right. But then he had always known that. He could bear her hatred, but her hurt—that was a lot harder. But Ned would bear it. He had borne much in his life. Things that would have made men like Devlin and Kit Northcote quail. He would bear it and know he had done all that he could. And that knowledge at least was something.

Ned did not drown his sorrows in gin. He did not stare aimlessly down on to the darkened street. He went to the desk and he found the papers that he needed. Then he sat there in that expensive leather-winged arm-chair, in a room that was bigger than any house he had lived in. He waited for the night to pass, and the dawn to come.

When daylight finally came he washed and dressed himself in fresh clothes. And with the papers safely stowed in his pocket he slipped out of the front door.

Emma stood at the edge of the window of her bed-chamber and watched Ned's figure disappear along the road.

She was still wearing the nightdress and shawl. Her feet were bare and tinged blue from the cold. Her head was pounding from a night filled with a storm of misery and disbelief and nothing of sleep. Her eyes were swollen and heavy from weeping. But she did not weep now. She was empty. Numb.

She stood there even after he was long gone.

She stood there because she did not know what else to do.

What *did* a woman do when she discovered that the man she loved was not who she thought him? That everything upon which their life and love was based was a lie?

I have never lied to you. I never will.

Maybe not in words. But he had deceived her just the same. And she did not know where they went from here. Because she did not know what it was she felt for him any more. Because she was his wife and he her husband and nothing could change that.

He was her husband.

He was her lover.

And he was the man who had taken her family's money.

She thought of her father having to give up their family home in Berkeley Street and move to a string of increasingly cheaper accommodations. And of the slow ignoble decline to obscurity.

She thought of Kit's running away, of what that had done to her mother, of first Spitalfields and the consumption that had taken her mother's life. And then Whitechapel, and the dockyards and the Red Lion.

'Kit.' She whispered his name in the quietness of the room, as if he would hear her. *Kit.* In her mind she saw his face, the laughing eyes that were so like her father's, the grin that he wore when he teased her.

No one put a pistol to his head and forced him to the gaming tables. Devlin's words sounded again in her memory. She tried to close her mind to that truth, just as she had always done, but this time there was something in the way and the door would not shut completely.

She closed her eyes and it was not her brother's face she saw, but that of another man. A face that was not refined or beautiful. A face that was rugged, with its own harsh handsomeness. It made the hole in her chest, where her heart had been, ache. But it could not change who he was and what he had done. It only ridiculed it all the more, even if what had brought them together really had been just a cruel trick played by fate. Did she even believe that?

The memory of the pain in Ned's eyes, the force of emotion pulsing through him when he had denied her accusation. A man on the edge. She believed him. But it did not change anything. He had kept the truth from her. And, in a way, that deception hurt more than what it was he had been hiding.

She thought of packing the little travelling bag with which she had arrived here. Of returning to her father.

She thought of turning up at the Red Lion and asking for her old job back. Of earning enough to rent a room with another girl.

But in the end she knew she could do neither of those things.

So Emma went through the motions and she washed and she dressed, and she waited for Ned to come home.

It was six o'clock in the evening when Ned returned to the Cavendish Square mansion.

The sky was grey outside, the light already beginning to fade even at this early hour. Rain pattered softly against the bow window, trickling down the panes of glass like tears. She sat on the Queen Anne armchair by the fire in the drawing room, pretending that she was reading a book, pretending that she had not been pacing and anxious.

'Emma.' He came to stand by the fireplace. She could see the sparkle of raindrops where they sat upon the shoulders and sleeves of his coat, not yet absorbed by the wool. His hair was damp, swept back as if he had raked his fingers through it.

The silence was strained.

'Where have you been all day?' He looked tired. There were shadows beneath his eyes. And she already knew that he had stayed the long night in his study.

'To see my man of business. And a few other people, too.'

There was the slow tick of the grandfather clock in the corner of the drawing room and the clatter of horses' hooves passing from the road outside. It felt everything that her relationship with Ned had never been—awkward, uncomfortable. The accusations she had thrown at him last night still hung between them, jagged and sharp, still cutting.

'I don't expect you to forgive me, Emma.' His eyes held hers for a moment and her heart began to pound and the pain was back, making a lump in her throat.

'I am not sure that I ever can.' She had to be honest with him.

The silence hissed.

He nodded, then looked away. Took some papers from his pocket, legal papers by the looks of them.

He sat them down on the table by her side. 'Everything is yours. To do with as you see fit. My only request is that you keep the businesses running. My man of business, Mr Kerr, will call upon you in the morning to explain the details. As far as everything else, if there are any problems, if you are ever lost, go to Rob Finchley in South Street. He will help you.'

'You are leaving?' Her heart contracted small and tight with shock and too many other confused emotions.

'I didn't think you wanted me to stay.'

The silence roared

Stay! her mind whispered, but her tongue held the word captive and would not let it escape. Her fingers were gripping so hard to the book between them that her knuckles shone white. Pride was all she had left. Pride and the pretence that he had not flayed her raw, that his leaving was not hurting her all the more.

That moment was the longest of her life. Stretched precarious. Painful. Cutting to the bone.

'Goodbye, Emma.'

Do not go! The plea pounded through her head. Whispered through her blood. But she sat there and said nothing, and let him walk away.

The drawing-room door shut softly behind him. She heard the quiet murmur of voices, then the open and close of the front door.

He could not be gone. So quickly. In the space of a few heartbeats.

She ran to the window, saw the familiar figure walking away down the street. Alone. No carriage. No travelling bag. Nothing save the clothes he was wearing. The darkness of his tailcoat disappearing into the grey gloom of the evening.

He could not really be gone, she thought again. Just like that. With nothing. He had to be coming back, for his clothes, for his possessions. Didn't he? But there was a terrible empty feeling in her chest because she knew, absolutely knew, that Ned was not coming back.

The book slipped from her fingers to thud on the Turkey rug below.

She did not stoop to pick it up. She did not even know

its title or a single word that was written within its blue-bound covers. The rain lashed harder against the windows like fists beating to gain entry.

And a little part of Emma's soul shrivelled and died.

Chapter Seventeen

Emma received Mr Kerr in the drawing room at ten o'clock the next morning.

He was a small tidy man, with short grey hair neat around a balding pate. His age was middling, but his eyes were sharp and honest. Everything about him exuded competence and efficiency.

His gaze moved to the documents that still lay untouched on the table where Ned had left them.

She met his eyes, held them. 'What are you here to tell me, sir?'

'Mr Stratham had this house and the other property, and all of his assets, moved into a trust. He then gave the trust into the management of Mr William Northcote, with the stipulation that it be all for the "separate use" of his daughter, Mrs Emma Stratham. It effectively means that legally you own it all.'

'But he is my husband, and as such, everything that I own is his.'

'Not in the case of the trust. It is one of the few devices that may be used to circumvent certain particulars of the marriage property laws.'

She looked at him as what he was saying sunk in. 'I own it all?'

'Down to the last farthing.'

She frowned. 'You mentioned another property.'

'A house in Berkeley Street. Number nineteen, as I recall.'

The house in which she had been born and grown up.

'Mr Stratham purchased it almost two months ago.' He slipped a pair of spectacles to his nose and peered down at his notes. 'On the thirteenth of September.'

A few weeks after she had come to work for the Dowager Lady Lamerton.

'I have taken the liberty of producing a summary of your financial situation, which I thought would be of assistance.' He passed her a single-page document. 'I think you will find everything to be in order, but if you have any questions or instructions please do not hesitate to contact me.' He removed his spectacles to the safety of his waistcoat pocket, put his papers away in his leather folder and rose to leave. 'I will bid you good day, Mrs Stratham.'

Emma's eyes moved over the sheet, scanning the figures written there. 'A moment, sir.'

He stopped and looked at her with polite enquiry.

'These figures...the sums in the bank accounts... They cannot be accurate.'

'I assure you, madam, they are entirely correct.'

'But...' Her father had been wealthy enough, worth five thousand a year. She totted up the balances of the bank accounts. 'One hundred thousand pounds?' she said weakly. It had to be an error. It made no sense.

'Your husband is a very shrewd businessman. There are not many men who could grow an investment twentyfold in the space of two years.'

She stared at him. 'How did he do it?'

'A nose for knowing what to invest in and when.'

'He spoke of "businesses."'

'A variety throughout the East End—a vinegar manufactory, a dye house, several timber yards, a cooperage, a large brewery and a distillery. He also owned several mills—for wool, cotton and silk. Investments in the East and West Indies, and in the Americas. Shipyards in Portsmouth. And then there were the London Docks with all the warehousing, storage and loading operations located there. As I said, a very shrewd gentleman.'

She sat very still.

'So it seems,' she said and thought back to the conversation that had passed between her and her father on the day of her wedding, specifically to that one subtle slip. She understood it now, although she had barely noticed it then, let alone understood what it meant—that her father knew that Ned Stratham was the man who owned the dockyard and provided employment to him and all those men in the warehouse.

'Are there any other questions with which I may help you, Mrs Stratham?'

'No, thank you.' She let the butler show him out before untying and opening the uppermost legal document. It was the trust deed that Mr Kerr had spoken of.

Her eyes scanned over the list of all it encompassed. All the monies and properties and businesses. Bonds and shares and investments. Everything that Ned had owned. Wealth that must best almost every other man in England. And then her eye saw the date on the document.

The house was silent. Empty. Not another sound within it save the sob that caught in her throat.

Ned had signed the document on the morning of their wedding.

The days passed and Ned did not return. Everything went on in the house just as before, everything running like clockwork. Well oiled and efficient without her. The servants never asked when their master would be returning. If they knew he was not, they made no mention.

After a week of hiding behind closed doors she left Cavendish Square and went to visit the house in Berkeley Street.

The family to whom her father had sold the lease had changed much, but some things were still the same. As she walked from room to room there were echoes of memories from far-off days: her mother smiling and entertaining in the drawing room; Christmas Day with twenty gathered round a banquet in the dining room; Kit pulling her ponytail and laughing as he chased her down the stairs; cold winter evenings in the parlour with her father telling them stories as they all sat round a roaring log fire, drinking warmed milk with honey. And the feeling was bittersweet because all those times, all that happiness, and what had Ned been doing in those same years?

Children are not children for long round here.

A boy alone in a harsh world. With no warm cosy house. No proper home at all. A foundling. A runaway. No banquets at Christmas. No love.

The thought scraped at her insides. She closed her eyes, tried to suppress it, but it remained there silent and stubborn.

Poverty. Struggle. Hardship. What would a man not do to escape that life?

The house was empty now. A past gone never to be reclaimed. Inside Emma was keening. But it was not that long-lost life of plenty that she grieved. It was the loss of something much more precious. And it did not matter if she closed her eyes because she still saw him standing there with those intense blue eyes. And it did not matter if she blocked her ears because she still heard the gentleness of his voice.

She hugged her arms around herself, clutched her skin tight, but she still ached for his caress. A man stronger and fiercer than any she had known. A man who she did not doubt could kill another. And yet towards her she had never known a more gentle man.

She left Berkeley Street and knew she would not return. The past was just that. Gone, as much as Ned.

Emma sought out Rob Finchley in his house across town in South Street the next day.

He received her in his drawing room.

'Mrs Stratham.' For all the polite tone of his voice she could see his reserve and judgement when he looked at her. He knew Ned had left and why.

'Is something wrong, ma'am?' Worry flashed a frown in his eyes, there, then masked.

She did not waste time in niceties. There was little point in that for either of them. 'Where is he, Mr Finchley?'

'If you are referring to Mr Stratham's whereabouts, the answer is I don't know.'

'You came with him from Whitechapel. You are his friend. You must know where he has gone.'

'He would not tell me.'

She held his gaze, not sure whether he was telling her the truth. 'And if you did know…would you tell me?'

'I'm afraid I wouldn't, ma'am,' he said.

They looked at one another.

'I just want to know that he is all right. That he is… safe.'

'Ned is a survivor. He was on the streets alone at four years old. His home was a corner in a derelict manufactory. He's survived things you couldn't even begin to imagine.'

She said nothing. Because she knew it was the truth. And nothing she could say could make it better, only worse.

'Ned is hardly blameless in all of this,' she said to justify herself against the accusation she sensed in him. 'He did take the money.'

'He took the money all right, the money your wastrel brother would have drunk and whored and gamed elsewhere…'.

'My brother—' she began in Kit's defence, but Rob Finchley kept on talking.

'The money that you would have frittered on fancy frocks and balls and fripperies. Yes, he took it, and he did something good with it. He created jobs for those that had none. He set up soup kitchens for the hungry, and is building a children's home for those that live on the streets of Whitechapel. You may think what you will of him, but Ned Stratham is a better man than any I've ever known.'

'A home for children?'

'His project with Misbourne. An annexe of the Foundling Hospital. Ned's idea, Ned's money and means. But no matter how worthy the cause, he still needed a title to sway the prejudice of the powers that be. Misbourne is chief amongst the Hospital's governors.'

'I did not know,' she said softly. So many things she had not known about him.

'Happen you didn't. But you should know how hard he tried to do right by you.'

She thought of all the times that Ned had saved her.

'He would have married a title. Achieved the influence and acceptance he needed to drive his charities forward, to grow his businesses and provide more employment for the poor. And then you appeared…and everything changed.' Rob Finchley stopped. Reined himself in. 'Forgive me, ma'am, if I've spoken out of turn. But it's a matter close to my heart.'

And a matter close to her own. She felt cold and alone. She felt the battle of conflicting emotions—of hurt and anger, of love and longing. *An annexe of the Foundling Hospital.* He was a villain; a rogue whose every action only proved all the more why she loved him. There was an ache in her heart that grew only worse, but Emma showed nothing of it. She gave a dignified nod and, with her head held high, walked away.

Emma rose early the next day, despite another night in which she had managed snatches of sleep and nothing more. Entered Ned's study for the first time since he had left. Just needed to have a sense of being near him.

The autumn sunlight was cool and pale through the window. The trees that lined the Square were ablaze with fiery leaves rustling in the breeze, a last show of colour before they withered and fell.

She stopped where she was. Felt her heart turn over. For there on the great desk lay a letter. One small pale shape upon that stretch of dark polished wood, just like Kit's IOU that had lain there on that terrible night.

She knew before she walked closer, before she stood before it and read the single name, written in a hand that was cramped and uncomfortable with writing, that it was for her. And she knew, too, who it was from.

Her heart was pounding hard and heavy. Her stomach clenched and twisted. She bit her lip to stop its tremble. Reaching out, she lifted the letter. Something slid and moved within its folds.

On the back it was sealed with a blob of red wax, the letter S imprinted within the waxen circle. She broke the wax and carefully opened out the letter. Inside, the paper was blank. Not one word written there. Instead, in its centre was a small ivory disc, dented and scraped, its edges unevenly clipped. The shape of the diamond carved within it was worn smooth by his touch through the years, its red stain now faded to the faintest blush. The only thing Ned's mother had ever given him. Ned's lucky token.

She took it in her hand and held it as if it were the most precious thing in the world. And the tears welled in her eyes and overflowed to spill down her cheeks because she knew then that he really had given her his everything. All that he owned. All that he was.

Rob knew he was coming and yet he jumped as Ned stepped out of the shadow of the wall beside him. The narrowness of the mews behind the house in Cavendish Square was quiet at this time at night.

Ned glanced towards the house with its lights that glowed behind blind closed windows, then asked the question. 'How is she?'

'She's like a ghost.'

Ned closed his eyes at that. 'The pain and anger will fade eventually.'

'Will it?' asked Rob.

'For her, I hope.'

'And for you?'

Ned said nothing to that. He had no anger. Only pain, and that was unremitting. He held it to him and would never let it go because it was entwined with her memory.

'You haven't told her anything, have you?'

'Just as you instructed.' Rob glanced away to the side. 'She asked me where you had gone.'

Ned's eyes met those of his friend. 'And what did you say?'

'The truth—that I don't know.'

There was a little silence.

'Where are you staying, Ned? If you need some money—' Rob began to pull some banknotes from his pocket, but Ned stopped him with a touch to the shoulder.

'No.'

He could see the worry in Rob's eyes. Knew it was time to go. 'Thank you for doing this for me, Rob. For looking out for her in these early days until I know she's going to be all right.'

Rob gave a nod. 'It's the least I can do.'

They looked at each other for a moment longer, before Ned gave a final gruff nod. 'Take care of yourself, Rob.'

'You, too, Ned. You, too.' Rob stood and watched while the figure of his friend walked away to be swallowed up by the night.

She went to Whitechapel the next day. Walked there to the dockyard.

'Emma?' Her father took one look at her face, gestured the other two men in the office to leave and closed the door quietly behind them before turning to face her. 'You look tired, my dear.'

'I am well enough.' She brushed away the observation, forced a smile to her face. 'I am here to ask you to come home with me to Mayfair. You do not need to work, Papa.'

But he shook his head. 'I may not need to work, Emma, but I want to. I like it here. I am useful. I have purpose. I am good at what I do and what I do makes a difference, to the men that work here, and more. My home and life is here now. Life moves on, Emma. There is nothing for me in Mayfair. Not any more.'

'There is me,' she said.

He touched the back of his fingers to her cheek. 'You are my daughter wherever we are. Nothing will ever change that.'

'Do you have no wish to resume your life as a gentleman?'

'What makes a man a gentleman is not his birth or right, not his money or wealth or abode. It is the way he lives his life. And I live my life as a gentleman, Emma, whether it be in Mayfair or Whitechapel.'

A vision of Ned swam in her mind. Not dressed in the finery of Weston's tailoring, but in the shabby old leather jacket and trousers. Standing up for her honour that night with Black-Hair in the Red Lion. Protecting her from drunken sailors in the alleyway. His expression grim and measured. His voice quiet. And his face when he had opened the door of Colonel Morley's library and saved her from Devlin. She forced the thoughts away. Tried to swallow down the sudden lump in her throat. But when she looked into her father's wise old eyes, he seemed to see too much.

She glanced away. Folded her fingers together in the semblance of a composure she did not feel inside. Tried to find the right words.

Her father did not rush her. Just waited. Let the silence act like a cushion around her.

'The man who is my husband...' *My husband*—the words sounded strained upon her lips. She swallowed again. 'He owns this dockyard. But then you already know that, do you not? I should have realised when you referred to him as *Ned* Stratham on the day of the wedding. How could you not know, working here?'

'Ned Stratham does not own this dockyard, Emma. I do.'

She stared at him in shock.

'The business is mine. The money. The responsibility that all I employ here earn a decent wage in decent conditions. Ned transferred it to me, just before the wedding, when he came to speak to me.'

There was a resounding silence while she took in the magnitude of what he was telling her.

'Is he here, today…?' She tried to make the question sound casual and unimportant.

'He has not been here all week.' But he misunderstood her reason for asking. 'You may rest assured our conversation will not be interrupted by Ned or any other.'

Her stomach squeezed tight.

There was a silence. She knew she had to tell him, all, not just a part.

'It was not Ned that tried to…compromise me…in Colonel Morley's library. It was Devlin.'

'Devlin?' Her father frowned.

She nodded. 'Ned stopped him, then swapped their roles. He took the blame and made Devlin the hero.'

'He did not tell me that part of it.'

'There is something else I need to tell you, Papa. About Ned.'

He did not ask what. Waited with his usual restful patience that helped ease the hard heavy beat of her heart.

'You had better sit down.'

But he did not move. Just stood there, with an almost peaceful expression.

She touched her knuckles to her mouth. Then let her hand fall away. Took a breath and looked up into her father's face. 'Ned…' She swallowed. Took another breath. Tried again. 'Ned Stratham is the man Kit gambled against that night, Papa.'

Her father's face registered nothing of shock. Only calm acceptance.

'You already know?'

He nodded. 'Ned told me who he was when he came to ask for your hand.'

'And you let him wed me?' She stared at him aghast.

'Would you rather have faced ruin and condemnation?'

'Why did you not tell me?'

'Because you would not have married him had I done so.'

'And you wanted me to marry the man that ruined us?' She could not believe what she was hearing.

'No, Emma,' he said gently. 'I did not want that.'

'But that is what you got. What we both got.'

'Is it?' he asked, his eyes raking hers. 'If we are honest with ourselves, hard though it is to admit, my dearest girl, we both know that is not true.' He touched a light kiss to her cheek. 'You should go home to your husband, Emma.'

She could not tell him that Ned had gone. She just took her leave of him and began the long walk home.

Home. To the mansion in Cavendish Square. But her mind was a myriad of confusion and her cheeks were damp from silent tears when she got there.

She kept his bedchamber exactly as he had left it. Stopped the maid changing the linen on the bed. Where Ned's head had lain upon the pillow still held the faint scent of him. In the long dark hours of the night she held it to her. And her body throbbed for him. And her heart ached for him. And her soul felt small and empty without him.

There were so many thoughts going round in her head. So many emotions conflicting and confused. Love and anger. Blame and injustice. Guilt and regret. Grief and loss. They clamoured relentlessly through her body, stoked her mind in constant motion. One thought more than all the others.

There could be nothing of sleep. She rose. Pulled a shawl around her nightdress. Crossed the darkened room. She opened the curtains and stood there at the window, looking out into the darkness of the night.

The street lamps had extinguished. There was no moon. Only a scattering of tiny stars, silver-bright sparkling pinheads on the black velvet of the sky.

Her father's words whispered again through her head: *If we are honest with ourselves, hard though it is to admit, my dearest girl, we both know that is not true.*

She understood. She had always understood. All of the rest of it had been excuses and misplaced blame. She had lied to herself because it was easier than facing the truth.

Ned Stratham was not the man who had ruined her family. It was Kit who had done that. She allowed the thought freedom for the first time. It hurt. But the hurt was less than she had expected. It was pale in comparison to the rest of what she was feeling.

Ned might have taken the money, but coming from where he did, how could she honestly blame him? Had she walked in his shoes, would she have turned away so readily from such temptation?

And her heart ached all the more for the man who was her husband.

At five o'clock the next morning Emma sat at Ned's desk. She was still wearing yesterday's dress and her head throbbed with fatigue.

The house seemed dead. The street outside had not yet woken. Silence hissed in her ears. She glanced down at where her hands lay upon the desk, and the token within them. Rubbed her fingers upon it, wondered if it really would bestow luck.

'Bring him back to me,' she whispered. 'Please, God, bring him back to me.' Because he might be the man who had faced Kit across a card table in a smoky gaming den, he might be the man who had won her family's money, but none of that changed the fact that she loved Ned Stratham. And none of it changed the fact that in her bones she felt he was a good man.

She tried tipping the token along her knuckles as Ned always did, but it fell off and rolled to land upon the desk's surface time and again. So she left it where it lay. Stroked a finger against it. An old gaming token. What had his mother lost that she would give up her child? She thought of Kit and the night he had left for the gaming hell with Devlin and Hunter. She thought of Kit facing Ned across a table in Old Moll's Den. She lifted the token and flicked it to spin upon the smooth dark polish of the desk.

She did not hear its soft whir, only the whisper of the words Devlin had spoken, *No one put a pistol to his head and forced him to the gaming tables.*

Devlin had been there that night. Devlin must have known exactly what had happened. The thought only struck her then. So obvious that she wondered that she had not realised it before.

If Devlin was there that night, then he must always have known who Ned was. It explained Devlin's contempt, the tension that had always crackled between him and Ned—indeed, between Ned and the rest of her brother's friends who had been with him on that fateful night.

It explained, too, why Devlin had tried so hard to keep her away from Ned.

What it did not explain was why Devlin did not just tell her that fact? He must have known that telling her that one truth would have worked far better than any warnings or threats or innuendoes.

If Devlin wished to save her from Ned, what better way than that? And yet Devlin had not.

Something uneasy stroked down her spine. That sense that there was something she was missing. A feeling that something was not right. That there was more to the story than Ned had told her. The token stopped spinning and landed flat on the desk before her with a soft clink.

The air rippled with mystery. She frowned and stared down at the token as if it held the answer. It did not, of course, but she knew who did and she knew, too, where to find him. She smiled a grim determined smile and, scooping the token up from the desk, placed it safe inside her pocket. Then she rang for the carriage and went to fetch the long dark winter cloak that Ned had bought for her.

Chapter Eighteen

The footman who opened the door of the St James's town house had a face that did not betray the least shock to find a woman standing on the doorstep at six o'clock in the morning, almost as if it were not so unusual an occurrence.

'If you would be so good as to call back later, madam. His lordship has not yet risen.'

'Then you had better wake him and tell him that Mrs Stratham is here to speak with him.'

Only once she was inside did she push back the hood of the cloak and look around her.

It was a distinctly masculine drawing room. Dark red walls. A black-onyx fireplace rather than the usual white. And above it a painting of an exotic-looking woman in a shockingly intimate pose. Emma studied it in horrified fascination.

He appeared some fifteen minutes later, smartly dressed in a shirt and cravat so white that they gleamed in the soft autumn daylight. But his dark hair was ruffled and his chin and cheeks were blue shadowed with beard stubble.

'Devlin.' She tried not to think of the last time they had been alone together.

'Emma.' His voice was gravelled in a way that hinted at his excesses of the night before. 'Or rather I should say Mrs Stratham.' He smiled in that easy way of his. 'Coffee, or perhaps you take chocolate in the morning. Kit always did.'

'No, thank you. I am not here for refreshment.'

'No, I rather suspected as much.' He walked over and poured himself a brandy. Glanced up and saw her watching him with disapproval. 'Hair of the dog. I over-imbibed last night,' he said by way of explanation, and took a swig. 'Does your husband know you are here?'

'He does not.'

'I see.'

She should have been afraid. Given what he had done to her, being here with him alone was a foolhardy position in which to place herself. But she felt nothing of fear because, with Ned's confession, she finally understood.

There was a small silence in which he topped up his glass again and moved to stand before the fireplace. He looked at her. Waited for what she had to say. Almost as if he knew.

'In Colonel Morley's library that night…' she began. Stopped. Glanced away in embarrassment.

'My sincere apologies over our little…misunderstanding.' He looked as uncomfortable as she felt at the mention of what had happened between them that night.

'It was hardly that.'

He dipped his head, raised an eyebrow, half-agreement, half-disagreement, and took another sip of brandy.

'You said I should have married you.'

'And so you should have.' There was nothing of jest or humour in his face now, only a deadly earnest. 'But it is too late now. You should go home, Emma. Married woman or not, I do not need to tell you what it would do to your reputation were you to be seen here.' He looked remote, cool, emotionally detached. A world away from the man that night in the library.

But she just stood there. 'You really were trying to save me, just as you said.'

'You know,' he said so softly that it was almost a whisper. 'Who he is. That is why you are here.'

She nodded. 'He told me.'

Devlin closed his eyes momentarily. And when he opened them he glanced away. 'I did try to save you from him.'

'I know.' She understood everything that Devlin had done had been to save her from Ned. 'That is why you proposed marriage.'

'Yes.'

'Why you tried to compromise me when I refused— to force me to the altar.'

'Monteith and the others were supposed to interrupt us kissing. I am sorry for forcing you, but I would have done anything to stop him getting his filthy hands on you.'

'Anything,' she said. 'And yet all you had to do was tell me who he was. That he was the man who won against Kit that night. Why did you not just tell me, Devlin? That one small fact?'

'Because of the oath, of course.' He finished the brandy from his glass. Moved to the decanter and poured himself another. 'Had I told you, Stratham would have made Kit's cheating public and none of us could allow that.'

The world seemed to fall away from beneath her feet. Her stomach plummeted to meet her shoes. There was a cold seeping dread of realisation through her blood. She stared at Devlin as the full horror of his words hit home.

'Kit cheated?' The voice that asked the question did not sound like her own.

'Ah,' said Devlin softly. 'Stratham did not tell you that bit.'

'No,' she said. 'He told me nothing of any cheating. But you are going to tell me what happened that night, Devlin. You are going to tell me it all.'

And he did. How they had taken to frequenting Old Moll's Den in the East End. How Stratham had toyed with them, and baited them, winning from them, night after night.

'Sitting there, tumbling that token of his over his fingers without cease. Taunting us.' Devlin's face was hard at the memory. 'We would have called it quits, but Kit would not have it. He was convinced he could beat Stratham. I laughed at him. Ridiculed him. *Like you did the last time?* I said to him. I did not realise what it would push Kit to do.' Devlin closed his eyes, but not before she had seen the guilt and pain in them. 'He persuaded us to go back to Old Moll's. *One more time*, he said. *Knew he could win*, he said. So we went. And we played again against Stratham and his friends. And low and behold, Kit did it, just as he said he would. He won. Then Stratham and his toughs accused Kit of cheating. We thought at first it was just bad form on their half, just a ruse to get out of paying.'

There was a grim tortured look on Devlin's face, and a faraway look in his eyes, as if he had gone back two years and was there once more in the smoky haze of Old Moll's Den.

'*Pull up your sleeves*, Stratham commanded. Kit refused, of course, as every one of us would have done. We were all incensed on his behalf. All of our honours slurred. All ready to fight.

'*Pull up your sleeves or I will do it for you*, said Stratham again. And Kit did.'

Devlin met her eyes. 'There were cards hidden there. He had cheated.'

There was a deafening silence in the room.

She swallowed down the bitterness in her throat.

'Have you any idea what happens to men that cheat at cards in Whitechapel, Emma?'

'I think I might hazard a guess.' But she knew. She knew in detail and it sent a chill through her bones.

He looked away, his expression hard, reliving the memory of that night. 'He would have been found washed up on the banks of the Thames.'

And that would have been a mercy after what else they would have done to him.

'They were going to lynch him. But Stratham said he would settle for all or quits. Everything that Kit had staked on that table. One turn of the cards. Just Kit and Stratham.

'They would not trust Kit to deal. We would not trust Stratham. So Stratham had me deal the cards.' Devlin held her gaze hard. 'I dealt your brother that final hand, Emma. Not anyone else. I dealt and he lost.'

Lost the money, but kept his life and all of his limbs, she thought.

'Stratham struck a deal. We were to say nothing of who he was and how he had come by his wealth. In exchange he would keep quiet on Kit's cheating. But he never lost an opportunity to remind us. He was a card shark who played us. Then, and now. Every time I look at him I remember.' There was both loathing and guilt in his eyes as he spoke the bitter words. Then he met her gaze. 'But better to lose every penny, Emma, than bear the other disgrace.'

Of being a cheat. Within a society which deemed gambling debts ones of honour, there was no greater disgrace. She nodded, knowing that if it ever got out that her brother had cheated at cards there would no way back for any of them.

'I am sorry, Emma, for Kit, for the marriage to Stratham and for the rest of it.'

She gave another nod. 'I blamed you for corrupting my brother, but the truth was Kit needed no corrupting. You tried to protect him…and me.' And she had blamed Ned for taking the money, when what he had done was something much more.

'But not well enough,' said Devlin quietly. 'I did not stop Stratham when it came to you.'

'And I am glad of it,' she said. 'He is not what you think him, Devlin. He is a man of integrity and honour.'

Devlin said nothing, but she could see in his eyes that he did not believe her.

'I love him, Devlin. I love him with all my heart.'

Silence echoed her admission.

'I cannot pretend to agree with your measure of Stratham, but I am glad of your happiness,' Devlin finally said.

They looked at one another for a moment.

'You should go to him.'

'Yes,' she said. 'I should. I will.'

'I wish you all the best,' he said and bowed.

Emma pulled up the deep hood of her cloak and, with her identity hidden from any early morning prying eyes, she slipped away from the St James's town house.

She did not go home, but went instead to another man's house in a respectable street not so very far away.

'Mrs Stratham.' Rob Finchley received her as uneasily as the last time.

'Mr Finchley. Ned said I was to come to you, if I had a problem.'

'How may I be of help?' He gestured to the red-covered sofas in the neat and tidy drawing room.

But Emma shook her head and stayed where she was.

'You can tell me where Ned is.'

'I've already told you, Mrs Stratham, I don't know where he is.'

Silence.

'You were there that night in Old Moll's Den.'

'I was there.' His expression was cool, his jaw stiff and tight.

'Ned did not tell me that my brother was a cheat.'

His eyes moved to hers. 'Who told you?'

'Devlin let it slip. He thought Ned had already told me.'

'Ned would never have told you.'

'I know.' And she knew, too, why. 'I love him, Mr Finchley. I want him to come home. So you see why I need to find him.'

An uncomfortable expression crossed Rob Finchley's face. He looked away.

'Please, sir. I am begging you. Please tell me where he is.'

Rob Finchley swallowed. She heard him blow out a breath. He raked a hand through his hair before finally meeting her gaze once more; and when it did she saw compassion in his eyes.

'I really don't know the answer to your question, Mrs Stratham.'

'But he must have left a means for you to contact him.'

Rob Finchley shook his head.

She stared at him, feeling her hope shrink and diminish with what she saw in his face.

'Loving you, knowing who you were…it tore him apart.'

Just as she was tearing apart. She had spoken such cruel words to him. She had let him walk away when he had looked at her for one single word to stay.

'I have to find him, Mr Finchley.'

'I wish you luck, truly I do, ma'am. But if Ned doesn't want to be found, I don't think that you will find him.'

Panic was rising in Emma, and cold dread. Back in Ned's study in Cavendish Square she pulled open every drawer, rummaging through them, emptying the neat piles of legal papers that Mr Kerr had left on to the surface of the desk. There was nothing else there. She opened cupboards and checked the shelves of the library with their blue leather-bound books.

She searched his bedchamber and dressing room, went through the pockets of every tailcoat in his wardrobe. But there was nothing.

She worked her way through his clothes' chest, through each pair of breeches and every waistcoat folded neatly within, and found not a single clue as to where he might have gone.

She pressed the waistcoat to her nose, inhaling the scent of him. She would not let herself weep, just pressed on with an utter determination to find him.

She moved to the wardrobe. Inside hung the shabby leather jacket and trousers he had worn in Whitechapel. Once they had been brown, now they had faded to a soft silvered birch. She traced her fingers against the jacket, remembering the very first time she had seen him, remembering the first moment those blue, blue eyes had looked into hers and tilted the axis of her world, and made beautiful butterflies flutter in her stomach.

Just as with everything else, the pockets were empty. But these clothes were not like all the others. Because they whispered to her another place she might seek him.

'Emma.' Nancy glanced up from behind the bar of the Red Lion Chop-House. 'Didn't expect to see you back here, girl.' The older woman's eyes darted over Emma's fine clothes, over her face, taking it all in in an instant.

The hour was still relatively early. Three diehard regulars sat at a table, eyeing Emma with curiosity. Other than them the place was empty.

There was the sound of the cleaver chopping against the wooden block and Tom's cheery whistling coming from the kitchen. A new girl was mopping a spill from the floor without enthusiasm.

Paulette wandered over from where she was scraping wax from a table in the corner. 'All right, Em? Look at you! Ain't you the fancy lady!'

Emma gave both Paulette and Nancy a hug.

'I'm looking for Ned Stratham.'

'All right.' Nancy raised her brows. 'You and him still walking out?'

'In a manner of speaking.'

'Is it serious?' asked Paulette.

'Very,' said Emma. 'I need to find him. Urgently.'

She saw Nancy and Paulette exchange a look.

'Like that, is it?' Nancy set the cloth she had been wiping the ale taps with down on the counter.

'Has he been in?' Emma asked.

'We've had neither sight nor sound of Ned Stratham in months,' Nancy replied.

'Since I told him you'd gone for a lady's maid, he ain't been back,' said Paulette.

Emma closed her eyes and took a breath. She knew both women were staring at her. 'If he does come in… if you see him at all, will you tell him I am looking for him? Will you ask him to come to me?'

'Does he know where to find you?' asked Nancy.

'He knows.' She paused and then added, 'Will you tell him that I love him?'

They looked at her with eyes agog and nodded.

Emma did not go to bed that night. She sat in Ned's chair in his study. The drawers all still hung open from her earlier frantic search, the legal papers still lay scattered across the desk. She made no effort to tidy them.

All the accusations she had thrown at Ned. All that she had believed of him. When all along her heart had known the truth of him, if only she had listened to it.

Ned had gone because of her and he was not coming back. And she would have to live with that knowledge for the rest of her life.

She had blamed Devlin and Hunter.

She had blamed Ned.

She had blamed Kit.

But when she stripped everything away and looked at the bones of what lay beneath, there was only one person she could blame and that was herself.

She had as good as sent him away; the man whom she loved, the man who had saved her brother's life and protected her honour. The man who loved her and had given her every last thing that he could.

The knowledge cut deep in her soul. She knew she never would forgive herself.

Her gaze moved over the documents that covered

the desk's surface, documents that made her one of the wealthiest women in the country. She had every material thing. All that her family had lost and far more. And it was all as dust. Because the only thing that mattered was who one loved.

She loved Ned and she had as good as sent him away. He could be anywhere, anywhere in the world. And she did not know how to find him. Rob Finchley's words echoed through her mind. *If Ned doesn't want to be found, I don't think you will find him.*

On the desk lay the deeds from the house in Berkeley Street that he had bought back for her, the details of manufactories that he had built to give men in the East End work, the returns from the London Dockyards where he had given her father back his dignity. And the plans for the children's home in Whitechapel—*the most important deal of his life*. All the money he had made and all the good he had done with it.

She closed her eyes, but the tears still leaked down her cheeks. She rummaged in her pocket for her handkerchief and as she pulled it out Ned's lucky token came with it and fell on to the mess of papers on the desk.

She picked the little battered token up, rubbing it between her fingers as she had seen him do so many times. But it would not bring him back, no matter how much she wished.

Emma let it fall from her fingers back down on to the papers.

Her eyes lingered on where it lay, then shifted to the paper beneath—the plans for the children's home. She looked a little closer. Moved the token aside and opened out the folded paper to reveal the plan in full.

It was a technical drawing, detailed and carefully executed by a draftsman. It showed what the building would look like when finished. It showed the layout of the rooms and corridors and their scaled dimensions. It showed the playgrounds and the gardens—and the note for the planting to contain violets. It showed, too, the precise location in Whitechapel where it was to be built.

I grew up here. It reminds me of my childhood. The words he had spoken on a summer morning echoed in her mind. Now she understood what he had told her in a way she had not at the time.

A hand squeezed around Emma's heart. The tears flowed all the more down her cheeks as the tiny spark of hope kindled in the dark despair of her soul. She did not fan it. Dared not allow herself to hope too much. But the beat of her heart was strong and in her bones was a knowledge that she was afraid to admit. That she knew where he was. That she should always have known. For where else did a man go other than the only place he felt his home?

He had told her with his own lips and she knew now, in truth, that Ned Stratham was a man who had never lied to her.

She lifted the gaming token and pressed a kiss to it. Then she slipped it in her pocket and went to ready herself.

The morning bell sounded from the distant view. From his stone bench Ned watched the men moving about like ants in the dockyard below. The sky was a clear blue, the sun warming something of the autumn chill from the air. Overhead the leaves hung like red-and-gold pennants fluttering in the breeze.

He heard the carriage before he saw it. There were not many fine town coaches in this part of London. He recognised it before it came to a halt at the end of the road.

Knew that she had come before the footman opened the door and she climbed down.

Emma stood there for a moment and looked at him. Just as she had done on that summer's morning. She even wore the same sprig muslin and shawl she had worn then, the same faded straw bonnet trimmed with the matching ribbon. The sight of her squeezed tight at his heart. Made him think that she was a vision and this was a dream.

He got to his feet. Stood there. Everything else around him faded to nothing. There was only Emma.

She walked towards him, never taking her eyes from his, and he could not look away even had he wanted to.

She walked and everything seemed to slow and quiet so that all he could hear was the beat of his own heart.

She walked right up to him. Stood there two feet before him. Her soft brown eyes striped golden in the dappled light of the sun.

'You found me,' he said.

Her mouth did not smile, but her eyes…her eyes held things he dared not hope for. 'I would have searched a lifetime to find you, Ned Stratham.'

He swallowed.

She moved to the bench, sat down next to where he had sat.

He resumed his seat by her side.

'The old vinegar manufactory.' She looked across the road to the tumbling derelict walls. 'It was where you lived as a boy, when you ran away from the Foundling Hospital to come back here to Whitechapel, was it not?'

'It was,' he admitted.

'And it is the site of the children's home you are funding and organising.'

'There are too many homeless children in Whitechapel.'

'There are.'

They sat in silence for a little while, looking out over the scene.

A gentle breeze blew, rustling the leaves above their heads. From the dockyard came the sounds of hammering and the creaking of cranes and the sound of men at work.

'You should have told me about Kit, Ned. That he cheated that night.'

'You love your brother. I did not want to hurt you. I would have given anything that you were any other woman than Kit Northcote's sister.'

'I would not.'

He looked at her. 'I took his money. I bankrupted his family. I sent you to a life of poverty and hardship, while I pretended to be a gentleman.'

'You saved his life. We both know what happens to men who cheat at the card tables in Whitechapel.'

He did not deny it.

'And as for pretending to be a gentleman… My father told me that what makes a man a gentleman is not his birth or right, not his money or wealth or abode, but the way he lives his life. And you, Ned Stratham, are more of a gentleman than any other man I know.'

He looked into her eyes. Felt her hand move to cover his where it lay upon the stone bench between them. He took her hand, entwined their fingers together.

'I regret my cruel words to you, Ned. I never meant for you to go, but my foolish pride would not let me tell you. I came here to ask your forgiveness.'

He stared at her in amazement. 'I am the one who should be down on my knees begging before you.'

'My brother made the decision to go to Old Moll's. He made the decision to cheat. My family suffered because of the decisions he made that night, not yours. And we would have chosen the same path a hundred times over to save Kit's life.'

He could feel the pulse of her blood where their hands held, feel the warmth of this woman whom he loved so much.

'I love you, Ned. Please come home.'

He reached a hand to cradle the softness of her cheek. 'I love you, Emma Stratham.' He slid his hand beneath her bonnet to the nape of her neck and his mouth moved to hers and he kissed her, sitting there on the quiet stone bench beneath the flaming spread of the old beech trees.

He kissed her with all the love that was in his heart. And then he scooped her up into his arms and he carried her down the road to the waiting carriage.

Later, when day had faded to night and the moon glowed like a giant opal in the sky, Emma and Ned made love with a tenderness and understanding beyond anything else. And afterwards as the moon bathed them in its soft silver light Emma lay in the warm protection of her husband's arms, her face resting upon his chest, listening to the strong steady beat of his heart.

He stroked her hair and kissed the top of her head.

'How did you know where to find me today?' he asked.

She reached her arm across to the bedside cabinet, felt with her fingers until they closed upon the small battered token. As he watched she looked up into his eyes and pressed it to her lips. 'Just a lucky guess,' she said and tossed the token to spin in the air above them.

Ned reached up and caught it.

'With maybe a little help from destiny,' she added.

They laughed together.

And then they kissed, and showed each other how very much they loved one another all over again.

* * * * *

*If you enjoyed this story,
look out for Kit Northcote's,
coming soon!*

THE LOST
GENTLEMAN

Chapter One

The sea was a clear green-turquoise silk, rippling and sparkling with crystal-flecked waves. The sky overhead was vast and expansive; the type of sky that only this part of the world held, a vivid never-ending blue, cloudless. It was only ten in the morning, but the sun had already unfurled its bright strength, bleaching the oak of the small American pirate schooner *Coyote's* wooden deck pale and baking it.

Kate Medhurst could feel its warmth beneath the bare soles of her feet and was grateful for the shade of the dark awning that stretched over this section of the quarterdeck—that and the cooling sea breeze. It sent the dark silk ribbons of her straw bonnet flicking and dancing against her neck and the muslin of her black skirts hugging her legs, but Kate noticed neither. Her attention was fixed solely on one thing—the ship coming into view in the distance.

There was the sound of a raven's caw, a slightly sinister call, out of place here in the middle of the ocean.

'A raven on the mizzen mast. A portent that our luck is about to change,' one of the men murmured from the deck before her. Kate knew the superstitions the same as every man on the ship. But unlike them she did not touch her forehead, making the sign to ward off evil. She did not believe in such omens, but superstition was a very real thing to most of those who spent their lives on the waves, so she did not mock them.

'For the better,' she said, 'if what is coming our way is anything to go by.' Through the spyglass she held to her eye she followed the course of the large black-hulled merchant schooner, struggling against the wind.

She snapped the spyglass shut and turned to Tobias, standing by her side. He was a tall man, over six foot in height, with a skin lined and weathered to a nut brown and hair that hung, from beneath his tricorne, in long matted braids interwoven with beads and feathers. His nose was flat from it having been broken in too many drunken fights in the past. With his looks and his faded, frogged frock-coat, Tobias was the very image of what one expected a pirate captain to be, with a temperament to match. He was still staring up at the raven with a vicious look in his eye.

'She's flying the Union Jack, but I cannot see her name.' Kate spoke not to Tobias, but the small, sturdy older man standing on her left-hand side—Sunny Jim. The bandanna wrapped around Sunny Jim's bald head had once been red, now it was a grubby faded pink, pale in comparison to the mahogany-darkened leather of the skin of his face and neck. She passed him the spyglass. 'Can you?' She frowned, knowing the name of every British ship she had ever attacked.

Sunny Jim frowned even more than usual, shaking his head as he passed the spyglass to Tobias for appearances' sake. 'Not yet, ma'am.'

'What does a name matter?' Tobias asked as he peered through the glass.

'Probably nothing.' But it bothered her more than the large black bird that still sat on the mast top watching them.

At the sight of the ship, Tobias grinned, revealing his missing front teeth. His gold-hoop earring glinted in the sunlight and reflected golden dots of light to dance upon the tattoo inked upon his neck. 'Nice,' he hissed.

'A straggler from the merchant convoy that passed at dawn, no doubt,' she said.

'Fallen behind, all alone, without the protection of those mean, son of a gun, Royal Navy frigates.' Sunny Jim almost managed a smile. 'Oh, dear, oh, dear, oh, dear. We can't leave her out there all on her own now, can we?'

'We certainly cannot,' Tobias agreed. 'We should slit their English throats.'

'There will be no slitting of throats.' Kate exchanged a glance with Sunny Jim, then shot Tobias a fierce curbing look.

Tobias's upper lip curled. 'You are too soft on them.'

'Not soft at all,' she countered. 'Hit them in their pockets and leave them alive to bear the pain and witness to the fact that America's seas are just that. America's. It is enough.'

'And supposing I disagree?' He looked at her with angry challenge in his eyes.

'Again? You seem to be disagreeing with me over much these days. This is not the time to be having this discussion. We will deal with it when we get back to Tallaholm. For now, you are on my ship, under my command and you do as I say.'

'Do I? When so many think *I* am *Coyote's* captain?' He stepped closer, trying to intimidate her.

'You do, you young cur,' Sunny Jim said with soft deadly menace and pulled his cutlass free from its scabbard. 'You would do well, Tobias Malhone, to remember that you're a nobody playing a part. There's only one true captain of this ship and, for all your fancy coat, it ain't you. So if the Captain says it's enough then it's enough. *Comprendez?*'

Tobias gave a sullen nod and backed off from his challenge, for now. 'If you say so, *Captain*.' He placed just a slight sneering emphasis on her title.

'I do.' She met his gaze unflinching. 'Are you going to be a problem for me today, Tobias?'

He looked at her for a long second before answering. 'No.' He sneered at her. 'Not today.'

She understood well the implication. Not today, but another. But unbeknown to Tobias, the problem would be gone by then. 'Then we can get on with the job at hand. They are low in the water line.'

'Heavily laden with cargo,' said Sunny Jim.

'Our favourite kind of merchantman.' She turned her gaze from the prize to Tobias. 'Make ready. Let us see if we cannot lighten the merchantman's load a little to speed her on her way.'

'Aye-aye, Captain,' Tobias said softly and without the cynicism this time. He grinned almost to himself, then spoke more loudly to the men who stood poised and waiting, 'Take her about, boys, we've got a date with an English merchant schooner.'

There was a raucous cheer of approval, before the small loyal crew raced to action. Kate pushed her worries over Tobias to the back of her mind for now and watched from her place beneath the awning, with Tobias standing ahead, giving the small orders. The black canvas sails unfurled to catch the wind and the ship began to move.

'Hoist the flag,' she commanded.

A smile curved her lips as *Coyote* sped towards her prey.

* * *

Kit Northcote, or Captain North as he now went by, snapped his spyglass shut and slipped it into the pocket of his faded leather coat. The coat had once belonged to a pirate, now it was worn by someone markedly different—someone leaner, harder, honed; although he still wore the black shirt beneath, the shabby buckskin breeches and his tall boots.

'They are coming.' His gaze was fixed on the distant ship.

'Is it La Voile?' Reverend Dr Gabriel Gunner, his friend, asked.

'The hull is a single black-striped sienna brown, the sail is black, and she is flying the Stars and Stripes as well as La Voile's own flag.'

'A skull with a mouth that is the smiling curve of a cutlass painted red with dripping blood. He is artistic. You have got to give him that.'

'I will give him more than that when he arrives.'

Gunner laughed. 'The captain is going to get the nice little surprise that he deserves. Does he think he can just keep attacking British merchantmen and get away with it?'

'I expect that is exactly what he thinks.'

'Do you know that La Voile is thought to be single-handedly responsible for reducing British transatlantic trade by almost twenty per cent? How can that be? How is it even possible?' Gunner asked. He was tall and surprisingly slender for a man who had spent many years at sea. Freckle-faced and with hair that in colder climes was red, but now in the bright sun of the waters off the Gulf of Mexico was golden beneath the straw hat he always favoured. He had clear, honest blue eyes and long bony fingers that could wield a prayer book, scalpel and cutlass with equal precision.

'La Voile operates under the protection of both a pirate overlord and authorities who turn a blind eye to his illicit actions. He has one vessel and a small loyal crew—low costs, tight control. He hits fast and hard. Takes what cargo he wants and leaves the merchantman and crew intact and *in situ*—a novel concept in the pirate world. He's clever. Clever enough to hit only easy targets and leave the big well-defended jobs to others. Clever enough to find the inevitable stragglers every convoy leaves behind. And clever enough to avoid being caught despite the best efforts of His Majesty's navy.'

'Lucky for us,' said Gunner.

'Very lucky,' agreed Kit and thought of the astronomically large sum they were being paid to do this job.

La Voile's ship, *Coyote*, was no longer a speck on the horizon. 'My, but he *is* fast.' Gunner spoke aloud what Kit was thinking.

'Almost as fast as us,' said Kit.

Gunner smiled. 'Do we take him dead or alive?'

'Alive,' said Kit. 'The bounty is higher. They want to make an example of him and hang him in irons themselves. Be gentle with this particular American pirate, Reverend Dr Gunner.'

'If you insist, Captain North.'

The two men exchanged a wry smile of understanding.

The crew on the deck hurried about as if in panic, feigning a ship that was trying to escape the jaws of a predator. The Union flag fluttered from the jack, its red, white and blue crosses and diagonals clear in the Caribbean sunlight. Men appeared as if they were trying to adjust sails.

'Is everything ready?' Kit asked.

'Exactly as you specified.'

Kit gave a nod and, slipping the spyglass from his

pocket once more, studied the black-sailed *Coyote* as she closed the distance.

'Interesting,' he murmured and focused on the three figures standing at the ship's helm beneath the black awning. 'They appear to be arguing over a woman.'

'A woman?' Gunner screwed his face in disbelief.

'And a respectable looking one at that.'

'A hostage?'

'She is neither bound nor gagged.'

'Abducted,' pronounced Gunner.

'More likely.' Kit could see the distinct threat in the body language of the taller pirate towards the woman. The sunlight glinted on the steel of both men's half-drawn cutlass blades.

'Is La Voile one of them?'

'I believe so. Look for yourself.' He passed the spyglass to Gunner that he might study the three figures.

'How big a fall in the bounty if we deliver him dead?'

'Enough.'

'You convince me, but I cannot deny that I would prefer a more personal approach to the spilling of his blood.'

The two men stood together on the deck of *Raven* and waited for La Voile to step into their trap.

It was the sight of the captain of the merchant schooner that sent the first shiver of apprehension rippling down Kate's spine. There was something about the dark steady focus of his eyes that reminded her of the unnerving stare of the raven that had sat overhead on the mizzen mast not so long since. She pushed the absurd thought from her head and tried to ignore the unease that hung about her like a miasma in the air. This was a hit, just like any other, she told herself, but her eyes checked again for long guns, despite the spyglass having already told her they were absent.

'Not a gun in sight,' said Tobias as if echoing her thought. 'Not a hint of resistance. They are yielding just like all the rest of the British yellow bellies. Cowards! For once I wish they would give us a real fight!' He spat his disgust on to the deck.

'Unarmed and faced with our long guns pointing straight at them? Don't be a fool, Tobias. We should be thankful that their common sense makes things easier for us,' she said.

Coyote's long guns had that effect on the British merchant ships Kate selected, allowing an easy progression to locking the two ships together by means of grappling hooks before throwing down the boarding planks. The nameless ship was no exception.

Kate's crew followed the same procedure, the same routine they were so practised at they could have undertaken it with their eyes shut. She watched the Tallaholm men disappear down the merchantman's ladders to her cargo deck. All they had to do was take their choice pick of the goods being carried and *Coyote* could sail away. Same as ever she did. Easy as taking candy from a baby. Yet that same unfamiliar apprehension and anxiety pulled again at Kate, stronger this time.

Her gaze scanned over the merchantman's deck, finding nothing out of the ordinary, before returning to the ship's captain once more. There was something about him, something she could not quite figure out. She examined him more closely. He was lean of build with that stripped, strong look that came from years of hard manual work. She could tell by the way his shabby faded coat sat on his broad square shoulders, from his stance, and the way the shadows cast from his battered old tricorne hat revealed sharp cheekbones and a chiselled jaw.

Under his hat his hair was dark, and his skin had the

golden tanned colouration of a man who had spent time at sea. Beneath his coat she could see a shirt and neckcloth, both black as any pirate's. Buff breeches were tight on muscular legs. On his feet he wore leather boots that had once been brown, but were now salt- and sun-faded to a noncolour that defied description. The long scabbard on his left hip was empty. Its sword lay with the other weapons her men had taken from him and his crew, thrown in a paltry pile on the deck before them. The tip of young John Rishley's sword hovered close to the captain's chest, should any of his crew decide to defy their captors. John had proven himself a valuable member of *Coyote's* crew, but Kate still wished Tobias had sent an older, more experienced member of her crew to hold the merchantman's captain.

All of these thoughts and observations took place in seconds, her gaze absorbing it in one swift movement before returning to his eyes. Dark eyes beneath the brim of that hat. Eyes that were looking right back at her. The shiver ran over her skin again. Someone walking over her grave, her grandmother would have said. She did not break the gaze, because it was his eyes that were ringing every warning bell in her body. There was something about those eyes of his. What was it…? As she stared into them, she realised.

The captain did not look like a man who was nervous for his life or his livelihood. There was nothing of fear in him, not one tiny bit. His stance was relaxed and easy, too easy. There was an air of quiet, almost unnatural calm that she could sense even across the distance that separated them—him on the deck of the merchantman, her watching from beneath the awning on *Coyote*. What she saw in that resolute, unflinching dark gaze of his was cold, hard, very real danger. She glanced at Tobias.

'Something is wrong. Get the men out of there.'

'What…? Hell, woman, nothing's wrong.' Tobias was looking at her in disbelief, as if she had run mad.

'Do it,' she insisted.

He glared at her but, at last, grudgingly gave the command.

But it was too late. In that tiny second everything changed. It happened so fast that there was nothing she could do. One minute the situation aboard the merchantman was quiet, controlled, run of the mill, the next, all hell had broken loose. The British produced weapons, and such a host of weapons that she had not seen aboard any mere merchant schooner before. They fought, hard and fast and with an expertise that surpassed *Coyote's* crew. It was over almost as soon as it had begun. Easily handled, so that within a minute her crew on the deck of the merchantman were lying face down on its deck; all save young John Rishley, who was being held like a shield before the dark-eyed captain, the boy's head pulled back to expose his pale vulnerability. A cutlass now glinted in the captain's hand, as the wicked curve of its blade pressed against the youngster's throat.

'Sweet heaven!' Kate whispered beneath her breath as her blood ran cold at the sight.

At that moment the rest of the British emerged from the schooner's lower deck and cargo hold. Her men, who had ventured down there for the prize, were being led, bound and gagged.

It was not a situation in which Kate had ever found herself before. Her mind was whirring, her eyes flicking this way and that, seeking a means of escape for them all, but there was nothing. No way out—not with the merchant captain's blade hard against John Rishley's throat, if the man really was just a merchant captain, because Kate had seen a lot of British merchant captains, but never one like him. The boy was nineteen years old. Kate knew his mother and his sisters, too. His Aunt Rita taught Sunday School back home in Tallaholm. And Kate had sworn to them that she would do all she could to keep the boy safe. Now a British blade was pressed to his throat and the sight of it stirred such dark terrible memories that almost paralysed her with fear.

He frogmarched John Rishley before him, crossing the boarding plank over which *Coyote's* crew had walked without the slightest suspicion of what was awaiting them on the other side. A lanky fair-haired fellow, who wore the robe and collar of a priest, followed in his wake.

'When did you add abducting women to piracy, La Voile?' The merchant captain's gaze was fixed on Tobias. His English accent sounded foreign to her ear, but even so she could hear there was something educated about it. His voice was low-toned, serious, unemotional.

They thought her abducted? She opened her mouth to tell him the truth, to step up to the mark and own responsibility, for everything about him told her he was not just going to let *Coyote* and her crew go. There was a blade at a boy's throat. This was serious. The masquerade was over.

But Tobias stepped forward first. 'Who the hell are you to question me?' he growled, donning the role of the captain he was coming to believe he really was.

As she and Tobias and Sunny Jim watched, the raven flew down from its perch high on the top of the mast, to land gently upon the merchant captain's shoulder. He did not bat an eyelid at the raven's presence. The bird sat there quite happily, preening its black feathers that shone blue in the sunlight, as if it were his usual perch.

The breath caught in Kate's throat. She felt her heart kick, then gallop fast. Her stomach dropped right down to the deck beneath her feet. *Not a merchant captain, after all.* She knew who he was. She should have known the minute she set eyes on him.

'He is the one they call North.' Her throat was so dry that her voice sounded husky. Because she knew in full the implication of the man standing before them with his sword ready to slit John Rishley's throat—for her crew, and for herself.

'Lord help us!' Sunny Jim whispered on her left-hand side.

She could hear the murmur that spread through her crew, could see the widening of their eyes, could hear someone beginning to pray.

Lord help them indeed.

Those dark eyes turned their attention to Kate. Now that she knew who he was she could have retreated from that gaze, but her pride would not let her.

'At your service, madam,' he said, and gave her a tiny bow of his head before returning his gaze to Tobias. 'Let the woman go.'

Tobias laughed. 'You can have her…if you leave my ship.'

'I will leave your ship.' North smiled and it was a smile that was colder and more cutting than other men's glares. 'You *are* the pirate La Voile?'

'I'm La Voile, all right.'

'Good,' said North. 'I would not want to take the wrong man.'

'Like hell am I coming with you!'

North pressed the blade harder against John Rishley's neck. 'You want me to slit his throat while you watch? Or will you yield to spare him?'

Kate had to press a hand over her mouth to stop herself from crying out. Her heart was racing. She felt sick with fear and horror and rage. As her hand tightened against the handle of the long knife hidden beneath her skirts, she felt Sunny Jim's grip around her wrist.

'Don't!' he whispered fiercely. 'Let him think you abducted. There's too much at stake, Katie.' The old man's slip of the tongue, to use her girlhood name, showed just how serious the situation was. His crinkled pale blue eyes stared meaningfully into hers, reminding her of exactly how much was at stake both here and back at home in Tallaholm.

'Go ahead. Slit it.' Tobias grinned and shook his head, an excited expression on his face. He glanced down at the long blade of his cutlass, as if watching the way the sun glinted on the sharpness of the steel. Then suddenly with a great swing of his cutlass he ran at North, yelling, 'But I'll never yield to you, you English dog!'

'No!' Kate screamed, knowing Tobias's foolhardy action would cost John Rishley his life.

It happened so fast that she could not have told how. One minute John Rishley was North's shield, the next he had been thrown, alive and well, into another British grasp and a single slash of North's blade had felled Tobias. She could see the dark stain spreading rapidly across Tobias's chest, see the blood growing in a glistening pool on the scrubbed wooden deck beneath him.

Shock stole her breath.

The silence that followed was deafening. The seconds seemed to stretch.

Nobody moved.

Nobody spoke.

Kate stared. Tobias's eyes were still wide open, dead and unseeing, staring with the same shock that she felt freezing like ice through her blood.

The priest, who seemed to be North's second-in-command, walked over to where the body lay. Crouching down, he touched his fingers against Tobias's neck.

'Dead as a doorpost, I'm afraid,' he pronounced softly, and gently swept the man's eyes shut before murmuring the words of a final prayer and getting to his feet.

'More is the pity. But we'll take him dead just the same.' North gave a nod.

With incredulous horror Kate watched as four of the British crew lifted Tobias's body between them and carried it across the boarding plank to the bigger schooner.

North's eyes shifted to where Sunny Jim's hand still held Kate's wrist. 'Release her to us.'

'And if we don't?' Sunny Jim demanded. His grip was gentle for all the ferocity of the part he was playing before North.

North's gaze flicked coldly to Tobias's lifeless form before returning to Jim's. 'We'll kill every last man amongst you.'

She did not doubt North's assertion, neither did anyone else. Every pirate and privateer who sailed these oceans had heard the stories of North the Pirate Hunter.

Sunny Jim's eyes slid momentarily to Kate's in veiled question. He would fight for her to the death, they all would, but she could not allow that, not all these men who had served her so loyally.

'I am not worth one man's life, let alone thirty,' she answered. 'Surely you see that?' Words that could be those of a prisoner held against her will.

But Sunny Jim's expression was stubborn. He had known both her grandfather and father and he was not a man to cut and run.

'Give us the woman and the rest of you may go free,' said North.

'You think we would believe a story like that?' Sunny Jim sneered at North.

'You should—it is the truth. I have no interest in bringing in *Coyote* and her crew as a prize. My commission is purely for La Voile.'

She felt the hope that North's words sent rippling through her crew. They did not fully believe him, but they wanted to. She knew it with a certainty, because she felt the same way, too. North could not be trusted, but, if he wanted, he could kill them all anyway and take her just the same.

Sunny Jim knew it, too. But still he wavered.

'You must yield me to them,' she said, as if pleading with her captor, when in truth it was the command he needed to hear.

He gave a nod, his gentle old eyes meeting hers in understanding and salutation. 'If you want her so much, take her. And let us pray you do not lie, Captain North.' In the role he was playing Sunny Jim threw her hard towards North.

The force of it made her stumble and almost fall, but North caught her and in one movement swept her behind him.

'Oh, I do not lie, Mr Pirate. You need have no fear of that.' She could hear the ironic curve on his mouth as he uttered the cool words.

But he was not smiling when he glanced at the priest. 'Escort the lady to safety, Reverend Dr Gunner.'

The priest gave a nod and when he gestured ahead, she had no choice but to follow him, leaving behind *Coyote* and safety, and step with feigned willingness across the breach that divided her world from his.

On the British ship Kate stood by the bulwark, her grip so tight upon the rail that her fingers ached, watching them, watching North, watching what would come next.

Those crew who had been captured upon North's ship

were returned across the plank to *Coyote*. All of her men were lined up there, on their knees, most still bound and gagged. There was nausea in her stomach, an icy dread in her blood.

'Will he kill them?' she asked the priest, her eyes lingering on the scene on *Coyote's* deck.

'North does not lie. He will not take their lives, ma'am.'

But priest or not, Kate could not trust the words.

North moved.

Her heart missed a beat.

But he did not spray the deck red with blood as she feared. Instead, true to his words, he sheathed his cutlass and walked away, leaving them there as he returned to his own ship. In less than a minute all physical connections between the two ships had been severed, the boarding plank and pricey grappling hooks sent plummeting into the waves without a second glance.

As North's ship manoeuvred carefully away from *Coyote*, Kate's gaze held to Sunny Jim's, but neither of them dared show one single sign. Behind her she could hear the creaking of the rigging and the crack of unfurling canvas and the movement of men busy at work. And before her, the distance of the ocean expanding between them as North took sail.

She was aware that North and the priest were somewhere behind her, but Kate did not look round. She just stood there and watched while the wind seemed to speed beneath North's sails to leave *Coyote* further and further behind.

Until, at last, the dark shadow fell across her and she knew that North had come to stand at the rail by her side.

One second. A deep breath.

Two seconds. She swallowed and hid all that she felt.

And only then did she turn to face the man who was the infamous pirate hunter North.

Those dark eyes were looking directly into hers with a calm scrutiny that made her nervous.

'North, Captain Kit North,' he offered the unnecessary introduction. 'Under commission from the British Admiralty to bring in the pirate La Voile.'

The hesitation before she spoke was small enough not to be noticed. 'Mrs Kate Medhurst,' she said, using her real name because it would mean nothing to him and because successful deception was best attained by sticking close to the truth.

He took her hand and just the feel of his fingers against hers made her shiver.

'You are cold, Mrs Medhurst, now that our speed increases.'

She hated that he had seen it, that tiny sign of weakness, of fear. 'A little,' she agreed by way of excuse.

Before she could stop him he slipped off his coat and wrapped it around her shoulders.

She could feel the warmth of him still upon it, smell the scent of him too much in her nose—leather and soap, sunshine and masculinity. It surrounded her. It enveloped her. Bringing him close to her, making it feel like a gesture of intimacy that she did not want to share with any man, least of all him. She itched to tear his coat from her, to dash it at his feet, this hard-eyed handsome Englishman who was her enemy in more ways than he could imagine. But Kate knew she could not afford to yield to such impulses of emotion and controlled herself as carefully as ever she did.

'Thank you,' she said, but she did not smile.

'You are safe with us.'

Safe? The irony of the word would have made her laugh had the situation not been so dire. 'Even if I am an American? And there is—' she hesitated in order to choose the word carefully '—disharmony between our two countries?'

'Even if you are an American and there is disharmony between our two countries.' There was the smallest hint of a smile around that hard mouth. 'You are welcome aboard *Raven*, Mrs Kate Medhurst.'

'*Raven*,' she said softly. *Of course.*

'The name of the ship.'

The name that, had she seen it, would have made all the difference in the world.

'They said there was no name upon your ship,' she said.

'La Voile was not meant to see it.'

'It was a trap,' she said slowly, her blood chilling at the extent of his cold calculation.

North smiled. 'The name would have tipped him off.'

'Yes,' she agreed. 'I am sure it would have.' And knew it for the certainty it was. 'Why take just La Voile and not *Coyote* and the rest of her crew? Why leave behind the greater part of the prize?'

'I am not interested in prizes. My commission is for La Voile and only La Voile.'

'I did not realise he was so important to the British. Surely compared to Jean Lafitte, he is just small fry?'

'He is a big enough burr and one with the potential of becoming a rallying anti-British figurehead, much more so than Lafitte. Admiralty wish to cut off the head and leave the body in place to tell the tale, leaderless and ineffective. Which suits me. One man is easier dealt with than an entire crew and ship,' he said.

'So it seems.' But things were not always as they seemed.

Her gaze held his for a moment longer, looking danger in the eye and seeing its ruthless, dark, infallible strength. She swallowed.

The tiny moment seemed to stretch.

'Reverend Dr Gunner will escort you below to a cabin where you may rest. If you will excuse me, for now.'

She shrugged off his coat and gladly returned it.

A bow of his head and he was gone, moving across the deck to speak to his men.

Kate felt the tension that held her body taut relax, letting out the breath she had not known she was holding.

'Mrs Medhurst…ma'am.' The priest moved forward to her side.

One last glance of hope and longing out across the ocean to where *Coyote* and safety had diminished to little more than a toy ship upon the horizon.

The priest saw the direction of her glance and misconstrued it. 'You really are safe with us.'

'So Captain North reassures me.' But if North were to realise the truth of who she was, of what she was… Captain *Le* Voile, as she always thought of herself. Such a subtle difference from *La* Voile, but one that was important to her. Le Voile or La Voile, it made no odds when it came to North. Either way she was the pirate captain of *Coyote* whom he sought.

You really are safe with us.

Kate gave a smile of irony. For what place could be more dangerous than aboard *Raven* with the deadly British pirate hunter who had been sent to capture her?

It was a sobering thought. She forced it from her mind and, with a nod, followed Reverend Dr Gunner below deck.

Chapter Two

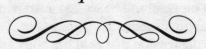

'I put her in my cabin. I'll sleep on the deck with the men—naturally.' Within Kit's day cabin Gunner was lounging in a small wooden chair. The priest pulled a silver hip flask of brandy from his pocket, unstopped it and offered it to Kit as a formality. They both knew that Kit would refuse.

'There's a cot in the corner—you are welcome to sleep there.' Kit was seated in his own chair behind the plain mahogany desk.

'Are you suggesting I could not manage a hammock?' Gunner downed a swig of brandy.

'A man does not forget such things,' said Kit and thought of the past years and all it had entailed for them both.

'He certainly does not.' Gunner grinned. 'They will bury us in those damned hammocks.'

Kit smiled. 'No doubt.' He moved to the large rectangular window, looking out over the sea. 'How is our guest?'

'Resting. She has a remarkable resilience. Most women would be suffering the vapours at the mere suggestion of the ordeal she has endured. But maybe the shock of it has not hit home yet. Delayed emotional response following trauma—we have both seen it.' Gunner came to stand by his side and met his gaze meaningfully. They both re-membered the horrors of the year in that Eastern hellhole.

'Has she any signs of physical hurt?'

'None that I could see. I did explain I was a physician and enquired whether she had need of any assistance, but she declined, saying she was well enough.'

'A lone woman amongst a crew of pirates… How well can she be?' said Kit.

Gunner's mouth twisted with distaste. 'I am rather glad that you killed La Voile.'

'I am not. They would have taken his life just the same in London.' And Kit would have welcomed the extra money that would have paid.

'Always the money,' said Gunner with a smile.

'Always the money,' agreed Kit, and thought of what this one final job would allow him to do. All the waiting and planning and working, and counting every coin until the target was in sight, and the time was almost nigh. He pushed the thought away, for now. 'I will have the day cot set up for you and space cleared for your possessions and clothes. If you will excuse me, I have got work to do.'

'And always work,' said Gunner.

'No rest for the wicked.' There was a truth in that glib phrase that few realised, Kit thought wryly. No rest in-deed. Not ever. 'La Voile is dead, the job is done. We go back to England and claim our bounty.'

'And Mrs Medhurst? We cannot touch port in America. We'd be running the gauntlet with the flotilla of French privateers and pirates patrolling their coast. Even with all *Raven's* advantages, she cannot match such numbers.'

Kit smiled. 'We will drop the woman at Antigua when we victual. Fort Berkeley there will organise her return home.'

'A good plan. But it has been so long since we were

in the presence of a respectable woman, one cannot help speculate how her presence would have lifted the journey home. It would certainly have kept the men on their best behaviour.'

'You are too long from home, my friend,' said Kit drily.

Gunner gave a smile. 'Perhaps.' He was still smiling as he left the cabin, closing the door behind him.

Kit returned to his desk and the navigational charts that lay there. But before he focused his attention on studying their detail he thought once more of Kate Medhurst with her cool grey eyes: proud, appraising, wary and with that slight prickly hostility beneath the surface.

Disharmony between our two countries. He smiled at that line and wondered how a woman like her had come to be abducted by a shipload of pirates. And even more, how she had fared amongst them. For all the strength of character that emanated from her, she was not a big woman. Physically she would not have stood a chance.

Maybe Gunner had a point when it came to La Voile. Kit thought of his blade slicing through the villain's heart. Maybe it was worth the gold guineas that it had cost him, after all.

He gave a grim smile and finally turned his attention to the charts that waited on the desk.

Kate forced herself to stop pacing within the tiny cabin in which they had housed her. She stopped, sat down at the little desk and stilled the panic roiling in her mind and firing through her body. *Stop. Be still. And think.*

Her eyes ranged over the assortment of medical books, prayer books and the large bible on the shelf fixed to the wall above the desk. On the desk itself were paper, pen and ink and a small penknife. She lifted the knife and very gently touched a thumb to test the sharpness of the blade. The priest kept the little knife razor sharp, potentially a useful weapon, but it was nothing in comparison to her own. The feel of the leather holster and scabbard, and their precious contents, strapped to her legs gave her a measure of confidence.

She would not hesitate to use either the knife or pistol on North if she needed to. Not that she thought it would come to that.

Coyote would come for her. It is what she would have done had one of her crew been taken. Regroup, rearm, follow at an unseen distance, then come in fast for the attack. Sunny Jim would do the same. She knew her men—they would not abandon her.

They would come for her and it was vital that Kate be ready. All she had to do was watch, wait and keep her head down. Not today, perhaps not even tomorrow, but soon. It was just a matter of time before she was back once more on her own ship, maybe even with Captain Kit North as her prisoner. She smiled at that thought. The Lafitte brothers, the men who oversaw most of the mercantile, smuggling, privateering and pirate ventures around Louisiana, would pay her well for him. With North off the scene it would be a great deal safer for them all. She smiled again, buoyed by the prospect.

She pleaded fatigue that night so as not to have to join them for dinner, eating instead from the tray he sent to her cabin. *Coyote* would not come tonight, and as for North… An image of him swam in her head and she felt nervousness flutter in her stomach…she would defer facing him until tomorrow.

But of North the next morning there was no sign. It was the priest, Reverend Dr Gunner, who sat with Kate at breakfast and the priest who offered her a tour of *Raven*.

She accepted, knowing the information could be useful both to *Coyote* and to all her fellow pirate and privateer brethren.

'I could not help noticing that Captain North was not at breakfast.'

'North does not eat breakfast. He is a man of few needs. He takes but one meal a day.'

'A man of few needs… What else can you tell me of the famous Captain North?'

'What else would you like to know?' He slid her a speculative look that made her realise just how her question had sounded.

'All about this ship,' she said.

Reverend Dr Gunner smiled, only too happy to oblige.

Raven was bigger than *Coyote*, but the lower deck was much the same. There were more cabins and the deck contained not cargo, but long guns. Better gunnery than *Coyote* carried. So much better that it made her blood run cold. Two rows of guns, some carronades, others long nine pounders, and a few bigger, longer eighteen pounders, including two as bow chasers, lined up, all neat on their British grey-painted, rather than the American red-painted, wheeled truck carriages and secured in place by ropes and blocks. There were also sets of long oars neatly stored and ready for use, something that made the hairs on the back of her neck stand up.

'You are oared,' she said weakly.

'They do come in handy at certain times when the wind does not blow. And we are sufficiently crewed to man them easily enough.' The priest smiled. 'We are also carrying extra ballast to make us lie low in the water,' he explained. 'To give the illusion we are heavily laden with cargo.'

'You were deliberately posing as a merchantman.'

'Captain North's idea. He said that when you have a

whole ocean to search for La Voile the easiest thing would be to have him come to us. He said it would work.'

'And it did.' A shiver ran through her at North's cold, clever calculation and how easily and naïvely she had stepped into his trap.

'It did, indeed, Mrs Medhurst,' Gunner agreed with an open easy smile as he led her into a room that was lined with wooden and metal hospital instruments.

Her eyes ranged around the room as he spoke, taking it all in, and stopping when they reached the huge sealed butt in the corner. The sudden compassion on Reverend Dr Gunner's face and his abrupt suggestion that they progress to the upper deck confirmed the butt's macabre contents: Tobias. She was relieved to follow the priest up the ladder out into the fresh air and bright sunshine. But the relief was short lived.

North was already out on deck, taking the morning navigational reading, chronometer, sextant and compass clearly visible; a man absorbed in his task. The blue-sheened raven sat hunched on his shoulder, as if it were party to the readings.

His shirt was white this morning, not black, and he was clean shaven and hatless, so that she could see where the sun had lifted something of the darkness from his hair to a burnished mahogany. It rippled like short-cut grass in the wind. In the clarity of the early morning light his golden tanned features had a harsh handsomeness that was hard to deny. But even a rattlesnake could look handsome; it did not mean that she liked it any the more.

North saw her then, cutting those too-perceptive eyes to her in a way that brought a flutter of nerves to her stomach and prickle of clamminess to her palms.

He gave her a small nod of acknowledgement, but he did not smile. Indeed, his expression was serious, stern almost. Nor, to her relief, did he make any movement towards her. Instead he turned his attention back to his measurements and calculations.

'Do not mind North,' said Gunner with good humour. 'It is his manner with everyone. He is a man who takes life too seriously and works too hard.'

As she followed the priest over to the stern of the ship, her eyes scanned the ocean behind them and saw the distant familiar shapes of islands across the water, but nothing else.

She leaned against the rail, feel the cooling kiss of the sea breeze, noticing both its strength and direction as she watched the frothy white wake *Raven* left behind her. Just looking at the ocean, just being on it, never failed to comfort her. Her gaze dropped to the tall lettering that named North's ship, tall and clear and stark white against the rich black paint of the stern. *Raven*.

'There was no name upon this ship when the pirates approached.' She looked at the priest with a question in her eyes. 'I am sure of it, sir.' But was she? Had such a basic mistake brought her to this situation? 'At least, I thought I saw nothing and I sure was looking to see who you were.'

'Do not doubt yourself, madam. There was no name for the pirates to see. Look more closely.'

She walked toward the stern and leaned over it to examine the painted name, and saw exactly the device North had used. 'There is a long black plank, like a frame fixed above the lettering.'

'Largely invisible from elsewhere. It can be flipped down to cover the name.'

'How clever.' So clever that it frightened her.

'It is, is it not? North is clever.'

'How clever?' she asked, needing to know the full measure of the man who was her enemy.

'Do you know anything of ships Mrs Medhurst?'

'I do,' she admitted with a nod. 'Both my father and grandfather were shipwrights and sailors. There have been sailors in my family for as far back as can be remembered.'

He smiled. 'Then look up at *Raven's* sails and rigging.'

She did as he bid and what she saw stole the words from her tongue. Gone was the tatty patched ordinary canvas found on many merchant schooners, and in their place was a large spread of pristine-looking sails. She felt the prickle of cold sweat at the sight.

'And our hull is longer and sleeker than most ships of this size. North's own design. The combination of the hull design and the sail spread allow us uncommon speed and manoeuvrability, making us faster than most pirate ships.'

'I did not see any gun ports either for the guns below.'

'Optical illusion.' Reverend Dr Gunner smiled again. 'We are carrying eighteen big guns, as well as several small swivel guns.'

Compared to Coyote's arsenal of eight guns.

'Our men are drilled to fire one-minute rounds. And—' he could barely contain his excitement '—we have a special powder mix that extends the range of our shot.'

'Oh, my!' she said softly.

'Not to mention our personal weaponry.' He pulled part of the enormous cutlass from the scabbard that hung from his left hip, to expose a small section of the silver shining blade. 'It is a special high-tensile steel from Madagascar. There is nothing to match its combined hardness and flexibility. And we carry an armament that would kit out an army. We are the very best, or, depending on whose point of view one takes, the very worst of what sails upon these seas. We can best any pirate.' He smiled again.

Kate thought of *Coyote* out there somewhere behind, following *Raven*. 'I see.' She forced the curve to her lips, but inside her stomach was clenched with worry and there was a cold realisation spreading through her blood.

'Wonderful, is it not?'

Wonderful was not the word Kate was thinking to describe it. The priest was awaiting her reply, but she was saved from having to make one by the arrival of a call that rang out from the crewman in the rigging.

'Ship ahoy!'

It was the words that until only a few minutes ago Kate had been praying to hear. Now, in view of what Reverend Dr Gunner had just told her, they left her with mixed emotions.

'South-south-west.'

Kit scanned the horizon in that direction and saw the tiny spot. Raising his spyglass to his eyes, he trained it hard upon the ship and focused.

He heard the familiar tread of Gunner's boots strolling over towards him. He heard nothing of the woman, but knew she was there from the reassurances Gunner was speaking to her.

They stood there quietly by his side, the woman between him and his shipmate. Gunner, not wanting to interrupt Kit's concentration, stood content and quiet in his own meditations.

The silence stretched.

It was the woman who broke it.

'What do you see, sir?' she asked.

'A schooner.'

'Is it the pirates? The same pirates...?'

He snapped the spyglass shut and turned to look at her. 'It is difficult to say at this distance.'

He felt that same slight prickle of tension and hostility that emanated from her.

'Mrs Medhurst is understandably a little nervous,' Gunner said. 'I have tried to convince her of our superior strength, but...' He smiled and gave a shrug of his shoulders.

'Rest assured, ma'am, if *Coyote* is fool enough to come after us with vengeance in mind, then, as I am sure Reverend Dr Gunner has already pointed out, we will have disabled her before she is within range to fire her own guns. She has only eight small ones, mainly four and six pounders, nine if you include the swivel gun on the rail, to our eighteen larger.'

'How can you know that?' She looked pale in the bright morning sun.

'I have a very good spyglass.' He smiled. 'And I counted.'

She swallowed and did not look reassured.

'Calm your nerves, ma'am, if La Voile's crew threaten violence they will go the same way as their captain.'

He saw the flicker of something in those eyes trained on the distant ship before she masked it, something that looked a lot like fear, there then gone.

'Have I convinced you, Mrs Medhurst?'

'Yes, Captain North, I do believe you have.' Her eyes held his and she smiled, but it was not an easy smile. 'May I?' Her eyes flickered to the spyglass in his hand.

She could not have known what she was asking. A sea captain did not lend his spyglass lightly. But she stood there patiently waiting, with those Atlantic grey eyes fixed on his. There was no sign of any fear now. She seemed all still calmness, but he sensed that slight tension that underlay her. Her hands were steady as she accepted the spyglass and peered through it, adjusting its focus to suit her eyes. She looked and those tiny seconds stretched.

At last she closed the spyglass and returned it to him, their eyes meeting as she did so.

'Thank you.' Her American lilt was soft against his ears. 'If you will excuse me, gentlemen. I think I will retire to my cabin for a little while, if you don't mind.'

They made their devoirs.

His eyes followed her walking away across that deck to the hatch, the gentle sway of her hips, the proud high-held head. Despite the faded black muslin, chip-straw bonnet and bare feet, she had an air about her of poise and confidence.

'She is afraid,' said Gunner softly.

'Yes,' agreed Kit, his gaze still fixed on her retreating figure. She was afraid, but not in the way any other woman would have been afraid. There was a strength about her, an antipathy, and something else that he could not quite work out.

He glanced up to find Gunner watching him.

'Is it *Coyote*?' Gunner asked with just the tiniest raise of his brows.

'Without a doubt,' replied Kit smoothly.

Kate closed the door of the cabin behind her and leaned her spine against it, resting there as if she could block out North and the situation she found herself in.

If La Voile's crew threaten violence, they will go the same way as their captain. North's words sounded again in her mind, and she did not doubt them, not for an instant. Not because of rumours or reputations, but because she had seen the evidence with her own eyes.

Her men were coming for her. And they would most definitely threaten violence. *Raven's* sails made her fast. But not faster than *Coyote*.

Sunny Jim was an experienced seaman. He would see the change in *Raven's* sails, but he would not see anything that was designed to stay hidden. Not the long-range guns or their number, or the fact *Coyote* would be hit before she could fire a shot. Not the weaponry aboard, or, worse than any of that, the mind of the man who was a more formidable enemy than any fireside tale foretold.

He would not realise that *Coyote* did not stand a rat's chance against *Raven*.

Have I convinced you, Mrs Medhurst?

He had more than convinced her. She had seen the cold promise in those eyes of his, the utter certainty.

Fear and dread squirmed in her stomach. She thought of Sunny Jim and of how much she respected the old man who had been her grandfather's friend. She thought of young John Rishley and how he had his whole life to live in front of him. She thought of each and every man upon *Coyote*. She knew them all and their families, too.

'Sweet Lord, help them,' she whispered the prayer aloud. 'Make them turn back.'

But they wouldn't turn back. She was their captain. They were coming. She knew it and North knew it, too. If her men reached *Raven*, their fate was sealed and the knowledge chilled her to the bone.

She couldn't just let it happen. She couldn't just let them sail unwittingly to their deaths.

So Kate sat down at the priest's little desk and she thought and she prayed, but no answer came. And then she remembered the distant islands and how all of the attention of North and his crew would be on *Coyote* growing steadily bigger. The first tiny hint of an idea whispered in her ear. She knew these waters, all of their layout and what was in them and on them. Any good Louisiana privateer or pirate did. And Sunny Jim was a good Louisiana pirate, too.

It was not the best of plans, she knew that. It was risky. It could go wrong in so many ways. But it was the only plan she could think of, and she would rather take a chance with it than sit here and let her men sail to their doom. Anything was better than allowing their confrontation with North.

Pulling up her skirts, Kate unbuckled the leather straps of her holsters and hid them with her weapons beneath the cot. Then she smoothed her skirts down in place, and, with a deep breath, made her way to the upper deck to wait for the right moment.

'We need to veer to the north,' said Kit. He stood on the quarterdeck with Gunner, the two of them pouring over the navigational chart that covered this area. With one of his men dedicated to watching *Coyote* full time, Kit could get on with navigating *Raven* through these waters. 'Regardless of what the charts say, we do not want to be too close to that cluster of rocky outcrops, or what lies beneath.'

Gunner gave a nod. 'One cannot always trust the charts and it is better to be safe than sorry.'

'Bear to larboard, Mr Briggs,' Kit gave the command to his helmsman. *Raven* began to alter course ever so slightly, taking her in a broader sweep clear of the rocks.

'Clearly visible in daylight, but at night, in the dark… I bet there have been more than a few gone to meet their maker by that means.'

The two of them mulled that truth for a few minutes in silence as they watched those dark, jagged, rocky bases ahead. Kit would not mind meeting his maker. Indeed, over the years part of him had wished for death. But not quite yet.

His gaze wandered to *Raven's* bow, to where Kate Medhurst had stood for so long, staring out at the ocean ahead of them. Now the spot was empty. He scanned the deck and saw no sign of her.

'Where is Mrs Medhurst?' His eyes narrowed with focus.

'She was right there…' Gunner stopped. 'Maybe she wanted some shade from the fierceness of the sun.'

'Some shade…' Kit murmured the words to himself and in his mind's eye saw the dark awning fixed across *Coyote's* quarterdeck. Something about the scene niggled at him, but he could not put his finger on why.

'Probably returned to her cabin.'

'When the cabins are like sweat boxes and there is shade behind us?' Kit raised an eyebrow and met Gunner's gaze. 'How long has she been gone?'

'No idea. Could be two minutes, could be twenty. Some time while we were engaged with the charts.' Gunner was looking at him. 'Call of nature?'

'Perhaps.' But he had a bad feeling. 'Better to take no chances.' They both knew he was responsible for her safety while she was aboard *Raven*.

'Has anyone seen Mrs Medhurst?' Gunner asked of the crew.

'Lady went below some time since,' Smithy answered from where he was holystoning the deck.

Kit and Gunner exchanged a look and went below.

Kit gestured his head towards Gunner's old cabin that, for now, belonged to Mrs Medhurst. Gunner nodded and went to knock on the door.

There was only silence in response. Gunner opened the door, then glanced round at Kit with a shake of the head.

'The head?' suggested Gunner. 'I will let you check that one.' He grinned.

'You are too kind.' But Kit didn't balk from it. He headed to the bow and knocked on the door that led out onto the ship's head. There was no one outside. But folded neatly and tucked in behind the ledge was black dyed muslin. Kit lifted it out and Kate Medhurst's dress fluttered like the black flag of a pirate within his hand.

'What in heavens…?' Gunner shot him a worried glance.

The two men looked from the dress outside to the open platform of the head.

'She cannot possibly have… Can she?' Gunner whispered in horror.

Kit stepped out first on to the ledge of the head with Gunner following behind.

'Hell!' Kit had not cursed in eighteen months, but one escaped him now. For there in the clear green water a distance from *Raven* was Kate Medhurst, swimming smoothly and efficiently with purpose. Oblivious to the two men that stood watching her, and oblivious, too, to the sinister dark shape beneath the water out near the rocky outcrops.

Kit and Gunner's gazes met and held for a tiny fraction of a second and then they were running full tilt for the upper deck.

Chapter Three

The water was colder that Kate had anticipated and the distance to the rocks looked further in the water than it had done from up on *Raven*. The cotton of her shift was thin, but it still caught around her legs and swirled in the water enough to slow her progress. But the dive had been seamless and quiet and she was a strong enough swimmer, taught by her father when she was still a girl. He had seen too many people drown and insisted that it might save her life one day. It might save several other lives, too, she thought wryly, if she made it to those rocks unnoticed and was able to flag down *Coyote* when she passed.

Each stroke of her arms, and each kick of her legs, was careful and as smooth as possible, trying to avoid any splashing or noise that would draw a stray glance from *Raven* as she cleared the shadow of the ship.

Quiet and smooth.

Breathe.

Keep going.

The three-line mantra whispered through her head. She did not look up and she did not look back. Instead, she kept her focus fixed firmly on the closest of the group of tiny rocky islands that lay in a direct line ahead. All she had to do was swim to it. North and his crew's attention would all be to the larboard and stern. Kate was starboard and swimming clear. She would have to be real unlucky for them to see her.

Quiet and smooth.

Breathe.

Keep going.

And then she heard the shouts.

Her heart sank.

Keep going. They had what they thought was La Voile's body; it was enough to secure their bounty. They did not need her. And North was an Englishman and a scoundrel to boot. He would not come back for her, but sail right on.

But the shouts grew louder, more frantic, so that she could no longer pretend she did not hear them. She glanced behind and saw what looked like every man on the ship crowded on to the upper deck. And there, at the stern, she could see North, his coat stripped off to expose his white shirt beneath, busy with a rope. The black-robed priest was by his side helping him and she knew in that moment, whatever else North was, he was not a man who sailed away and left a woman in the water.

She stopped swimming and trod water, knowing that to swim on would only make things look worse for her. One last glance at the tiny rocky islands and freedom. A movement flickered at the side of her eye. She shifted her gaze and saw across the beautiful clear green water the tall grey dorsal fin heading directly her way.

Time seemed to stop. For a tiny moment she froze, then turned and swam as fast as she could back towards *Raven* and North and all that she had fled. Her enemy had turned, in one split second, to her only hope. She could feel the beat of her heart and the cold sensation of terror as all of her life flashed before her eyes in a multitude of tiny fast frozen scenes. Ben and little Bea. Wendell. Her mother and father. Sunny Jim. Tobias with his dead unseeing eyes. And North. Why North, she did not know, but he was there with that sharp perceptive gaze of his.

She did not look back. She did not need to. It did not matter if North sent the jolly boat down. In maritime stories people always swam fast and made it to the safety of the boat just in the nick of time before the shark reached them. And she wanted so much to believe those yarns right now. But the truth about sharks was that one moment they were two hundred yards away and the next they were right there in your face. They could swim real fast; faster than any man, and faster than a boat could be rowed. If you were in the water and they wanted you, then your time on this earth was over. Those who survived only did so because the shark let them, so her grandfather said. And he should know since he was one of those that did not taste so good to sharks. They took his foot, but not the rest of him.

Fear was coursing through her body, fatigue burning her muscles like fire. Her breathing was so hard and fast that she could taste blood at the back of her throat. She knew the shark must be right there, but she would not yield, not when she had so much to fight for. Not when Ben and little Bea still needed her.

Something big and hard bumped against her, knocking her off course. She pushed it away, flailing beneath the water, holding her breath, eyes wide open to see the big dark shape. The lazy flick of its tail was so powerful that she felt the vibration of it through the water. Her head broke the surface, her mouth gasping in great lungfuls of air as she watched the enormous white-tipped dorsal fin head towards *Raven's* stern.

Something landed in the water between her and the

shark. Something that was swimming towards her. Something that was North. She stared in disbelief.

A few strong strokes of his arms and he was there before her.

'What are you doing?' she gasped.

'Stealing a shark's meal.' He pulled her to him. There was no smile upon his face, but there was something in his eyes that did not match the deadpan voice.

They stared at one another for a tiny moment and she felt as if he could see everything she was, all that she kept hidden from him, from her men, from all the world. As if her very soul was naked and exposed before him. As if he were not North, and she Le Voile. As if he were not British and she American. As if he were just a man and she just a woman with raw honesty and attraction between them. Making her forget about Wendell, making her forget about everything she had sworn, everything she was. All of this revealed, stark and sudden and undeniable in the tiny moments left of their lives. It shocked her, the depth of it, the absurdity of it in this situation.

Someone shouted a warning from *Raven's* deck.

Beyond North, where he could not see, the shark circled and came heading straight for them.

'It is coming back,' she murmured to him. The dorsal fin disappeared as the shark submerged for attack. Her eyes held to North's for her last moment on this earth.

North's arm gripped around her waist. 'Hold on tight,' he whispered into her ear, then turned his head to yell, 'Now!'

She gasped as they were suddenly yanked hard out of the water and suspended in mid-air, swinging precariously. Below them the great jaws of the shark snapped shut as it sank beneath the waves once more.

Only then did she notice the rope around North's waist that was hauling them slow and steady up to *Raven's* deck.

She closed her eyes to the image of the shark and held tight to him, her body pressed to his, her legs wrapped around him in the most intimate way. Nothing mattered other than that they had made it to safety.

She was alive and she could feel the beat of her heart and his. She breathed the freshness of the air and the scent of him where her cheek was tucked beneath his chin. North's arms were strong around her, securing her to him. His body was warm after the coldness of the ocean. He was strength. He was safety. And by holding to him she was holding on to life.

Her breath caressed his neck. Her lips were so close to its pulse point that she could feel the thrum of his blood beneath them, so close that she could taste him. She was alive, and so was he. And she clung all the tighter to him and to the wonder of that realisation.

But at that moment the voices of the men intruded and she felt her and North's merged bodies being guided as one over *Raven's* rail.

They were safe.

The ordeal was over.

Her face was so close to North's that she could feel his breath warm and moist against her skin, their bodies so close as to be lovers. Breast to breast. Heart to heart. Thigh to thigh. In a way no other man had ever been save Wendell. She stared up into his eyes, frozen, unable to move, unable to think.

Wendell.

She tried to right herself, but North maintained his grip around her and she was glad because her legs when they touched the solidity of the English oak deck had nothing of strength in them and her head felt dizzy and distant.

Somehow the rope was gone and North was sweeping his dry coat around her and lifting her up into his arms, as if she were as light as a child.

'Let me take her from you, Captain. I will carry her.' Reverend Dr Gunner's voice sounded from close by, but North did not release her.

'I will manage,' he said in his usual cool way. 'It is your other skills that are required.'

She did not understand what North meant, but the faces of the men were crowded all around, staring at her, and exhaustion was pulling at her, and it felt such an uphill struggle to think. Every time her eyes closed she forced them open. She knew she was over North's shoulder as he descended the deck ladder. When she opened her eyes again she was lying on the cot in the cabin they had given her. North was standing over her and Reverend Dr Gunner was there, too, in the background.

North's hair was slicked back, dark as ebony and sodden. Seawater had moulded the cotton of his shirt to the muscular contours of his arms and his broad shoulders, to the hard chest that she had been pressed so snug against. Only then did she see the scarlet stain on his shirt.

'You are bleeding.' Her eyes moved to meet his.

'No,' he said quietly, and gently smoothed the wet strands of hair from her face. 'Rest and let Gunner treat you.'

Before she could say a word he was gone, the door closing behind him with a quiet click.

Gunner opened up a black-leather physician's bag and stood there patiently. Only then did she understand that the blood was her own.

'You are a physician as well as a priest?'

'Priest, physician, pirate...' He gave an apologetic smile

and a little shrug of his shoulders. 'I never could quite decide.' He fell silent, waiting.

Kate gave a nod of permission and laid her head back against the pillow.

Up on the quarterdeck, having changed into dry clothes, Kit stood watching the distant ship creep closer. It was discernible as *Coyote* now without the need for the spyglass.

He thought of Kate Medhurst lying bleeding and half-naked upon the cot. And he thought of her in the water, her body so slender and pale against the large dark silhouette of the shark. And the way that, even as he dived from *Raven's* stern, the scarlet plume had already clouded the clear turquoise water. And more than any of that he thought of that look in her eyes of raw, brutal honesty, exposing the woman beneath with all her strengths and vulnerabilities, and the sensations that had vibrated between them. Desire. Attraction. Connection. Sensations with a force he had not felt before. Sensations that he could not yield to even if what had just happened had not.

As he watched *Coyote*, his eyes narrowed in speculation. He was still thinking about it when he heard Gunner's approach and glanced round.

'It is an abrasion only.' His heavy leather coat hung over his friend's arm. Gunner chucked it on to the floor and spread it out to dry in the sun. 'The shark's skin has grazed one side of her waist—from beneath her breast to the top of her hip. And the palms of her hands, too, where she must have pushed against it.'

'How deep?'

'Mercifully superficial,' Gunner replied. 'She will be sore for a few days, but she will heal.'

Kit gave a nod.

'What I do not understand is what on earth she was doing in the water.' Gunner shook his head as if he could not understand it.

'Swimming,' answered Kit.

'Surely not?'

'You saw her.'

'Maybe she fell.'

'She did not fall. Her dress was removed and neatly folded.'

'Not necessarily,' countered Gunner.

'She might have removed it for other purposes.'

'Such as?'

'Bathing.'

'With no means to reboard the ship?'

'A woman might not think.'

'Kate Medhurst certainly doesn't strike me as woman who might not think—quite the reverse. I would say, rather, that she has a shrewd intelligence lacking in many a man.'

'I concede you may have point there. She was not bathing,' said Kit. 'She was swimming. With purpose. Away from *Raven*.'

Gunner nodded. 'But there is nothing out there save those rocks. Even if she reached them, what would have been the point?'

'The rocks are not quite the only thing out there.' Kit's gaze shifted pointedly to the horizon and the small dark shape of the pirate ship that followed.

'You cannot seriously be suggesting that she was trying to escape us to wait for them.'

'I am not suggesting anything.'

'But you are thinking.'

'I am always thinking, Gunner.'

'And what are you thinking?'

'I am thinking we need to discover a little more about Mrs Medhurst and her presence upon *Coyote*.'

When Kate woke the next morning she thought for a minute that she was aboard *Coyote* heading back to Tallaholm and Ben and Bea, and her heart lifted with the prospect of seeing those two little faces again and hugging her children to her. But before her eyes even opened to see the truth, the sound of English voices faint and up on deck brought her crashing back down to the reality of where she was and what had happened. She remembered it all with a sudden blinding panic: *Coyote* and Tobias and North; and the shark; and that North had saved her life by risking his own.

Yesterday seemed like a dream. She might not have believed it had truly happened at all were it not for the ache in her body and the prickle of pain in her side every time she breathed; a dream in which she could not get the image of him appearing in the ocean between her and the shark out of her mind. What kind of man jumped into the water beside a ten-foot shark to rescue a woman he did not know? Not any kind of man that Kate had ever met.

She thought of the way he had pulled her to safety with no concern for himself. She thought of how she had clung to him, in a way she had never been with any other man save Wendell during their lovemaking. But most of all she thought of the gentleness of his fingers stroking the sodden strand of hair away from her cheek. Such a small but significant gesture that made her squeeze her eyes closed in embarrassment and guilt. She thought of Wendell and the memory reminded her that she hated the English and she hated North. She had to remember. Always. She could not afford to let herself soften to him. Because of Wendell and because of who she was.

Yesterday had been an aberration caused by the shock of the shark…and the rescue. This morning she was back to her usual strong self. She was Le Voile. With images of Wendell, little Ben and baby Bea in her mind, she hardened her resolve.

On the hook of the cabin door hung her black dress, her newly dried shift with its faint bloodstain and her pocket. The sight suddenly reminded her of the rest of what she normally wore. Her heart missed a beat. Throwing back the bedcover, and unmindful of her nakedness or the way her newly scabbed side protested, she sprang from the bed and got down on her knees to check her hiding place under the cot, but the holstered weapons were still there just as she had left them. With a sigh of relief she sat down on the bed. And thought.

North was not stupid. He was going to ask questions. About what she was doing in the water. And the thought frightened her. But one of the best forms of defence was attack and so Kate had no intention of just sitting here waiting meekly for the interrogation.

On the washstand in the corner, someone had sat a fresh pitcher of water, brandy and some fresh dressings. Kate wasted no more time. The dressings Gunner had applied had stuck to the dried clotted blood. She eased the mired dressings from her side using the water and dabbed the fresh flow of blood with the brandy, ignoring the sting of it. The wound made wearing her holsters an impossibility. Much as she would have felt more comfortable with them in place she left them where they were. Then, she quickly dressed, tying her pocket in place beneath her skirt, and fixing her hair the best she could with her fingers and the few pins that remained. She stood there, looking into the small peering glass fixed to the wall, for a few moments longer. Calming herself, waxing her courage and determination, readying herself. One final deep breath and she went to face North.

'Come in.' Kit did not raise his eyes from the open ledger before him when the knock sounded at the door. He was expecting Jones the Purser with a list of the supplies needed. It was the silence that alerted him to the fact that it was not Jones that stood before him. He marginally shifted his gaze and caught sight of a pair of feminine bare feet peeping from beneath the hem of the black dress he had hung on the back of Kate Medhurst's cabin door.

'Mrs Medhurst.' He set his pen down, rose to his feet and bowed, as if they were in a polite sitting room of one of London's *ton*. 'Take a seat, please.' He waited until she lowered herself on to one of the chairs on the other side of the desk before resuming his own seat. 'I did not think you would be recovered enough to be out of bed today.'

'I am very well recovered, thank you, sir.' Following yesterday's lapse, her armour was back in place. Her head was held high with that slight underlying hostility that was always there for him. There was the same expression in her clear grey eyes, politeness flecked with strength and defiance, wariness and dislike.

Most women would have still been abed, waiting for Gunner to dress their wounds. Kate Medhurst had not waited for Gunner...or for him and his questions. The grazes on her hands were the only visible evidence of what she had endured the previous day.

'How are your hands?'

'Healing.' She held out her hands before her, palms up for him to see, a gesture of revealing herself to him, a clever tactic given that he suspected that, aside from yesterday, Kate Medhurst had revealed nothing of the truth of herself.

'And the rest?' His eyes held hers.

'The same.' She did not look away.

He let the silence stretch, let that slight tension that buzzed between them build, until she glanced away with a small cynical smile.

'I came to thank you,' she said, taking control of the situation and looking at him once again.

'For what?' He leaned back in his chair, watching her.

She raised her eyebrows in an exaggerated quizzing. 'For rescuing me.'

'Is that what I did?' he said softly. *Rescuing her...or preventing the escape of a prisoner.*

The ambiguity of the words threw her off kilter for the tiniest moment. He could see it in the *frisson* of doubt and fear that snaked in those cool, unruffled eyes of hers, before she masked it.

'How else would you describe it, Captain?' she asked.

'A lunchtime swim,' he said.

Despite herself she smiled at that and averted her gaze with a tiny disbelieving shake of her head.

He smiled, too. And then hit her with the question. 'What were you doing in the water, Mrs Medhurst?' His voice was soft, but the words were sharp.

Her eyes returned to his. The hint of a smile still played around her lips. 'Swimming. At lunchtime.'

'As I suspected,' he said.

They looked at one another, the amusement masking so much more beneath.

'Tell me about Kate Medhurst.'

'What do you wish to know?'

'How she came to be aboard *Coyote*.'

'In what way do women normally found upon privateer or pirate vessels come to be there?' she countered.

'Were you abducted?'

'Abduction is a delicate question for any woman.'

She was good. 'As is the question of allegiance, I suppose.'

'I do not know what you mean, sir.'

'I am sure that you do.'

She said nothing. Just looked at him with that calm unruffled confidence that hid everything of what was true or untrue about her.

'Where are you from, Mrs Medhurst?'

'Louisiana, America.' She said it with defensive pride, wielding it like a weapon. 'And you?'

'London, England.'

Her eyes narrowed ever so slightly at his answer.

'Why do I get the feeling that I am not your favourite person?' he asked.

'Delusions of persecution?' she suggested, and arched one delicate eyebrow.

He laughed at that. And she smiled, but the tension was still there simmering beneath the surface between them.

'I don't expect you can take me home to Louisiana,' she said.

'No.'

'Too dangerous for you?' she taunted.

'Most definitely.'

'So, Captain North,' she said in a soft voice that belied the steel in her eyes, 'what are you planning to do with me?'

'We are for Antigua to replenish our water and stores before our journey to England. There is a British naval base there, they will arrange your transport home.'

'Thank you.' She gave a single nod of her head.

The conversation had been conducted on her terms. Now she terminated it at will. 'If you will excuse me, sir...' She rose to her feet.

And as manners dictated he did the same. He waited until she reached the door and her fingers had touched to the handle before he spoke again. 'I had presumed you would be happy to travel with us to Antigua. Is that the case?'

'Of course. Why wouldn't I be?'

'Why, indeed?' he asked.

The quiet words hung in the air between them.

Her eyes held his a moment longer and the tension seemed to intensify and rustle between them. About unanswered questions, implications and the physicality of yesterday.

'Good day, Captain North.'

'Good day, Mrs Medhurst.' Her bare feet were silent upon the floor. The door closed with a click behind her.

He stood where he was, his eyes fixed on the closed door. In his mind he was seeing the one moment when Kate Medhurst had let her mask fall, in the ocean faced with death. Then there had been nothing of poise or polish or clever tricks. Only a pair of dove-grey eyes that had ignited desires he thought long suppressed. Eyes that made him remember too well the press of her half-naked body against his and the soft feel of her, and the scent of her in his nose. Eyes that were almost enough to make a man forget the vow he had sworn...as if he ever could.

He sat back down at the desk and, picking up his pen, curbed the route his thoughts were taking. He wanted her, he acknowledged. But he could not have her, not even were she not hiding something from him. Not even if she were available and she wanted him, too. He thought of that vow, forged in blood and sweat and tears.

A knock sounded at the door, pulling him from the darkness of the memory. This time it was Jones, and Kit was glad of it.

Kate Medhurst was not being entirely truthful. But whatever it was she was hiding, she and it need have no bearing on his returning La Voile to London.

The afternoon was as beautiful as the morning. Every day was beautiful around this area, except when hurricane season came. Kate did not have to feign that she appreciated the view as she stood at the stern, watching the crystal-clear green waves and the intense warm blue of the sky so expansive and huge…and the distant speck of a ship against its horizon.

North was on the quarterdeck, issuing commands to his men. Her muscles were still tense, her blood still rushing, her skinned palms still clammy from their confrontation in his cabin that morning. Part of her wanted to stay hidden below decks in her cabin, not wanting to face him, but Kate knew she could not do that. *Coyote* was coming. So she stood on the deck, brazening it out, watching Sunny Jim struggle to catch them, and breathed a sigh of relief that Gunner seemed to be right about *Raven* having the superior speed.

As she watched she thought of North's cabin, a cabin that she would have mistaken for that of an ordinary seaman had it not been for its larger space. Everything in it was functional. There were no crystal decanters of brandy on fancy-worked dining tables, no china plates or ornamentation, no crystal-dropped chandelier as she had expected. Everything was Spartan, functional, austere as the man himself. He did not seem given to indulgences or luxuries. Maybe that was why the men liked him. Or maybe they were just afraid of him. She slid a glance at where he stood with his men, seeing the respect on their listening faces, before returning her gaze to *Coyote*.

There was no tread of footsteps to warn her of his approach, nothing save the shiver that rippled down the length of her spine as North came to stand by her side, his body mirroring her own stance, his gaze sweeping out over the ocean.

'Enjoying the view, Mrs Medhurst?' The Englishness of his accent, cool and deep and dark as chocolate, sent a tingle rippling out over her skin.

'Indeed I am, Captain North.' And she was, now that there seemed little danger of *Coyote* catching *Raven*.

Those dark eyes shifted to look directly into hers. Watchful, appraising, making her feel as though he could see through all of her defences, all of her lies, making her remember who he was, and who she was, making her shiver with awareness that his focus was all on her.

She glanced down, suddenly afraid that he could see the secrets she was hiding, her eyes fixing on his feet that were now as bare as her own and the rest of his crew's. Her mother always said you could tell a lot about a man by his feet. North's were much bigger feet than hers, tanned and unmistakably masculine, with long straight toes and nails that were white and short and clean. Strong-looking feet, grounded and sure as the rest of him. Their feet standing so close together, and bare, looked too intimate, as if they had just climbed from bed. The thought shocked her.

She swiftly raised her eyes and found him still watching her. He smiled, not the arctic smile, or the cynical one, but one that told her he knew something of the direction of her thoughts and shared them. Swallows soared and swooped inside her stomach and her cheeks burned hot. Kate was horrified at her reaction. And North knew it, damn him, for the smile became bigger.

With an angry frosty demeanour she turned her attention back to the horizon and focused her thoughts on Wendell and his sweet kind nature: her husband, her lover, the only man for her. She thought of what men like North had done to him and the weakness was gone. Touching the thin gold wedding band she still wore upon her finger, turning it round and round, she drew strength from it and did not look at North again.

The two of them stood in silence, contemplating the view, watching *Coyote*.

She hoped that he would leave, go back to the work he was normally so busy with, but North showed no sign of moving.

The scene was beautiful and peaceful, but as they stood there seemingly both relaxed it was anything but ease that hummed between them; or maybe the tension was just all in herself.

'She makes for interesting watching,' he said eventually, his gaze not moving from where it was fixed on *Coyote*.

'I wasn't watching her in particular,' she lied.

'No? My mistake. Pardon me.' He flicked a glance at Kate.

'Have you identified her yet?'

'We have.'

Her eyes met his.

'La Voile's pirates.' He paused. 'They are following us.' He waited for her reaction.

'Why would they do that?'

'Why indeed?'

She kept her nerve. 'Vengeance? Or maybe to reclaim their captain's body.'

'Maybe,' he agreed, and shifted his gaze to *Coyote*.

'But they will not catch us, will they? Not with *Raven's* superior speed. I mean...we are quite safe from them... are we not?'

'Oh, rest assured we are safe.' He smiled at her, the small cool dangerous smile. 'But *Coyote* is not.'

She felt the cold wind of fear blow through her bones. 'What do you mean, sir?' She worked hard to appear cool, calm and collected.

He glanced pointedly at *Raven's* sails. Her gaze followed his and she saw to her horror that they were reducing the sail. *Raven's* speed was already dropping.

Her heart missed a beat. Her stomach dropped to meet her shoes.

'You intend to let them catch us!' She stared at him, feeling the horror of what that meant snake through her.

'Not entirely. Just to let them get within range of our guns.'

'Why?' she whispered.

'*Raven* is fast, but not fast enough that *Coyote* will not fathom our direction to Antigua. Better a confrontation out here under our terms than risk her stealing upon us at anchor in the night.'

'She would not...' Antigua was a British naval base, filled with warships that *Coyote* normally avoided. But given the situation she was not sure that North was not right.

'Not when we have finished, she will not,' he said grimly.

She felt the blood drain from her face. When she looked again at the distant horizon *Coyote* was already a little larger. She kept her gaze on her ship rather than look at him, so that he would not see the truth in her eyes.

It took all of her willpower to stand there beside him, watching her men creep slowly closer to their doom, and betray nothing of the feelings of dread and fear, impotence and anger that were pounding through her blood. Instinctively, her hands went to her skirt, reaching for the weapons that were not there. Instead, she forced them to relax by her sides.

Glancing across at North's profile, she saw that he watched *Coyote* with cool, relaxed stillness. Only his dark hair rippled in the wind.

'What is the range of your guns?' she asked, her heart beating fast with the hope that she had overestimated *Raven's* range of fire.

'Our eighteen pounders have an effective penetrating range of five hundred and fifty yards,' he answered without looking round.

Far greater than the two hundred and eighty yards that *Coyote's* six-pounders could manage. She felt sick. Her mind was thrashing, seeking any possible way to stop the impending slaughter. But short of putting a gun to North's head… Her gaze dropped to the large scabbard that hung against his leg, and the leather holster above it…with the pistol cradled within. It was a much larger weapon than her own, but she could manage it all the same…if it was loaded. She glanced up to find his gaze was no longer on *Coyote*, but on her.

'I hope that pistol is loaded,' she said.

He smiled as if he knew it for the question it was. 'Always. But it will not make any difference to *Coyote's* fate. Bigger guns are already aimed and waiting.'

She swallowed, her mouth dry as ash, her heart thudding hard as a horse at full gallop. *Coyote* would see the guns, but she would not realise their size, or the special powder, or their range. She would not know what she was sailing into before it was too late.

Raven was barely moving now, making the distance between the two ships diminish fast. Too fast. Even with the naked eye, no one aboard *Raven* could doubt that the identity of the closing ship was anything but *Coyote*. Every second brought her closer.

Kate's fingers found her wedding band again. *Oh, God, please stop them.* But *Coyote* kept on coming.

'Eight hundred yards!' came a shout from the rigging.

She bit her lip, trying to stop herself from crying out. Stood there still and silent as a statue while her mind sought and tunnelled and tried to find a way out for them all.

'Seven hundred yards!'

She thought of Sunny Jim. She thought of young John Rishley. And the rest. All of them men from Tallaholm. Men with wives and children, with mothers and fathers, and brothers and sisters. Men who would lose their lives trying to rescue her.

'You can't just kill them!' The words burst from her mouth.

'Why not?' He turned to look at her, his calmness in such contrast to the rushing fury and fear in her heart.

'For the sake of humanity and Christian charity.'

'You care for the lives of the men who abducted you?'

'Some of them are barely more than boys, for pity's sake. Have mercy.'

'Your compassion is remarkable, Mrs Medhurst.'

'Reverend Dr Gunner is a priest. He will tell you the same as me, I am sure. Where is he?' Her eyes scanned for Gunner.

'He is on the gun deck,' said North, 'making ready to fire.'

She could see the fifteen horizontal red-and-white stripes and the fifteen white stars against the blue canton of the American flag and the skull and smiling cutlass of her own flag.

'Six hundred yards!' the voice called, followed by another from over by the deck hatch, 'Ready below, Captain! We fire on your command.'

'Do not!' Her hand clutched at North's wrist. 'If you sink them, they will all die. And no matter what they have done, they are just men seeking to make a living in difficult times.'

He looked at where she held him so inappropriately. Her fingers tingled and burned with awareness. She loosened her grip, let it fall away completely. 'Please,' she said quietly.

Their eyes locked, their bodies so close that she could feel the heat of his thighs against hers.

'I do not intend to kill them,' he said with equal softness to hers. 'Only to disable them.'

'Five hundred and fifty yards and in range!' the call interrupted.

North turned away and gave the command, 'Fire!'

Her heart contracted to a small tight knot of dread. She heard the echoing boom of a single long gun and watched with horror as the iron shot flew through the air towards its unsuspecting victim.

But the round shot had not been aimed at *Coyote's* hull. Instead, her foremast was cleaved in two, the top half severed clean to fall into the ocean. Canvas and rigging crumpled all around. The men on deck rushed around in mayhem.

Her hands were balled so tight that her nails cut into her skinned palms. She did not notice that they bled as she braced herself for the echoing cacophony of shots that would follow, standing there knowing that she owed it to *Coyote* and her men not to look away, but to bear witness to their valour. She waited.

But there was only silence.

Kate glanced round at North in confusion.

'She is, no doubt, too small to carry spare spars and canvas, but these waters are busy enough that they should not have too long to wait for help. Either way *Coyote* shall not be following us into port, or anywhere else for that matter.' He paused, holding her gaze. 'If you care to check, you will be relieved to see not a pirate life was lost.' He passed her his spyglass and stood watching her.

She looked at the spyglass, knowing she should not accept it. But she could no more refuse than she could stop breathing. The responsibility of a captain to her ship and men ran deep. So Kate took the spyglass and checked for herself the damage to the men and the ship.

North was right. There were no casualties.

'Let her run with the wind,' he commanded his men.

'Aye-aye, Captain,' came the reply as they ran to increase the sails.

Kate returned the spyglass without either a word or meeting North's eyes. She was aware of how much she had betrayed, but all she felt right now was wrung out and limp with relief for her men. She offered not a single excuse or explanation.

'If you will excuse me, sir.'

He did not stop her, but let her walk away without a word.

Because they both knew that she was not going anywhere other than her cabin. They were on his ship. At sea. He could come and question her anytime he chose. And that there were questions he would ask, she did not doubt.

Chapter Four

Within his cabin Kit sat at his desk, the paperwork and ledgers and maps upon it forgotten for now. Gunner sat opposite him, leaning his chair back on to its hind two legs and rocking it. The afternoon sunlight was bright. Through the great stern window the ocean was clear and empty, the disabled *Coyote* long since left behind.

There was a silence while Gunner mulled over what Kit had just told him of Kate Medhurst's reaction up on deck earlier that day.

'Women are the gentler sex. Their sensibilities are more finely honed than those of most men,' said Gunner, 'but...' He screwed up his face.

'One might have expected a degree of either fear or animosity towards the boatload of ruffians that took her by force and held her against her will,' Kit finished for him.

Gunner nodded. 'It is possible she has an unusually meek nature.'

I hope that pistol is loaded? Kate Medhurst had looked at the weapon like a woman seriously contemplating snatching it from its holster and holding it to his head.

He thought of the essence of forbidden desire that whispered between the two of them, the barely veiled hostility in those eyes of hers and the way her body had responded so readily to his.

He thought of her plunging from *Raven's* head and swimming so purposefully towards those rocks. And of their interaction in his cabin, with her skilful deflection of his questions to reveal nothing of herself.

'I would not describe Kate Medhurst as meek.' Intelligent, determined, formidable, capable, mysterious, courageous and passionate, most definitely passionate. But not meek. 'Would you?'

'No,' Gunner admitted.

'Mrs Medhurst was not so unwilling a guest upon *Coyote*.'

Gunner's gaze met his. 'You think she is lying about being abducted?'

'She never told us she was abducted. We made that assumption. Mrs Medhurst did not correct it.'

'But you saw how the pirates treated her.'

'La Voile would have given her to us easily enough. The rest did not wish to yield her.'

'She was afraid of them.'

'She was afraid, but not of them...*for* them.' He thought of the desperation that had driven her to grab his wrist, to plead for the lives of those men. 'There is someone on *Coyote* that she cares for, very much.'

'A lover.'

Kit thought of the way Kate Medhurst touched so often to the gold wedding band upon her finger. 'Or a husband.'

Gunner looked at him in silence for a moment. 'You think it was not La Voile's body his crew were intent on retrieving. You think it was the woman.'

'It would explain much.'

'But not what we saw between her and La Voile on *Coyote's* deck that morning.'

'Does it not? If we remove our assumptions, what did we see, Gabriel?' Kit asked.

'An argument between two men over a woman,' Gunner said slowly. 'The other pirate...'

'It is a possibility.'

'The only fly in the ointment is her mourning weeds.'

'Are they mourning weeds? A ship that flies a black sail is not in mourning.'

Gunner looked at him and said slowly, 'A pirate's woman might dress as a pirate.'

Kit said nothing.

'And if she is a pirate's woman?' Gunner asked.

'It makes no difference. As long as we have La Voile's body she is not our concern. We offload her in Antigua in the morning. Let them ship her back to Louisiana. We have bigger things to think of.' Like getting La Voile's body back to London. Like returning to face what he had left behind. 'Post a guard on La Voile's body in the meantime.'

'You think she is capable of sabotage?'

'I think we should not underestimate Kate Medhurst. I will breathe easier when she is gone.' And he would. Because every time he thought of her, he felt desire stir through his body. She was temptation, to a life he had long left behind, to a man he no longer was. And that was a road Kit had no intention of revisiting.

The purple-grey-green silhouette of Antigua loomed large before them. The haze of the early morning would burn off as the day progressed, but for now the sun sat behind a shroud that did not mask the brightness from the daylight. Within the rowing boat there was no sound other than the rhythmic creak and dip of the oars and their pull of the water. No one in *Raven's* small party spoke.

The wind that was usually so mercifully cooling seemed

unwelcome at this hour with the lack of sun, making Kate's skin goosepimple beneath the thin black muslin. Or maybe it was just the sight of North in his place at the other end of the boat.

His eyes were sharp as the raven's perched upon his shoulder and strayed her way too often, making her remember the lean strength in his body, and the scent of him, and the feel of his skin against hers...and the way he had stroked the hair from her cheek. Making her feel things she had never thought to feel again; things that appalled her to feel for him of all men. And she was gladder than ever that this was the end of her journey with him.

But there was a small traitorous part of her that, now she was safe, wondered what might have happened between them were it not the end. Just the thought turned her cold with shame and guilt. She pushed it away, denying its existence, as much as she denied the tension between them was not all adversarial. And turned her mind to wondering as to her crew and *Coyote's* fate.

North was right, these waters were rife with Baratarian pirates and privateers; one of Jean Lafitte's boys had probably already found and helped the stricken ship. Sunny Jim knew what he was doing and would get them all back safe to Tallaholm, and she felt better at that thought.

'Something is not right,' Kit said softly to Gunner as they stood before Fort Berkeley on the island not so much later. Jones the Purser and five ordinary seamen who had rowed across with them had stayed in the main town, St John's, to procure water and the list of required victuals. Kate Medhurst stood just in front of him, surveying the yellow-washed walls of the fort that guarded the entrance to English Harbour. She was more relaxed than he had seen her, now that they were about to part company, her secrets intact. He wondered what they were. He wondered too much about her, he thought, as his eyes lingered on the way the wind whipped and fluttered the thin black muslin of her skirt against the long length of her legs. He turned his focus back to the fort and what it was that he did not like about it.

Gunner gave a nod. 'I get that same feeling.'

'No guard outside the gate.' His eyes scanned, taking in every detail.

'And apart from the lookout in the watchtower, not another soul to be seen,' murmured Gunner.

'Silent as a graveyard, and a gate that should be opening, demanding to know our business by now.'

Kate Medhurst glanced round at him, as if she was thinking the same.

'Wait here with the woman, Gunner. If I am not back in fifteen minutes—'

'I'm coming with you,' Kate Medhurst interrupted, as if she did not trust him.

'Maybe Mrs Medhurst has a point,' said Gunner. 'You should have someone at your back.' He touched a hand lightly to his cutlass.

Eventually they were admitted through the fort's gate by a lone marine in a coat faded pink by the sun and taken to see the admiral. The distant dry docks were empty, not a man could be seen working in the repair yards, not a man on the tumbleweed parade ground. Within the yellow-painted building every room was deserted. Not one other person did they pass along those corridors and staircases lined with paintings of maritime battles. And for all of that way there was a faint smell of rancid meat in the air.

'It's like a ghost town,' Kate Medhurst whispered by his side and she was right. 'Is this normal for a British fort?'

'Anything but,' replied Kit softly.

'Something is definitely off.' Gunner's quiet voice held the same suspicion that Kit felt.

He shifted his coat so that his hand would have easier access to both the pistol holstered on his hip and his cutlass and saw Gunner do the same.

The marine eventually led them through a door mounted with a plaque that read Admiral Sir Ralston.

The office was large and more grandly decorated than many a *ton* drawing room. Ornate, gilded, carved furniture filled it, along with a massive sideboard that looked as though it might have been brought from Admiralty House. There was a large black-marble fireplace, although the hearth was empty save for a pile of scrunched balls of paper which were clearly discarded letters. The windows had roman blinds of indiscriminate colour, pulled halfway up the glass, and were framed by fringed curtains that might once have been dark blue, but were now somewhere between pale blue and grey. From the ceiling in the centre of the room hung a crystal chandelier. But despite all of this faded opulence there was an unkempt feel about the place.

The great desk was littered with a mess of paperwork and documents. A thick layer of dust covered the window sill and every visible wooden surface. It sat on the back of the winged armchair by the fireplace and turned the ringed, empty crystal decanter and silver tray that sat on the nearby drum table opaque. It hung with cobwebs from the chandelier. But the two things that concerned Kit more than any of this were the stench of rum in the room and that the man that sat on the other side of the desk was not Admiral Sir Ralston.

'Acting Admiral John Jenkins, at your service, sir. I am afraid Admiral Sir Ralston died a sennight since.' Jenkins was younger than Kit, no more than five and twenty at the most, with fine fair hair that stuck to a sweaty brow, red-rimmed eyes and thick determined lips.

'I am sorry to hear that, sir. My condolences to you and your men.'

Jenkins gave a nod and gestured to the chairs on the other side of the desk. 'Take a seat. May I offer you a drink?' He produced a bottle of rum from the drawer of his desk.

'There is a lady present, sir,' said Gunner.

'Beg pardon,' Jenkins said and sat the half-empty bottle on top of a book on the desk. 'How are matters in London?'

'I have no idea.' Kit had no intention in wasting time in small talk. 'What has happened here?'

'We are awaiting reinforcements. They are due any day now.'

'You have not answered my question. Why do you need reinforcements?'

'We have lost almost all the men.'

'How?'

There was a silence while Jenkins stared longingly at the rum.

'What happened to the men, Jenkins?'

'Dead,' he said, and did not take his eyes off the bottle. He reached a hand to it and began to absently pick at the wax near the rim. 'It will have us all in the end. Every last one of us, you know.' He smiled softly to himself.

Cold realisation stroked down Kit's spine. He understood now, not the detail, but the gist. Too late. He was here now, and more importantly so were Gunner and Kate Medhurst.

'Get up,' he snapped the order to them by his side, already on his feet. 'We are leaving.'

'What?' She looked aghast. 'But—'

'I said we are leaving. Now.'

'So soon?' interrupted Jenkins. 'You are welcome to stay and dine with Hammond and me.' He smiled at Kate and walked round to their side of the desk. 'It would be a delight to have the company of a lady at our table.' He offered his hand to Kate.

Kate moved to accept, but Kit grabbed her hand in his and pulled her away from Jenkins, placing himself as a barrier between them.

'Captain North!' she protested and tried to break free.

'They have a pestilence here,' he said harshly to her. 'A pestilence that infects both men and women.'

She ceased her struggle, shock and fear flickering in her eyes.

'Which disease, sir?' Gunner asked Jenkins, the scientist and physician in him coming to the fore.

'Yellow Jack.'

'May God have mercy upon your souls, brother,' whispered Gunner.

'Amen to that,' said Jenkins.

'What were you thinking of, admitting us?' demanded Kit. 'You know the drill when it comes to pestilence.'

Jenkins smiled again and this time it held a bit of a leer. 'Hammond said you had a woman with you. A white woman. An English woman.' His gaze travelled brazenly down Kate Medhurst's body to rest on the small bare toes that peeped out beneath the hem of her dress.

In a prim angry gesture she twitched her skirt to cover them. 'American,' she corrected with a look of disgust that Kit could not tell whether it was due to Jenkins's appetite or the fact he had mistaken her as English.

'How many of you are left?' Kit shot the question at him.

'A handful.'

'How many infected?'

Jenkins gave a shrug.

Gunner slid a look at him. They both knew there was nothing they could do, that it was too late.

'Quarantine the place. Let no one new in and no one infected out. Burn the bodies of the dead,' said Kit. It was the most he could offer. He pitied Jenkins. He wanted to help and were he alone he would have stayed, for all the difference it would make, but he was not. He had Gunner and a shipful of men to think of. And he had Kate Medhurst.

'It is too late for that.'

Kit met Jenkins's eyes and said nothing. Given his own past he could not condemn any man for a weakness of character, especially not under such circumstances.

'I pity you, sir, but your attitude is despicable,' said Kate Medhurst quietly.

'I suppose that means a mercy shag is out of the question?' Jenkins said.

Kate did not flinch. 'As I said—despicable.'

'And dead,' said Kit as his hand tightened upon the handle of his cutlass. He controlled the urge to pull it from its scabbard and hold it against Jenkins's throat.

Gunner was already on his feet, poised for action.

'But not by our hand,' finished Kit, then, to Kate Medhurst and Gunner, 'Move. We have already spent too long in here.' Not trusting Jenkins not to attempt some last, defiant, contemptuous action, Kit kept his eye on the man until they were out of the office and making their way back down the corridor. Moving quickly, they retraced their earlier steps across the deserted yard and through the gate.

The hired horse and gig still waited where they had left it. In silence Kit picked up the reins and began the drive back to St John's.

'So what happens now?' Kate asked the question after ten minutes of driving during which no one had uttered a word. She was more shaken by what had happened at the fort than she wanted to admit. A whole garrison, wiped out by Yellow Jack.

One summer, when she was a child, Yellow Jack had come to Tallaholm. Some were taken, some were spared. Kate had been lucky enough to recover. She remembered little of it, but her mother still spoke of how terrible that time had been and how she had nursed Kate. *I sat by your side and bathed your body with cold stream water all the nights through to cool the fever.* It made her all the more anxious to get home. But she was very aware that there was no British navy ship here on which she could hitch a ride.

She saw the glance Gunner exchanged with North and a little sliver of apprehension slid into her blood.

'You heard what he said. Your country is sending re-inforcements and that will encompass not only the fort, but those frigates that patrol the waters near to Louisiana,' she said.

'No doubt.' North did not look round at her, but just kept on driving, eyes forward, expression uncompromising.

'Indeed, many of the British naval frigates in this area use English Harbour as their base. It's just a matter of time before one comes into port.'

'True. But that time might be weeks or even months.'

'Unlikely,' she countered.

'Very likely, given that word of the pestilence will have passed through the fleet.'

'I'll wait,' she said stubbornly.

'But I will not. *Raven* leaves Antigua tomorrow, Mrs Medhurst.'

'Fine,' she said. 'I am not asking you to delay your journey.' Indeed, the sooner he was gone the safer she would be.

He pulled gently at the leather reins wrapped around his hand and brought the horse to a stop. Only then did he look at her, his gaze meeting hers with that searing strength that always made her shiver inside. 'You are a woman, with no money, no protection and no knowledge of the island. Are you seriously suggesting that you wait here alone?'

That was exactly what she was suggesting, but when he said it like that it made it sound like the most idiotic idea she had ever had in her life; when she knew that honour belonged to her decision to attack an unnamed ship with a raven circling its masts.

'Next you will be telling me you are planning on staying at Fort Berkeley with Jenkins.'

'Don't be absurd!' she snapped. 'I am not a fool.'

'Then do not act like one.'

She glared at him. 'Are you offering to take me home to Louisiana, Captain North?'

'No.' No superfluous explanation.

'So just what is it that you are proposing, Mr Clever?'

'We take you with us to England. Admiralty will put you on a frigate escorting one of the convoys bound for America.'

'England?' She could not believe what she was hearing. 'You expect me to travel all the way to England and hope that I may find my way back from there?'

'There is nothing of hope involved. I will ensure that you obtain safe passage.'

She stared at him with utter incredulity. 'But that will take months.'

'So will waiting here amidst the pestilence for a frigate to drop anchor.'

What he said made sense, yet the thought of sailing thousands of miles to England…and with him of all people… She bit her lip, torn between the devil and the deep blue sea.

His gaze held hers, unwavering and steadfast, cool and perceptive, stroking all of the nerves to tingle in her body. 'And the longer you stay here the greater your risk of contracting Yellow Jack, or carrying it with you when you eventually do find passage back to Louisiana.'

To her children, to those she loved, to a community that was already struggling against hardship and feared the disease more than any other.

'The choice is yours to make, Mrs Medhurst. There is a place for you on *Raven* should you wish to accept it.'

But the reality was that her choice was already made. Kate could not risk either her children or Tallaholm. So she swallowed her pride and quashed the trepidation that gnawed deep in her belly. 'You are right, sir,' she admitted even though it galled her to do so. 'I would be a fool, indeed, if I did not accept your offer.'

He gave a nod and said nothing more. The rest of the journey continued in silence.

Only once they reached the main street of the town did he speak again, addressing his words to Reverend Dr Gunner. 'I will return the gig and do what must be done.' From his pocket he produced a purse that looked heavy with coin and threw it to the priest. 'Find Mrs Medhurst a dressmaker.'

'That will not be necessary, sir!' She felt her cheeks flush with warmth. Only husbands and lovers bought women clothes.

His gaze met hers, then dropped lower from her face to slowly sweep the length of her body before returning to her eyes once more. It was not a leer—a leer she could have handled with a smart put down—but his usual cool, intense, serious appraisal made her blush glow even hotter.

'The Atlantic is a harsh and cold environment. Your attire will not suffice.'

Always so cold and clinical, and yet there was something at the back of his eyes that hinted he was not as devoid of passion and feeling as he would have the world believe. Something dark that made the memory of his strong arms around her and the feel of their bodies pressed tight and close whisper between them, that made her remember the tenderness of his fingers against her face. The butterflies danced in her stomach. Her whole body seemed to quiver.

'And as Gunner is clearly a man of the cloth your reputation should not be so damaged.'

Pulling her gaze from his, she looked at Gunner, who smiled a sheepish smile. She glanced down to her bare toes next to the dusty leather of North's boots.

'Very well. But your money is a loan only. I will pay you back every last coin.'

'If you wish.'

Cool as a business deal to any observer, but what she felt inside was a heat of embarrassment and awareness of a dangerous sensual connection. It made her manner cold almost to the point of rudeness.

'I do, sir.' She climbed down from the gig and walked away without so much as a backward glance.

She did not want to think about being enclosed upon *Raven* for the entirety of a transatlantic journey with him. She did not want to think of the dangers that posed for her. Because if she thought of the enormity of it the fear would overwhelm her. Even now, the seeds of panic stirred in her belly. She stifled them and followed Gunner into the crowded, dusty market square of St John's.

And then, through the mass and press of bodies and woven baskets filled with brightly coloured produce, she saw a face that she recognised and she smiled. Maybe God had heard her prayers, after all.

With one eye on the face she bided her time and, as the crowd pressed closer, she slipped away from Gunner.

'What do you mean, you lost her?' Kit raised an eyebrow and stared in disbelief at his friend.

'Exactly that,' replied Gunner calmly. 'One minute she was right there behind me, the next she was gone without a sign. It is market day. The square could not get any busier.' He paused before adding, 'You do not think that she might have been abducted?'

'Again?' Kit said the word with heavy scepticism. They both knew that Kate Medhurst's presence aboard *Coyote* had not been through abduction.

'She did not seem so enamoured with accompanying us to England.'

'Hardly surprising.'

'Had she refused, would you really have left her here alone?'

Kit did not answer that one. 'There is another ship newly anchored. She is flying the Stars and Stripes and listing herself as a merchantman, but with a name like *Gator* and the fact that she is here at all, means she is more probably a pirate making the most of the fort's misfortune.'

'There are pirates in town…? We need to find her fast.' Gunner understood what that meant. That American or not, men newly come ashore were always looking for a woman. And Kate Medhurst stood out from the rest of the women in this place.

'You cover the east side, I will take the west.'

Gunner nodded.

Together they set out across the square.

* * *

'Bill Linder!' Kate called the name clear and strong before the two men could head into the tavern.

Linder stopped and glanced round at her. 'I thought I heard a home-grown Louisiana voice. Well, if it ain't little Kate Medhurst.'

'You sly old dog, Billy Boy,' the other shorter man, built like a bear, said with a lascivious tone. 'You didn't tell me that you had a girl here.'

'I'm not his girl,' corrected Kate and moved the small distance down the lane towards them. 'I am allied with Jean Lafitte the same as the two of you. Aboard *Coyote*.'

'La Voile sails *Coyote*,' said the bear man.

'True,' she said, and thought it better to keep quiet about Tobias's death for now. 'You still with McGaw on *Gator*?'

'I sure am. She's out in the bay.' He looked at her with a puzzled expression. 'What you doing here, Kate Medhurst?'

'Looking for a ship home to Louisiana. Fast.'

'You sound like you're escaping someone.'

'Maybe,' she conceded. 'Can you help me?'

'Can I help you? Honey, what did I always say to old Wendell? You have come to the right man, Kate Medhurst.'

She gave a sigh of relief at his words.

He smiled and she saw his gaze meander down over the dusty muslin of her dress, lingering a little too long on the fichu that covered her décolletage, before dropping lower to where the wind had moulded her skirt with a degree of indecency to her legs, all the way down to her dirty bare feet. There was something in that gaze that made her realise that Bill Linder's attitude towards her had changed. Something that was all too obvious when his eyes met hers again.

'How's your wife, Mary, and your two little ones?' she

said, trying to keep things a bit safer and casting her mind back across the years to the last time she had seen this man.

'They're good.'

'Please pass on my best wishes to her.'

'I don't think so. She's the jealous type.' The words made her feel uncomfortable and set a warning tattoo beating in her breast.

'She's got nothing to be jealous of. You were a good friend of my husband's, Bill Linder. I thought you were my friend, too.'

'I was. And I am. But you see—' he leaned in closer, as if to share a secret '—I always did have an eye for Wendell's pretty little wife. And Mary knew it.'

She stared at him, shocked at what she was hearing.

His fingers brushed lazily against the tie of her fichu as if he were toying with the idea of loosening it.

'What the heck do you think you are doing?' She slapped his hand away, but in that moment he changed from lazy insolence to fast striking snake, grabbing hold of her wrist and twisting it up behind her back at the same time as the weight of his body barrelled her into the nearby shady alleyway.

'I think I'm doing what I've waited a long time to do, little lady.' His hands moved over her body, his fingers rough against the still-tender wound on her side, searching for her pocket and finding it empty save for a handkerchief.

'She got a purse of money?' his bear companion asked.

'Nope,' said Bill Linder.

'Oh, dear,' said the bear man. 'She's going have to find some other way of paying her passage on *Gator*. I suppose we could pay her coin for her and in return...' He licked his thick dry lips slowly and deliberately.

'In return...' said Bill Linder with a grin that showed his uneven teeth.

The stench of unwashed men was strong. She could see the grime caked upon their sun-baked skin and feel the length of Bill Linder's dirty fingernails cutting into her wrist.

He threw her further into alleyway so that she stumbled against its wall.

A quick glance told her it was blind-ended. No way out other than through the two pirates from *Gator*.

She backed away, giving herself a little distance, and pulled up her skirts.

'That's right, darlin', you get yourself nice and ready for us,' Linder drawled and began to unbuckle the belt of his trousers.

'Oh, I'm ready for you, boys,' she said, pulling the pistol and knife from their leather holsters on her thighs. 'You wait till Lafitte hears about this. He'll hang you both by your scrawny necks.'

'Lafitte ain't going hear nothing. Put the weapons down, darlin', before you get hurt,' Linder sneered.

'You back out of this alleyway right now, or I will shoot.'

'And then what?' Linder asked.

The two men exchanged an amused grin with one another.

'We got you all to ourselves, Kate, honey. Haven't you heard? The navy boys are down with Yellow Jack. Ain't no one going to come and help you.'

Linder's eyes held a nasty glint and the bear man laughed as the two of them closed towards her.

Kate aimed the pistol…

'There you are, Mrs Medhurst. I wondered where you had got to.' North's voice was smooth and quiet and cool, but its authority cut through the situation in the alleyway.

Her finger hesitated upon the trigger.

'She's already taken, friend. You're interfering in something that's got nothing to do with you. Go get your own.' The two men turned with a swagger, ready to chase off the intruder come to spoil their fun, but what they saw checked their cocky attitude.

North was standing there, his faded leather coat pulled back to show one hand resting on the handle of his pistol and the other on his cutlass. In the shade of the alleyway his eyes were black as the devil's. With his dark shirt and his buckskin breeches, his battered tricorne hat and the large black-feathered bird that perched silent and beady-eyed upon his left shoulder, he looked every inch what he was: downright dangerous.

He stood there silent, still, his stance relaxed yet poised for action, and emanating such an air of threat that even Kate felt a shiver of fear go through her.

'You are mistaken, gentlemen. You see, this is everything to do with me...given that this lady is under my protection.'

It was his eyes, she thought; there was something in them, something deadly, like the eyes of a shark. Linder and the bear man could feel it, too. She could sense their sudden discomfort and suspicion and fear and see it in the way they glanced at one another.

'I don't think we've been introduced, sir,' said Linder.

'Think very carefully about what you are asking for,' said North.

The raven cawed as if to mock the men.

'Merde,' she heard the bear man whisper as the penny finally dropped and they realised what they should have known straight away from the sight of both him and the raven. 'He's North.'

'Still want that introduction, gentlemen?' North said quietly.

'Begging your pardon, Captain North. We didn't realise that the lady was…in your care.' Linder sounded pathetic.

'We surely did not, sir,' agreed the bear man. 'Our apologies.'

'Not to me,' said North. With a single curt gesture of his head towards her, 'To the lady.'

'Our apologies, ma'am,' they murmured, turning to her. Then quieter, to her, but not North, 'God help you, Kate Medhurst.'

'Get down before her,' North instructed.

They glanced at one another again, but did as he said, kneeling in the sandy soil of the alleyway.

'Lower,' said North. 'On your bellies.'

She saw them swallow their pride, saw the humiliation in their eyes as they obeyed, to lie face down in the dust.

'Did they hurt you?' he asked her.

She shook her head, not trusting herself to speak.

'Then they get to live,' said North. He bent over, and whispered the words quietly to the prostrate men, 'But if there is ever a next time, gentlemen of the *Gator*…' He let the words hang unfinished, but they all understood too well his promise. 'Now, I think you should leave me and the lady together.'

The two of them got to their feet and ran out of the alleyway as if the devil himself, or North, were on their heels. The raven flew off, following them.

Leaving Kate facing North alone, knife in hand, pistol aimed directly at his heart.

Chapter Five

His gaze held hers, yet he spoke not a word.

Her heart was pounding hard and fast. Beneath the grip of both the pistol and knife her palms were clammy. Her mouth went dry.

'I had it under control. I can defend myself, sir.'

'So I see,' he said in that quiet sensual voice that made the goosebumps break out across her naked skin. His gaze dropped to the weapons still clutched tight within her fingers, before coming back to her eyes. 'Do you want to put them away now?'

She was not sure that she did. Not because she thought he would hurt her, but because of what might happen when she did. The tension seemed tight enough to break between them. They were standing alone, too close together, in a place shielded from the eyes of others. She could feel the heat of him, sense the dark passion that lurked beneath that cool calm control.

She swallowed. Took a couple of steps back to put some space between them. Turned her back to stow the weapons safely once more.

He was leaning against the wall of the alleyway, waiting, when she faced him once more.

Their gazes held, his with such dark intensity that

she feared how much he might have overheard before he stepped into the alleyway.

Neither of them spoke.

Neither of them moved.

She felt like she was trembling inside, from the shock of what Linder had almost done and from the feelings that overwhelmed her when she looked in North's eyes. Of attraction. Of desire. Of a need so raw and guttural she could no longer deny it.

He walked closer.

Kate knew she should move away, but she didn't. She just stood there, knowing what was coming, her eyes never leaving his.

Reaching a hand out, he threaded it through the back of her hair. He hesitated only a moment longer before his mouth met hers and their bodies came together, and he kissed her just as she wanted, exactly how she needed. A kiss that was inviting and passionate and filled with all of the stormy intensity that was in her own soul.

He tasted of something divine, his tongue enticing her own. He was masterful yet not forceful, gentle yet passionate. And his kiss woke other parts of her, parts she had thought long laid to rest. Needs and desires, passions and longing. The feel of him, the touch of him, the scent of clean man and leather and sunshine and sea…and just *North*. And then she caught what she was doing—kissing him. Kissing the first man since Wendell…the only man other than Wendell. And not just any man—North. An Englishman. A man who made his money from killing privateers and pirates.

She broke the kiss, backed away, confused and embarrassed and ashamed, and angry, too, with herself more than him.

'We should go,' he said.

'We should.' Her voice was cool and firm to hide the quiver and flux of conflicting emotions inside.

'But I will have your weapons first.'

'And you think I am just going to hand them over?' She stared at him.

'You will if you do not want the dressmaker to see them. What would she think?' he asked silkily. 'A pirate ship at anchor and a woman with a pistol and a knife strapped to her thighs turning up in her shop.'

Pirate's moll. The words whispered unspoken between them.

She gritted her teeth and, sliding her hands into the slits in the seams of her skirt, produced the weapons. She looked at him for a moment, almost tempted to use them, before reluctantly yielding them.

'And the holsters,' he said as she watched her weapons disappear into the pockets of his coat.

'What?'

He looked at her.

With an exclamation of disgust, she turned her back, rustled beneath her skirts to unfasten the buckles and finally dropped the leather strapping into his waiting hand.

'Still warm.' He smiled.

She glared at him.

As they walked out of the alleyway together and re-entered the crowded square she felt his hand close firm, but gentle, around her wrist.

'Just in case,' he said softly by her ear. 'I would not want to lose you again.'

Kit was careful not to look at Kate Medhurst again until he had cut a path through the crowd to Gunner.

'Change of plan. You check on the procurement and the men. I will take Mrs Medhurst to the dressmaker.'

He saw the way his friend's eyes moved to Kate Medhurst and Kit's grip upon her, before returning to Kit, and the hint of both curiosity and speculation that was in them, but Gunner was wise enough to say nothing.

Beneath his touch he felt her stiffen and saw the rosy bloom, that had not yet faded from her cheeks since the kiss they had shared, intensify. 'That will not be necessary, Captain North.' Outraged antagonism flashed in her eyes.

'It is entirely necessary.'

Gunner cleared his throat. 'I will see you back on *Raven*.' With a nod, he hurried away, his tall fair frame standing out amongst the shorter dark crowd.

'This way.' Kit directed Kate Medhurst onwards.

'You're not a priest,' she said.

'You noticed,' he replied, but he did not look at her and he did not stop leading her towards the only dressmaker in town.

'Allow me to go in there alone.'

'No.'

He felt the slight resistance in her arm. 'For pity's sake, North, you must be aware of the impression it will give if we enter the shop together.' Her eyes met his, part-appeal, part-indignant anger.

'Fully aware.' He looked at her then—at those beautiful soft grey eyes, and her kiss-swollen lips that tasted like the sweetest thing on earth, and the sensual disarray of her sun-kissed tawny hair from its pins—and felt the urge to take her hand in his own, lead her from this square into the quiet intimacy of an alleyway once more. He wanted to put her against a wall. He wanted to pull up her skirts and make her his own.

'There is a wedding band upon your finger. And we are together, my hand on your arm. What impression do you think it will create?'

'Do you honestly expect me to pretend to be your wife?' Beneath the cover of the frumpy fichu her breasts rose and fell with increasing rapidity.

'I do not expect anything other than you choose your clothes quickly.'

The dark woman at the other side of the counter flashed her gaze between them, taking in Kate's hair that had escaped its pins and the way North stood too close to her, before fixing on North. Her smile was wide and very white in her pretty dusky face.

'You are looking for a dress for your wife, sir?' Her English was smooth with just a trace of an accent, taking them as man and wife just as North had said. Kate could feel the heat in her cheeks, but better this than they thought her his whore, she told herself. And no amount of explaining was going to make it seem anything otherwise. She swallowed and touched at her wedding band for reassurance.

'My lady's wardrobe was lost. We are looking to replace it. But we are only in port for a few hours. We sail tonight.'

'Such a little time.'

'Not a full wardrobe, just a few items for traversing the Atlantic,' Kate clarified. 'Respectable...and black if possible.' She did not look at North. She was too aware of him and the proximity of his body that proclaimed an intimacy between them beyond the fact that he was buying her a wardrobe of clothes. His kiss still burned upon her lips, her skin still tingled everywhere he had touched. She tried to smooth her hair tidy, tucking the strands behind her ears.

'Fate smiles on you today, ma'am.'

Not with the fort or Bill Linder, she thought. But with North's timely arrival in that alleyway, the little voice in her head whispered, and she knew it spoke the truth. Her pistol was small, its single shot at best only able to cut the attack by fifty per cent. Her knife, to fend off the other barrelled brute of a man, would have been sorely tested. Despite her protestations, and whether she wanted to admit it to herself or not, North had saved her. Again.

'I have the very thing.' The dressmaker smiled again. 'A customer of mine was unable to return to collect her order, a lady of a similar size to yourself. A full wardrobe all finished and ready.' Her gaze dropped to Kate's bare feet. 'Slippers, too.' She looked at Kate with curiosity. 'Dark in colour—a mourning wardrobe, in fact.'

Kate twisted the wedding band harder around her finger and stared down at it, thinking of the man she had lost. 'How appropriate—it will suit my needs perfectly.'

'As would the yellow silk,' said the dressmaker as she saw North glance at a bright yellow dress draped upon a mannequin in the corner.

'No,' said Kate.

'We'll take both,' said North and paid the woman for the clothes and to wrap them.

'After you, my dear,' he said as he tucked the parcels beneath his arms and opened the door for Kate.

'You are too kind to me, sir,' she replied with heavy irony.

He leaned closer as followed her through the door out into the square and said quietly. 'You know very well, Kate Medhurst, that I am not kind at all.'

She felt the shiver ripple through her both at the coldness of the words and the heat in his eyes.

The afternoon was done and the evening begun by the time that the provisions were all aboard. A whole stockroom of sacks of flour and grains, of fruits and vegetables. Livestock, too. The cages containing the hens had yet to be taken below. Kit could hear their soft clucking from where he stood on the quarterdeck.

The cool white-blue of the daytime sky was yielding to the warm orange and glorious red of sunset. The aqua-green of the ocean was silvered in this cobwebbed light of dusk, a swirl of colour bigger and more vivid than anything that could be seen at home in England. Colours there were softer, more muted, like the land and the people. Here, as in the East, life was more immediate, more intense and bold. To be lived all the freer or snatched away in the blink of an eye.

The wind was mellow, but enough to billow in *Raven's* sails and carry her away from Antigua and *Gator*, anchored not so very far away.

'The men are grumbling about missing out on a night in the town's taverns,' said Gunner by his side.

'Tell them they can go back in the jolly boat for their night in the taverns, but Raven shall not be here waiting for them tomorrow morning. Nor will their share of the bounty. And remind them of our trip to the East Indies.'

'Where the local brothels were hotbeds of pestilence even if the women themselves showed nothing of the symptoms,' said Gunner. They both remembered too well what it had done to the crew in the days before they turned hunters.

There was a silence while they both watched the silhouette of the island recede into the distance.

'What happened with Mrs Medhurst…in the square back there?' Gunner asked, without shifting his gaze from the view.

'She had a run in with a couple of *Gator's* boys.'

'You got to her in time?' Gunner's gaze shot to his, his brow creased with concern.

'I got to her as she was about to put a shot through one

of them and take her chances against the other with a knife. She is capable, but even so the scoundrels would have had her eventually.'

'Had you not shown up. Where did she get the weapons?'

Kit glanced round at him. 'She was holstered beneath that skirt of hers.' He remembered the flash of those pale legs in the dim shade of the alleyway and was very aware of the leather, within his pockets, that had been strapped so intimately to her thighs.

Gunner's eyebrows rose. 'She really is wife to one of *Coyote's* men.'

Kit thought of the way Kate Medhurst touched so often to her wedding band. He thought, too, of the look of sadness in her eyes following the dressmaker's reference to a mourning wardrobe and of her response— *'How appropriate...'*

'I am not so sure of that,' said Kit.

'She seems too respectable for a pirate's lightskirt.'

'Appearances can be misleading. But I do not think she is a pirate's lightskirt.'

'Then what?'

'A widow.'

There was a silence during which he could feel the weight of his friend's gaze.

'So the dress was mourning weeds, after all.'

'It is now. I am not sure if it was when we first saw her in it aboard *Coyote*.'

'You think she is La Voile's widow?' whispered Gunner.

'That is what I need to discover. I will speak to her after dinner. Until then, I have work to do.'

'Kit.' Gunner's voice stayed him. There was a ripple of embarrassment in Gunner's eyes. 'I think perhaps you should know—her belly bears the signs of having borne a child.'

Kit gave a nod. 'Thank you.'

'Will you not stay and watch the beauty of the sunset? It will be gone within the quarter of the hour.'

Kit was almost tempted. Whilst stood on the deck of a ship he had seen the sun set across the oceans and countries of the world and it truly was a wondrous sight. But to stand here and indulge himself in the pleasure…? He clapped a hand against Gunner's upper arm in a token of their friendship. 'You stay. Enjoy it.' He had work to do. And the problem of what he had overheard in that alleyway to think of.

He left Gunner standing where he was and went to find his desk.

Kate sat on the cot in her cabin, haunted by thoughts of Kit North saving her from Linder, by his hard handsome face and the feel of his mouth on hers.

She touched her fingers to lips that even now still seemed to tingle and burn from his kiss. It seemed she could still smell the scent of him, still feel the strength of his arms around her. Her breasts felt heavy and sensitive, and there was an insistent ache between her legs that could not be denied.

North awoke a longing deep inside her that should not be there, a longing that made her burn with shame and anger and frustration.

She thought of the vow she had sworn. She thought of the love that was in her heart.

Beneath her fingers the gold of her wedding band felt smooth and warm. She looked at the ring on her finger and, pushing North from her mind, filled it instead with Wendell. His presence seemed to surround her, giving her strength. She thought of Ben and Bea and the weakness was gone.

Three-and-a-half-thousand miles of Atlantic Ocean lay ahead of her with North. And given what he had seen he was going to ask questions, a lot of questions. She worried how much he might have overheard in the alleyway. Regardless, he would be more than certain by now that she had not been aboard *Coyote* by abduction. But he had Tobias and that would mean he would not push too hard. She knew it looked bad for her, but shrewd as those dark eyes were, she was confident that they would not guess the truth. No one had ever guessed the truth.

Kate would just have to be very careful how she answered his questions.

Someone knocked at her cabin door and she started.

North. His name whispered through her mind, making her heart race, making birds take flight in her stomach, making her afraid that it was not questions he had come to ask.

Taking a deep breath, she composed herself, reminding herself of what men like him had done to Wendell. Opening the door, she was ready to do battle.

But it was not North that stood there. The level of her gaze dropped to the young cabin boy.

'Begging your pardon, ma'am, but Captain North wishes to know if you will join him for dinner.'

Couched in terms of politeness, Kate understood the message for the command it was. It was the summons she had been expecting.

The boy's face and frame were thin. He could barely have been older than nine or ten years of age and his mop of blond hair and freckled cheeks reminded her too much of what she had left behind in Louisiana.

She smiled him. 'What is your name, boy?'

The boy's eyes widened. 'Have I done something wrong, ma'am?' There was fear in his voice.

'You have done nothing wrong.' She reached a hand to his arm to reassure him, but the boy jumped beneath her touch and pulled away as if burned. 'I only ask that I might know what to call you.'

The boy was regarding her with the suspicious wariness of a trapped animal. 'They call me Tom,' he said after a moment.

Heaven only knew what manner of treatment to which the child had been subjected, to warrant such a reaction.

I am not kind. North's own admission seemed to echo in her head. All of the stories and rumours she had heard surrounding him came whispering back. Of his cruelty and his temper. Of all those things he was reputed to have done to men doing their best to reclaim the living denied them. It reminded her just who he was, and more importantly who she was. That knowledge and the sight of the child before her fuelled her determination, hardening her will, sharpening it, focusing it with precision.

'Well, Tom,' she said, crouching down to his level, 'please tell Captain North that I accept his invitation.'

'Yes, ma'am.' The boy nodded and, with a tug of his forelock, ran off across the gun deck to where the dining tables were ready and waiting with hungry men.

The usual screens were not in place. North glanced over from where he sat at the head table, his dark eyes meeting hers and sending that shiver of sensual awareness rippling down her spine.

Kate stood there for a tiny second, holding his gaze coolly, bold as a pirate about to wield a cutlass and shield, knowing what was coming and tempted to close her cabin door and make him wait for the skirmish. But the crew were not eating, the dishes sat covered, awaiting her arrival. And she could not be so petty.

Taking a breath, she left the illusion of safety her cabin offered and went to eat with North and his men.

There was only polite small talk during the meal. She sat in the empty space that had been left for her, close to North and directly opposite Gunner, engaging in the politeness and listening to the surrounding conversations, aware that the men's language was careful on account of both her and their captain's presence at the head of their table. The time passed until, at last, Gunner cleared his throat and, setting down his napkin, got to his feet.

'If you will excuse me, Mrs Medhurst…Captain North?' Gunner's eyes shifted between Kate Medhurst and Kit.

The men eating at all the tables finished their food and, with a respectful nod to their captain, followed Gunner. The men that were serving table also disappeared so that not one soul remained on that gun deck with Kit and Kate Medhurst.

Now that they were alone there was a subtle shift in the atmosphere—a tightening of that multifaceted tension that shimmered between the two of them.

She swallowed, but made no attempt to run. Holding her head up, she faced him calmly across the table, with cool grey eyes and a small defiant curve to those honey-sweet lips.

'I'm getting the impression that there is something that you wish to discuss with me in private, Captain North.'

'Am I so obvious?'

'Just a little.'

He smiled and so did she.

'Do you wish something to drink?' he asked.

'I will take a brandy, thank you,' she said, no doubt to shock him.

He poured her one and himself a lemonade, acknowledging her derisory glance at the lemonade with a smile.

She sipped the brandy. 'You wasted your money, and mine, on that dress. I do not wear yellow.'

'Why not?'

'It does not suit.'

'On the contrary, I think it would suit very well.'

The silence stretched.

She met his gaze directly and dispensed with the small talk. 'So what exactly is it that you wish to ask me?'

He smiled at her tactic and then supposed with her he should always expect the unexpected. He studied her face closely and saw a mask of beautiful composure. She was cooler under pressure than any man he had known. She revealed nothing, not a flicker of a tense muscle, not a swallow in a dry throat. Not the slightest tremor of her voice.

'Those men in the alley today. You knew them.'

She did not miss a beat, held his eyes with confidence. 'I recognised them as being from Louisiana.'

'They were pirates.'

'Really?'

'Really. How do you know them in Louisiana? Friends of yours, were they?'

She smiled again. 'We're all friends in Louisiana.'

'Or perhaps of your husband's.'

The mask slipped for a tiny second. Something flickered in her eyes, something raw, before she glanced away to hide it, her fingers rotating the thin gold wedding band on her finger. 'My husband is dead, Captain North.'

'Tell me of him.'

She looked at him again, the emotion gone, her cool composed self once more. 'I would rather not,' she said in a voice that beneath the soft velvet held a hint of steely strength.

The silence hissed between them. She held his gaze, bold and stubborn in her defiance. They could sit there all night and she would say not one word. He tried a different tactic.

'You know Lafitte.'

'Everybody in Louisiana knows Jean Lafitte and his older half-brother Pierre.'

'Pirate overlords.'

'I would describe them more as trade facilitators.'

'They are French corsairs.'

'They might have been French born, but they are of New Orleans and everything they do is for the good of Louisiana. And I am sure you are well aware that Louisiana is now a part of the United States of America.' Anger and pride flashed in her eyes. 'They are not violent men, not murderers.'

'And are these non-violent trade facilitators La Voile's overlords?'

'How would I know?'

'Because you knew La Voile. Because you were with him, willingly, on his ship.'

She did not deny it.

'What manner of man was La Voile?' he asked.

'Not the manner of man most would expect, that's for sure.'

'Did he treat you badly?'

'He did not.' There was confidence in her eyes and wariness.

'And yet that morning *Coyote* attacked *Raven*, there was a disagreement between you and him.'

'Was there?' She arched an eyebrow, brazen and cool.

He let a small silence stretch between them before the

important question. 'Were you La Voile's wife, Kate?' he asked softly.

The shock in her eyes was real. She blinked for a moment and then she gave a little laugh, half-incredulity, half-amusement. 'His wife?' She glanced away and shook her head.

'Are you telling me that there was nothing between you and La Voile?'

Her eyes shifted to his once more. 'On the contrary, I am not telling you anything, Captain North.'

'You certainly are not,' he agreed. 'I wonder why.'

'I wonder,' she said.

The silence seemed to hiss between them.

She looked beautiful and pale and proud.

Their gazes held, and for all their stab and fish and parry of words there was the whisper of that other underlying tension between them. That same thing that had made him take her in his arms in the alleyway and kiss her. She could feel it, too. He could tell by the look in her eyes. In the flicker of the candlelight they looked not dove-grey, but charcoal-dark and serious and sensual.

He slid his hand across the table and took her fingers gently in his.

She did not snatch it away, just looked at where their hands lay there together.

The tension pulsed strong between them in the silence.

She swallowed. 'I am a respectable and loyal widow,' she said slowly before she raised her gaze to meet his. 'So you may ask your questions, all you will, but you will hear no answers.' Her hand withdrew from his, but her fingers were soft as a caress in their parting.

He did not doubt it for a minute.

'For all you are English and a bounty hunter, you seem an honourable man, Captain North.'

His smile was small and tight and cynical. 'Do I?' But appearances could be deceptive.

'So I am sure you will understand when I tell you I will not compromise mine.'

'Perfectly,' he said. He knew what it was she was saying. That she would not betray anything of her connection with La Voile…and that she wanted nothing to come of the passion that was smouldering between her and Kit.

The latter suited Kit perfectly well. The desire was there, palpable and thick and real between them, but he wanted nothing to come of it, either. Kit Northcote would have, but Kit North did not. And North had business in London to think of and a vow to honour.

'You offered me safe passage, Captain North. Do you rescind it?'

'The offer remains unchanged.' Whoever she was, and whatever she was hiding, did not matter. He had La Voile pickled in a butt at the other end of the deck. And that was all he needed to return to London and do what was required.

'Thank you.' She gave a small nod of acknowledgement. 'If you will excuse me, sir, it has been a long day and I would like very much to retire for the night.'

He rose, his eyes holding hers. 'Goodnight, Mrs Medhurst.'

'Goodnight, Captain North.' Her bare feet made no sound as she walked across the deck to her cabin.

Whoever she was, and whatever she was hiding, did not matter, he thought again.

But whoever's widow she was, it was not La Voile's.

Chapter Six

Kate awoke to the morning bell ringing up on deck. The warmth and comfort of the dream was still upon her, of her children and her home back in Tallaholm. She clung to its soft remnants, pressing her lips to Bea's plump baby cheeks and breathing in the scent of Ben's tousled mop of golden blond hair as she ruffled it and told him to be a good boy for Grandma. But the images faded too soon and she was left lying alone in the tiny cabin aboard Kit North's ship.

How long would it be before she saw them again? Weeks, maybe even months, stretched ahead—weeks in which she was trapped here with Kit North. A dangerous man in more ways than one.

She thought of last night's encounter, of questions asked and unanswered, of the louder unspoken tension between them. She had more or less blatantly told him she would not sleep with him and that he should stay away from her. She could scarcely believe her own audacity.

Would he honour her request? She touched against the fingers that his had held, seeing again the cool cynicism of his smile at her admission of his honour despite being English and a bounty hunter.

She thought of the way he ate with his men, not apart

on some high captain's fancy table, sharing the same plain food, not fine fare prepared by a personal chef, as she had believed all British captains did.

I am not kind. The words sounded again in her mind, with their brutal ring of honesty.

He was North the Pirate Hunter. He was not kind. But he had not hesitated to dive into the water with a ten-foot white-tip shark to save her. And she was under no illusion as to what would have happened in that alleyway with Bill Linder and his sleazy companion had North not arrived.

He was not kind. But the caress of his fingers and the touch of his lips were all gentleness.

He would honour her request, she thought. And that, more than anything else, was the one thing that would make the three-and-a-half-thousand-mile journey that lay ahead easier.

In those first few days, as their journey got properly underway, she was proved right in her estimation of his honour, for North kept his distance just as much as she had hoped he would. And Kate was relieved. For the sake of her children, for the sake of her mama, and for all who waited in Tallaholm. And for the sake of the vow she had sworn to Wendell.

It was Gunner who sat with her at meals and Gunner who came on occasion to speak to her when she stood at the rail, looking out over the endless ocean and all she was leaving behind.

In the evenings, when the work was done and the daylight gone, the azure-blue of the sky curtained with midnight velvet and diamond stars, *Raven's* crew got together in the dining room, screened off from the rest of the deck, and drank a little grog and talked and laughed and sang old songs of love and loss, of drink and women, and the sea. Gunner played the fiddle and an older man, called Pete, played a little flageolet. They did not seem English. In those evenings she forgot they were her enemies. They were just men the same as those from Tallaholm that crewed *Coyote*.

But North was not there, not on any of those first evenings of *Raven's* journey. Not at dinner time, when he ate at the opposite end of the table to her, their seats too far apart to allow conversation. Nor later for the singing and the music and camaraderie.

On the fifth evening when she came from her cabin to join the social he was over talking to Gunner, but when he saw her approach he left the gun deck, giving her a small but cool nod of acknowledgement as he did so.

Her eyes lingered on the deck ladder up which he had disappeared, realising that his absence from the leisure time was because of her presence. She should have been glad of it, but instead all she felt was a curious empty kind of sadness.

Aware that she had been staring too long after him, she glanced round to find Gunner watching her.

'Maybe I will just spend the evening in my cabin reading one of those books you were kind enough to lend me, sir,' she said.

'You will do no such thing, Mrs Medhurst,' he countered, lowering his voice a notch before adding, 'North never joins us in the evenings.'

'Not ever?'

Gunner shook his head and poured her a small glass of grog. 'He prefers to work.'

'But he cannot always work. There must be times when he—'

'There are not,' Gunner cut off her words gently. His

brow furrowed in worry and there was a far-off look in his eyes as he stared at the table between them. 'North is a hard man, Mrs Medhurst, but hardest of all with himself. He is…driven, relentlessly, without rest, without mercy.'

'What brings a man to such a place?'

'His past.' Gunner looked into her eyes.

'What happened in his past?' she asked quietly.

'Things you could not imagine, Mrs Medhurst.'

She stared at him.

'Where's that fiddle of yours, Reverend Dr Gunner?' one of the men called.

Another was starting up the first notes of another traditional folk song.

Gunner's confidences were over. Lifting his fiddle from its battered case, he began to play.

The men joined in, singing and stamping their feet in time to the rhythm, smiling and laughing, enjoying the jolly tune.

Kate watched them, her tankard of grog sitting on the long scrubbed wooden table before her. Just the same as the previous nights, but this night was different. Gunner's words seemed to ring in her head, sending a discomfort through her.

All of this camaraderie and bonhomie while North was elsewhere, alone, working. She should be glad he was not present. He was dangerous. This was what she wanted, for him to stay away from her, wasn't it?

What happened in his past?

Things you could not imagine.

She was still pondering on it when Gunner sat down beside her an hour later.

'Reverend Dr Gunner, are you feeling all right?' Even in the mellow soft light of the lanterns the priest looked too pale around his eyes, but with the telltale flush of cheeks that boded ill. It was warm on the gun deck, but not enough to account for the sheen of sweat that glistened upon his face. The hour of playing seemed to have drained all of his energy.

He shook his head as if to shake away her concern and set his fiddle on the table surface, something he never did; he always was careful to keep it in its case. 'I do feel a little under the weather,' he admitted, and with that his eyes rolled up into their sockets and he slid from the bench to collapse on to the deck.

The dancing and the singing stopped abruptly. The flageolet, too.

Kate got down on her knees, laying her hand against his forehead and feeling how hot he was.

'Go fetch Captain North,' she instructed the nearest man, then turned Gunner on his side in case he should be sick and choke upon it. The men were all crowded around, worried but not knowing what to do, Gunner was the physician, after all; he was the one who normally dealt with such occurrences.

North came immediately. The men cleared a path for him as he made his way to where she knelt by Gunner.

They carried the priest to his cot in North's day cabin and Kate followed.

'Go back to your cabin, Mrs Medhurst. The matter is in hand,' North instructed.

'If you do not mind, Captain, I'll stay.' Her eyes met his meaningfully. 'I think you're going to need my help.'

She waited until his crew were gone before she spoke. 'He is burning up with fever.'

They looked at one another, both realising the awful possibility—that what had wiped out the naval fort and yard on Antigua was now here on *Raven*.

'It might be a coincidence,' she said.

'Unlikely.'

'Either way he has a fever that needs to be cooled.'

'This is not work for you.'

'I had Yellow Jack as a child. I will not contract it again.'

He just looked at her.

'For goodness' sake, I was a married woman. I have seen a man's body before.'

'He is a priest.'

'And a friend to us both. I am not going to sit in my cabin doing nothing. We need a basin of cold water and clean rags. And some boiled water that we can leave to cool.'

For a moment his eyes held locked to hers, the expression them unreadable.

She did not back down, just held his gaze steady. Gunner had been kind to her.

'Do you know what you are doing, Kate Medhurst?' he asked.

She swallowed, understanding the layers of meaning in the question.

'I do,' she said, still holding his eyes. 'I have seen fever before.'

But they both understood that was not what he was asking.

After a long moment, North gave a nod. 'I will fetch what is needed.'

Did she know what she was doing?

There was no time to think about it. A man's life was at stake.

Kate moved to Gunner's side and began to roll up her sleeves.

The night seemed very long.

Kit held the small cup to Gunner's mouth and tried to

pour a few drops of the cooled boiled water between his friend's cracked dry lips, but most of it just spilled down the side of his face. He sat the cup down on the surface of his nearby desk.

'A little is better than nothing,' Kate Medhurst said from his side.

'But not enough.'

'Drop by drop,' she said.

His eyes moved over the thin sheet that covered Gunner's naked body and was already drenched with sweat although they had not long changed it.

'I will mop his brow and sit with him, while you go get some rest,' she said, her American twang soft and lilting in the room.

'I am staying.' Gunner was his friend, his shipmate and the man who had saved his life. And even if he were not, it would not matter. He held out his hand for the wrung-out rag she was holding, ready to wipe away the rivulets of sweat that ran down Gunner's brow and cool the fever that burned beneath the pallor of his skin. 'You rest.'

'I do not have a ship to captain in the morning,' she pointed out.

'This is my responsibility.'

She stood there silent for a moment and he could feel the weight of her gaze upon him, even though he kept his focus fixed on Gunner.

She passed him the cloth. 'You are a stubborn man, Captain North.' The words, uttered soft as a caress, felt like a compliment rather than a criticism. She walked quietly away then, pausing when she reached his door. 'I will be back at dawn.'

His eyes met hers across the cabin, glad of her words, and her strength and her capable practicality.

He nodded his acknowledgement and turned his attention back to Gunner.

But what neither of them knew in that moment was that by dawn hell would have come to *Raven*.

Kate Medhurst came back long before that hour.

Eighteen of his fifty men were struck down with the same fever that held Gunner.

Kit North had not slept. His eyes held their same steady resolve and determination, but also an unmistakable fatigue, and beneath them was the smudge of smoky shadows. He looked bone weary beneath that rigid backbone of his.

She told herself she was not doing this for North, that it was purely selfish interest. For if *Raven* did not complete her journey safely, how was she going to get back to her children and to Tallaholm?

'Eighteen of your men are affected so far, not including Reverend Dr Gunner. It could go higher. You are undermanned with them down and, on top of that, the ill need nursing and you've still got to sail *Raven*. You cannot do all of that alone.'

He did not shoot her down, just let her speak. 'I get the feeling you are about to offer me a solution.'

'Let me take charge of nursing the ill. I'll need six men who will do what they are told.'

She waited for him to refuse. Most men that didn't know her always did. They judged her on the fact she was a woman, not on the strength that was inside.

But he did not refuse.

'And Gunner?' he asked.

'I will nurse Reverend Dr Gunner myself.'

He gave a nod of acknowledgement.

They worked together.

Those men without symptoms were massed on the lower deck. North informed them of the situation and how it would be managed, while Kate watched on. A captain to his men, a commander, a natural leader, his men hung on his every word, their faces grim with worry, yet eyes that spoke of a deep-seated trust in him. Unlike most captains he ruled with a firm hand of fair justice rather than through undeserved or unending lashings and beatings, and the difference was clear. His leadership was instinctive, easy and unquestioned.

'Move the hammocks of those afflicted to the aft. Those who are clear bunk to the fore. Keep a clear boundary between. We are fortunate to have Mrs Medhurst amongst us as she has much experience of nursing the ill.' A deal less experience than North's words implied.

The crew's gaze turned to rest on her as he spoke and she looked at them with the confidence of a woman who had had nursed a shipload of men with Yellow Jack a hundred times before. They needed to believe in her as much as North. They needed to believe they could beat this and sail on and not panic and give up or bail for their lives.

'Riley, Horse, Sandbatch, Gilley, Henhead and Scrobe,' North instructed, 'you are assigned to assist Mrs Medhurst. Do as she commands. For the rest of us it is business as usual.'

His eyes met hers fleetingly and alongside the usual complex dark feelings of attraction was respect and the knowledge that the fate of *Raven* rested in both their hands.

Kate Medhurst was still on her feet, wiping down Gunner's face when Kit finally made it back to his cabin. Through the big stern windows the night sky was tinged with a beautiful deep azure. Stars big and bright and numerous as a sprinkled bag of diamonds twinkled in the sky. The ocean was dark, a deep pitch-black that made men think of the darkness of their own souls and the monsters that lay hidden in the realms beneath.

A single lantern burned on the table. Beside it Gunner lay naked on the cot that had been stripped of all sheets. Only a cloth draped across his hips preserved his modesty; his thin pale body looked so corpse-like that it made Kit fear the worst.

'How is he?' he asked as he came to stand by her side.

'He was sick again earlier, hence the lack of sheets. We have no clean ones left.'

'That, I can do something about.' He passed her the fresh linen he had brought with him.

'Thank you.' She smiled a small smile.

For three days she had nursed his friend and organised and run an operation of caring for the rest of his crew, who were afflicted with the pestilence, with the efficiency and expertise of a captain running his ship. And in all of those three days and nights he had not seen her sleep, not once.

Her face was shadowed with exhaustion and worry, the same worry he felt twist deep in his gut over Gunner's fate.

'Is he going to make it?' He glanced at the man to whom he owed so much before looking into Kate Medhurst's eyes for the truth that words might hide.

'I do not know,' she said with bare honesty. There was no attempt to deceive, whether through kindness or otherwise, nothing of that edge of conflict that was usually there between them. Fatigue had blunted it, exposing something of the woman beneath the armour. It felt like, in this at least, they were fighting on the same side.

'When will we know?'

'Probably by the end of this night.' She set the linen down on table.

He swallowed down the bile that rose at the thought

of Gunner dying. Turned away so that she would not see how much the prospect affected him. 'I will stay with him. You get some sleep.' His voice was gruff. He did not look at her.

'We'll both stay with him,' she said quietly, and he heard the movement and glanced round to see her sit down in her chair.

He should have insisted. But he was too tired to argue and, in truth, he was not sure that he wanted to face the dark hours ahead alone. He sat down on the chair beside hers.

'How long have you been friends?' she asked.

'Three years. It does not sound long, does it—three years out of a whole lifetime?'

'Long enough,' she said. 'There is much that can happen in three years.' There was something about the way she said it, something sad and reflective, that made him think that she was talking not only about him, but about herself, too.

'Very much.' His eyes lingered on Gunner, remembering all that they had been through together—the worst of times, and the best.

'He means a lot to you.' Her voice was gentle.

'He saved my life,' he admitted.

'Saved you from a shark, did he?' *Like you did me.*

He glanced round at her, his eyes holding hers, remembering that moment between them.

'Threw me to them, more like,' he said.

'And that saved you?'

'Without a doubt.'

She said nothing, but her silence, like her presence, seemed comforting in a way he did not understand. It seemed to reach out to him. It seemed to connect them as much as the way that she held his gaze and did not look away.

'I would have destroyed myself otherwise.' He smiled, but the bitterness of shame and guilt was still there. 'Along with everyone else I cared about.' And the anger, too, even through the tiredness.

'The dreaded drink,' she said, misinterpreting his abstinence from brandy and other spirits.

'Amongst other things.' He looked at Gunner in silence for a while, at the way the tremors still shivered through his friend's body and the labour of his breath. Death seemed to hover close in that cabin. Even Bob the raven, sitting on his perch in the corner, was silent and brooding.

Kit felt helpless and too aware there was nothing he could do to help. He got to his feet, needing to do something, so tired he could not think straight and yet knowing he could not rest, that this was his friend, his ship, his responsibility, his duty.

'In many cultures the raven is associated with battle and death,' he said.

'Is that why you captured and trained your raven—as a symbol of such?'

He gave a small soft laugh. 'The raven I trained when I was in prison. Bob came to the bars of my cell one day. We became friends.'

'Bob?' she said with a teasing arch of her eyebrows that, despite everything, made him smile.

'What is wrong with the name Bob?'

'Nothing. I guess I was expecting something a little darker or more Gothic or mystical.'

'I think he is more of a Bob.'

'I think you are probably right.' She glanced across at where Bob sat hunched and watching. 'And your boat is named for him?'

'My boat was a black sail, built to fly fast and to scavenge.' Wringing out the cloth in the clean cold water, he held it to Gunner's forehead, trying to cool the fever that raged beneath the flush on that pallid skin. 'He is going to die, isn't he?' The question was not really for her, was not really a question at all, more a trying to come to terms with the hard fact himself.

He felt gentle hands take the cloth from him and place it once more in its basin.

'Sit down, Kit North,' she said softly. 'There is nothing more we can do except wait. And pray.'

'I do not pray.'

'Why not?' she asked.

'I have no right to pray.'

'Everyone has a right to pray.'

'Not everyone.'

'You are very hard on yourself.'

'Not hard enough,' he said, his eyes holding hers, daring her to argue or question.

She did neither. She sat down in her chair and reached her hand to his, taking it in her own. It was a small hand, slender and soft, but a practical hand, a hand that worked rather than frittered away time in leisure. A hand that was gentle yet firm. No woman had touched him like that. Even in the old days, when he had bedded the best of whores with the worst of rakes, it had all been about selfish gratification. This felt like something very different. He knew he should remove his hand from hers, but he did not; he could not.

With his eyes on Gunner he sat down beside her.

The long hours of the night stretched ahead, the time when men's lives were weighed in the balance and taken or given. But for the first time in such a long time, he was not alone. Kate Medhurst, with her strength and her calm practicality, was by his side. He threaded his fingers through hers, and was glad of it.

'Why in heaven's name am I lying here naked as the day I was born?'

The imperious demand dragged Kit from deep slumber to the cabin aboard *Raven* once more. Kate Medhurst's head rested on his shoulder, her soft breath warm and moist against his cheek. His arm was curled protectively about her, while her hand rested against his chest. Their legs were entwined like lovers. There was an ache in his back as though someone had kicked him with an iron-clad boot, where the wooden chair frame had pressed against his spine for hours. And, worse than any of that, he had an erection that would have dwarfed Mount Olympus.

She woke when he tried to move, her eyes soft at first, her mouth smiling, then, as reality intruded, that changed. She hastily disentangled herself, springing to her feet, her cheeks blushing red, as if caught *in flagrante* while he adjusted his coat to disguise his awkward predicament.

'Gunner?' North's voice sounded hoarse as if he had not used it in eons. She forgot her embarrassment as she watched him. 'Gunner!' He smiled. A proper smile, a real smile. Full of joy and relief and gladness. It was the first time she had seen it and the man it exposed beneath. It changed his face from one of hard determination to one that she could not take her eyes from. He looked in that instant like the weight of the world had been lifted from his shoulders. He looked happy. Like a man who could have swept her off her feet with laughter and made the world all right again. She watched the transformation in amazement.

'Thank God,' he whispered. A man that did not pray,

but she remembered the soft murmur of his words in the night and felt his strength surround her.

'I am naked before Mrs Medhurst, Kit!' Gunner complained. 'Grant a priest some dignity.'

'You have been ill, old friend.'

'Not any more.' Gunner's voice was weak, his face skull-like and just as pale. But the fever had passed and he was still with them. 'My apologies, ma'am, for my state of presentation,' he said to her. Then smiled. '*Quid pro quo* for my treatment following your encounter with the shark.'

'We are even,' she joked. 'Welcome back, Reverend Dr Gunner. You had us scared for a while.'

'I had myself scared for a while.'

She smiled. 'We were waiting for the fever to pass before replacing your bedsheets.' She could feel the heat flush her cheeks and did not look over at North, knowing how they had awoken together. 'I am glad you are returned to us, sir.'

Gunner smiled weakly with dry cracked lips.

'I will leave you in Captain North's capable hands.' Then, to North, 'I must go and check on the others.'

The smile was gone, the hard, determined, emotionless pirate hunter back once more. But something had changed between them. Something small and yet important, something in the depths of those dark eyes that made the blush heat her cheeks all the more. He gave a nod and turned back to Gunner.

She slipped away and left the two friends together.

Six of Kit's men were not as lucky as Gunner. He buried them the next day in the traditional maritime way that they would have wanted, their bodies sewn up in their hammocks. Those of the crew well enough to walk collected on the upper deck for the funeral. Men, even pirates and sinners, deserved dignity in being laid to rest, especially when there had been nothing of dignity in the manner with which the pestilence had taken their lives.

Kit stood there before the assembled crew, feeling, as did all of his men, the loss of those who had been taken. The leather-bound book of prayer was alien in his hand, shaped and used to the touch of another. He could feel the slight dents worn by the press of Gunner's fingers. This was a priest's territory, but Gunner was still too weak to climb from his cot.

Across the deck, some little distance behind the crowd, Kate Medhurst stood. The shabby black muslin she had worn all of the past days and nights was gone. In its place she had donned a fresh dress, one of those from the wardrobe bought in Antigua. A black silk and matching bonnet with her own familiar black fichu fitted in place to cover her décolletage. The colour intended to mourn another now a mark of respect for the men she had nursed and lost.

He opened the book and the men fell silent before him, bowing their heads, hats and caps clutched in hands.

All we can do is wait and pray. Her soft words sounded again from the previous night. And his own reply, *I do not pray.*

Yet here he was with the prayer book. The irony was not lost on him. He wondered if she was thinking the same. She had every right to. But when his eyes met hers it was not mockery that he saw there, but understanding—that this was a captain's duty to his men.

She gave a small nod. Of acknowledgement, of encouragement, of support. Her face was etched with fatigue, the shadows beneath her eyes blue in the brightness of the daylight—from working to help his men, from being there to help him. All those nights without sleep and yet her shoulders were squared and her head held high as ever it was, with strength and dignity and unwavering stead-fastness. In all of his life, Kit had never seen a more beau-tiful woman.

He put aside his own discomfort and spoke the words from the prayer book.

There were tears in the eyes of some of the men as the canvas-shrouded bodies slid into the clear green ocean, sinking down to disappear beneath the waves.

When it was done and over, he looked again for Kate Medhurst, but the place on the deck where she had stood was empty.

Chapter Seven

In the few days that it had taken Gunner to regain something of his strength *Raven* had long left behind the balmy climes of the Caribbean. The waters of the mid-Atlantic were not aqua-green but darker, deeper, a grey-blue that did not invite swimmers. The wind was stronger, colder, biting even, but for today, at least, the sun still shone and she could understand Gunner's insistence in coming up on deck to lean against the rail and look out over the vast endless surround of ocean.

'Only for a little while,' she reminded him. 'And then you should rest again.'

'I do nothing but rest.'

'You can work on your scientific papers.'

'You nursed me well, Mrs Medhurst.'

'Captain North did more.'

He smiled.

'I guess there is a bond between men who have saved each other's lives.'

Gunner glanced round at her with a quizzical expression. 'What makes you think I saved Kit's life?'

'He told me so. "By throwing him to the sharks," I believe was the precise expression.'

Gunner chuckled at that.

'What happened?'

'So much,' said Gunner, and looked away over the ocean again.

'How did you meet him?'

'In a tavern in Portsmouth three years ago. My ship was in port and I was making the most of the last of my land leave. He was not North then.'

'Who was he?'

'A different man altogether.'

'In what way?'

'In ways he would not wish me to divulge.'

She said nothing, knowing better than to persuade any man, let alone a priest, to break a confidence, no matter how much she wanted to know the answer to the question.

'I did not trust to leave him there. So I took him with me. And threw him to the sharks.'

'I do not understand.'

He smiled again as he glanced round at her. The wind fluttered through his short blond locks, the bright clarity of the sunlight revealing in his face the ravages of his fight with the Yellow Jack. 'Priest, physician, *pirate*...' Those same words he had said to her once before.

'I did not think you were being serious.'

'Entirely serious, my dear Mrs Medhurst. I was a pirate, part of a black-sailed cutthroat crew and I suppose you might say that I press-ganged Kit into joining us with the help of more than a few bottles of brandy. He did not know what he was signing up for. And by the time he realised, it was too late. We were well on our way, heading for the riches of the East. Superb plunder. A fine living for almost a year.'

'What happened?'

'We intercepted a jewel load belonging to the Sultan of

Johor. The Sultan, quite rightly, took exception and sent his navy after us. Our captain was hanged, drawn and quartered while we watched. The rest of us were imprisoned in the Sultan's gaol, death by labour. In this case the labour was shipbuilding for his navy.

'Kit had changed by then, his body grown strong from the hard work on the ship. He stood up against the tyrant guards, for the older men of the crew, for the injured and the sick. And in return they punished him, with solitary confinement and more.'

She felt her stomach twist in horror at the word punished and all that it suggested.

She closed her eyes, remembering what North had told her of Bob the raven coming to him when he was in prison.

'More than any other man could have endured. He survived. Not as he was. He became the man he is today. All those months alone, all that time to explore his own mind. He designed *Raven*, in that cell, and an escape plan. When they let him out eventually, we built her. Right beneath the noses of the guards, as if she was just the same as every other ship we worked upon. After she was completed and taken to the harbour, Kit broke us out of there. We took the ship. It was not stealing, you understand. We had built it. It was Kit's.'

'And the pirates became pirate hunters.'

'Kit's idea. As I said, he was a changed man. He did not drink, did not game, did not so much as look at a woman. He said we would earn our money honestly. You might take comfort in the fact that La Voile is our last job. A special commission. Once Admiralty pay the bounty on him Kit will hunt pirates no more.'

'What will he do?'

'I do not know. You will have to ask him that question.'

Her thoughts swirled around Kit North, what Gunner

had just told her turning all of what she had believed on its head. Glancing up, she saw that the priest was studying her face.

'I do not know your story, Kate, nor will I ask you, but I believe you suffer as much as he does, in your own way.'

'I do not—' she began.

But he shook his head and pressed a finger to his own lips to stop her denial.

She looked into the truth in his pale-blue eyes.

'Now, I think you were right.' He took a deep lungful of air. 'I have ignored my scientific papers for too long.'

She nodded and took his arm in hers while he leaned on his walking stick with the other. Slowly they made their way across to North's cabin.

She helped Gunner inside, settling him in his chair, before her eyes met North's where he sat working behind his desk. Met and held.

So much that she had not known about him. Her heart seemed to swell with the newfound knowledge.

'Mrs Medhurst.' He got to his feet, all formal in front of Gunner, but what was between them, what had always been between them, seemed to whisper louder than ever.

'Captain North.'

Their eyes held for that moment too long before she dipped a curtsy and departed the cabin.

Kit watched while Gunner leaned back in his chair and, fitting his spectacles on to his face, lifted the small pile of papers from the occasional table by his side.

'How are you feeling?'

'All the better for some fresh sea air...' Gunner smiled. He still looked tired and thin, but the colour of his skin was healthier and his eyes were his old self. 'And the company of Mrs Medhurst.'

Kit moved his focus back to the log book that lay open before him. 'It seems she is good for you.'

'Even if she is the widow of La Voile,' said Gunner.

'She is not the widow of La Voile.' Kit did not look up.

'You are sure?'

'When it comes to Kate Medhurst I am not sure of anything. But whoever she was wed to, I do not believe it to have been La Voile.'

There was a small silence before Gunner said, 'I told her how we met, something of how *Raven* and Kit North came into being, and that La Voile is our last job.'

'And what did she tell you?'

'Nothing.'

Kit gave a hard smile and kept on writing.

'You are attracted to her.'

'Because of the other morning? You may be a priest, Gunner, but even you know better than that.'

'And she is attracted to you, too.'

Kit's hand paused midword, only a tiny pause, but enough for the ink to blob.

'I may be a priest, but I have eyes in my head. And even had I not, the atmosphere between the two of you is thick enough with passion to cut a knife through it.'

'You are imagining things, Gunner. It is the after-effects of the fever.'

Gunner laughed in his usual good-humoured way and, looking down at his scientific paper, began to read.

Kit stared at the page before him without seeing anything of it. He was thinking of Kate Medhurst by his side through the long hours of the night; a woman who refused to explain anything of herself to him, not her presence on La Voile's ship or her acquaintance with *Gator's* men, not the fact she knew Jean Lafitte, and especially not anything of the man to whom she had been married. What did he really know of her? Nothing.

But that was not entirely true. He knew that she had eyes that made a man forget the darkness in himself and lips that were the sweetest he had ever tasted. He knew that she was more courageous than most men he had met and that her mind was sharp and clear and intelligent. He knew that she had a sense of honour and had borne a child. And that something niggled in his mind about the very first time he had seen her, standing beneath that black awning with La Voile and the other pirate.

But most of all he knew that Gunner was right—he was attracted to her, all of her, despite everything of his situation and hers. He was attracted to her with a desire that seemed to be escalating. And she was attracted to him, too.

And that was why it was more important than ever that they stay well apart.

The wind had dropped, and *Raven's* progress slowed. The last of the Yellow Jack had left the ship and all of those Kate had spent her time nursing were recovered enough to return to their normal quarters and duties. What had been her infirmary vanished into storage deck once more.

Kate sat on the edge of her cot, staring at the wood of the cabin door when she should have been readying herself for dinner. Everything had returned to normal, although not for Bowes and Ashton, Lyle and Smithy, or Rimmer and Caxley. She thought of the young men whose bodies lay somewhere at the bottom of the clear green waters near the Caribbean. Nothing would ever be normal for them again. Maybe not for herself, either.

Only now that the emergency was over, and her role in it done, did it hit her. She was so tired, so very tired. And she could not get what Gunner had told her yesterday of Kit North out of her head. He had been press-ganged to a pirate against his will. He had endured months of solitary confinement. He had designed *Raven* in his prison and built her. He had got his men out of there and back home against all the odds. No other man could have done such a thing. Kate knew that with all of her heart and soul.

He was not the man she had thought him, but one that had risen from conditions that would have crushed others: one with integrity, trying to do what he believed was right as much as all of those who worked in the trade with the Lafittes did. As much as Wendell had done and herself after he was gone. She had to admire that and his strength and his care for his men. She had been misled by her own prejudices. Because he was English. Because he did not understand their cause or why they were forced to go about it as they did. The plain truth was that Kit North, the pirate hunter reviled across the Gulf of Mexico and the Caribbean, was a fine man.

She rested her head in her hands; the knowledge gnawing at her because it didn't change the fact of who they both were. Nothing was ever going to get round that one. He was a very fine man, indeed. A man she wanted as a friend…and a whole lot more than that if she were being entirely honest. But if she let down her barriers, if she let him get close, there was every chance that a man as intelligent and shrewd as Kit North would see exactly who she was. And right now, that was something she could not risk.

This was not about her. This was about her children waiting for her back in Tallaholm. This was about being there to guide and guard them into adulthood. And it did not even start to go anywhere near Wendell.

She thought of Ben and baby Bea, and her heart ached for them.

And she thought, too, of Kit North. And the ache in her heart seemed to intensify.

A knock sounded on her cabin door.

North. Her pulse leapt at the thought.

'They are waiting for you at the dining tables, ma'am,' came one of the crew's voice.

'Thank you, sir. Please tell the Captain that I'll be right there.'

The sound of footsteps receded across the deck.

She pulled the black evening silk that he had paid for from the little wardrobe and changed, fitted the fichu carefully in place, before combing, winding and pinning her hair tight into its pins. She wrapped a long dark shawl around her shoulders against the evening chill. Then, slipping on a pair of long black evening gloves, she took a deep breath and went to dinner.

Kit tried hard to keep his eyes from where Kate Medhurst sat at the other end of the dinner table.

She was quieter than normal during the meal, probably worn out by the days that she had worked so hard to save his men, to save Gunner. Yet too often her eyes moved to meet his across that small distance.

She was in his mind, with the strength of the passion that, tonight, seemed stronger than ever between them, despite that she was allied in some way with Lafitte and La Voile and the rest of the Baratarian pirates. Despite the fact she was keeping her dark secrets as much as he was keeping his.

'How is your scientific paper coming along, Reverend Dr Gunner?' she asked. And Gunner was only too happy to tell them all. It relieved something of the slight tension that seemed to hover about the table.

Young Tom was playing footman, bringing a dish of

sweet potatoes to the table when the dish slipped from the boy's hands, and crashed to the floor. The china smashed into pieces, its mashed orange contents splattering far and wide.

'Daft lad!' Wilson, who was also serving table, uttered without malice.

But Tom being Tom froze, a look of terror on his face, cringing before Wilson. 'Please don't beat me, sir. I'm sorry, sir.'

'Come here, Tom,' Kit commanded.

The boy crept to stand before him.

'You forget where you are, boy,' he said.

The lad nodded.

'Remember, as I told you the last time.'

Tom took a breath and looked around him. 'I am on *Raven* and I am one of her crew.'

'And what do you know of *Raven*?'

'That no one is beaten without just cause here. That it is safe.'

'It is safe,' confirmed Kit. 'So hear what else it is that Mr Wilson has to say to you.'

'Yes, Captain.' Tom nodded and went dutifully to stand before Wilson.

'Best get a shovel and a cloth, and clear it up, lad,' said Wilson.

The boy bobbed his head, 'Yes, sir, Mr Wilson, sir.' Flashing Kit a toothy grin, he rushed off to do as he was bid.

Kate Medhurst seemed frozen at the other end of the table, her face filled with compassion for the boy.

'The boy requires uncommon gentle treatment on account of his rather traumatic past. We found him being cruelly treated in the Johor prison—the lone survivor from his family, all of which had been killed. North rescued him and is equipping him with the means to survive. I have it on good authority he will make a fine sailor one day,' he heard Gunner say.

The men round the table all grinned and raised their glasses with murmurs of, 'Aye, sir, he will that.' But Kate Medhurst just made a choking sound. Her eyes were filled with tears when they met his across the table.

'Please excuse me, gentlemen,' she managed in a strangled voice and, with her face averted so that it could not be seen, she fled the dining room.

The men all glanced around, awkward, uncomfortable, tough, strong, leathered men who had sailed through the worst of storms and could cleave a man in two and think nothing of it, helpless before the tears of a woman. They wanted to aid her, but did not know what to do. They all looked at him. Gunner's eyes, too, met his down the length of the table.

A single nod of his head and he went after her.

Kate was mortified. She didn't even know why she was crying, just that the tears would not stop. She needed to pull herself together, up by her bootstraps as her mama always said. She had never shown weakness in front of her own crew. Now here she was making a fool of herself before those against whom she should remain strongest and keep up all her defences.

A knock sounded against her door and she knew it was North even before he spoke.

'Mrs Medhurst.'

'Go away.' She did not even glance at the door, just scrubbed the tears from her eyes. She didn't want him to see her like this—weak and vulnerable. She could not let him see her like this—not when her guard was down and when she couldn't think straight, let alone protect her secrets.

But he did not go away. The door opened and Kit North stepped into her cabin, his eyes taking in her and her damnable tears. She turned her back to him that he wouldn't see them.

'Kate.' His voice was quiet.

She sniffed, tried to get a rein on herself. 'I will be all right in a minute. Go back to your dinner, Captain North.' Her voice was husky and on the verge of breaking. She wanted him just to turn around and leave. The only sound was the quiet click of the door being closed. But he had not left. She could sense his presence standing there.

His hands were gentle as they turned her to him, so that she could not hide from him any more.

'It's nothing,' she said, although he had not asked the question. She did not meet his eyes.

'It would take a great deal more than nothing to make a woman like you cry.'

She kept her gaze on the wood of the door behind him, willing herself to be strong.

'Something of the boy, Tom, upset you,' he said, as perceptive as ever.

She swallowed. 'Was what Gunner said of him true?'

He nodded. 'Unfortunately so. He was a passenger aboard one of the ships the Sultan of Johor's men captured.'

She squeezed her eyes shut, trying to stop the tears, but they welled and leaked to roll down her cheeks just the same.

'Do not let it distress you. Tom will always have a place with me. He is safe and well cared for. And always will be. I promise you.'

And she believed him. She truly did. The sob escaped her.

'Kate,' he said softly, He pulled her against him, wrapping her in his embrace.

He passed her his handkerchief while she cried in earnest, for the boy Tom, and for her own little Ben and Bea, and for the man before her.

He held her, just held her, in his warmth and support and strength. Held her until the tears were all cried and the shudder of the sobs echoed though her body, and the terrible twisting, gnawing tension that had been tight in her all these days since that morning of *Coyote's* capture had loosened its grip upon her. Until she felt empty. And calm.

Standing there in North's arms. It felt like a safe harbour from the storm. She knew that was all wrong and that he was the storm who could destroy her. But in that moment the knowledge seemed small and inconsequential. What she felt, what pulsed through her heart, what filled her every pore, what was deep inside the marrow of her bones, that was all that mattered.

'This is about more than Tom,' he said. Not a question, just a fact.

Her cheek was pressed against his shirt, against the hard muscle of his chest, against the beat of his heart. She nodded.

'He reminds you of another.'

She pulled back, and looked up into his eyes. 'How do you know?'

'Gunner told me that your body bears the marks that you have carried a child.'

'Two children,' she said. 'Ben is six years old. Bea is four. Both are as blond as young Tom and as their father was. Both the cutest little pumpkins you ever could meet.'

'Where are they now?'

'Back home in Tallaholm. My mama looks after them while I'm away. It is a good arrangement. It gives her purpose since my papa died a few years back.' She took a breath. 'I miss them so much. They are the reason I was in such a hurry to get back to Louisiana, the main reason at least.'

'You should have told me.'

'Why? It would not have made any difference. I knew you could not go into Louisiana waters.'

'I would have found a way.'

She looked up into his eyes, so dark and intense. 'I believe you would have, Kit North,' she said in a voice that was barely more than a whisper. 'You are not the man I thought you were.'

Their gazes held and locked.

The next step was inevitable and unstoppable. She knew it was coming and she wanted it. She needed it.

His mouth lowered to hers and she met his lips with all the tenderness and feeling that throbbed in her heart.

She gave herself up to him. She gave herself up to all that her body had been deprived of these past three years. All that her heart missed and craved.

He kissed her with tenderness and gentleness and, beneath it, the same fierceness of passion that she felt; their lips igniting those sparks to flames that could not be doused. She was lost in its heat and so was he.

And when he snuffed out the lantern light and unlaced the black silk from her, stripping it off...when his hands caressed her naked skin with reverence and tenderness and desire...when his mouth closed upon her breast to pleasure them both...when she pulled the shirt from him and ran her hands over the toned hard muscle of his body, feeling bumps and ridges and welts on his skin, feeling his strength, feeling the power that was in him...it was more than want, more than desire. It was a need so guttural and raw that she could no more deny it than wilfully stop herself from breathing.

Everything in him mirrored what she felt. As though he understood, as though he was just the same as her. As though his strength could feed her and mend her and make everything all right again when it hadn't been all right for such a long time despite all of her pretences.

Their bodies spliced together as if they had been made to fit that way.

There was only Kit North, only this healing that was happening between them as their bodies merged. They moved together, their rhythms perfectly in tune, reaching, striving, needing what only the other could give. A journey together. A journey that faded everything else to oblivion.

'Kit.' She called out his name as they finally reached their destination and she exploded in a surge of white light and stardust and sunbeams and a pulsing pleasure that overcame the entirety of her being as he pulled out just in time to keep her safe.

And afterwards, when the urgency and madness had passed, when their bodies parted and they both realised what they had done, awkwardness and embarrassment replaced passion. She clutched the covers to her, hiding her nakedness even though it was dark.

'I should go.' She felt him leave the cot, felt the dip of the mattress as he sat on its edge and pulled on his drawers and breeches, quickly dressing himself. Then rose to leave. There was a small hesitation, as if he had turned to say something, then thought better of it. He did not say another word, just left, closing the door quietly behind him.

She lay there, her body warm and sated, while a cold wind of horror blew through her heart at what she had just done. Lying there, naked beneath the sheets, his scent strong upon her, her skin still flushed from his touch, she stared up through the darkness towards the low wooden planks of the ceiling above. Everything she believed of herself was shaken. All of her values and her standards. If someone had told her two weeks ago that she would have behaved like a wanton, forgetting everything that was important to her, forgetting the vow she had sworn, so driven by the need to couple with Captain Kit North that she would lay herself down before him and go at it like a barnyard animal, she would have laughed in their face at the utter absurdity.

What have I done?

Betrayed the memory of her husband. Betrayed her children. Betrayed her own self.

She was Le Voile. He was the man the British establishment had sent to capture her.

Lord help me, what have I done? The question whispered again and again through her mind as the full horror of it sank in.

Her anger was not at him, but herself. For her weakness.

But she knew the answer, and worse than that was the fear that, despite that knowledge, if he were to kiss her again and whisper her name with such tenderness, she would do it all again.

In the darkness of the tiny cabin Kate shivered and, wrapping her arms around herself, curled on her side. She did not weep, there were no more tears left to cry.

She just stared into the black night and wondered how on earth she was going to get through the rest of this journey with what lay between her and Kit North.

Kit did not return to the dining tables. He did not want any of the others to guess what had just happened between him and Kate Medhurst, both for her sake and his own. Instead, he climbed the ladder that led to the upper deck and sought the sanctuary of the open night sky.

Briggs was at the helm, Collier on watch, but neither

would bother him. Through the darkness that submerged him they would see nothing of the truth. He stood by the rail, feeling the whip of the wind against his face and through his hair and staring out into the dark roar of the ocean.

He thought he was a man who had righted his course. He had sailed so far and never felt temptation to veer from that course, not once, until he met Kate Medhurst. And now he had faltered, fallen. So close to home.

'There you are.' Gunner's voice was quiet as he came to stand by his side, handing Kit his lantern so that he could lean between his stick and the bulwark to look out over the side at the dark night seascape.

'You should not be up here. You will exhaust yourself,' Kit said.

'I thought I was the physician here,' Gunner said, and he could hear the smile in his friend's voice.

They stood in silence for a little while, with only the creak of the timber and the flap of canvas and the ever-present roar of the ocean.

'Is she all right?' Gunner asked softly after a few moments.

'I hope so.' He hoped, but he feared what he had done had only made matters worse.

Another silence before Gunner spoke again. 'Are *you* all right?'

'Why would I not be?' He would not lie, deception went too close to the tear in his soul that could not be mended, but he would do all that he could to protect Kate Medhurst's reputation; he owed her that, at least.

'No particular reason,' said his friend. But he had the sensation that Gunner knew something had happened between them, maybe not the full extent of it, but something that should not have happened all the same. He should not have bedded her. He should not have loved her. It whispered of dishonour, in more ways than one. He would have put his head in his hands were there no one to witness it.

'Seeing the boy, Tom, upset her.'

'You were right. She is a mother, with two young children back in Louisiana—a son and a daughter. She misses them.'

'I am sorry for her. It cannot be easy.'

'More difficult I would guess than either of us can imagine.'

'Did she tell you anything else of herself or her circumstances?'

'A few things,' he said, staring out at the blackness. 'But nothing that changes my thinking on her.' He could still feel the softness of her skin, he could still smell the clean womanly scent of her and feel her in his blood. What had happened in that cabin felt like a lot more than just sex. It felt like something he had no damn right to experience.

'Well, I suppose we should be glad of that.' Beside him he could feel the weight of Gunner's gaze upon him.

'Yes, I suppose we should,' he said, but supposing and being were two different things.

'Come on, old man, best get this old crock back down below,' said Gunner.

Kit took hold of his friend's arm to help guide him through the darkness.

Slowly the two men moved together across the deck towards the ladder.

She could not hide from him for ever. She had to face him sooner or later, and the sooner it was done, the better. Kate rinsed her face in the cold water and stared at her reflection in the small looking glass that hung over the cabin's washstand.

The night spent sleepless with regret and remorse, with guilt and shame, with anger and all sorts of other confusing emotions, had left its mark on her face. Her eyes were ringed with shadows, her complexion too pale and ashen.

The soap and water had washed North's scent from her body easily enough. But no amount of scrubbing could erase the knowledge of what they had shared together. It felt like that was engraved on her soul.

Lord, help her, she cringed at the thought of seeing him again.

But not once in her adult life had she hidden from what had to be done. Fear was a thing that lurked behind you, in shadows and round corners, the only way to deal with it was to turn round and confront it. She did not know any other way. So she dried her face and dressed in her own black muslin and fichu and the black shawl, and tidied her hair all neat and respectable. And with her head held high she went to face the crew of *Raven* and its captain, too.

Gone was the bright sunshine of home. In its place were grey skies and a churning charcoal ocean beneath, both of which matched the sombre mood that hung about the ship this morning.

North was in his usual place on the quarterdeck, peering into the distance through his spyglass when she emerged from the deck hatch. There was no sign of Gunner, although the rest of his crew seemed at busy industry. Bob the raven sat perched on North's left shoulder.

Her heart was beating harder than normal with the illogical fear that somehow what had happened between her and North was branded there on her face for all to see, almost making her turn right around and hurry back to her cabin.

But none of the men treated her with anything other than their normal respect.

North's eyes met hers across the deck. She gave him a small polite nod of acknowledgement, as if nothing had happened last night, then walked to stand by *Raven's* larboard rail, not too close that might be construed she was angling after him, but not far enough away that might be thought avoidance.

A few moments later and she heard his footsteps. Her heart began to race in earnest, part of her praying he would walk on by.

All her blood rushed and tumbled, and she felt her cheeks blush rosy as any green girl's at the sight of her lover, as his footsteps came to a halt by her side.

She did not trust herself to look round at him, not until she could be sure of her composure.

'Last night—' he began to murmur quietly.

'Should not have happened,' she said, finishing the sentence, taking control of the situation. She knew what she was going to say, had rehearsed the words a hundred times through the night, but still her throat was dry. 'We were both tired and our sensibilities were running high.' She said it quietly, but with a firmness of confidence that brooked no disagreement. 'It will not happen again.'

'It will not,' he agreed. It was what she wanted to hear, but those words upon his lips made her feel strangely bleak. 'I hope you do not feel that I took advantage of you. It was not my intention.'

She met his eyes then, seeing that there was a gravity in them that matched the darkness of the daytime sky. 'You know you did not,' she said, angry that he could think such a thing. 'Do you honestly think me so weak as to be so easily coerced against my will?'

'No, Kate,' he said. 'I do not think any such thing.'

She gave a tiny nod. 'Please do not let me keep you from your duties, Captain North,' she said, effectively dismissing him.

'You know I could not allow such a thing, even were I

to wish it otherwise, Kate Medhurst,' he said softly, and there was such a look in those dark eyes of his that made her feel as though she had just had a glimpse of some deep personal truth in him—a look that held both intimacy and pain.

He walked away, returning to his charts and his spyglass.

She wanted to retreat to her cabin, but she stayed where she was, looking out over the grey swell of the ocean, for the sake of appearances and pride.

You know I could not allow such a thing, even were I to wish it otherwise, Kate Medhurst. It was not so much the words that haunted her as that look in his eyes.

Her bonnet's black ribbons fluttered wildly in the wind. Her skirts moulded themselves to her legs and beneath the dark shawl she shivered from the cold and from other things, too. But still she stood there, and would do so for the next half-hour until, with her pride intact, she could go below. She shivered again, the shiver bone deep and cold as ice this time, as though someone or something had walked over her grave. And then she saw it—the ship that sailed out of the bank of clouds in the distance, the ship on which Kit North had trained his spyglass. And her mouth went dry and her stomach gave a somersault and she understood the reason for the men's mood and intensity of focus. And her heart leapt at the same time as there was something sad beneath it.

For the ship heading straight for *Raven* was one that Kate recognised. Although it was sailing under French colours and flew neither black sails nor any flag to proclaim its privateer status, she was under no doubt as to the identity of the schooner—*La Diligent*. Only one man commanded that vessel: Captain Jean Lafitte. And there could only be one reason why Lafitte was this far across the Atlantic and flying not the bloody flag but the white one of *parlez*.

The ship heading straight for *Raven* was coming for Kate—to save Le Voile from North the Pirate Hunter and take her home to Louisiana.

Chapter Eight

Kit watched Lafitte's ship, judging the distance with an expert eye, aware that there could only be one reason big enough and important enough to bring Lafitte chasing all this way across the Atlantic.

'Continue to hold our current course and speed, and ready the guns,' he commanded.

'Aye, aye, Captain.' The men moved smooth and efficient as cogs in a clock. Everything timed to precision. They all knew who was coming and that Lafitte had not carved a name for himself amongst the Baratarian pirates for nothing. They all knew that *La Diligent* was a match for *Raven*. They knew, too, that her long guns were big enough to come close to the range of those that *Raven* carried.

Kate Medhurst stood statue still, her hands gripping the rail, her focus fixed all on the pursuing ship.

He moved to stand by her side. 'Go below, Kate.'

She glanced round at him, meeting his gaze briefly, but with an intensity that mirrored what he was feeling himself. 'You know who that is, right?'

'I know,' he said. Then, to Briggs, 'Escort Mrs Medhurst to her cabin.'

'No.' She turned to where Briggs was advancing towards her, stopping him in his tracks with a look before returning her gaze to Kit. 'That will not be necessary, sir.'

Briggs looked at Kit.

'As the lady wishes,' he murmured, knowing that short of slinging her over his shoulder and carrying her down that deck ladder by force she was going nowhere.

Briggs hurriedly returned to his station.

'Six hundred yards!' shouted Collier from the crow's nest, whose eyes were trained on the approaching ship.

'Stand ready with the guns,' Kit ordered.

Kate stared round at him with a look of incredulity. 'Do you not see the white flag of *parlez*?'

'I see it.'

'And yet you mean to shoot at him?'

'Just as he means to shoot at us.'

'You are mistaken!'

'I do not believe so.'

'He wishes to *parlez*,' she said, not understanding what it was Lafitte had come to do.

'He wishes anything but to *parlez*. He knows who I am. And the cargo I carry. He intends to stop me reaching London with La Voile.'

'You don't know what he wants until you listen to what he has to say,' she implored. 'Jean Lafitte is an honourable man. I give you my word on it.' Desperation made her careless.

'Men are not always as honourable as they might seem, Kate.'

But she still did not understand what was happening here and no amount of words would ever convince her. But she would see soon enough, *La Diligent* was already within penetrating range for her own guns.

'Kit, please...' Her hand touched his arm and stayed there, betraying them both.

He did not look at her, just kept his gaze fixed on the closing ship, gauging distances and direction with finesse, knowing that although *Raven* had the advantage of being on the windward side, with less hull exposed and more manoeuvrability, this was still a very dangerous situation.

'You should brace yourself, Kate.' Lafitte would fire; Kit was convinced of it.

'Have you no honour?' she demanded.

He froze at the words that stabbed with stiletto precision into his weakness, his darkness, his Achilles heel. He turned to her, meeting her eyes directly, forgetting in that tiny sliver of a moment about *Raven* and *La Diligent*, about where they were, or how much he was revealing of himself.

'No,' he said in a cool quiet voice. 'My honour is lost and cannot be redeemed.'

She looked at him with disbelief and disgust and contempt and he took it, accepting that judgement unflinchingly because it was completely warranted.

'God have mercy on your soul, Kit North.'

'I sold my soul a long time ago. For me there can be no mercy, Kate.'

Their eyes locked in the moment of painful truth and revelation before with a measure of disgust and disbelief she turned and walked away from him. He watched her go, knowing that whatever she might have felt for him was no more. And rightly so. He returned his focus to *La Diligent*, now much closer.

Something glinted in her rigging, tiny and brief, and Kit realised that he had misjudged Lafitte's plan by one small important point. The sudden truth of it became clear as he identified the glint as a sharpshooter, the long-barrelled rifle in the man's hands, so carefully taking aim.

'Get down, Kate! Now!' he yelled, but it would be too

late, he knew that even as he sprinted the distance to reach her. The shot rang out, like the clear snap of a branch in a silent wood.

She was turning towards him, her face looking to his.

With all the force he could muster he threw himself forward, shielding her, taking her down, twisting as he clutched her to him and they fell together. He landed heavily, the pain like a hard heavy punch to his shoulder pinning him there when he would have got up.

She lay on top of him, like they were making love. Her face inches from his own, her eyes wide and staring with shock.

'Kit…?' she whispered, her breath warm against his cheek. 'Kit…!' as the realisation began to hit her.

He tightened his arm around her. She was safe.

'Three hundred yards,' he heard Briggs's voice shout from somewhere far in the distance.

'Fire the guns!' he instructed. The echo of his command ran down the line. *Raven* roared as her guns let loose on *La Diligent*.

The dizziness and darkness roiled in his head. He fought to clear it.

The guns were sounding and the stench of smoke and saltpetre had drifted up from the gun ports to sting her eyes and fill her nose, but Kate barely noticed. She stared with horror at the pool of blood spreading out so dark and wet on the pale scrubbed wood where Kit lay.

'Lafitte's fleeing, heading back from where he came.' The voice seemed so faint she barely registered it.

She could not take her eyes off Kit as she trembled from shock and horror and the need to help him, to save him. She did not remember getting to her knees by his side or bunching her shawl to form a pad. The fine cotton of his black shirt was sodden where she pressed the pad firm against the white-and-red flesh that gaped at his shoulder.

His face was pale, his eyes dark as jet as they looked into hers. 'I am fine,' he said. 'I just need a little assistance to reach my cabin.'

By the time Gunner arrived Kit's men had laid him out on the cot within his night cabin. They stood in the background, caps in hands, afraid to leave, their faces, usually so strong and merciless, haunted with the same gut-wrenching, blood-chilling fear that was trembling through her own body.

'Maybe we should we move you below to the surgical room,' she said quietly, seeing the never-ending leak of blood that was spreading over the sheets.

'No.' His tone was adamant.

'It is just a flesh wound that needs to be cleaned and bound,' said Gunner as he stood by Kit's side. Then, to the men, 'We need basins of water—cold and fresh boiled— and the packets of linens from the cabinet in my medical room.'

They nodded and hurried away, easier in activity than idleness. The door clicked shut behind them.

'If you would be so kind as to assist me in stripping off his coat and shirt,' said Gunner.

'Your strength is not yet fully recovered. I will call one of the men back to help me.' She moved towards the door, but Kit's quiet voice stopped her.

'No, Kate.'

He exchanged a glance with Gunner before Gunner said, 'We cannot let them see how bad it is.'

Her stomach dropped, her blood froze. She stared at the

priest. 'You said it was just a flesh wound.' But she understood even before he answered the unspoken question.

'I am afraid I lied,' Gunner said softly.

'They are men with pasts, Kate,' said Kit. 'They need a strong leader. Without it, *Raven* would be a very different place for you and Gunner.'

A ship of leaderless ex-pirates in the middle of the Atlantic would be no place for a priest who had not yet regained his strength, or a woman. 'How bad is it really?' she asked.

He glanced at Gunner for the answer.

'We will not know until I get a proper look at him.'

She nodded.

Between the three of them they prised the thick leather coat from him, cut the shirt from his blood-smeared body and pulled off his boots and stockings, covering him with a blanket so that when the men returned they would see nothing. But even that exertion brought an ashen sheen of perspiration to Gunner's face and left him breathless.

Once the water and the linens had arrived and the door was safely shut once more, Gunner closed his eyes and leaned against the bed, catching his breath. When he opened them again he met her gaze, holding out his hands before him, revealing openly for the first time the extent of the tremor that beset them.

'It is a delicate operation to probe the wound and one that requires precision if it is to be successful.'

'I will do it myself,' said Kit.

'You will do no such thing,' she said firmly and stepped forward. 'I will be your hands, Reverend Dr Gunner.' Although she spoke to Gunner her eyes never left Kit's, holding them with determination until, at last, he gave a tiny nod of assent.

Gunner's pale-blue eyes looked into hers. They both knew Kit's life hung in the balance.

'Tell me what to do,' she said.

And he did.

As she washed the red smear of blood from Kit's chest and shoulder, she saw for the first time what her fingers had felt the night they made love—his body was a lattice of raised and ragged scars. And she understood at last that solitary confinement had not been the only way the prison guards had punished Kit North.

The sight made her throat feel thick and tight with emotion, almost broke her heart, but she hid it from him, refusing to meet those dark eyes lest they saw the truth in her own. She swallowed down the rock in her throat, stowed away the deluge of tears that would have fallen, silenced the sobs that crammed tight in her chest for release, for none of those would help him. But strength, practicality and caring hands—they would. Summoning up all of her strength and self-control, she got on with the task, doing what must be done.

He lay there not saying a word, not flinching from either the pain or the past revealed so clearly all over his body. The blood welled and leaked from the wound constantly. She cleansed it as best she could, moving the basin and cloth aside when she was done, before standing ready before him.

'Now for the real fun,' said Kit, cool and calm as ever. As if his life blood were not dripping all over the floor. As if a bullet had not torn its way through half his shoulder.

'Are you sure you want to do this, Kate Medhurst?' he asked and there was an undertone there that made her understand something she did not want to.

'Are you sure you want to let me, Kit North?' she replied, never shifting her gaze from his.

He laughed, but the laugh became a cough, laboured and painful so that she felt the cold fear for him spasm again and caught hold of his hand in her own, squeezing it tight as if she could give him something of her strength.

When the coughing stopped he laid his head back on the pillow, his eyes holding hers. 'Do it,' he said, then glanced across at Gunner with a nod of his head.

Gunner passed her one of the horrible hooked metal devices she had seen in the glass cupboards down in his surgical room. Such an instrument of torture that she quailed within at the thought of what she was going to have to do with it.

'Having second thoughts?' Kit's voice taunted.

'Are you?' She parried his too perceptive question with one of her own.

'No,' he said. 'Not over you. Not any more.'

Their eyes clung together. She wanted to weep, she wanted to tremble, she wanted both to hold him to her and to flee this room, this situation and him. She did neither of them.

Instead, she took a deep breath and glanced over at Gunner. 'I am ready.'

Gunner moved to insert a piece of wood between Kit's teeth so that he might bite down on it and not his own tongue when the pain got too bad. But Kit refused it with a shake of his head.

So Gunner stood behind her and spoke the instructions in a slow, clear, calm voice.

Taking a deep breath, she moved the metal probe to the wound and then closed off a part of herself to follow Gunner's every command.

She probed the raw pulp inside Kit's body, with one instrument and then another, and he made not one sound. Deeper, further, harder, she probed and probed, until, at last, after what seemed an intolerable lifetime, she saw the dark, misshapen lead ball.

'I found it,' she said.

Gunner passed her a pair of small pointed tongs. 'Prise it out.'

Her eyes flicked up to meet Kit's. 'How are you managing there?' she asked softly.

'Have you started yet?' He smiled, but his face was devoid of colour, leaving him powder white, as if the wound had indeed bled every last drop of blood from him, and the sheen of sweat upon his skin glistened in the daylight that flooded through the porthole.

She returned her focus to the wound, blanking out everything, save Gunner's voice, and listened carefully to what he was telling her to do.

With steady hands she dug out the bullet that Jean Lafitte's sharpshooter had put in him, dropping it with a clatter into the waiting metal dish. Then with the merciless care and the relentless tenacity that Gunner demanded, and Kit deserved, she began examining the wound, removing every tiny fibre of cotton and leather that she could find.

Every time she thought she was done, Gunner had her go back in with that sharp metal probe, poking and prodding in that bloodied, raw, gaping hole of flesh until it looked like a piece of butcher meat. And she did it. Like the men in Johor who had tortured him, she tortured both him and herself in doing so. And she did it willingly because she would have done anything to save his life.

The pain must have been unbearable, but not once did he flinch. Not once did he cry out, or groan or even murmur. She could see the knotted muscles and strained tendons tight beneath the skin of that shoulder and could feel the strain that gripped his whole body and the sweat that trickled in rivulets. She prayed that he would know the mercy of passing out, but he did not take what mercy offered. With what must have been utter relentless determination, he stayed right there, aware and awake the whole time.

It was the longest wait. An agony of suffering that was like nothing she had ever known. Not like birthing her two children. Not like hearing the news that Wendell had been killed. Because here with this was the terrible weighty burden of guilt. For she knew that Kit North had taken that bullet for her.

At last Gunner pronounced the probing finished. At last she placed the probe down into the dish and he passed her the black-threaded needle, and she sewed him up as if she were sat back in the homestead in Tallaholm, stitching curtains for the windows.

'No.' Gunner touched a hand to her arm, stopping her when she would have fetched a dressing for the wound. 'No dressing. The air will heal it better than anything. Keep the bedcovers clear.

'There is nothing more we can do,' Gunner said. 'Except pray.' Practically the same words she had said to Kit when they sat by Gunner's side that night.

'You know that would be wasted on me, Doc,' murmured Kit. He managed a smile. His face was grey. Sweat was beaded on his forehead and upper lip. His voice was weak, but the look in his eyes was strong and dark and determined as ever.

'One of these days, my friend,' teased Gunner, but she could see the toll just being on his feet all that time, watching carefully over her shoulder, had taken on the priest–physician. He was almost as pale as Kit.

'Go, get some rest, Reverend Dr Gunner. I will look after our captain.'

Gunner gave no argument, only staggered through to the day cabin to collapse on to his own cot.

The water in every basin was scarlet. The pile of stained rags on the floor was too large. Her hands were stained and wet with Kit's blood. She stared at them. So much blood. Surely too much for a man to lose and still live? The fear squirmed in her stomach.

'So, you are going to look after me, are you?' he said.

She forced herself to swallow the fear down before she let herself look up at him.

He was watching her, his eyes on hers.

'Shouldn't you have passed out from the pain by now?' she asked softly.

'Sorry to disappoint, Kate. Pain is my friend.'

'So it seems.' She smiled.

And so did he.

'Sit down,' he said.

But she was afraid to face him. 'When I have cleared up and washed up.' She moved to gather up the rags.

'No,' he said, his voice quiet, but still with command.

She stopped, leaving the rags where they were.

Her eyes moved to his face, scanning his eyes, fearing what she might see there.

'Sit down now, Kate, before you fall down.'

'I'm fine, really, I am,' she insisted, but she sat down on the little wooden chair by his bedside all the same. Her eyes scanned the cabin, moving over the pile of scarlet-soaked rags, over the blood that had run down his arm to drip from his fingertips to pool on the bare deck planks below the cot. And the marks of everywhere her bare feet had trodden. The deep dark stain of the blood pool and her own bloody footsteps would be preserved in the wood for the rest of *Raven's* life, she thought as her gaze travelled over her bare toes smeared red with his blood. So much blood that she feared there could be none left in his veins. So much blood that she feared…

'Are you?' His voice was soft, but held a timbre that seemed to reach into her chest and stroke a finger against her heart. He had just endured what would have sent most men out of their minds. Pain that was beyond imagining. Blood loss to drain a body dry. And his concern was not for himself, but for her…the woman who was the cause of it all!

She looked up into his dark, dark eyes, eyes that were intelligent and perceptive and tender. 'You need to rest, Kit.' Her voice was hoarse in her struggle to stop herself breaking down. He needed her strength, her care, her reassurance, nothing else, not right at this moment in time. That would all come later…if he survived.

'We both need to rest, Kate.'

She looked at where his bloodstained hand lay loose and open, palm up on the cot's sheet. She reached her own hand to gently close around it. Their fingers, so engrained with blood, entwined. 'Maybe you are right,' she admitted.

Only then did he close his eyes and take the rest his body must have been screaming for.

She sat there, exhausted physically, emotionally and spiritually; her eyes on his face, knowing in that moment that she was bound there by much more than their linked hands, or the stain of his blood that marked half her body.

His face was ashen, his breathing shallow. The bullet was out, but the danger was far from over. A cliff edge stretched ahead, for them both.

Gunner was right—all they could do was pray.

The shaft of cool silver moonlight behind his eyelids woke Kit in the solitary cell of the Johor prison. The press of the poker in his shoulder was white-hot, bringing a sweat to prickle and run over his skin, holding his breath hostage in his throat, clouding the thoughts from his brain, obscuring the other pain ever present and mammoth in comparison to anything they could do to him.

He embraced it. Suffered all that they could do to his body. All their paltry efforts. All their taunts, their threats, their promises of how they would make him suffer, what they would take from him before they took his life. They were supposed to terrify him. They were supposed to make him cower and beg. They were meant to break him. But nothing of it touched him.

Take it, he could have said to them. *Take it all*. It meant nothing to him. Not what they could do. Not when it went nowhere near the real torture. He did not fear death, but welcomed it and the relief it would bring from the real torment that churned in his soul.

Regret. Remorse. Guilt. He could not forget. Not for a minute. Not even for a second. What he had done.

It had taken those long days and nights locked alone in the tiny cramped cell for him to look into his soul and see what he really was. Only then had he finally realised the man he had been and fully appreciated that the fault was all his own and no one else's. Enlightenment. And a vow sworn. Kit Northcote had died in Johor and Captain Kit North been born.

He thought again of what he had done and the shame of it was excruciating in a way none of their knives or pokers or whips ever could be.

Devlin, Hunter and all the rest of the men who had been there that night to witness it were present there in the cell with him, their mouths silent, but their eyes speaking volumes. And present, too, were those he had brought to their knees—his own father and mother, his own sister…

That pain was unbearable. He cried out against it and in

the midst of the torment he prayed for the poker to touch again that it might distract him from that real pain, prayed for the stench of burning flesh that would follow, but the only smell was that of the sea and the wind and dampness of night. There was no clank of metal or rake of hot coals, only the quiet roar of the ocean; no dripping damp wall at his back or hard press of manacles, but a soft mattress and the comforting rock of the waves. There was no relief, only the pain, and the one thing that sustained him through it was the vow he had sworn.

The moonlight through the porthole shone its gentle silver light into the cabin. The bloody rags were gone, the red-water basins, too. Not one of Gunner's instruments of life and torture remained. The only evidence of what had taken place all those hours earlier were the stained planks beneath her feet and the half-naked man lying on his back upon the cot.

Kate could not sleep despite the exhaustion that pulled at her body. There were so many thoughts crowding in her head, so much confused emotion vying in her breast, so much fear and guilt, so much she did not understand—about that sharpshooter's shot; about the man who had saved her from its bullet…and the way she felt about him. If he died… Something contracted in her chest at the thought and there was an ache there, dull but persistent.

A man so unlike any other. A man she had expected to hate; a man she should hate. He represented everything she despised—the British, a hunter whose prey was honest, hardworking, American citizens who had been driven to justifiable forms of privateering and piracy; he was ruthless, hard, emotionless, someone who put money and a bounty above all else. There was no denying he was all of those things. And he was everything that she respected and admired, too—a man of integrity, a man who had risked his life to save hers, be it to dive into an ocean to snatch her from the jaws of a shark, or to use his own body to shield her from a bullet—a bullet from a privateer she had defended and for whom she had pled. A man of initiative and intelligence, who had not left his crew to rot in an Eastern prison, but had broken them out and got them home. A man who had rescued a small boy to whom he owed nothing.

A tear escaped as her eyes moved over his torso. What had they done to him in that prison? Too much pain and suffering for any one man to endure.

Her gaze travelled higher to his hard handsome face. There was nothing of peace in his slumber. The place that it took him was not a good one. And little wonder given the scars that marked him. Kate watched the troubled dreams and saw the pain that etched his face, sleep revealing the truth he hid so well in waking. He hurt, she realised. He hurt the same as her, just as Gunner had said.

'Emma…Devlin…' The garbled murmurs escaped his lips, fast, troubled, his level of distress so evident that it shook her.

'Hush, I am here,' she whispered the words softly and soothed a hand against his troubled brow, as she did to little Ben when a nightmare struck.

And in his dark place of sleep Kit seemed to hear her and calmed beneath the gentle brush of her fingers.

He was the man she should hate, but what she felt for him was very far from hate. What she felt for him…

'Hush, my love,' she whispered, soft as a summer breeze through palm leaves and pressed a butterfly kiss to his forehead.

And she wept, for him and for her children, for Wendell and for the damnable mess she was in.

* * *

It was Gunner who woke her, with his light knock on the door before he entered the night cabin.

She woke with a start, her dreams confused and troubled. Images of Ben and Bea and Wendell, of Jean Lafitte and Bill Linder…and Kit all too clear in her mind and her heart beating too hard with raw emotion, and her chest too tight with the knowledge of what had changed between them.

The moonlight had long gone, replaced instead with the bright light of day, harsh and unforgiving.

She was slumped in the chair, her head resting on the edge of the cot near Kit's legs. As she righted herself she took a breath, preparing herself, screwing her courage to the post before she moved her eyes to Kit.

He was awake, his gaze fixed on hers. His face was still pale, but not grey as it had been the day before. Something fluttered inside her heart.

'So, you are still with us, Captain North.' Her voice was soft and husky from sleep and the tears she had shed in the night.

'For my sins,' he replied softly, but there was something in the way he said it that made her think the words were not in jest and brought the memory of what she had seen etched upon his face flooding back.

'How is our patient this morning?' asked Gunner with his usual cheeriness. He did not wait for an answer. 'I brought you breakfast.' He set a bowl of blood-soaked oatmeal on the little bedside table. 'You should eat while it is still warm.'

She could smell the metallic stench of the pig's blood, the tingle of it hitting the back of her throat, making her head swim and her stomach revolt. Ironic, for what was a little pig blood in comparison to the crimson tide that had washed the floors of this cabin?

Gunner leaned closer, peering at the ragged wound with its blood-encrusted black stitches and the newly appeared surrounding bruising. 'No discolouration, no pustulation. Healing nicely.'

'I had a good surgeon,' she heard Kit say, and when her eyes moved to his it was to find them on hers. Their gaze lingered, so many words unspoken between them.

'I will take over from here,' Gunner said.

She did not argue, but gladly left.

Chapter Nine

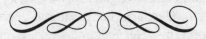

'I did not mean to interrupt,' said Gunner once the door closed behind Kate.

Kit eased himself up to a sitting position. 'You did not interrupt.'

'She saved your life, Kit. I could not have got the bullet out.'

'I know.'

'And she has not left your side.'

He knew that, too. He thought of the fatigue shadowed beneath her eyes. He thought of the sight of her there, sleeping, overcome by exhaustion. He thought of the feel of her hand within his own. Of all that she was and all that she made him feel.

There was a silence while Kit ate, the pig blood replacing some of his own which had been lost.

'That shot Lafitte's man fired. His aim was true. The bullet was meant for Kate Medhurst.'

'It was.'

'It does not make any sense.'

'Quite the reverse,' said Kit. It made perfect sense, once one rid oneself of the blinkers. The truth was glaringly obvious and had been right from the start.

'Care to enlighten me?'

'Not yet.' Not until he had got his own head around it.

He finished the oatmeal and the grog, then, ignoring the protests his body made, swung his legs over the side of the bed.

Kate poured the water from the jug into the little basin in the washstand and sponged away the rusty stains from her naked skin. Her face, her neck and décolletage, her hands and forearms. Her feet and shins. Even her thighs where the blood had soaked through the layers of black muslin. She washed her hair, too. At the end of it, her skin was white again and the water in the basin crimson. She rolled the muslin to a tight ball and stowed it beneath the bunk where her holsters and weapons had been hidden, remembering that it had once been her intention to put a bullet in Kit North's chest herself. Now everything, and nothing, had changed.

He was still North the Pirate Hunter. She was still Le Voile. And he knew. Even though he had not spoken the words. It was there in his eyes when he looked at her. She could feel it in the very air between them.

He knew. And he had still taken that bullet for her. Jean Lafitte had come, but not to rescue her.

She was confused, so confused. Everything in her life had been so simple before. Everything made perfect sense. But not now. Now, she did not know what to think any more. All that she had believed had been turned on its head. Friend and foe. Betrayal and loyalty. Love and hate.

She lay down on the cot and closed her eyes. But no matter how long she lay there she could not sleep. And she could not stop the thoughts that twisted and spun in her head. So, after a while, she rose and dressed herself in the black silk from the Antiguan wardrobe. Black stockings tied in place with black tapes. The matching black slippers upon her feet. She combed out her wet hair, leaving it long and loose to dry. Then ate the light breakfast Gunner had left before eventually heading up on to the upper deck.

She stood there, looking out over the grey Atlantic Ocean, the rhythmic roll and spray of the waves lending her some sense of relief.

The tap of Gunner's stick sounded as he came to stand by her side

'Here you are,' he said quietly.

'Here I am,' she said, without looking round. 'How is he?'

'He is typical North,' said Gunner in a voice that made her smile despite everything else that was in her chest.

They stood in companionable silence for a while.

'It was my fault that he was shot,' she said.

'Men make their own choices, Kate.'

'He told me to go below. He told me Lafitte meant to fire. But I would not listen. I…' She could not tell Gunner the truth of her words in those final moments. No doubt Kit would tell him soon enough. 'I thought I knew better,' she finished instead. Then looked round, meeting his eyes for the first time, saying what every man on *Raven* already knew, 'He took that bullet for me.'

Gunner's silence was an agreement.

She sighed and returned her gaze to the grey roll of waves, watching them in silence for a few minutes. 'Does Captain North have a woman?'

'No. I have already told you the way it is with him and all the usual vices of a man at sea. Why do you ask?'

Emma…Devlin… 'No reason.'

Voices sounded. Men moving to the quarterdeck. She glanced over and saw Kit standing there in his faded leather coat and his hat, and Bob the raven on his shoulder. As if his shoulder were not torn apart. As if he had not been hovering so close to death's door all through the night.

'What is he doing?!'

'Taking the morning briefing,' said Gunner quietly.

She shot a look of accusation at the priest. 'You should have stopped him. He is not well enough—'

'He is the captain. And these men need to be led.'

She made to move past him, but he stopped her by the lightest touch upon her arm. 'If it is any consolation, I have seen him rise the next day after a lot worse.'

'What could be worse than yesterday?'

'Much more than you could imagine, Kate,' said Gunner softly so that she remembered the scars upon Kit's body.

Her eyes moved to where Kit stood, at the helm of his ship. Those dark eyes met hers for the briefest of moments, before he turned away and got on with giving his orders.

'If you will excuse me, Reverend Dr Gunner.' She left and headed back down to her cabin, needing to be alone, needing time away from the man who affected her too much.

In the days that followed Kate Medhurst steadfastly avoided him. She did not come to the dining tables. She spent too much time in her cabin, and the minutes during which she did surface on deck was when it was busy, overrun with crew, and she kept well clear of wherever he was to be found.

Part of him was relieved by it. But it was just putting off the inevitable. She knew it every inch as much as him. His eyes traced her silhouette against the prow, the black silk dark and sheened as Bob's wings in the dying sun.

'Take over, Reverend Dr Gunner,' he instructed. 'Carry

on, Mr Briggs.' He made his way up the length of the ship to her, aware that the eyes of his crew were watching.

'Mrs Medhurst.' He stopped by the rail only a few feet away from her, sharing the same view.

'Captain North.' She did not look round at him. 'I was just leaving.' She began to turn away.

'You cannot hide in your cabin for ever, Kate,' he said quietly.

The words stopped her in his tracks. She did not flee. Just stood there very still for a moment before resuming her position at the rail. 'No, I suppose I cannot.' She closed her eyes for a moment, then opened them again, and took a deep breath before she glanced at him.

'Tell me about your husband,' he said softly.

Their gaze held for a long second until at last she gave a nod and looked out once more to the vast grey expanse of the ocean.

'His name was Wendell Medhurst. He was born and raised in Tallaholm, the same as me. We married when I was twenty-two years old and had our son, Ben, a year later and our daughter, Beatrice, Bea for short, a couple of years after Ben. He was a good man—a kind husband, a loving father. We owned a small general store. It earned us a good living. And then with all the political trade blocks—first the French, then the British, and finally our own government. So many blocks as to be a stranglehold—we could not make ends meet. Could not put food on the table for our children. It was the same for all of Tallaholm, as much as New Orleans. So Wendell did something about it.' She glanced round at him, something of the old light of defiance in her eyes. 'He stood up to you British.'

'He became a pirate,' he said.

'He became a privateer, with a letter of marque from

the French consul. He might have flown French colours, but everything he did was to benefit Louisiana.'

'He plundered British merchant vessels.'

'He stood up for his family and his country against tyranny.'

'He became one of the Lafittes' men.'

'He worked for himself, not Jean or Pierre Lafitte. The Lafittes helped with the set-up, the storage and distribution of goods, and offered a measure of protection. They know people in high places, powerful people.'

'The overlords.'

'In a manner of speaking I suppose they are.' She nodded.

'What happened to Wendell?'

'He was murdered by the British.' She met his gaze. 'A naval captain boarded his ship and slit his throat in front of his crew.'

Just as he had feigned with the boy on *Coyote*. Only then did he realise how much it must have affected her to see his blade held to the boy's throat. The threat had been an empty one, but she could not have known that.

'I am sorry, Kate. That never should have happened.'

'It should not. But it did.'

There was a silence.

She met his gaze. 'So you will understand something of my feelings towards the British.'

He said nothing. He did understand. Too much.

'I loved him,' she said, and looked down to where her fingers twisted the plain gold wedding band on her finger. 'I still do.' She swallowed. 'I always will.'

Her eyes met his again and he saw her pain and her grief, and the strength that had driven her.

'I know,' he said.

'How many days until England?'

'A week at most.'

She nodded and looked out again at the ocean.

They stood in silence together.

He felt her pain as keenly as he felt his own.

He understood, but understanding changed nothing. He walked away, left her standing there and returned to his duty.

At the dining table a few evenings later Gunner was sitting opposite her and little Tom beside her, keeping her company at the dinner table, now that she had given up hiding in her cabin. It made her heart swell to see how much the boy had come out of his shell.

'If you're not wanting that...' Tom eyed the chicken pieces in gravy sauce that she was poking round her plate, like a starving dog staring at a food-laden table.

'Take it.' She pushed the plate towards him. 'A growing boy needs to keep his strength up and I am not hungry tonight.'

'You weren't hungry last night, neither. Nor any of the nights since the captain got shot.' He looked at her with concern creasing between his brows.

'Eat the chicken, Tom,' Gunner said.

She forced a small smile to her face. 'My appetite does seem to have deserted me these days. I cannot think why.' But she knew why.

She glanced down the length of the table to where Kit sat with Briggs, Collier and Hastings. On the surface he was his usual self. Cool, strong, remote almost. A captain in every sense. And yet she noticed he looked pale and there was still a slight stiffness in the way he moved.

As if sensing her gaze, Kit moved his eyes to hers. Across the small distance the tension vibrated between them. So much unspoken. So much he had not asked her. Not one question on Jean Lafitte. No mention of Le Voile.

She returned her attention to Tom and to Gunner, to find the priest watching her.

'You cannot go on like this,' Gunner said softly.

'I cannot,' she agreed. It was time to take matters into her own hands.

Kit was alone when he came into the day cabin, just as she had known he would be. From the shadows that obscured her she watched him close the door behind him and lean back heavily against it, closing his eyes, his shoulders slumping as if he carried the weight of the world upon them. The sunset that blazed through the huge stern windows washed the pallor of his face rosy and revealed the darkness of the shadows that smudged beneath his eyes. It touched mahogany streaks to the darkness of his hair and showed the full extent of the vulnerability only revealed now he thought himself alone. The sight of it touched raw against her heart. She swallowed.

He must have heard it for she made no move or any other sound, yet his right hand slid quickly to the handle of his cutlass and his posture changed.

And then his eyes were open and trained on her standing there in her black dress in the shadows where the sunset did not reach. She stepped out into the rosy glow of light.

His hand dropped away from the cutlass but he did not revert to leaning against the door.

They looked at one another in the silence.

'You know, don't you?' she said. 'Who I am.'

'Captain La Voile,' he said softly.

She gave a smile that had nothing of mirth in it. 'I have dreaded this moment, since first you brought me aboard *Raven*. But now that it is finally here, it is almost a relief.' She took a breath. 'Does Gunner know?'

'Only me.'

She gave a sigh. 'You already know why. I guess I should tell you the rest of it.'

He said nothing. But she wanted him to know, this part of it, at least.

'*Coyote* was always mine, built by my grandfather. I had sailed her in those waters from the time I was a little girl. I knew them better than anyone else. When Wendell died I had my children to provide for and a very good reason to hate the British. I wanted to sail under American rather than French colours, but as our countries are not officially at war I could not obtain an American letter of marque. So, officially, I became a pirate. Unofficially, Mr William Claiborne, the Governor of Louisiana, gave me his blessing. I had the knowledge and the ship. But no self-respecting privateer or pirate would have crewed for a woman, so I gave them the captain they expected.'

'A player.'

She nodded. 'All he had to do was look the part and do what I told him.'

'I should have known the very first time I saw you on *Coyote*, with the dark awning above the quarterdeck, a screen for the woman who habitually stood in a captain's place.'

'In my defence the sun is very fierce in our Louisiana waters. I did not want to burn.'

'Who have I got pickled in my medical room?'

'Tobias Malhone.'

'I would not have killed him had he not been fool enough to attack.'

'I know.' She nodded. 'He was a violent and brutal man. It was not supposed to be about killing, but about trade and honour. Tobias was starting to believe he really was La Voile. He was trying to cut me out. Even if you had not come along I was closing down the operation, so that he could not destroy my good name.'

He came to stand before her, the toes of his boots touching the dark hem of her skirt.

'How did you know?' she asked.

'You are a widow who still wears her wedding ring and dresses in mourning. You told me that your children were both fair-haired like their father, your husband. The man in the butt is not fair-haired. And Jean Lafitte would not have got in his ship and sailed halfway across the Atlantic to stop me reaching London with a dead La Voile. Imagine what it would do to his reputation if it was revealed that the prime operator amidst the Baratarian pirates was a woman with two children at her skirts.'

'It took me a while to work that one out. I thought he had come to rescue me.'

'I underestimated him, too. I thought he meant to "lose" La Voile in a skirmish.'

Neither of them mentioned the bullet. They did not need to. It was there thick in the atmosphere between them, mixed with the passion and everything else.

'I am Le Voile.' The admission was finally out there in the open between them. Now she just had to ask the question they had both spent the last days avoiding. 'What are you going to do about it, Kit?'

He took her gently in his arms, and he leaned his forehead against hers, his eyelashes brushing hers as they shuttered. 'I do not know, Kate. I honestly do not know.'

It was cool and grey the day they landed at Plymouth.

For all it was summer it did not seem so. England was a place so alien to her. She missed the boundless blue skies of Louisiana. She missed the sunshine and even the stifling humid heat that she so often complained about. But most of all she missed her children and her mama and her friends; and all of her life that was wrapped up in Tallaholm. Devon, England seemed every single one of those three-and-a-half-thousand miles away.

She climbed from the little rowing boat and stood there in the harbour's yard, looking around her. Men hurried here and there over the damp ground. Carts, coaches and gigs crowded the road leading in and out—both delivering and collecting from the boats and ships waiting to leave and just arrived. Officers in the dark-blue uniforms of the British royal navy, their men in dark jackets and the wide trousers and striped tops of seafarers.

'So many of your King's men,' she said, and felt a shiver ripple down her spine to be standing there in their midst, like a spy who had infiltrated the garrison of her enemy.

'This is the Royal Navy's dock. Merchantmen use the harbour just a little along the coast,' Gunner explained.

'*Raven* is not a Royal Navy vessel.'

'We have special dispensation given that we sail on Admiralty business.'

She understood now why the ensign had been hoisted before they approached the harbour. 'Who would have thought that the American pirate Le Voile was so important to the British Admiralty?'

'So important that they'll hang him by his scrawny pickled neck and pay us handsomely for the privilege,' said Briggs from behind her.

Collier and the others nodded and smiled, practically rubbing their hands at the prospect. 'Very handsomely indeed. When North says he'll deliver he does. Ain't it so, Captain?'

She swallowed.

A muscle tightened in Kit's jaw, but he said nothing in reply.

The men turned their attention to shifting sea chests and the great oak butt that contained Tobias's body. But their words remained.

The ground seemed unsteady beneath her, the way it always was after so many days at sea. Except that it was not only sea legs on dry land making her feel like her world was tilting. The men's words stripped everything else away, paring it down to the danger she was in.

Run. The word whispered in her head. *Escape.* Kate watched Tobias's coffin no longer, but turned away. And found her nose practically touching Kit North's chest. She made to sidestep, but his hand captured her elbow fast and firm, preventing her flight.

She looked up into his eyes, knowing that whatever else he might do, he was not going to let her go.

They made it as far as the end of Dartmoor. Kit stopped short of heading into Exeter, choosing, instead, to spend the night in the small market town of Chudleigh at the edge of the moor. The quieter location of the Courtenay Arms Inn meant there would be fewer problems in securing stabling for both the cargo and horses.

The first hint of trouble came once they had booked in for the night and were sitting in the taproom, and the landlord and his wife brought them their plates of mutton pie and potatoes they had ordered.

Kate was sitting by his side.

'Thank you,' she said as the woman set the plate down on the stained and pitted table surface.

'American?' the landlady asked, her dark brows drawing together.

'Yes, I am, ma'am.' Kate held her head high and proclaimed it loud.

A hush seemed to spread across the tap room.

The landlady's fingers fixed upon Kate's plate, lifting it back on to the great wooden tray she carried. 'I don't rightly know that we serve Americans in here. Not with them causing our boys such a trouble across the sea.'

Suddenly there was a dangerous atmosphere in the inn. *Raven's* crew's hands let go their tankards of ale to close upon the handles of their muskets and knives.

Kit got to his feet and spoke not to the landlady, but across the room to her husband behind the bar. 'If you do not serve the lady, you do not serve any of us.' His fingers rested lightly against the handle of his cutlass.

'It's late and you'll be hard pushed to find accommodation elsewhere at this hour,' the man answered.

'We will,' agreed North. His eyes held the landlord's. 'As pushed as you to find others to fill your empty rooms and stables.'

The landlord seemed to understand that the threat was not idle. He gave a nod to his wife. 'Serve her. I don't suppose there's much harm in having her under our roof for one night.'

The woman nodded and banged the plate down before Kate with a surly expression.

The standoff passed.

The locals drinking at the bar and through in the snug glanced their way too often, but Kate showed not one sign of intimidation.

His men grew rowdy, the earlier threat diluted by ale.

A serving wench came to clear the empty plates from the long wooden table. Beneath her apron the girl's bodice was tight and low cut, her grubby chemise laced so low and loose that her huge soft breasts were in danger of spilling free. With a sly glance at Kit's face she leaned over, presenting him with a full view. She leaned closer, deliberately brushing them against his arm, offering herself to him. The men sniggered, their gazes locked on those breasts, licking their lips. His gaze moved beyond the girl to another woman, whose eyes, the colour of the ocean they had just crossed, were watching him.

The girl's gaze followed his before returning to his face.

'A fine man like you...' Her fingers reached to toy against the lapel of his coat. 'You want to get yourself a nice English whore instead of an American.'

'I am not his whore.' Kate's voice cut like a blade through the jollity and laughter.

Silence descended upon the table.

'What are you, then?' the girl demanded, turning to her with narrowed eyes. 'His prisoner?'

'She is my betrothed,' said Kit coldly and removed the girl's hand from his coat.

'I beg your pardon, sir,' the girl said coolly and, lifting her tray, left in a hurry.

Silence hissed. The whole of the crew was looking at him and Kate.

Gunner raised his tankard. 'It seems congratulations are in order.'

Kit said nothing.

'To the Captain and his lady,' said Gunner.

'The Captain and his lady,' the men all chorused and toasted them with their tankards of ale, stamping their feet and cheering.

'Calls for a celebration, I reckon,' said Briggs.

'I will leave you to celebrate, gentlemen,' Kate said, getting to her feet. 'It has been a long day. I think I'll turn in for the night.'

The men all stood, as if they were gentlemen and she their captain's lady in truth.

Kate's expression revealed nothing, but when her eyes met Kit's he saw the flash of resentment in them.

'Gentlemen.' Kit rose and followed close behind her, so that all of those locals who watched her too much left well alone.

Kate was very aware of Kit walking behind her. All the way up that rickety staircase. All the way along that long narrow corridor. They walked in silence past closed doors until they found the one they sought. When he opened the bedchamber door for her and she saw the sea chest sitting there on the floor she thought it was his, she thought...

'Your wardrobe,' he said from where he still stood out in the narrow corridor of the landing.

She glanced round at him, relieved that he had no intention of coming in, the atmosphere thick and cagey between them with so much that remained unclear. 'Thank you.'

The wardrobe he had bought for her in Antigua. The words pulled all that was unspoken into the little distance between where they each stood. All they had shared: the shark, the alleyway, their bodies united in lovemaking, the bullet in his shoulder and the biggest of all, the thing that neither of them was mentioning and that was there, huge and obvious as a mountain—*I am Le Voile... What are you going to do about it, Kit?*

The question still whispered without answer, growing more insistent and louder and tenser with each passing day, twisting tighter in the pit of her stomach now that they were on British soil.

She would not beg. She would not plead. She had her pride and her integrity. And so did he. But it did not make all those dark long hours of not knowing any easier. She turned her mind from that and thought of her vow.

'You should not have told her we were betrothed.' The sight of the serving wench touching him had made her throat tighten and her fingernails cut into her palms. *A fine man like you*... She swallowed down the memory and fidgeted with the wedding band on her finger, reassuring herself. It was not as if it was a real betrothal.

'What would you rather I had told her?' *The truth?* He did not say the words, but they were there just the same.

She glanced away, knowing what that would mean. Her fate would be sealed. The crew of men downstairs would not stand so ready to defend her honour. There would be nothing of friendship or respect.

'Lock the door behind me. And do not open it again until morning.' His voice was unemotional, instructional, cool almost, as if the enormity of the dilemma did not rage between them. As if he did not hold her life in his hands. He made to close the door and leave.

'Why do you have a care for my safety?' Her words stopped him in his tracks, but he did not turn round. 'Oh,' she said softly. 'I forgot. You get a bigger bounty if I am alive.'

He turned to her then, his face all cool, hard dispassion, but those dark eyes fixed on hers held a conflict so deep and serious and tortured that it resonated right through to her core.

The silence hissed loud.

He did not say a word to break it, just looked at her and then closed the door and she heard his booted steps recede along that narrow passageway.

She locked the door just as he had said, then leaned her spine against it and stood there, with her eyes on that sea chest, knowing full well that a bigger bounty was not the reason he was safeguarding her.

Moving to the bed, she eased off her slippers, blew out the candle and crept beneath the thin blanket.

The smoke from the extinguished candle drifted in the darkness, lit grey and curling by the moonlight that showed through the small dirt-hazed window. The flimsy curtains that framed it on either side stirred in the draught. From the taproom below came laughter and the rowdiness of men's voices. From outside came the creak of the heavy wooden inn sign swaying, and the wind's low howling from across the moor.

Kate lay there in the darkness, until the taproom downstairs emptied and voices and hooves faded across the moor. Lay there unmoving and silent for so long, until the men had ceased their singing and the footsteps had faded and internal doors had opened and closed again. Until there was only the creak of the sign and the moan of the wind. And only then did she let herself think of Ben and Bea back home in Tallaholm so far across the ocean and what would happen to them if she did not return. Only then did she close her eyes and silently weep.

All that he was. All that he had become. All that made it possible to live with the knowledge of what he had done. All of it hinged on integrity…on honesty. On a vow he had sworn in a prison on the other side of the world, the words of which were seared upon his heart, as raw and meaningful as if he had spoken them only yesterday. He would never be Kit Northcote again. He would not lie. He would not cheat, not in the smallest of things…or in the largest.

He had signed a contract with the Admiralty and taken half the payment up front. There was no getting out if it. He was promised to deliver them the pirate La Voile. He could give them Tobias; all of his crew would stand witness that the man in the butt was La Voile. And the Admiralty would pay the money. But Kit would know the truth—that he was lying, that he had conned them. That he had *cheated* them. Just the thought made him feel sick.

But if he delivered them what they had paid for… He

swallowed. The fact that she was a woman would not save her. They would hang her, privately, if not publically. The most courageous woman he knew. A woman of integrity and strength. The woman to whom he had made love. The woman who had dug a bullet from his shoulder. He balled his fists. How could that be right? Where was the integrity in leaving two children motherless? Where was the honesty in a man betraying his lover?

She was La Voile. And she was also the woman he cared for.

So he was damned if he did, and damned if he did not. He either cheated Admiralty or he sent Kate Medhurst to her death.

That was the crux of the decision before him. Stark and brutal, no matter how many ways he might try to disguise it and name it otherwise.

Chapter Ten

'Briggs is watching the door that leads up to the bedchambers as you instructed. You really think that the anti-American feeling is so strong as to be a risk to her?' Within the stables Gunner leaned back against the wooden partition and watched Kit strapping the saddle on to his horse.

'I do not wish to take the risk. Hostility is in the air, stoked, it seems, by a series of sensationalised stories of what La Voile and his pirate friends have been doing to the British merchant vessels in their waters.' He did not like the way she had been treated over her nationality. And no matter the risk to her safety Kate would refuse to keep quiet or pretend she was anything other. But protecting her from attack was not the only reason he was keeping a close eye on her.

He could not trust that she would not try and make a run for it. No other woman would risk it, but Kate Medhurst was not any other woman. She would not balk at the dangers for a woman alone and penniless in a foreign country. Just the thought of her alone out there, at the mercy of men who would hurt her… He tightened the buckle and moved on to the next strap around the horse's girth.

'This betrothal—' Gunner began.

'Feigned. To save her reputation,' he interrupted in a harsh voice.

'That is a shame,' said Gunner. 'When the two of you are such a good match for each other.'

Kit ignored the words and kept his focus on the strap he was buckling

Gunner got the message and turned to leave.

'Gunner,' Kit said, his fingers stilled against the horse's belly.

His friend stopped and glanced back.

'The vows you swore as a priest... The vows that define a man...'

Gunner waited.

'Is there any way you could break them and live with yourself?'

The morning sunlight spilled across the straw-strewn floor. Outside a blackbird was singing.

The two men looked at each other.

'No,' said Gunner softly. 'I could not. Why do you ask?'

But Kit just shook his head and turned his attention once more to the horse before him.

The little column of men and horses and the carts wound their way across those narrow bumpy highways, creeping slowly but surely towards London. Kit rode out in front, keeping his distance from Kate, checking on her welfare, but leaving her to ride beside Gunner. But too many times during that long day that took them out of Devon and halfway across the south coast of England, she glanced at him to find those dark eyes upon her.

The Cardinal's Cap Inn in Milbourne was busier than the one at Dartmoor had been, and its guests, a little more mannerly. But she was still very aware of the looks her accent drew. And of the slightly threatening message that

Kit's protective presence sent them. He paid extra money that she did not have to share a bedchamber with other women travellers and walked her there after they had eaten. But whether it was as a man protecting the woman he cared for or a guard escorting his prisoner, she did not know.

Neither of them spoke.

The tension seemed more strained than ever.

There was not a single word. Only the sound of that door closing. Only the sound of his booted steps walking away to leave her there alone. Only the knowledge, as she made her way through the candlelight to lie on the bed, that in two days they would be in London.

Would Kit really give her up to hang? A man who had made love to her body with such tenderness, a man who had saved her life and who looked into her eyes as if he felt things for her. Part of her could not really believe he would do it. And part knew him a man who would not flinch from doing the hardest thing. It was not about the bounty, for Tobias's body would secure him that easily enough. It was about integrity. And whatever else she knew, or did not know, about him, she knew that he was a man of integrity. It was the thing she admired most in him. And the thing she most feared, for it was his integrity that could hang her.

There had to be a way out of this. But no matter how many times she turned the problem round, no matter how many different angles she looked at it from, she could find no solution. There was no rest to be found on that lumpy over-warm bed. With a sigh she abandoned the elusive quarry of sleep and moved silently to stand by the small window.

The moonlight shone across the coaching yard, bleaching the gaudy inn sign to more muted hues and showing the empty dark carriage bodies lined up there like beasts crouched ready to pounce. Over by the stone wall a lone figure stood looking out over the nocturnal English countryside. The silhouette of a man in a shabby leather coat, wearing an old-fashioned tricorne hat—a pirate's hat, or more accurately a pirate hunter's hat, for upon the man's left shoulder sat the dark shape of a raven. Sleep eluded Kit North as much as it did her.

For a few minutes she stood there and watched his familiar figure so still and silent. And then, lifting her dark shawl from the chair on her side of the bed and slipping her feet into her shoes, she unlocked the door and crept from the bedchamber.

At the sound of her footsteps Bob flew up to perch on the inn's sign and watch them.

She came to stand beside Kit where he stood overlooking road and field and hedgerow, but seeing nothing of them.

'You should not be here, Kate.'

'Probably not,' she agreed, but she made no move to leave, nor did he want her to.

She stood by his side, watching out over that same view, just as they had stood together on *Raven*, looking out over the ocean.

'A man has got to sleep some time,' she said.

'Not always.' He could not remember the last time he had slept.

The wind howled across the fields, blowing a rustle through the hedgerows that lined the road and divided the fields.

'Who is Emma?' she asked.

He shifted his gaze to her, to study her profile.

'My sister.' He wondered what else of his secrets he must have spilled in his nightmares.

She gave a nod and asked no more.

They stood in silence a little while longer, contemplating the view, before she spoke again. 'We will be in London the day after tomorrow.' She did not glance round, nor ask the question. That she could be so cool, so controlled, was a measure of her strength and made him realise that he was making the right decision. It had to be tearing her up inside; it was certainly doing as much to him and she was the one whose life hung in the balance.

He swallowed. 'We will.'

She turned to him then, her eyes moving over his face, down over his open coat, down over his shirt as if she could see the scars beneath, down to his holsters and his weapons before coming back up to his face.

They stood so close, facing one another, in that deserted dark coaching yard, arms loose by their sides.

'Integrity,' she said.

'Integrity,' he echoed.

'Such a difficult decision to make…whether to compromise it.'

'It was.' More difficult than she could ever imagine.

'Maybe I should have made it easier for us both. Maybe I should have taken the decision out of your hands. Since you are the only one who knows the truth of who I am.' Her gaze dropped to his holsters again, to his pistol, just as it had done that day on *Raven*, before coming back up to meet his eyes again.

'You know it is always loaded,' he said quietly.

'Yes.' All that had happened on *Raven* seemed to whisper in the quiet breeze of the night around them.

He took the pistol from its holster, turning it in his hand so that he was holding the barrel as he offered her the handle.

She inhaled a deep steadying breath, staring at it for a moment before she accepted it from him.

He opened his coat, exposing his chest.

He saw her swallow as she removed the safety catch, saw the slight tremor that ran through the pistol as she aimed it at him.

'Close your eyes if it makes it easier.' He guided the muzzle to press against his heart. 'One squeeze of the trigger and it is done.'

She stared at his heart with determination in her eyes, but he could feel how much the pistol's muzzle trembled against his chest.

The moment stretched between them.

'Do it, Kate,' he urged.

She glanced at his eyes, then looked at where the pistol pressed to his heart and, giving a sigh, let it drop away before making it safe. Stepping closer, she slid the pistol back into its holster, before meeting his gaze once more.

They stood there and those short dark seconds of the night stretched longer.

They stood there and there was the thud of his heart and of hers.

'Tell me,' she said.

'I will cheat Admiralty and give them Tobias. Kate Medhurst was just another of his victims. They will send you home with the next convoy.'

Her eyes closed tight as the relief flooded through her. 'Thank God,' she whispered.

'I cannot deprive children of their mother.'

'And were I not a mother?'

'My decision would be the same.'

They stared at one another.

'Go back inside, Kate. It is late and we have many miles to cover tomorrow.'

But still she stood there.

'You might be giving them Tobias but the seas are free of Le Voile. I have already told you that her piracy days are over. I give you my word on that. So you are not cheating them. Not really.'

He smiled a bitter ironic smile at that because it did not change what was written upon the contract he had signed. And it was not La Voile he was delivering.

'Go,' he said with quiet command.

She nodded and walked away.

He watched until he saw her face appear at the small lead-latticed window and knew she was safe.

Bob swooped down to resume his perch on his shoulder. And Kit turned his gaze once more to the dark roll of fields.

Kate breakfasted with Gunner the next morning in the Cardinal's Cap Inn's dining room.

The bread was fresh baked and soft, the warmth it still held from the oven melting the fresh pale-yellow churned butter that she spread thick upon it. The tables had been wiped down of last night's spills and tankard rings of dried ale. The worn and uneven stone-flagged floor had been swept and washed, and the windows opened to let the morning air chase away the stale odours of pipe smoke and soured ale and lend a brisk chill to the dining room. A maid was sweeping out the ashes from the great hearth on the other side of the room. The landlady was busy in the kitchen, and the landlord, with a drying towel in his hand, could be seen in the doorway that separated the two rooms.

Raven's crew occupied the other tables, their normally robust manner subdued this morning, but whether it was due to a surplus of ale the night before or another cause she could not tell. Of Kit there was no sign.

'Does Kit sleep late this morning?' she asked Gunner quietly, wondering at what hour he had finally gone to bed.

Gunner shook his head. 'He is in the stables, checking over the horses and the cargo. He was already out there when I came down at five.'

She wondered if he had slept at all.

Something of last night's overwhelming relief had faded. This morning what she could not seem to get out of her head was that look in his eyes when he had pressed the muzzle of his pistol to his heart. And those soft words.

And were I not a mother?

My decision would be the same.

'Mrs Medhurst... Kate...' Gunner lowered his voice. 'Please do not think me impertinent... Kit seems... Did something happen between the two of you? A disagreement, perhaps...?'

She shook her head, knowing that what was between the two of them would remain that way. She could not tell him. 'Why do you ask?'

'Because there is something in his eyes this morning that I had not thought to see there again.'

'What do you mean?'

But Gunner just gave a little sad smile and shook his head in reply.

Her appetite waned, but she finished her bread and butter, and drained her coffee cup, not knowing when they would next get to eat.

The big wooden door banged as Kit came through it. 'We need to get moving. Now.'

'Aye-aye, Captain.' The men did as he bid, finishing up their food and making their way out to the yard.

'Gunner... Mrs Medhurst.' He did not look at her. His manner was cool, hard, efficient. Almost like the very first time they had met. Almost. But something was different, something she could feel the essence of, but not quite define. 'The bill has been paid. I will wait for you outside.'

The door banged again and he was gone.

She shot a glance at Gunner, but he was already on his feet and waiting for her. His pale blue eyes met hers and she felt a chill of unease stroke against her heart where there should only have been relief.

Ignoring the feeling, she fastened her bonnet on her head, slipped her gloves on to her hands and followed Gunner towards the front door.

Kit urged his horse onward. Now that the Cardinal's Cap and Milbourne were far behind the sun slipped from behind the clouds to brighten the day. Early morning had turned to late, but still his train of horses and men and carts pressed on, knowing they had Whitchurch to reach tonight.

He led from the front, keeping his distance and his eyes from Kate.

They rode for another hour before they stopped to water and feed both the horses and men, eating the great chunks of bread and cold ham and cheese for which he had paid the Cardinal's Cap landlord handsomely.

He studied his map, checking the roads that lay ahead, eating the bread, keeping his mind fully engaged on the task in hand so that he did not have to think of the other darker things that lay ahead in London.

'When is the wedding to be, sir?' Briggs asked.

'The wedding?' He glanced up from the map.

'Between you and Mrs Medhurst. What other wedding could there be?' Briggs teased with a grin.

Kit had glanced across at Kate before he could stop himself. Her eyes met his and held so that the secrets they were hiding seemed to vibrate in the air between them.

Only the two of them and Gunner knew there was never going to be a wedding.

Only the two of them knew the truth.

He should say the words, *When we get to London*. Or some other lie. Once an oath was broken the floodgates were opened to release lie upon lie, cheat upon cheat, until a man had no hope of saving his soul, or living with the deeds he had done. But he could not. The weight of his own darkness pressed down heavy upon him. He would damn himself to save her a thousand times over, he thought, and wondered that the decision had taken him so long.

'Captain North and I have yet to make that decision.' It was Kate who answered, with neither a lie nor the truth.

'Are we invited, ma'am?' little Tom asked. '*Raven's* crew, that is.'

Kit was glad the question was not directed at him. He saw the way the little boy looked at her. When she left it would break the lad's heart as much as his, had he a heart to break.

'At any wedding of mine and the Captain's I am sure that all of *Raven's* crew would be very welcome guests.' Again, no lie. Her clever use of words ensured it, cleverer than his had ever been.

He was glad when the time came to put away the map and ride on.

All day he rode out ahead alone, apart from the rest of them.

All day she could feel the wedge that was between them.

She should have been glad of it. She should have been willing the hours to pass all the quicker, for the sooner they reached London and she was aboard a frigate bound for America the better. She would be safe, heading home to her children and her family. And she would leave him behind, never to see him again.

He was British. She was American.

He was a pirate hunter and she the pirate he had been paid to capture.

And he was a man who had compromised his integrity to save her.

She had known that it would cost him to compromise himself, but to see it, to feel it, this difference in him… She thought of how she would feel had she to stand up and renounce all that she believed in, her cause and country, to save him.

Being closer to London, the White Hart Inn at Whitchurch was much busier than those of their previous stops. No one accosted or challenged her on her accent, but she saw the glances that were shot her way when she spoke and heard the dark murmurs. There was an air of threat about the place and no locks upon the doors, so that when Kit escorted her to her bedchamber that night and did not leave, she was glad of it.

'There is a bad feeling about this place. You should not be alone.' He did not say anything of her nationality.

He jammed a wooden chair beneath the handle of the door so that it could not be opened from outside. She watched the care he still took in private over his weakened shoulder as he removed his heavy leather coat and laid it down on the floor before the chair. She knew what he was doing as he unsheathed his cutlass and positioned it on one side of the coat.

'Planning on undoing all my hard work with your shoulder?' she said, walking over to stand before him.

'It is healed.' His expression was cool and dispassionate, his eyes did not meet hers. He laid the pistol at the other edge of the coat.

'Even so, there is a perfectly good bed over there. You can sleep above the covers, I can sleep below. I promise I will not ravish you.'

He glanced at her then. But he did not smile. Just gave a nod of his head.

And so that is what they did. She, fully clothed beneath the blankets, he, wearing his coat above them. Lying on that bed together, a thousand miles apart in the darkness.

There was a two-foot gap between them. At no point did they touch, but she could feel the tension that hung about his body, as if it were her own, feel the darkness of his turmoil.

She tossed and turned.

He lay still and unmoving, but awake. She could sense it, hear it, feel it, all through the long slow stretch of those hours until at last, when he thought her asleep, he gave up the pretence and walked quietly to stand by the moonlit window, staring out into the darkness. She watched him standing there for a few moments, like a man who had sold his soul, like a man who was haunted. And then she rose from the bed and went to stand beside him.

'I did not mean to wake you,' he said.

'I was not asleep,' she admitted.

He glanced round at her then and there was something so tortured in those dark eyes of his that it was as if a hand had taken hold of her heart and squeezed.

She slid her fingers to cover his. 'In all the time I have been Le Voile I have never regretted it, not once. Indeed, it has been my salvation. But only now, only when I see you, do I wish with all my heart that it were not so.'

She felt the caress of his thumb against hers.

'La Voile Noire—the black sail,' he said quietly.

'Not quite,' she said. '*Le* Voile Noir—the black veil. My little joke. I was a grieving widow and a pirate captain, and I was obscuring what was there in plain sight before all the world.'

He stared at her, a hard look of shock on his face.

'Please do not feel bad, Kit, everyone made the same assumption. No one looked beyond the black sail.'

'And when they referred to *La* Voile…'

'I did not correct them. It is what they wanted, what they needed to believe. Part of the illusion.'

'The illusion of Tobias.'

The silence echoed between them. She could feel the change in him, feel the stillness and sudden increase in tension, feel intense heavy weight of his gaze.

She looked up into his eyes. 'It started out right and justified, but…' She bit her lip. 'Things are not so clearly delineated any more. Who is friend and who is foe. What is right and what wrong.'

'So all these three years you have been *Le* Voile,' he said very carefully. He stepped up close to her, staring down into her face with sharp urgent eyes.

'You know I have.'

'And Tobias, La Voile.'

'I guess.'

He rummaged in an inner pocket of his coat, pulling out a folded document that was pale in the moonlight, and crossed the room quickly.

With fast efficient fingers he lit the candle stub using the tinderbox. She saw him swallow before he opened out the document, and, in the flickering candlelight, carefully scan the neat penned black lines.

His eyes shuttered. His body relaxed. He gave a sigh of relief.

'What is it, Kit?' she asked, her eyes staring into his.

'My salvation,' he said, and he smiled as he passed the document into her hands.

Her gaze moved over the rusty stain that marked the paper, the same stain that was preserved upon the deck of Kit's night cabin on *Raven*, before she read the words written there.

And then she smiled, too. His salvation, indeed.

For the document was his contract with the British Admiralty. And the name of the pirate he had been contracted to capture and rid the seas of, written clear and without ambiguity in every single instance throughout, was *La* Voile.

He smiled, that same smile she had once seen him give on *Raven*, of happiness and relief, a smile that lit her soul and made her heart swell for him. It was as if he had stepped out of the darkness of a terrible oppressive shadow into the light. She was so glad for him, so relieved. She knew how much this meant to him.

Reaching a hand to cup his cheek, she felt the roughness of the beard stubble that shadowed and darkened his cheek, his chin and above his lips. She slid her fingers against it, caressing the harshness and masculinity that made him the man he was. Anchoring that man now he had returned, never wanting him to leave lest the darkness of that unfathomable torture swallow him up again.

He smiled and, reaching a hand round her waist, pulled her to him, stroked the long loose strands of hair and stared down into her eyes.

Tomorrow they would reach London. Tomorrow they would go before the Admiralty. And she would start her journey home to Louisiana. She longed for it and she dreaded it, too. Because of this man standing before her.

After tomorrow it would be as if she had never met him and everything would go back to the way it should be. Her heart belonging to Wendell. Her life devoted to raising Ben and Bea and caring for her mama. She would be the person she had always been. Strong and loyal and true—to her children, to her country and the memory of the man she had sworn she would always love.

All of that came tomorrow. But tonight…she was here and looking into those dark, dark eyes with all their secrets and integrity and her heart was filled with tenderness for him and her body alive with desire for him. Tomorrow she would step back into her old life. But tonight…tonight she followed her heart and the longing in her soul.

He blew out the candle and they kissed and stripped off their clothes, and they loved together beneath the light of the silver moon.

The hour was still early, too early to wake Kate.

Kit thought of their lovemaking of the night. She had loved him, giving herself and her heart with an intensity of meaning that matched what was within his own body and mind and soul.

Today she would go home across the seas and he would face what it was he had spent the past three years both running from and to. It had to be this way. He could not weaken. Not now. Not when he was so close, in the home straight. And besides, he had nothing he could offer her. If she knew the man he really was, she would not look at him the way she did now. She would revile him. She would lock her door and her heart against him, not open her soft arms and hold him to her breast. He did not deserve a woman like her. And more importantly she did not deserve a man like him.

Last night was a dream that would sustain him for the rest of his life. This morning, life was there again, waiting with all its harsh reality.

He slipped quietly from the bed and, taking care not to wake her, washed in the basin of cold water and shaved the last of the blue-shadowed bristle from his face. Splashing the water through his hair, he smoothed it back from his face and stared at the man reflected in the looking glass. Always his life was a battle against the weakness within. It always would be. But today he would go to the Admiralty and deliver them La Voile in truth. Le Voile would never sail again. And he would let her walk away and turn his face to London and all that he had worked the last years to do. He stared at the man and knew he would always be glad he had known Kate Medhurst.

He smiled to himself and with a deep breath rolled down his shirt sleeves, tied his neckcloth into place and pulled on his coat.

Out on the window ledge, Bob gave a caw and Kate stirred to waking, looking over at Kit with sleep-misted eyes and a shy smile.

Kit walked over to the bed. 'Bar the door behind me,' he whispered as he dropped one final kiss to her lips.

She nodded.

Kit walked out of her bedchamber for the last time.

Gunner was sitting alone at a small table in the corner of the White Hart's dining room when Kit entered. Those of the crew who were up and ready sat together at a larger table in the centre of the room, largely in silence and looking dog-eared as seamen always did on those first few days ashore.

Gunner's normal calm expression was gone. In its place was a tense worry that stroked foreboding through Kit.

With a nod at his men he sauntered over to Gunner's table and sat down opposite him. He ordered only coffee from the serving wench who appeared from the kitchen doorway in her apron. When she was gone he asked, 'Something wrong?' He wondered if Gunner knew that he had stayed with Kate last night and disapproved. He would not let a slur be cast on her.

'We have a problem,' Gunner said quietly.

'What kind of a problem?'

In reply Gunner handed him a newspaper folded over to reveal half a page, and pointed halfway down a column of print. 'That kind of a problem.'

Kit's eyes read the words with quick precision and all of his assertions about cursing were forgotten. 'Hell!'

'Not good.'

'And with such impeccable timing,' he said sardonically and set the newspaper aside.

'What time are we due at Admiralty?'

'Three o'clock.'

A silence stretched while they both contemplated the magnitude of the development and how it changed everything for Kate.

'You could plead her case. Admiralty might make an exception given that you are delivering them La Voile.'

'They will not,' said Kit. 'You have had dealings with them before. You know they will not.'

'If you turn up with Mrs Medhurst at Admiralty this afternoon…'

'It is not Louisiana to which she will be sent,' finished Kit.

'It is not,' agreed Gunner quietly. 'She will not be going home anytime soon.'

'She has two children waiting for her there. Six and four years old.'

Gunner shook his head and glanced away, the compassion clear in his eyes. They both knew Kate's children would not remember her by the time she returned to Louisiana

...*if* she ever returned. 'We need her as a witness. And even if we did not, we could not leave her here. She would not be safe. The government have probably already started rounding up all the stray Americans.'

'Not all,' Kit said softly. 'They will not be arresting Lady Haslett.'

'Lady Haslett is not an ordinary American woman. She is a member of London's *ton*. Her husband is from one of the oldest and most powerful families in England.'

'My point precisely,' said Kit softly.

Gunner stared at him. 'Are you suggesting what I think?'

'It is seven o'clock. We have eight hours before we must be at Admiralty. Could it be done in time?'

'We passed a church on the way into town. A little gentle persuasion may be required...' Gunner's long bony fingers caressed the handle of his cutlass. 'But, yes, it could be done in time.'

They fell silent while the serving wench delivered Kit's coffee and left again.

'I will explain the situation to Kate. And ascertain whether she wishes to do what is necessary.'

Gunner gave a nod. 'God works in mysterious ways. I cannot pretend that America declaring war on Britain is in any way desirable, but marriage between you and Kate Medhurst might be no bad thing for either of you.'

But Gunner did not understand, not Kate and not him.

Kit's face was grim. He sipped his coffee and waited for Kate to come downstairs.

Chapter Eleven

Kate's first indication that something might be wrong was that there was not one man of *Raven's* crew in the inn's dining room. The second was the fact that Kit had secured them a private parlour for breakfast. The third was the look on his face—a dark intensity and tension so different to the man who had left her not so long since in the bedchamber.

She felt her cheeks grow warm at the memory of the intimacies that they had shared in the night. She had done things with him, given a part of herself she had sworn never to give again. It had seemed so right in the dark privacy of the night when all that had existed was him and her and their relief. Now in the stark clear daylight, with responsibility and respectability back in place, the wild abandon and tenderness of their bonding seemed to belong to another place and time.

Last night had been a different Kate Medhurst. This morning she was herself once again, but the echoes of the night still whispered between them.

'That coffee sure smells good,' she said with a smile, feigning a normality she did not feel as she sat down at the table.

But Kit gave no reply.

The serving wench delivered her a breakfast of warm bread rolls, a dish of strawberry jam and a fresh pot of coffee. Kit poured her coffee, adding a splash of cream and a tiny lump of sugar just the way she liked. And in all that time he did not say a word so that the skin on the nape of her neck began to prickle and a chill of foreboding seemed to spread across her skin and she was seized by the certainty that something was badly wrong.

She took a sip of coffee, but did not touch the bread.

Only when the door of the parlour closed behind the serving wench did he speak.

'There is something you need to know, Kate. Something that changes everything.'

A cold draught blew gentle across her heart, sending a chill through her blood. 'What do you mean? How much can have happened since last night?'

'A lot more than either of us could have anticipated.' From the table by his side he lifted a folded newspaper and passed it to her.

The cup of coffee sat untouched on the table as the printed words hit her. 'America has declared war on Britain!' Her heart stuttered. She stared at him, her mind stumbling over the implications of the headline.

Something that changes everything.

She wanted to deny it, to hope that all would be as they had planned. But she knew in her heart that he was right.

'The Admiralty are not going put me on a ship and deliver me home, are they?'

He shook his head, his eyes holding hers.

'What will they do?'

'Intern you with the other Americans who are here. For the duration of the war most likely. It is what happened during the War of Independence.'

A war that could last for years. Years locked in a prison

camp in England while her widowed mother struggled alone to bring up Kate's two children.

She was so close, so close, and now at this eleventh hour, it was all being snatched away. She wanted to shout out in anger at the injustice. She wanted to weep and cover her face with her hands. She wanted to rail against what was happening. But she knew if she let herself weaken then the floodgates would open and Lord only knew what would come out tumbling out then. So she kept herself together and took a steadying breath.

'There is a way around it, Kate.'

She looked at him. 'What way?'

'They would not intern you if you were married to a British citizen.'

Only the beat of her own heart sounded.

'A gentleman. Someone whose family was one of the oldest and most distinguished in England, and who could stand as your guarantor.'

'Where would I find such a man?' Her eyes held his. She held her breath, afraid that she had misunderstood what he was suggesting and even more afraid that she had not.

'Here, before you.'

Silence.

'Marry me,' he said.

She glanced away. Marriage, to another man. *Marriage.* She thought of all that she had done to avoid it. Becoming Le Voile and all that it had cost her. She thought of what marriage would mean to the memory of Wendell; of what it would say about her and her lack of loyalty. It would make a mockery of everything she had sworn—that she would stay true to him and only him. How could she then marry another? And not just any other, an Englishman, a man who hunted pirates and privateers—a man like those responsible for Wendell's death. And worse than that, a man for whom her feelings already invoked a sense of guilt when it came to the memory of her husband.

'There has to be another way,' she said quietly and saw something flicker deep in those dark eyes before he masked it.

'Believe me, there is no other way.' His voice was cool, clipped, focused. 'It would, of course, be a marriage in name only. As your husband, they would entrust me with your keeping. I have business to deal with in London, but I would arrange for Gunner to return you to Louisiana as soon as it was safe and have the marriage annulled.'

'Could it be so easily done?' A marriage dissolved as if it had never been? As if it counted for nothing.

'As long as it is not consummated.'

She could not meet his eyes. 'Is it not too late for that given we have already…?' She swallowed and tried again. 'That we have…' She rubbed a hand against the back of her neck, knowing that what she had done with Kit North, sleeping with him, loving him, would earn her the condemnation of every respectable citizen in Tallaholm. She knew what she had done was wrong, but when it came to Kit North it seemed all of what she thought she knew about herself and her morals and beliefs went out of the window.

'I believe the church and law consider only those relations that have occurred, or not, after the marriage ceremony.'

She nodded and finally met his eyes. 'You would be marrying a woman who is now officially an enemy of your King and country.' And more than that, much, much more than that.

'I brought you here. And, as I told you before, I have enough on my conscience without adding making your children motherless to it.' His voice was quiet and cool, the look in his dark eyes unreadable. 'I have no preference in the matter. The choice is yours to make.'

But there was no choice. Not as far as Kate could see. Without him, she stood no chance. She would be England's prisoner. But as his wife… She told herself that she was only doing this for her children, to get home to her country, for her freedom; that the marriage would be meaningless because it would be annulled.

And were all those things true she would have agreed to the plan without so much as a second thought. But she knew there was much more to it than that, maybe not for him, but for herself. Things that frightened her to admit. Things that she did not want to feel. Things that made guilt weigh heavy upon her shoulders.

She closed her eyes, swallowing down the guilt, feeling all those forbidden feelings whisper and smile their victory in that part of herself she would deny.

Forgive me, Wendell.

And when she opened them again she said, 'Then I choose you, Kit North. I will be your wife.'

He was silent for a moment, his dark eyes on hers. 'I will make the necessary arrangements.' Cool. Impassive. As if it truly were just a marriage name. As if they had not lain together and shared their bodies and shared their souls by the light of the moon over ocean and land. 'Be ready in an hour.'

So soon? Inside her guilt scraped at her again. She took a breath. Nodded. 'An hour,' she said with a calmness that belied all that was vying and fighting beneath.

'Remember to remove your wedding band.'

Her eyes met his in horror at the realisation. Her hand clutched to it to keep it there, the thought of taking it from her finger too much to bear.

He rose from his chair and walked away, closing the parlour door behind him.

She stared at the cup of cold coffee, scarcely able to believe how much her world had just turned upside down. She felt as though she had been standing in the middle of a quiet dusty street on a lazy sunny afternoon only to be hit, without the slightest whisper of warning, by a speeding mail coach.

In an hour she would marry the pirate hunter Kit North. The man for whom her body thrilled and longed, and her heart ached, and the man for whom she would betray the memory of Wendell and all she had sworn.

The scene was like something from a comedy. In the small country church of All Hallows the early summer sun flooded through the stained-glass windows to bathe the worn and ancient flagstones of the floor in a rainbow of heavenly light. Wooden carved statues of beatified martyrs and the Holy Virgin looked down with gentle expressions. Kit wondered how gentle their expressions would be if they could see the congregation that lined the pews of their church.

Raven's crew looked like the motley bunch of ex-pirates they were. Every one of them was armed to the teeth with pistols and knives. But they had smoothed their hair and wiped the dirt from their faces. Their jackets had been brushed and the dust washed from their feet. Most were even wearing shoes. Kit felt both proud and humbled by the sight of them standing there with their backs straight and their heads bowed in a house of God.

By his side Gunner was calm and serene, his expression so gentle, yet the way the priest before them in his black robes was sweating and the slight tremor in the Common Book of Prayer gripped so tightly between his fat white fingers told Kit that some degree of persuasion had indeed been required. Whatever Gunner had done, the sweating priest had found a way to overcome the not-inconsiderable obstacles of no banns being read and neither the bride or groom, nor a single one of the guests, being of his parish. Old Pete Pinksy was standing at the side with the flageolet on his lips, playing hymns softly.

'Had I known he knew such music aboard *Raven*...' Gunner whispered with a smile.

And then Old Pete stopped, and started playing 'The Queen of Love.' And Kit knew without Gunner's whisper that Kate had arrived.

He resisted the urge to look round, just kept his face pointed forward and tried not to think of her expression of horror when she had realised that she was going to have to marry him. He did not want this any more than she did, but he had brought her here and promised her safe passage home, and it was true that he did not need anything else on his conscience.

Marry her. Face Admiralty. Send her back to Louisiana. Then he could draw a line under all that had happened with her and return to his life in London. It was simple. It was the right thing to do. For the sake of two innocent children. Nothing else. He gritted his teeth and closed his ears to the other things that whispered within, the things to which he could not allow himself to listen, would not allow himself to listen.

The music was coming to a close. He should not have looked round, but he did, seeing her walking those last few paces that would bring her to stand by his side. Her face was pale. She was wearing the black silk dress from her Antiguan wardrobe and her black fichu, clothes for a funeral, not a wedding.

Her only concession to the occasion was the small

posy of wild pink briar roses that she clutched between her hands, their sweet perfume subtle and fresh in the mustiness and polish of the old church. Her tawny hair glowed golden in the sunlight, but her eyes were a resolute grey and they were filled with a determination and courage that no bride should have to wear as she walked down the aisle.

She was not alone. Young Tom walked in her father's place by her side. Kit saw the way the boy held his head up and the thin shoulders squared with pride at the honour of being chosen out of all the crew to perform this task of a man. The lad's eye caught Kit's and he grinned, his pleasure like a fountain flowing out of him to spread all around, such a stark contrast to the guarded look in Kate's eyes. Difficult though this time was for her, she had thought of the boy. Hers was the strongest of hearts, but it was gentle, too. There was not another woman in the world like Kate Medhurst. Had he not been the man he was... Had this marriage been in earnest... Had she not still been in love with her dead husband...

Her eyes met his, and he felt something tighten in his chest. The dust motes drifted between them like it was an otherworld scene. Kit called on his strongest reserves and with a will of iron turned his face forward once more. His gaze, cold and hard, moved to the fat priest.

'Marry us,' he commanded.

And the man did.

Kit went through the ceremony. Her fingers were cold within his, Wendell Medhurst's ring gone in material, but its presence still symbolised by the thin pale band of skin its absence had left beneath. He slid on his own ring to cover it.

Her eyes welled. Her lip trembled. She caught it between her teeth, biting on it to control the emotion, all of it for the dead man she still loved, a man with whom Kit could never compete.

He did not look at her again. Just said the words that made her his wife in the eyes of the church and the law and heard her voice soft and husky make the same vows.

They signed their names in the parish book. No one commented that he signed Northcote and not North, just as they said nothing over the name spoken during the ceremony.

They were man and wife in law. For now.

A marriage made easily enough and to be undone just as easily when the time came.

He kept his heart hard and cold. Because it was the only way he knew to survive.

Kate brushed her hand over her skirt, the same black silk in which she had been married not seven hours since, as if she would smooth away invisible creases. The afternoon sun glinted in through the window of the corridor in the Admiralty building, lighting the men that sat patiently waiting seated on the rows of hard wooden chairs still dressed in their best from the morning. All of *Raven's* crew had come to support their captain and gain their share of the bounty.

The worn old gold band on her finger glowed in the sunlight, light and bright against the darkness of the silk. Her hand stilled. She stared at the ring that Wendell had put there, the ring that she had sworn never to remove. Kit's larger ring was looped on to a thin leather lace tied beneath the fichu. The gold lay between her breasts, hidden well out of sight alongside her heart. No one had noticed the switch so far and she hoped no one would, but she slipped on her small lace day gloves, just in case.

The slow steady tick of the tall clock in the corner of the

room resonated through her body. It seemed that Kit had been in that office for an age. What if there was a problem? What if the Lord Admiral did not believe he had delivered them La Voile? What if they were refusing to pay him the bounty, with all his men sitting here waiting expectantly for their share of the hard-earned coin?

The air was too warm, the palms of her hands beneath the gloves already growing clammy. She smoothed a hand over her skirt again and was about to ask Gunner how long these things normally took when the office door opened and the young naval officer who had shown Kit in appeared once more.

'Reverend Dr Gunner, the first Lord of the Admiralty will see you now, sir.'

Gunner smiled his meek smile at the smartly uniformed younger man and, with a nod, rose and followed him into the office.

Eventually Gunner returned and then each of *Raven's* crew in turn were called within that office. The process took so long that Kate could feel her body tense all the more with growing worry. There was none of the usual convivial chatter and teasing. No jokes, just a feeling of absolute tension and importance, as if they all stood lined up at a cliff edge with a sheer drop on to jagged rocks beneath.

What if Kit had got it wrong and they meant to imprison her, after all?

What if they imprisoned him for trying to help her? She was an enemy of the state now, after all; a foreign combatant in their midst and that was before they knew anything of Le Voile. A feeling of panic twisted in her stomach.

'What will I say to them when it is my turn?' Little Tom,

sitting by her side, whispered the question and looked up at her with a pale face and worry in his eyes.

She wanted to take his little hand in her own or put an arm around him, but she knew that would only embarrass the boy before the men of the crew. So she just smiled at him as if there was not a jitter in her body and told the lie calmly. 'There is nothing to fear. Just answer their questions with the truth.'

He relaxed and returned the smile with a nod of his head.

When Tom disappeared into the office and the crew all sat there in silence, she heard Briggs across the waiting room murmur, 'It's like the bleedin' Spanish inquisition in there.' And despite all she had told Tom she could feel the fear tighten in her lungs and tremble in her nostrils. Her hands clung tight together. She closed her eyes to try to control her nerves.

'Stout heart,' she heard Gunner whisper by her ear.

He was a kind man. A gentle man. A priest. And he did not know how much she was hiding, or how much Kit was risking, and all that was in danger of being discovered.

And then Tom came back with a relieved grin and the young naval officer was saying, 'Mrs North.'

In the expectant silence all faces turned to her and only then did she realise.

'Mrs North,' the officer said again and she realised that she was Mrs North and no longer Medhurst; no longer Wendell's name, but Kit's. Another pang of guilt twisted deep within.

Taking a deep breath, she followed the young officer into the first Lord of the Admiralty's office, to play her part in this masquerade.

Just answer their questions with the truth. In order to save herself and the man who was now her husband, Kate had to do anything but.

* * *

'So Captain North rescued you from *Coyote* and the pirate La Voile,' Mr Charles Philip Yorke, the First Lord of the Admiralty and president of the Board of Admiralty, said once Kate was seated.

'Indeed, sir. He rescued me from Le Voile.'

And the significance of what she had just said was not lost on Kit. *Le* Voile.

Everything about her was easy, relaxed, confident. That same air that sat about her always, Le Voile, the veil, in truth, except in those few rare moments when the two of them were alone and she had let the veil drop away to reveal the vulnerability of the woman beneath.

She was feigning it. He watched her and felt that same respect he had always felt for her. She had more courage than most men he knew.

There was a silence while Yorke steepled his fingers and held her gaze.

Kate returned his gaze, calm and steady.

'And how did you come to be aboard *Coyote*?' Yorke asked.

Kit waited for her answer. There had been no time for rehearsals or to agree a story between them. He just had to trust that she would tell it in the same way he had.

'How does a respectable woman normally come to be aboard a pirate ship?' she said quietly and kept her gaze on Yorke's, almost daring him to be so insensitive and brash as to ask her the details of what everyone imagined the pirate had done to the woman he had abducted.

Kit reached his hand to hers and gave it a little squeeze. 'To discuss the details of the matter distresses my wife,' he said coolly and knew that he was not lying. He felt a wave of protectiveness for her. *My wife*.

Yorke cleared his throat. 'Of course.' He had already heard from his crew that La Voile had been seen treating her roughly on *Coyote's* deck.

'And once you were aboard *Raven* with Captain North...' Kit could see the way the man's mind was working. He thought that Kit had compromised her, taken advantage of her and been left with having to do the honourable thing by wedding her.

'I found a man of integrity and honour.' She glanced across at Kit, her eyes meeting his. 'A man whom I admire and respect.'

More lies or the truth?

Silence.

'And you were married only this morning. The day the nation learns that America has declared war on England.'

'We were,' she answered, unruffled by the unspoken implication in his words. But every man of his crew had told the First Lord of the Admiralty the same story—that their captain and Mrs Medhurst had declared their betrothal on their first day ashore.

Yorke gave a nod. 'Thank you, that will be all, Mrs North.' He got to his feet alongside Kit as she left, treating her like the lady she was. Only once she was gone and the door closed behind her did he resume his seat and speak again.

'I will have the remainder of the payment released to you and your men before you leave. There is, of course, no question of your wife being interned. You are deemed guarantor for her.'

Kit nodded. 'Thank you.'

There was a silence as Yorke's eyes raked his. 'I did not realise you were William Northcote's son.' He could hear the slight rebuke in the older man's voice and see the shift in attitude from respect to something very different. The first portent of what was to come.

'I did not expect that you did.' Kit bowed and returned to his men and his wife.

Within the rented house in Grosvenor Street Kate stood by the window, looking out over the quiet road. London, with its sprawl and its streets with rows of town houses with their stonework and Palladian style, was quite literally a world away from Tallaholm with its wide dusty single street and her wooden homestead out on the edge of town.

The bounty had been divided and *Raven's* crew paid their share. The cart with its great wooden butt and gruesome contents had gone. She did not want to think of what they would do to Tobias's body. No matter what she had thought of him, he was still a fellow American.

The day's difficulty had not been helped by having to feign a true marriage, before all those at the Admiralty and in the hours after. But she had done it both for fear that word might get back to the Admiralty and because she did not want to destroy the happiness that the crew and Gunner and young Tom had over the union. Gunner had taken Tom with him for the night, leaving the newlywed couple alone for their wedding night.

Now, as they stood in the drawing room of the house Kit had rented, she felt as nervous as the green girl in the rough-hewn bedroom of the farmhouse that Wendell had taken her back to after their wedding seven long years ago.

She turned to face Kit. 'So what happens now?'

He stood by the great marble fireplace, the toe of one boot resting on the fender guard, the wrist of one arm resting on the pale carved marble that made the mantelshelf. He looked not at her, but into the empty grate.

'Now we keep up the pretence of living as a happily married couple until the Admiralty's surveillance wanes and Gunner's business is concluded.'

'You think they really will keep their eyes on us.'

'I know they will. You are American. And I am—' He stopped abruptly, biting back whatever it was he would have said. 'My family might be genteel, but I am something of an untrusted entity.'

Because he had once been a pirate, she supposed. But they had trusted him enough to let him turn hunter.

'How long will it take?' Only once the words were out did she realise how they sounded—that she was desperate to be gone from him and on her way home to Louisiana. The latter was true, the former was not.

He turned then, and looked at her. 'A little over a fortnight.' His voice was cool.

She gave a nod, glanced away and, twiddling her wedding band, swallowed. She saw his eyes flick to her left hand and the gold ring upon her finger that was not the one that he had put there, before coming back up to her face. He made not one comment upon the exchange but his expression was as closed and as unreadable as the first day she had seen him standing on *Raven's* deck.

'Console yourself with the fact that we must play our parts as husband and wife only when we are being observed. Rest assured I will not inflict my presence on you a moment longer than necessary.'

'Kit...' Her fingers twisted harder at the gold band.

His eyes held hers, waiting, giving her the chance to explain. He could not know how much she wanted to, or at least try to. But even just to say the words would have been to betray Wendell and she could not do it. And in the stretching silence any chance was lost, swallowed up into something else.

He gave a bitter smile as if he understood, when in truth he understood nothing at all.

'Matthews, the butler, will give you a tour of the house and attend to your every need. If you will excuse me…?'

She should have stopped him. She should have told him.

He bowed and walked away, leaving her standing there. She heard the thud of the front door closing, its echo ringing in the emptiness of the house around her.

Everything was as she had wanted—she had been saved from internment, her passage back to Louisiana was guaranteed, Kit would annul the marriage once it had served its purpose, and he was leaving her alone, with her loyalty to Wendell. But she had never felt more empty and solitary.

She sat down in one of the drawing room's little armchairs and looked at Wendell's wedding ring upon her finger. And she did not understand why when she was trying so hard to do this right, it felt so wrong.

After his business with the bank he walked to Whitechapel and stood there in the dusky light outside the place in Half Moon Alley where he had sold his soul to the devil and destroyed his world and that of his family. It was a shabby, filthy-looking hovel with boarded-up windows and the scent of piss and stale ale and pipe smoke hanging around the doorway. It always had been, but Kit Northcote had been too blind to see the reality. He had seen only excitement in a life of privileged boredom and the chance to make himself look big in the eyes of others.

The same two toughs loitered, leaning on either side of the doorway that led into the small smelly darkness within, like matching black-toothed sentinels. Their faces were scarred and unfriendly. Their eyes held nothing of recognition. They did not remember him, but he remembered them and everyone else who had been there that night.

They sized him up, not sure what to make of his shabby sea attire, or Bob sitting on his shoulder, and, most of all, of the cutlass that hung by his side.

He had thought it would be difficult to stand here and face it again, but it was not. He had thought he would feel that old terror that had haunted him for so long, but he did not. He felt almost disappointed in its ordinariness. Three years ago, it had been anything but. Extraordinary. Exciting. Dangerous. Just like the rest of Whitechapel that surrounded it. But the places that Kit had spent the intervening years made Whitechapel look safe and salubrious.

'Is Stratham within?' he asked, gesturing with his head towards the dark passage. The air seemed to hum as he waited for their reply.

'Who wants to know?'

'An old friend,' he said, and never took his eyes from the biggest man's gaze. He saw the man's eyes flicker down to where his hand, through force of habit, rested upon the handle of his cutlass.

When the eyes returned to his face once more, the man shook his head. 'You ain't been around these parts for a while, mister. Stratham's long gone.'

He should have been relieved, but what he felt was a curious sense of disappointment.

'You going inside, fella?'

'I will pass on the invitation, this time,' he said.

One of them gave a nod of acknowledgement. The other just watched him with sullen eyes. In the memory that had played a thousand times in his mind, they had been taller, bigger, tougher, and Old Moll's Place a dark enticing den of iniquity. The men were not so very different from the man he had become, and Old Moll's just a hovel where Whitechapel men went to ease their hard lives. And the man, Stratham, whose face Kit could recall in detail, from his dark blond hair to his bright-blue taunting eyes and cold sneering smile, was gone.

He should not have been surprised. Someone had probably slipped a blade between the bastard's ribs in a darkened alleyway late one night; just as they should have done to Kit Northcote.

Whatever it was he had expected, it was not this. Stratham was gone. And Old Moll's was nothing. But he had done what he came to do.

He made his way back on foot, walking from the narrow dirty streets of Whitechapel with its poverty and danger all the way across town to the wealthy haunts of the *ton*. He walked the same streets he had walked three years ago, walking past places in which he had gamed and womanised and drank, past the homes of those who had been his peers and his friends.

The watch was calling midnight by the time he approached the house he had rented in Grosvenor Street.

No light burned behind the curtained windows of Kate's bedchamber. All of the house was in darkness save for the lantern left burning to guide his return.

He dismissed the footman who was curled up in the hallway chair waiting for him and climbed the grand staircase.

It was his wedding night, but he did not hesitate by the doorway that led in to where his wife slept. Instead, he walked straight past and on into the master bedchamber. But he did not go to bed. He stood by the window looking down on to the empty street. Tomorrow it would begin. All that he had returned to London to do.

He slipped the neatly folded piece of paper from his pocket and glanced at it. The money was earned. By hard honest labour.

Tomorrow it would begin and he would face it alone.

He thought of Kate Medhurst asleep in the room through the wall, not Northcote, but Medhurst.

And for all that he thought he had grown as a man, for all that he thought he had learned of himself in Johor, he realised that he had not learned that much at all. He had not learned that he would be jealous of a dead man.

Chapter Twelve

Kate watched Kit across the breakfast table the next morning. They were married, living in the same house yet it seemed that there had never been a bigger distance between them.

He was polite enough, considerate of her welfare, but there was a part of him that was closed off to her, a part that she could not reach. As if they were two strangers rather than two people who had sailed across half the world together, who had shared their bodies and their secrets; who had risked their lives for one another.

Gone were the shabby leather coat, the cutlass and black shirt, the worn buckskin breeches and those kicked-in boots that looked as though they had walked a thousand miles. North the Pirate Hunter was gone and in his place sat Mr Kit Northcote, a gentleman she barely recognised. He was clean shaven, his dark hair cut short and tidy, his dark eyes guarded.

'You look like a different man.' He seemed like a different man. It seemed as if everything between them was different. 'You are a gentleman in truth.'

'Appearances can be deceptive,' he answered. 'I am no gentleman, Kate.'

'And yet your family is gently bred and one of the oldest in all England,' she said softly.

'It is, but neither of those facts makes me a gentleman.'

Her eyes moved over the dark tailcoat that was tight across his shoulders, the white shirt and cravat, the white waistcoat and dark pantaloons that were snug around the hard muscle of his thighs.

He seemed to read her thoughts. 'I arranged for a wardrobe to be readied along with the house when we landed at Plymouth.'

'This house was not always your home?'

'No.'

She thought of what Gunner had said about meeting Kit in Portsmouth. 'But you *are* from London?'

'I am from Johor.'

'And before Johor?'

'There was no North before Johor.'

'And Kit Northcote?'

'Kit Northcote ceased to exist a long time ago.'

'Then to whom am I married?' Her eyes held his, wanting to understand him.

He glanced pointedly at the worn gold wedding band upon her finger. 'Wendell Medhurst, I believe,' he said softly and, rising to his feet, threw a heavy purse of money on to the table between them. 'Speak to Matthews to recommend a respectable dressmaker. Buy yourself whatever you need. London society is a deal different from *Raven*.'

She stared at the purse, Wendell's name still ringing in her head.

'There is somewhere I have to go this morning. If you will excuse me, ma'am?' He bowed and made to walk away.

'I do not excuse you,' she said, stopping him in his tracks.

She rose from her chair and faced him with her heart beating so hard that he surely must be able to see it through the black-silk dress she was still wearing. She knew she had to stop him; she just was not sure how to do it. Everything was wrong between them and she needed to make it right.

'What of the Admiralty's spies? Or did you lie about them watching us?'

'I did not lie. I have not lied for the past three years.'

'Then what when they see you going out alone? Again.'

'They will follow me for my visitation and they will understand.'

A sense of foreboding whispered down her spine. 'Where are you going, Kit?'

'Home,' he said. Without her.

She held her head high, too proud to let him see how much that hurt.

He crossed the room until he stood right before her, so close that the toes of his slippers brushed the hem of her skirt, black merging with black to become one, as husband and wife were supposed to be.

'I have to do this alone, Kate.'

She nodded as if she understood, but she did not; not really. 'To warn them that you are married to an American pirate,' she said, trying to make light of it.

'I would give the world that it were so simple,' he said quietly. His eyes studied hers and in their dark depths she caught a glimpse of something so painful that it made her want to weep.

He leaned in and brushed a kiss against her lips. 'I would be proud were you truly my wife, Kate. Never think otherwise.'

And with that he walked away.

She looked down at the ring on her finger and at the skirts of her black dress, the symbols of her love for Wendell and, screwing her eyes shut, tried to conjure the memory of his face. But it was hazy and indistinct. The face that haunted her, the face she saw when she closed her eyes, and when she opened them too, was not Wendell's, but Kit North's. She pressed her hand to her heart to stop what was there from bursting out and making a mockery of the vow she had sworn: to stay true to her first husband.

As his carriage came to a halt in Berkeley Street Kit sat there for that tiny moment before the footman opened the door. This was it—the thing that had driven him through the years and made him choose survival over the easy darkness of death; the chance to right the wrongs he had done, at least in part. It had been over three years since he had last been in this street, outside this house. Three years and in one respect it felt like three times a lifetime, and in another, only three beats of his heart since he had turned his back on them and walked away.

Now the time had come. Kit had returned home.

The carriage door opened. Taking a deep breath, Kit stepped down from the carriage and went to face them, but even as he walked towards the bottom of the stone stairs that led up to the black-painted door he could see that his journey had been in vain. For where the gleaming brass door knocker should have been there was nothing. The striker had been removed, indicating that the family were not in residence.

He climbed the steps just the same, knowing that a caretaker member of staff would have been left in place. But the thump of the edge of his fist upon the door brought no answer. Only when he was this close did he see the street dust that clouded the black of the paintwork and the glass of the windows. From where he stood on the doorstep he could see into the drawing room. There was no furniture.

Where paintings had once hung were only empty hooks. But most telling of all was that the red-patterned wallpaper he remembered so well had been replaced with something else. Of his family's possessions not one sign remained.

He made his way to the front door of the neighbouring house in the smart terraced row. This time the brass knocker was intact. He gave it a loud thud.

Old Carter, the Fredericksons' butler, answered.

'I am looking for the Northcote family. They lived next door.'

Carter looked at him suspiciously as if he had not a clue as to the identity of the man who stood upon his master's doorstep. 'I am afraid they are no longer in residence, sir.'

'Where have they gone?'

Carter's lips pressed firmer together. 'Away.'

'That much is evident. Might you shed any further light on their removal?'

'I cannot, sir.' Then Carter peered at him closer, screwing up his nose in the effort to see. 'Is that *you*, Master Kit?'

'It is, Mr Carter.' Kit held the old man's gaze.

'You look different, sir. I barely recognised you.'

Kit said nothing.

'So you came back, after all,' the old man murmured almost to himself.

'I came back.'

The old man just looked at him as if he had seen a ghost.

'My family's removal…?' Kit prompted, hoping that now the old butler had recognised him he would get on with answering the question.

For the tiniest of moments something flickered in the old servant's eyes, before he lowered his gaze to the toes of Kit's boots. 'As I said, sir, I would not know anything of that.'

'Is Mr Frederickson at home?'

'I am afraid he is not presently at home, sir.'

'And were he at home, would he be able to answer my question?'

The old butler still would not meet his gaze. 'I could not say, Mr Northcote. If you will excuse me, sir...'

'Of course,' said Kit coolly. He expected nothing less once people knew who he was. Contempt. Condemnation. Turning away, he made his way down the stone steps to where his carriage waited. His footman opened the door ready for him, but before Kit climbed inside he glanced back at where old Carter still stood watching. Carter was finally looking at him but, contrary to what Kit had thought, the look in the old butler's eyes was not contempt or condemnation, but pity.

The Fredericksons' front door closed with a quiet click.

And a cold finger stroked against Kit's heart.

'How did it go? With your family.' Kate saw the distant distracted look in Kit's eyes as he stood by the window looking out over the streets in the drawing room and recognised it as worry he would never admit.

'It did not. The house was empty. They have moved to reside elsewhere.'

Whatever resolution he had hoped to effect, whatever reunion he had planned, had evaded him. 'How will you go about finding them?'

The question seemed to pull him back from the dark place in which he brooded. His eyes met hers. 'Ever practically minded.'

She gave a shrug. 'It is my nature.'

He gave a little smile at that, brief and small, but real.

'My mother has a cousin in London, a Mrs Tadcaster. She will know where they have removed to.'

She nodded. 'Kit…what happened to make you lose touch with them?'

'Life happened. Change happened. Kit Northcote died.'

'And Kit North was born?'

He smiled again, but this time it was hard and bitter. 'Indeed. If you will excuse me, I will pay a call upon Mrs Tadcaster.'

Wasting no time. He might pretend a relaxed indifference, but she was not fooled. He needed to find his family. She could feel the tension that emanated from him at just the mention of them.

'Take me with you,' she said on impulse.

His gaze moved to the untouched purse of gold upon the dining-room table, before meeting her own.

'Unless you are ashamed of me,' she challenged softly, her gaze holding his, never backing down for a minute.

They looked at one another across that sunlit drawing room, all sorts of subtle tensions playing between them, until he said, 'If you would care to accompany me, I would be honoured to introduce you to my mother's cousin.'

'I will fetch my shawl,' she said, 'and bring Tom along for the ride. A boy needs fresh air, especially a boy used to sailing the ocean. '

He gave a nod.

She felt his eyes on her as she walked from the room.

Kit drew a similar response from Mrs Tadcaster's man-servant as he had from the Fredericksons' butler. Making his way back to the carriage, he saw young Tom's face watching him and Kate's, so calm and strong.

'She left two days ago to take the waters at Bath and is not due to return for a couple of weeks.' He took his seat opposite Kate and Tom, seeing the boy's pride in the fact that Bob had settled upon his narrow shoulder.

'Will you wait that long?' she asked, the look in her eyes telling him she already knew the answer to her question. She thought like him. She was not a woman to sit back and wait for life to happen to her, but one who went out and did what was required.

'No,' he said. 'There are men one can hire to find people.'

She just gave a nod of understanding and did not ask for any details in front of the boy.

Tom stared around him with obvious curiosity and excitement, making Kit realise that Kate was right—a boy did need fresh air. Kit's problems were his own to solve. Neither Tom nor Kate should suffer because of them.

'What say you to a trip to the park?' he asked them both.

'Yes, please!' Tom grinned.

Kate's eyes met his in shared pleasure. She smiled. 'A trip to the park would be a fine way to spend the afternoon.'

'Hyde Park is just round the corner.'

The carriage rumbled round the park's paths, the breeze catching at the dark ribbons of Kate's bonnet and the tassels of her parasol. Her eyes were soft silver in the sunlight and there was something in them when she looked at him, which was often. The sunlight brought colour to the freckles that had faded across the bridge of Tom's nose.

The boy held up his face to the sun and took a great big deep breath of air. 'It smells different here, not a hint of ocean or waves.'

'What do you smell?' Kit asked.

'Grass and horses, dung and rot, chimneys and…' He sniffed again. 'Sunshine,' he finished.

They all laughed.

Kit stopped the carriage, and they climbed out and

walked along the path. Bob flew off to some nearby trees and Tom ran off chasing him, detouring around every bush and park bench he could find.

Kit and Kate walked side by side, close but not touching.

Kit offered her his arm. 'Admiralty will be watching and we need to look the part.'

She accepted his offer, resting her fingers on the crook of his arm, holding on to him, as if they really were a couple who had just married for love.

'You were right,' he said. 'A boy needs fresh air.'

'It is good of you to have him here to live with you as a young gentleman.'

'If you could have seen him in that Johor gaol…' He swallowed down that awful memory, hardened his voice. 'This is just another part of his training. He has learned how to handle life at the lower end. Now he must be equipped with the means to deal with those from money and breeding, those who consider themselves his superior in every way.' He said it with cool dispassion, but Kate's eyes were soft when they met his and she smiled in a way that made his heart swell.

There were few people about at this hour—those exercising their horses, servants hurrying on errands, nurses with children in their charge—and none of them recognised him. It was a strange feeling. Nice. With Kate on his arm and Tom laughing and running about them he could almost let himself believe in this illusion they were presenting to the world. He could relax into it for those few moments and enjoy them for what they were. Reality would intrude soon enough. He could not defer it. The music must be faced.

He felt her fingers caress against his arm and his hand moved to cover them. And he thought how much he would give to have this masquerade be the truth.

* * *

At five o'clock, they were back in the carriage, but they did not head home.

The ease of what had been between them for those couple of hours seemed to vanish. She sensed the return of the tension within him.

He faced her, his eyes, so dark and filled with their secrets, on hers, and she knew something important was coming.

'We have to make our appearance in society sometime and the sooner the better.'

Because the Admiralty's spies would be watching.

She glanced at Tom, who was stroking Bob's feathers and feeding him some titbits, and listening intently for all it looked otherwise. Tom did not know their marriage was a sham and she could not burden the child with a truth that would destroy his happiness. With the boy's terrible background she was determined to protect and care for him in the little time they would be together, to let him experience something of what it was like to be loved and cherished, as every child should be, as her own little Ben, of whom he reminded her so much, was.

'And show them all how happily married we are,' she said with a smile, and held Kit's eyes, knowing that the irony of the words would escape the boy. 'What are you proposing?'

'Five o'clock is the fashionable hour for the *ton* to be seen here in Hyde Park. It will be quite the parade at Rotten Row.'

'I always did like a parade.'

'Kate, there is something that I should warn…' He glanced at Tom, then back at her, as if whatever it was that he wanted to say could not be spoken in front of the boy.

Tom glanced up directly at Kit at that moment, waiting to hear the words, silent, a slight tension about him.

Kit shifted his gaze to meet the boy's. He smiled at Tom. 'I should warn you both,' he said, 'that some of those we shall see are rather high in the instep.' Then paused, leaning closer. 'Very high in the instep, if truth be told,' he said, lowering his voice as if spilling a confidence to them both, and gave a grin that made him so devilishly handsome that it made Kate's heart skip a beat.

'Do you think you will be able to suffer a few curious stares?' he asked.

'Oh, yes, sir.' Tom smiled. 'It's a shame you are not wearing your cutlass and me my knife. I reckon we would draw even better stares then.'

'I reckon we would,' said Kit with that same grin that did strange things to her heart. He was still smiling when his eyes shifted to meet hers.

In their dark depths she saw that whatever lay ahead was not as easy as he was pretending. And she wondered as to the true words of warning he would have spoken had Tom not been with them.

Kate had not long to wait to fathom something of an answer.

It was, as he had said, a swarm of fashionable people. Most in open-top carriages with matching teams of bays like those that Kit had hired. Some were small groups of gentlemen on horseback. Some were women in a cacophony of coloured silks and bonnets, all expensive and elegant, perfect sophistication. The gentlemen's attire was very like that of Kit's—dark tailcoats, white shirts and waistcoats beneath, with matching neckcloths, and black beaver hats, black pantaloons and shoes for those who rode in carriages and buff breeches and shiny high-top black boots for those who rode. But their clothes had a look of expense and luxury, as if they had been stitched on to their bodies by some top-end tailor.

She thought of the pouch of gold that lay on the dining-room table at the house in Grosvenor Street and knew Kit's choice of tailoring was not due to lack of funds, but more what he deemed it important to spend his money on. She liked the fact he was not strutting and preening like the men all around them. Just the way he sat there, everything about him… He was more of a man than any of them.

How those fashionable people stared. And with Bob perched upon Tom's shoulder she supposed she could not blame them. A tame raven was a novel sight, after all. But then, as those long-nosed women and puffy-faced men stared, she saw something change in their expressions.

She saw that they recognised Kit.

There were no nods of acknowledgement. No waves, or friendly smiles. Just wide-eyed stares and disapproving tight lips and gossipy whispers behind fans and gloved hands. A ripple of shock spread out through the park, with the carriage that contained Kit and Tom and herself at its epicentre.

She held her head high and kept a slight smile on her lips as if it was all nothing more than amusing, and was both relieved and proud when Tom did the same.

Kit met the eyes of all those they passed. He did not look away. He did not smile. But he nodded an acknowledgement. Some returned it. Others turned their faces away in obvious slight. Neither response seemed to make a difference.

He showed nothing, but she knew that this was what he had expected, that what was happening was no shock to him. And his eyes when they met hers and Tom's were strengthening, as though it was the three of them together against the rest of the world.

* * *

When they got home, Tom dined with them as he did most evenings. It had been her suggestion upon their arrival at the house, both for the child's sake and as a means of alleviating the awkwardness of her and Kit dining alone. But the boy's presence was double edged, preventing both matters she did not want to discuss and those she did. She was forced to bide her time, to wait for a chance to speak to him alone. Dinner seemed to stretch on for ever.

At last it ended and the hour was late enough to send Tom to bed.

The footmen stood sightless and deaf against the wall.

The butler hovered discreetly by Kit's elbow. 'Shall I fetch the port, sir?' The man's eyes shifted to where Kate sat at the opposite end of the long, polished mahogany table.

Kit did not take his eyes from her, even though his words were for the manservant.

'No, thank you. My wife and I are going out to the theatre.' Then, to her, 'If you are feeling quite up to it, darling?' Playing the masquerade before the servants, for in truth what better place to set a spy than in the house that was supposed to be their home? Not him and her against the world, after all, only him. Behind closed doors she felt the distance he put between them.

'Perfectly,' she replied. 'If you will excuse me, while I change…'

From her Antiguan wardrobe she selected the deep-purple silk with tiny glass beads scattered over a low-cut bodice. For the first time, she did not don the black fichu to cover her décolletage, aware of how much skin she was exposing. But if all of London was going to stare and point and gossip over her as an American, then she would hold her head high and give them something worth staring at.

She tucked the necklace containing Kit's ring into her pocket and had the maid pin her hair up high at the back, then pulled a few strands free, winding them round her fingers and arranging the resultant tendrils against her neck and décolletage. Her neck was bare, the darkness of the dress exaggerating the pale nakedness of her shoulders and breasts. Nothing relieved the starkness of the dress or the skin it revealed...only the thin worn gold band upon her finger. Wendell would be shocked at her, she thought. She was shocked at herself. But the woman who looked back at her from the peering glass did not look shocked; she looked...powerful and proud and unafraid, and ready to face down the sneers of London's *ton*. Kate smiled, then went downstairs to where the man to whom she was married waited.

Kit stared at the woman who walked down that staircase of the house in Grosvenor Street and the sight of her stole the words from his tongue and the breath from his lungs. He had always thought her an attractive woman, but... He stared at her, as though he was some greenhorn and she, a goddess.

'Cat got your tongue, Captain North?' she said softly as she came to stand before him, but she must have known the sight she presented; that she was sensual and powerful and spectacular.

'You look beautiful,' he said, and could not take his eyes from hers. He leaned in and brushed a kiss against her lips and then whispered softly and slowly in her ear, 'The footmen are watching.' But that was not why he kissed her, or why he could not take his eyes off her.

She smiled that smile of hers, not fooled for a minute.

'Thank you, darlin',' she said, accentuating her American accent. 'You are kinda irresistible yourself.' She stepped in closer just as he had done and brushed the back of her hand against the fall of his breeches as she whispered in his ear, 'For the footmen's sake, you understand.'

With a smile that said she knew her power, she walked with a saucy wiggle out to the waiting carriage, leaving him standing there with an enormous and obvious erection.

His gaze shifted to the footmen and butler, who were all watching goggle-eyed, but who shifted their gazes immediately to pretend that they had noticed nothing.

He smiled to himself. Suddenly the prospect of the night ahead did not seem bad. Not with Kate by his side.

He walked out into the night to join her.

The Theatre Royal in Covent Garden was relatively quiet, which was not surprising given that it was only a matter of weeks until Parliament and the Lords closed for recess, and most of the fashionable and powerful families took themselves off from London to spend the hot summer months on their country estates. But the attention of the *ton* that were there that night was not focused on the theatre's stage with the players upon it, but on the box on the first level in which he sat beside Kate.

'Oh, my,' she said, 'we do seem to be rather a spectacle of interest.'

'We do,' he said. He had been prepared to face their scrutiny and condemnation, to suffer it as was his due, but this did not feel like suffering. It felt… He felt…buoyed by Kate, proud of her, sitting there like some beautiful Boadicea who could have felled them all with one sensual glance from those ocean-grey eyes, soft and gentle and yet wielding such power. All the men in the place were craning their necks to stare at her and he knew that every single one of them would be wanting her; every single one of them aching to be in his shoes, for all that they knew of him. It was not what he had expected to feel, coming back to swallow down his shame and humiliation.

The matrons of the *ton* were peering blatantly through their opera glasses, making not the slightest effort to hide either their disapproval of him or their jealousy of the woman by his side.

'I feel sorry for those players down there on the stage, acting their hearts out…' she began.

'When no one is looking at them,' he finished.

She smiled.

'All those shawls and fichus, all those…coverings you wore on *Coyote* and *Raven*, I think I understand them now,' he said.

'To protect me from the hot beat of the sun on one ocean and the cold bite of the wind on another,' she said.

'That is not why you wore them.'

'No?' She arched an eyebrow.

'No'. His eyes held hers. 'No man could resist if he saw you.'

She shook her head, but she laughed.

The lead actor's voice was resonating through the auditorium, but beneath it was the murmur of scandalised voices from the stalls below and the boxes all around them. A matron across on the opposite side of the theatre was pointing at him as she gossiped behind her fan, as if he were blind and could not see her. Above them, young Frew was hanging out of his box so far that he was in danger of falling. He saw Kate's eyes glance up at Frew before returning to meet his.

'Do you think he is reporting back to the Admiralty?' she asked.

'Frew fancies himself as a romantic and a poet in the fashion of Byron. But who knows who Admiralty are recruiting these days? Do not let him spoil the play for you.'

'But this is not about the play, is it? Being here. Tonight.'

'No,' he admitted.

She leaned closer to him, her eyes searching his. 'Maybe we should give them something more to gossip about.'

'What have you got in mind?' he asked softly.

She kissed him on the lips, a deep, gentle, passionate kiss that made him want to wrap his arms around her and lay her down right there and make love to her. To make her his wife in truth. To hold on to her and keep her by his side for ever.

He kissed her with the truth that was in his heart, with all that he felt for her. He kissed her as if he really were worthy of winning her love from a dead man.

The actor on the stage stumbled over his words, but that was not what drew the gasps of shock and disgust from the audience.

She broke the kiss and, looking into eyes, she smiled.

And, despite everything, he smiled, too.

She had faced them down. She had held her head high and been proud of being an American in their midst even though their countries were at war.

But now that they were alone, facing each other across the carriage as it rumbled over the roads that led from Covent Garden back to the house in Grosvenor Street, she could feel the change in the atmosphere. The darkness of the night was interrupted by regular-spaced gas lamps with their warm yellow glow. Every few seconds it flashed across the hard handsome planes of his face like that of a warning beacon over rocks. Her body thrummed with the knowledge of him, of the temptation he presented. The bodice of her dress seemed too tight and restrictive, her breasts too sensitive.

She could remember the feel of his mouth upon them,

the stroke of his fingers over the skin of her hip, the thrust of him between her thighs. Turning her face away from the lure of those dark dangerous waters, she looked out at the passing sandstone houses, all uniform with their Palladian-styled fronts and black-painted window frames and glossy front doors. Beneath the long black evening gloves, she could feel the press of the old wedding band and moved her fingers to touch it, to turn it, to remind herself of vows once sworn that, at this moment, seemed so long ago that she could barely remember.

'I am sorry for exposing you to this, Kate. You should not have to suffer such scrutiny or be subjected to such harsh appraisal.' His voice was quiet in the darkness.

'I am not sorry. I am proud to be American.'

She heard the slight catch in his breath, as if he had given an ironic smile. 'They do not look at us because you are American.' She heard him smile again. 'They look at you because you are beautiful. But their attitude—the disapproval, the censure—it is because of me, Kate.'

She moved her gaze to meet his across the carriage once more. 'Why?'

In the silence that followed she did not think he would answer. And in that moment everything seemed to click into place and she knew that this was at the heart of everything that drove him, everything that he was. She did not ask the question again, just waited.

'Because of what I did before I left London.'

The words seemed to echo in the space between them. 'What did you do, Kit?'

The next flash of gas lamps showed him smile that bitter ironic smile, the one that hid the other things beneath. 'Do not ask me that question, Kate. Not tonight.'

Her heart was beating hard with awareness, with anticipation. She swallowed. 'Why not, Kit?' she asked softly.

'Because I cannot bear to tell you the answer. Because I want you with me for the little time we have together.'

'I am with you.'

'But you would not be were I to tell you. Trust me, Kate.' He smiled again, but the quiet darkness was in his eyes so that she believed him.

She nodded, knowing this was not the right time to push, but feeling a spasm of fear over what would cause North the Pirate Hunter, who had endured torture and thought it nothing, who could expel another man's life without so much as a blink of the eye, to speak in such a way. What he had done must be truly terrible on a scale beyond imagining. A chill crept across her skin.

'In two weeks Gunner will be back in London. In two weeks you will be on your way home to Louisiana and your children.' The distance was there again in his voice. Whatever ease and teasing sensuality was between them in public was lost in private, when temptations and truth and darkness returned to stand as unscalable barriers, reminding them that they were each in a place the other could not reach.

Wendell's name whispered in her ear. She turned her gaze to the passing houses.

They did not speak again.

Chapter Thirteen

A man was leaving Kit's study when Kate came downstairs the next day. She leaned against the doorway, looking at him. She was wearing the black day dress and fichu, her armour back in place, shielding herself from him as much as every other man.

'Your family,' she said, not a question, but a statement. She was quick, intuitive. She understood too much. And gossip would reach her eventually. It was only a matter of time. The *ton's* censure he could bear, but hers? He turned his mind away from that thought.

'I will know their whereabouts by the end of the week. Collins is a Bow Street Runner and good at his job,' he said.

She nodded.

'There is a charity musical being held in Almack's Rooms this afternoon. Much of the *ton* will be there. Gossip will have spread following last night and our appearance in Hyde Park. It will not be easy, Kate. You do not have to accompany me.' He wanted to give her a way out. This was not her punishment to take.

'I want to,' she said.

Their eyes held and too many things stirred between them across that small distance, before she turned and walked away.

He listened to the sound of her footsteps on the hard polished floors.

One week and Collins would have traced his family.

Two weeks and she would be gone.

This was the way it was supposed to be, he thought, and focused his attention on the ledger that lay open on the desk before him.

Kate wore a dark chocolate-brown dress to the musicale, and forwent the fichu again. Ironically, in facing this London society that was Kit's enemy and hers, and opposite to everything that she had needed to be Le Voile, her strength lay in her sensuality and confidence as a woman.

Kit had been right in his warning. She slid her arm into his, presenting a united front to those vultures that circled them and felt the warmth of his fingers as they covered hers.

Rows of chairs had been set out within the ballroom of Almack's. Kate and Kit did not sneak like thieves into the back rows, but took seats right at the front.

She did not fully understand what this homecoming was about for Kit, but knew that, whatever was going on, part of it was a need to face them, to stand before them all and look them in the eyes. And given all he had done for her, it was the least she could do to stand by his side and help him. She did not want to think of the other reasons she was doing this, the complications in her heart.

There was a string quartet that played with a vibrancy and immediacy of emotion and an opera singer who sang with the voice of an angel of love, all of it of love.

Without thinking she toyed with the thin gold band upon her finger, feeling the tug of guilt and longing and the turmoil that struggled within her. Her thoughts moved from the woman who was singing to the man who sat by her side, the man with whom she had stood before a priest and spoken the same words that made a mockery of those she had spoken to another man a lifetime ago.

She glanced up to find Kit's eyes on her hands, where she touched Wendell's ring. His gaze, dark and too perceptive, moved to meet her own. He smiled, his cool ironic smile, and, returning his gaze to the musicale, did not look at her again.

Kit accepted a glass of champagne from the salver the footman offered and passed it to Kate. He did not take one for himself.

'Mr Northcote, is that really you?' The voice sounded behind where they stood.

'Prepare yourself,' he whispered in Kate's ear as he turned. 'One of the *ton's* biggest gossipmongers.' And saw her smile.

Mrs Quigley, a tabby of renown, had not changed in the years he had been away.

'It is, indeed, Mrs Quigley,' he said smoothly.

'How…surprising.' She smiled a sickly sweet smile. 'And yet here you are, with your lovely companion.' She looked at Kate, still smiling, the question burning in her eyes.

'Here we are,' said Kate with a naughty twinkle in her eye. He could have sworn she was making her accent deliberately more American.

Mrs Quigley's eyes widened, the fervour of excitement of this latest discovery practically choking her.

'May I introduce my wife?'

Mrs Quigley pressed a plump white hand to her breast. 'Your wife?' she breathed.

Kate leaned forward, as if to confide a secret to the tabby. 'It was a love match,' she said in a voice loud enough for all around to hear.

The room was quiet enough to hear a pin drop. The women were practically straining closer and tucking their hair behind their ears all the better to see and hear what was unfolding in their midst.

'How—' Mrs Quigley scrabbled for an acceptable comment and found one '—romantic.'

'I thought so,' said Kate, and stroked a hand against his arm.

It was all he could do not to laugh at the way the woman's eyes riveted to the small gesture with a fascinated horror. It was with obvious effort that she managed to draw them away long enough to ask Kate the question, 'And do my ears deceive me, or are you not of these shores?'

'You noticed.' Kate smiled. 'I'm American.'

Mrs Quigley practically choked on that revelation.

'How…nice,' she managed to say.

'Isn't it just?' Kate smiled again.

'I heard tell you had a boy with you, a boy from the west country.'

'You heard correctly,' Kit said.

'Not America?'

'Not America,' said Kate.

The speculation in Mrs Quigley's eyes was obvious. If the boy was not his wife's… But even she was not crass enough to ask the question outright. Instead, she changed the subject.

'We did not expect to see you again.'

'Evidently not,' he said.

'Where have you been hiding all these years?'

'Here and there.'

'Such a shame over what happened.'

Kit said nothing. This is what he had come back to face and face it he would.

'Your family losing the house and moving to a…less fashionable…neighbourhood.'

'Quite,' he said as if he already knew and indeed, in a way, he did.

'And your mother's death—my heartfelt condolences on that.'

The world seemed to stop. His blood ran cold. A knife cut through the wall of his chest, exposing the scars of his heart for all to see. He schooled his face to show nothing.

'Such kindness, Mrs Quigley.' He knew he should move away. He knew he had to mingle, to face them all down. But he could not move. He just stood there. Frozen. Exposed.

His mother was dead. The words did not seem real. None of this scene seemed real. Except he knew it was. He deserved this, all of it. But his mother…she had deserved none of it.

'Kit,' Kate's voice sounded. He felt her hand thread through his arm, catching hold of him, pulling him up from the dark waters closing over him. Her eyes met his as she threw him the life line. 'I am feeling a little…hot. Would you be so kind as to escort me home?' And in them was strength and understanding.

'As you wish.' He turned to the tabby who was watching every nuance of their interaction with avaricious eyes. 'Excuse us, Mrs Quigley.'

He led her across the room, out into the fresh air and space of the street. Their carriage drew up, the footman jumping down and opening the door.

They climbed inside.

He was in control again, closing it all over, knowing this was just a part of it, telling himself he should have been prepared for such an eventuality.

The door slammed shut and they were on their way to Grosvenor Street.

He stared out at the passing streets, streets he knew so well, streets that were a part of his life, a part of his childhood.

'Thank you,' he said without taking his gaze from the houses and shops and carriages, from the horses and the men and women.

'I am so sorry about your mother, Kit.' Her words were as gentle as her hand that took his.

'So am I.' His voice was hard.

He withdrew his hand from hers because he feared what he would do if he did not. He feared what he would tell her. He feared what he would reveal. He feared he would break every damn vow he had ever made.

He thought of those vows he had sworn. This was just a part of what must be faced, all of it by him alone. Kit Northcote was dead. It was Kit North who had come back. And Kit North who would do what must be done.

Now that they were alone again he was shutting her out as ever he did. Kate knew that. But this time it was different. This time he was hurting, really hurting. For all his cool hard veneer she had seen the truth in that unguarded moment in Almack's Rooms when he had learned so cruelly of his mother's death. He was hurting, but the hurt seemed only to harden his resolve, to make him harsher and more determined to do whatever it was he had come here for, facing down London's society, running the gauntlet of their censure.

The rest of the journey was conducted in silence but when the carriage stopped outside the house on Grosvenor Street he took her hand in his and helped her down from the carriage, his fingers entwining with hers as if he would never let them go. She held to him, and he to her, proclaiming their union to the world.

She glanced up into his eyes and he did not look away, just held her gaze and, stopping still, touched his mouth to hers. He kissed her with an excruciating sweetness that belied all of his coolness. And she slid her arms around him and kissed him, too, her lips offering the comfort her words could not. She kissed him in the middle of that respectable street, oblivious to all else except the need to reach him. She kissed him. And when the kiss ended, their eyes just held, clinging to that moment they both knew would end when they stepped out of the public eye into the privacy of their home.

He raised their still-entwined fingers to his mouth, brushed a kiss to her knuckles and led her inside.

Tom came running down the staircase, abandoning whatever tasks Kit had set him to, as soon as the front door closed.

'Captain North, Mrs Medhurst.' He smiled, oblivious of the mistaken name.

Kit said nothing, but she saw the tiny tightening of his jaw before he spoke to the boy. 'As part of your duties it is necessary that you learn to ride. It is a most useful skill in life. How about we start the lessons this afternoon, in Hyde Park?'

'Yes please, Captain, sir!' Tom looked delighted as he stared up at his hero with admiration, belatedly remembering her. 'If that's all right with you, ma'am?' The boy glanced over at her.

'It's all right with me,' she said, but she wondered if Kit was not doing this in part to avoid her.

'If you will excuse me,' Kit said to her with a stiff bow.

She said nothing, just watched him walk away pretending that he had not just learned that his mother was dead and that his family had been forced to move due to reduced circumstances; pretending that everything was all right.

* * *

It was the same when they returned later that afternoon. Tom was there then and at dinner so that she could say nothing of it. Kit behaved as if nothing at all different had happened today, but he made his excuses and left before it was time for the boy to retire for the night.

She heard the front door close and knew he had gone out. From the window she watched his dark figure descend the stone steps. There was no waiting carriage or horse. He walked off along the street to merge with the darkness.

Kit was not going anywhere. He walked, just walked, because he needed to be alone. And he did not know what else to do. He walked every damn street in London, trying to straighten the thoughts in his head. He walked until his steps had returned him to the house in Grosvenor Street and the woman who waited inside.

There was no light behind the curtains of her bedchamber. She slept. At least one of them would.

He had spent three years getting back here. Three years for a chance to make it right. Except he was too late. It would never be right for his mother. She was dead and gone, never knowing how sorry he was, never learning how much he regretted it all.

He made his way quietly up the stairs and into his bedchamber. A bottle of brandy and a single crystal tumbler still sat on his bedside cabinet. He kept it there, the same set as in his study, to tempt him, to know the strength of his resistance. Now standing there in that moonlit room, for the first time he lifted the bottle, held it in his hand and stared at the neatly printed label, seriously contemplating breaking the wax seal and prising the cork from the slender glass neck.

He missed the rich sweet taste of brandy. He missed

the burn on his tongue and in his throat and stomach. He missed the oblivion it could bring, the numbing of the senses, the escape that he had lost himself in so many times after he had realised the magnitude of what he had done on that terrible night three years ago. The pain bit all the deeper for knowing there was now a part of it that he could never undo. His mother had deserved better, so much better.

He sat the bottle back down in its rightful place and walked to stand by the window, staring down on to those streets he knew so well. He deserved the pain. Every damn bit of it. And God help him, he would take it like a man and keep his mouth shut from whining.

Kate sat in the chair in the darkness of her bedchamber.

She knew Kit was in there alone. She knew he was shutting her out. And she knew why, at least in part.

Beneath the push and pull of her thumb and forefinger Wendell's wedding band slid this way and that around her finger, the habit so engrained in her across the years. Normally it soothed her. Tonight it did not. There was a tightness in her throat, an ache in her chest.

The scene from Almack's Rooms was there in her mind, just as it had been there all night. Every time she shut her eyes she saw that moment again, when Kit had stood there and heard that his mother was dead from the lips of a gossip; stood there with his face a mask of cool dispassion hiding the truth beneath. She felt his pain as sorely as if it were her own. And she knew he needed her for all he refused to admit it. But if she went to him this night… if she offered him comfort, she knew what would happen between them. And if they made love, there could be no annulment. And if she went to him knowing that, what did it say about how she felt about Wendell?

Betrayal. The word taunted her and it was true because she could feel his presence fading. And she had loved him, with all her heart. She still did. He was Ben and Bea's father. And she missed him. And she missed her children. She missed them so much that there was a hollow of aching deep inside her. But Kit was on the other side of that door.

He was such a strong man. She had never seen him weaken, not in all that he had endured. He pretended he did not feel, but she knew that he did.

In a fortnight Gunner would be here to take her home, leaving Kit here alone.

The barrier between them seemed higher than ever. But there was a way she might reach him. And after everything they had been through, he deserved to know.

She toyed with Wendell's wedding band upon her finger and rose from her chair.

A light knock sounded from the connecting door from Kate's bedchamber.

She did not wait for an answer, just opened it and came to stand there.

He knew from the fact she was wearing not her night robe, but the black dress that mourned the passing of her real husband, that she had been waiting for him to return.

'You should go to bed,' he said, his voice unnecessarily cool. He did not want her to see him like this.

'So you can shut me out?' she said.

'What is it that you want, Kate?'

'To talk.'

'About what? My dead mother? The things I have done? Your journey home to Louisiana?' He shook his head. 'If so, you are wasting your time.' He made to turn away from her.

'None of those things,' she said, stilling him. 'I came to talk about Wendell.'

He stood where he was and watched her walk right up to him. 'I think I already know all I need to about Wendell.'

'No, Kit, you do not,' she said, and looked up into his face.

He knew he should turn away from her. He knew he should insist she go back to her room. But he did neither of those things. He just stood there and waited for what it was she had come to say.

'I loved him. I still do.'

'As I said—nothing I do not already know.'

'When he died, I swore a vow that I would stay true to him and him alone, that there would never be another man for me. It is the main reason I became Le Voile. Because I had sworn that I would never marry again. I needed to support myself and my children financially.'

He swallowed, only now fully realising the position he had put her in by bringing her here, by marrying her, even if it had been with the best of intentions.

'I have never told anyone of my vow,' she said.

In the same way he had never spoken of his. Vows were private things. They were sworn in blood and kept in secret. No one understood that more than Kit.

'I know some folks would not deem such a vow binding. They would say it was made in a moment of grief and offer all sorts of excuses to get me out of it. But a vow is a vow.' She stopped, and met his eyes, facing him squarely while she told him this most private of truths. 'If I break it…'

'If you break it, you would not be the person you are. It would turn you into someone else altogether,' he said. 'Someone you do not want to be.'

'Yes.' She nodded, her eyes caressing his face.

'I understand. I have sworn a vow or two myself.'

The silence hissed with his chance to tell her, but he

could not. Because he could not bear to see the look on her face if he did.

'Thank you for telling me,' he said.

'There is more, Kit.'

He waited, not hurrying her, giving her the space she needed, even if he was not sure he wanted to hear the rest of it.

'Before you there was only ever Wendell. And now, there is not. I feel things for you. Things that make me feel like I am betraying him.'

So he said the words she needed to hear. 'Our making love, our sleeping together, it was just to satisfy our bodies' physical needs. Lust, not love. Wendell would understand. Your heart is intact, Kate. You have not betrayed him.'

'Lust, not love?' she whispered.

'Yes.' But he looked away to tell the lie.

She reached her hand to cup his cheek, turning his face back to hers. Tears leaked from her eyes, glistening like crystal as they rolled down her cheeks in the moonlight.

'But, you see, the problem is that my heart is not intact, Kit. I still love Wendell, but I love you, too. No matter how hard I have tried not to. I have to tell you. I have to make you understand.' Her voice was thick with emotion. 'I cannot break my vow to Wendell, but I love you, Kit.'

He pulled her into his arms and held her, cradling her against him, pressing his face into her hair. 'I love you, too, Kate.' But he did not deserve her love. And once she discovered the man he had been, once she learned what Kit Northcote had done, she would not love him any more.

He wanted to carry her to his bed. He wanted their bodies to merge. He wanted to show her the truth of his feelings with his body, but he could not be so selfish. 'But you know we cannot make love. There could be no annulment if we did.' He spoke the words into her hair. 'And we both have our vows.'

'I know,' she whispered and he felt the sob she stifled in her chest. 'But I don't want to be alone, Kit. And I don't care what you say, I know that you cannot be alone tonight. I want to be with you.'

'I want to be with you, too, Kate.'

She looked up into his eyes and he held her face in his hands and carefully captured each of those precious tears.

'We cannot make love, but we can hold one another,' he said.

'We can hold one another,' she echoed softly.

He took her hands in his and led her to his bed. They climbed beneath those covers and he held her. And she held him. All through those long dark hours of the night. And when she finally fell asleep in his arms he was not sure she had not been right. He was not sure that he could have made it through this night alone.

The next morning when Kate awoke, Kit was gone.

When she finally caught up with him at the breakfast table it was as if none of it had happened, not last night, not their admissions of love, not the death of his mother. All of his barriers were once more intact, built so high she wondered if she had ever really succeeded in finding a way through them, if he had ever really lowered them at all.

He smiled at her, but it was his smile that showed he was hard and tough, and strong and emotionless. The first three were true, the fourth, she knew for a fact, a lie. She knew it in the kind way he spoke to Tom, even now.

He took her and Tom around London in his carriage all that day, buying them ices and chocolate from Gunter's Tea Shop. The relationship between him and Tom was changing; the little boy seemed to have found a way to pierce through Kit's armour, for all that Kit would deny it. And even though the way it was between her and Kit was a masquerade, a pretence, the way his hand was warm around hers, the way his lips brushed her cheek, the way his eyes caressed her body and that secret smile that spoke volumes to all those around that stared so, it felt real. Or maybe it was just her own wishful thinking.

Regardless, she did not think, she just embraced the illusion and enjoyed their time together, acting out all that was the truth of what she felt for him. Laughing with Tom, hugging the boy, linking her arm through Kit's, wiggling her hips when he was watching, looking at him with eyes that said she wanted to loosen his neckcloth and lead him to her bed and do all sorts of wanton things. Everywhere they went people stared—and the black sheep returned, his American wife and the boy they were whispering was his adopted son of questionable origin, gave them something worth staring at and they had the time of their lives in doing so.

They took dinner at a chophouse, then bought iced cakes that they ate in the carriage on the way home. According to the baker the cakes were replicas of the very same sponge iced doves served at the Prince Regent's latest banquet but they all agreed that the doves looked more like white versions of Bob.

'No more cake,' she said to Tom as if he were her own little Ben, 'or you will make yourself sick. You have icing all round your mouth. Come, let me wipe it clean.' She pulled her handkerchief at the ready.

But Tom beat her to it, wiping the sleeve of his new tailcoat, that was identical to Kit's, across his mouth, to leave a nice white trail of icing over the black superfine. 'All done.'

'Tom!' She pulled a face.

Tom grinned like a Cheshire cat.

She looked at Kit and the two of them shared a laugh.

'This is like having a mother and father,' Tom said. 'We're like a real family, aren't we?'

But they were saved from a reply by the carriage coming to a halt outside the house in Grosvenor Street and the footman opening the carriage door.

Tom jumped down and raced up the stone steps to the front door of their home. Kit stepped down, then offered her his hand to assist her.

This is like having a mother and father. We're like a real family, aren't we?

Their eyes met and held, and there was a tightness in her chest and a lump the size of a boulder in her throat, and the prickle of tears in her eyes.

'What is that you are saying, Mrs North? You cannot wait to get me inside and upstairs?' he said, naughty play-acting for the Admiralty spies and the rest of London, distracting her from Tom's words and all they meant so that she would not betray them both by weeping. He threaded his fingers through hers. 'Very well. I acquiesce.'

She smiled and stoppered the tears. But when he turned away and tugged at her hand to take her with him, she resisted, pulling him back to her, knowing what would happen once they were inside and free from the eyes of servants and watchers, and needing this closeness with him, feigned or not, to last that little bit longer.

He came to her, stood close, indecently so, looking down into her face. 'We are attending a dance at the Argyle Rooms this evening,' he said quietly.

She nodded.

The teasing sensuality had vanished from them both. Their gazes held and all of the world around her seemed to vanish. She looked into those so serious, so strong, so deep dark eyes and her heart was aching so much.

He leaned in and kissed her. Not a teasing playful kiss. Not a kiss that was all hot hard desire. A kiss that was nothing of masquerade or pretence, but serious and honest. A kiss that told her that he understood and felt the same.

A discreet clearing of the throat sounded from the butler who stood nearby.

The kiss ended and the moment was over. She could no longer defer the inevitable. He released her hand and she followed him up the stone stairs into the rented house, holding on to the thought that they would not be inside for long. There was still this evening's outing to come. She knew he would dance with her. She knew he would hold her close. And probably even kiss her again.

And that at least was something.

In the Argyle Rooms that night Kate was wearing a deep midnight-blue silk that revealed just enough of her figure to torture all of the men in that dance room, and him, with all that would never be theirs. It was not play-acting when his eyes were hard and hot upon her, or when he stood that little bit too close or let his fingers brush against hers.

It was not play-acting when he led her out on to the dance floor and waltzed with her before them all, their bodies moving together, as natural and rhythmic as they had been in bed.

She was a natural seductress, lowering those long dark lashes, then meeting his gaze with boldness and strength. This woman who had defied a pirate's world of masculinity and hostility and rivalry to reach the top. This woman who could weave the ultimate illusion and hold true to a vow. He wondered if she would be able to sustain the pretence once she learned the truth about him. It was something of which he did not want to think, not right now, when the scent of her was in his nose and the satin of her skin beneath his fingers. He was all too aware that the grains of sand were slipping too fast through the hourglass, but he held to these small precious moments, committing them and everything of her to memory.

And then he raised his eyes from her face to glance across the floor and saw Devlin.

Chapter Fourteen

Kate felt the sudden change that rippled through Kit's body, the tightening and tensing of muscles, the honing of attention that came when one sighted the enemy. Following his gaze, she saw the four tall dark-haired men who stood tight-lipped and cold-eyed at the corner of the room watching them, waiting like the four horsemen of the apocalypse. The last notes of the music sounded.

She curtsied.

He bowed.

The dance was over. She had the sense that something else was over, too—the waiting. Whatever battle he had come back to fight involved those men.

'Friends of yours?' she asked.

'With whom I must reacquaint myself.'

Alone. Four against one was hardly fair odds. 'Introduce me,' she said.

He looked into her eyes, as if weighing her words. 'Very well,' he agreed at last.

Tucking her hand into the crook of his elbow, together they went to face the men.

'Devlin,' he said to the tallest, most arrogant looking of the men and gave a small nod of acknowledgement.

Devlin. The tortured words of a nightmare whispered

again in her mind and she felt an instant dislike and wariness towards the handsome-faced man.

'Monteith, Bullford, Fallingham.' He named them all in turn.

'Northcote,' the man he had called Devlin replied. 'Or is it North? There seems to be some dubiety over which name you are going by these days.'

Kit smiled his cold hard smile and said nothing.

She could feel the bristle of animosity in the silence that followed, feel the coldness that existed between them and wondered why Kit was even here talking to them.

'So you have come back.' Devlin's tone was arrogant and dismissive.

'As you see.' Kit's eyes were cold and hard, but that same hint of a smile played around his lips.

'And creating quite the scandal.' Devlin's eyes flicked to her.

She returned his gaze with frosty dislike.

'I succeeded in that before ever I left,' Kit answered. 'May I introduce my wife?' he said to them. Then to her, 'His Grace the Duke of Monteith, and Viscounts Devlin, Fallingham and Bullford,' he introduced each of them to her. 'My oldest friends, darling.'

Blue-blooded aristocracy and nothing of friends if the way they were looking at him was anything to go by.

They all bowed, the perfect noblemen, but it was not North they called her. 'Mrs Northcote.'

The atmosphere was thick enough to cut with a knife.

'Perhaps your lady should avail herself of the withdrawing room.' Devlin's eyes were fixed on Kit.

'Thank you kindly for having such a concern over my welfare, Lord Devlin, but I have no need to visit the ladies' withdrawing room.' She stepped a little closer to Kit and eyed the viscount coldly. 'You can say whatever it is that you want to in front of me.'

Devlin looked at Kit.

She saw the tiny muscle flicker in Kit's jaw and knew that he was not as cool as he was pretending. His eyes slid to hers, holding them for a tiny second so that all of the world seemed to roar between them in that moment, before he returned his gaze to Devlin and gave a nod.

'You should not have come back,' said Devlin.

'I disagree,' Kit said smoothly.

'Why are you here?'

'I have my reasons.'

'Whatever they are, you are no longer welcome in London, Kit Northcote.'

Kit smiled. 'No doubt.'

'Go back to wherever it is you have been hiding these three years past.'

'Not yet.'

'How dare you speak to him like that? You have no idea—'

'Kate.' Kit's warning stopped her.

'You have not told her. She does not know.' Devlin laughed and it was a cruel sound that sent a shiver all the way to the tip of her soul. 'I suppose I should have expected nothing other from you, Northcote.'

With a nod of his head, Devlin and the three other noblemen turned their backs in a way that was clear to all who watched was an insult.

But Kit did not leave. He stayed with her in those Argyle Rooms, dancing with her, remaining in that spotlight of disapproval and gossip, smiling his cool hard smile, his hand warm and possessive against the small of her back, but there was something in his eyes when he looked at her that frightened her, something that told her that they were both standing on the brink of something terrible.

This time when eventually they left and travelled home, there was no teasing sensuality, no loitering by the carriage, no kissing. Only that tight-wound sense of foreboding and the haunting echo of the mocking words that Viscount Devlin had spoken.

You have not told her. She does not know.

Neither of them spoke, not until they were in the drawing room of the house in Grosvenor Street with the door firmly closed and the curtains drawn and the staff dismissed for the evening.

A branch of candles burned upon the mantelpiece.

He stood by the fireplace, staring into the dark hearth with its carefully built pile of coal and kindling unlit upon it.

She came to stand there on the Turkey rug behind him.

'So, Kit,' she said softly.

He glanced up into the looking glass above the mantel, meeting her gaze in it. 'So,' he said.

Their eyes held.

'I deserve their contempt,' he said. 'I am not the man you think me, Kate.'

'Whoever you believe yourself, whatever heinous crime you have committed in the past, have you not punished yourself enough?'

'No.'

'I know you, and you are good and strong and a man of integrity.'

He laughed, a bitter cynical sound, and shook his head. 'No, Kate, I only wish that I were, but Kit Northcote is none of those things.'

'So what is he?' she demanded.

He turned to face her, holding her gaze. 'He is a liar, a cheat and a coward.'

She shook her head in denial.

'Yes,' he said.

'What did you do, Kit?'

'I was an arrogant weak wastrel who did nothing save drink, womanise and game. Three years ago I went to a gaming hell in Whitechapel with Devlin and the rest of my friends and gambled away my father's fortune. And when it was done, I ran away like a coward and left my family penniless, ruined and shamed.'

She stared at him. 'You were young and reckless, you made a mistake—'

'No,' he cut her off. 'You do not understand. I sold my soul to the devil, Kate.'

She felt a shiver run through her.

'I cheated,' he said. 'In that gaming hell, I cheated and I was discovered. I should have paid with my life—it is what they do to men who cheat at cards in Whitechapel. I deserved it. But the tough I played against struck a bargain—everything on one turn of the cards. I lost everything—my father's money, my honour, my soul. Devlin and the others swore an oath that they would never reveal the truth of that night—that I had cheated. And they never did.'

A small silence hissed.

'So now you know the truth of me,' he said quietly, and there was a terrible grimness in his expression.

'Now I know the truth,' she said.

She saw the regret in his eyes, the guilt…the self-loathing…and at last she understood. All that lay at the heart of him, the terrible burden he had carried through the years. And what it was he had come back to London to do. And it made her chest feel tight and crushed beneath the weight of sorrow. The tears spilled from her eyes. 'Kit…' There was so much she wanted to say.

The drawing-room door opened and Tom stood there in his nightshirt, his eyes moving from her to Kit and back again, the smile on his face fading to be replaced with concern. 'Is everything all right?'

'Everything is just as it should be,' said Kit as he walked from the room, tousling the boy's hair as he passed him in the doorway.

'Ma'am?' Tom stood there staring at her, shadows of fear in his eyes.

'Captain North is right,' she said, wiping away her tears. 'I was just telling him how much I missed my children at home in America.'

'You have children?'

'A little girl who is four years old and a boy who is not so much younger than you.'

'What are their names?'

'Why don't we go down to the kitchen and I will warm us some milk and tell you all about them.' She put an arm around Tom's thin shoulders and guided him towards the stairs.

There would be time to speak to Kit later.

Kit stood by the window of his bedchamber, staring down on to the moonlit street. The hands of the clock on the mantelpiece showed a quarter to one.

He heard the soft knock on the connecting door between his bedchamber and Kate's, but he made no move.

'Kit,' she said quietly through the wood.

But he could not bear to see the disgust and pity in her eyes. It turned out he was still Kit Northcote, after all, still that same coward. He might face down all of London. But he could not face down Kate Medhurst.

He heard the rattle of the handle, but he knew for certain that the door was locked and the key removed from her side.

She did not persist.

The silence that followed was loud.

He stared out over the London streets, wondering where his father and sister were, wondering how the hell they had managed all those years with ever-diminishing funds. In his pocket the bank cheque was neatly folded. Soon Collins would trace them; soon he would make the little reparation he could.

Kit might have told her his deepest darkest secrets. He might have laid his soul bare before her. But it had changed nothing. In the morning they sat at the long mahogany silver-set table in the dining room with Tom between them as if it had not happened. She realised that everything was rolling on like an unstoppable carriage running down a hill, heading towards a destination she could not change.

He discussed the day's schedule, the planned visit with Tom to an art exhibition at the Royal Academy with a smooth ease.

She did not know how he bore it. How he kept going, as if their whole world were not imploding. As if he felt nothing. But she knew he felt. And she knew that this was more of a torture to him than to her, facing what he had fled from, trying to right the wrongs. She also knew if she was going to reach him it was never going to be by a direct approach.

Within the main exhibition gallery at the Royal Academy of Art Kit and Kate stood before a massive, framed oil painting of naval ships in fast pursuit of a schooner. Tom was a little distance away, a frown on his face as he examined a painting of a ship of pirates being apprehended by a British naval frigate.

'Perhaps we should be looking at some still-life oils of flowers and fruit,' Kit said by her ear, knowing this was safe because they were in public.

'Or pastoral scenes of the English countryside,' she replied. 'Scared the Admiralty will hear of our racy preferences in art?'

'Terrified,' he said.

She smiled.

And so did he.

'That schooner has a look of *Coyote* about her,' she said.

'She does,' he agreed, and felt the brush of her fingers against his.

She did not look at him, only at the tall-masted ships, the billowing canvas sails and spray of ocean waves. 'Are you keeping any more dark secrets from me?' she asked.

'Were not the ones last night enough for you?'

'Nowhere near enough,' she said, and turned her face to look into his. 'I have not changed my mind over you.' Threading her fingers through his, she leaned in closer until he felt her breath, warm and sensual against his ear. 'Even if you do lock your bedchamber door against me.'

His eyes met hers and it was not pity he saw there or disgust. It was acceptance. It was strength. It was love. He raised their joined hands to his mouth and pressed a kiss to her fingers.

'Just in case the Admiralty are watching?' she asked.

'No,' he answered. 'I do not give a damn if they are watching or not.'

They stared into each other's eyes.

She knew the worst of him. She knew who he was, what he was. And she did not judge him.

'Are those King's navy men going to hang the pirates?' Tom asked in a loud voice.

'It looks like they are going to, doesn't it?' Kate replied as she pulled Kit to examine the picture Tom was worrying over. She lowered her voice, 'But I happen to know that they escape.'

'Are the pirates villains?' the boy asked.

'Some pirates are, but not those ones.'

'Not like the ones that captured you.'

'Not like the ones that captured me,' she agreed.

'You must be very glad that Captain North rescued you and captured their captain.'

'Very glad, indeed,' she said, and her eyes met Kit's again.

She knew and still she looked at him like that.

'No more veils,' she said.

'No more veils,' he echoed.

No masquerade. No pretence. Everything between them was real. Now, and for the days they had left together.

'Thank you, Kate,' he said quietly

'For what?' she asked, and held his eyes with that old defiance and strength so that he smiled to see it. 'Now, sir, we should take this boy to see some more peaceful paintings of the world.'

'How about Venice?' He smiled. 'There is a Canaletto exhibition in one of the smaller rooms.'

'Perfect.' She smiled.

The small room that led off from the main exhibition hall was covered with intricately painted canal scenes of Venice, all blue skies and translucent green water that reminded her of the ocean back home in Louisiana. There were magnificent pale sandstone buildings and red-tiled spired churches, and grey-domed cathedrals, but what drew her attention the most were the dark boats that crowded the canal water. Mostly small rowing boats and ferries and hooded dark gondolas, but larger sailing barges, too.

The room was quiet compared to the main exhibition hall. Only a single woman stood there, dark-haired, respectable, dressed in a pale-blue walking dress and cream spencer, her attention all on the painting before her, seemingly caught up in its scene.

Kit glanced at the lone figure and kept on walking. But then Kate felt the check in his step as he looked again at the woman.

Beneath her hand she felt his arm tense, felt everything about him still.

The woman only then seemed to sense that she was not alone. Glancing round, her eyes widened and fixed on Kit. She stared as if he were a ghost.

'Kit?' the woman whispered.

'It is good to see you, Emma,' he said quietly.

Emma.

'Oh, Kit!' The woman flew to him, wrapping him in her embrace, staring up into his face. 'Kit!' She wept and pressed her face against his chest, while he held her.

Tom stared in confusion. 'Who is that lady?' His hand crept into Kate's. He looked at Kit fiercely as if he were betraying them both.

'That lady is Captain North's sister.'

'Oh,' he said, and visibly relaxed. 'I suppose it's all right then if she hugs him.'

'I suppose it is,' said Kate with a smile.

'I never had a sister,' Tom said wistfully.

'Maybe you will one day,' said Kate, for she did not doubt that Tom truly had become something of a son to Kit. When she had gone home to Louisiana and Kit was with another woman. Just the thought made her want to weep.

'I would like that.' Tom smiled.

She nodded, not trusting herself to speak.

A tall, muscular, fair-haired man walked into the little Canaletto room. Kate knew by his fine-tailored, expensive clothes that he was a gentleman, but the scarred eyebrow above his sky-blue eyes and the air of danger about him suggested otherwise.

'Emma?' the man said.

'Oh, Ned, it is Kit! He has come home at last!'

But when Kit's eyes rose to see the man standing there everything changed.

'Ned Stratham?' he said in a soft dangerous voice.

Emma released her hold of him and moved to take the man's arm.

Kit's eyes were arctic as they went between his sister and the man.

'It is not what you think, Kit,' Emma said quickly. 'Ned is my husband. We have been married these six months past.'

'Your husband…?' Kit did not look at his sister, only at the man who stood by her side. The promise of violence was suddenly thick in that little room, along with danger and tension. Kate knew something was about to explode.

'Kit,' she called his name, trying to prevent it, but knowing enough of warring men to realise it was fruitless. She reacted instinctively, her outstretched arm shielding Tom, backing him against the wall, away from where the little group stood. 'Kit!'

'You bastard, Stratham!' he whispered.

Ned Stratham knew what was about to happen, too, for in one swift move he had placed his wife behind him. 'Get out, Emma,' he said in a harsh London accent unlike any of the others Kate had heard in the *ton*.

But Emma was shaking her head. 'No, Kit!'

'Me, Stratham, yes, but not my sister,' Kit growled. 'She was innocent of any wrong, damn you!' And he launched himself at Ned Stratham.

'No!' screamed Emma and tried to grab her husband back. 'Do not hurt him, Ned!'

Kate ran to Kit, putting herself between the two men, moulding herself to him as a barrier so that he could not reach Stratham. 'Look at me, Kit.' She took hold of his face, steering it to hers. 'Look at me,' she commanded, knowing she had to break the death lock in his eyes before he would hear her.

She could feel the raggedness of his breath as his chest rose and fell hard against her breasts, but she did not let an inch of space open up between them.

'Think what you are doing, Kit. Think of your sister's reputation. Think of Tom who is watching.' She lowered her voice to a whisper. 'Think of your vow…'

He took a breath and she knew she had got through to him. His eyes finally met hers.

'There are better ways to do this, Kit,' she said quietly.

His nostrils were still flared with the scent of violence, his eyes dark as the devil's. She could feel the tension that strained through every muscle of his body. But he nodded and swallowed. His gaze shifted to the crowd that was staring in fascinated horror from the doorway before moving to Stratham again.

'My wife is right,' he said stiffly.

Emma's face was powder white, her eyes dark and huge in her face. She looked shaken. Stratham stood slightly in front of her, everything of his stance protective towards her.

'You, too, are married?' his sister asked.

Kit gave a nod.

In name only. The words seemed to taunt Kate. She slid her hand into his and held on tight.

'Your wife *is* right,' Emma said. 'Please, both of you—' her eyes shifted to take in Tom '—and the boy. Come home with us to Cavendish Square so that all of this might be explained.'

Kate looked at Kit.

He gave a nod.

Kate took Tom's hand in hers. The other she placed in the crook of Kit's elbow and let him lead them out through the silent crowd.

They did not speak another word until they were in their town coach, following after that of Stratham and his sister's toward Cavendish Square.

'Who is he?' she asked.

Kit looked into her eyes. 'He is the man I played against that night in the gaming hell.'

Her blood ran cold and her heart went out to his.

'Oh, Kit,' she whispered and understood his reaction in the art exhibition. 'Maybe it is not as it seems.'

'Maybe,' he said, but he did not look convinced.

In a drawing room at the back of a massive mansion house in Cavendish Square the two couples sat facing each other on dark-red-and-gold-striped sofas. Tom was outside in the garden, playing in the sunshine with a puppy and a footman that both belonged to Ned Stratham and Kit's sister.

Four tea cups filled with tea sat untouched on the occasional table between them.

The servants had vanished out of sight.

'It is not what you think, Kit,' Emma said again. He saw where her hand rested upon Stratham's. 'I know who Ned is. I know what he did. And I know what you did, too.'

He closed his eyes at that and felt Kate's hand tighten around his.

'And I still love him, Kit. Just as I still love you.'

'Even knowing the truth of what I am?' he asked.

'What are you other than my brother?'

'A fool, a cheat, a coward,' he supplied.

'We've all been a little of those in our lives,' said Stratham.

He looked at Stratham.

'I own my share of the blame,' Stratham said. 'If I could go back and undo that night in Old Moll's, I would.'

'The blame was mine, Stratham, all of it. I went to look for you in Whitechapel earlier this week to tell you. I know they would have lynched me were it not for your intervention. But Emma is a different matter.'

'I know you will never believe it, Northcote, but I do love her. And if you were not her brother I'd break your damn neck for what you've put her through.'

'Ned,' Emma chastised softly.

'If you ever hurt her, I will be the one breaking necks.'

Stratham smiled. 'You've grown some balls, Northcote.'

The two men looked at one another with a grudging mutual respect.

Kate rubbed her fingers against Kit's, her gaze touching to his before saying to Ned Stratham, 'It looks like you have a delightful view of a wonderful garden. May I...?' She got to her feet, gesturing towards the further of the two windows in the room.

Stratham was already on his feet, understanding what it was she was doing.

Kit needed time and privacy to talk to his sister and discover what had happened in his absence. He needed to learn the details of his mother's death and his father's welfare and whereabouts.

'I would be delighted to show you the view, ma'am,'

said Stratham. Kate smiled at Kit and Emma, too, before she walked with him to the window at the far away end of the drawing room.

'A beautiful house and garden,' she said.

'Thank you.' said Stratham. 'A fine boy.' His eyes were on Tom running the length of the lawn with a glee that matched that of the small, brown, scruffy dog by his side.

'Yes.'

They could hear the soft murmur of voices and knew that Emma Stratham had moved to sit by her brother's side.

'Kit rescued him,' she said. 'As he rescued me.'

Stratham said nothing.

'Do not judge my husband so harshly. He has suffered in ways you could not begin to imagine.'

'And you think that Emma did not? You have no idea what he left them to. So do not seek my sympathy, for him I have none,' said Stratham and switched those cold too-blue eyes to hers.

'It is not sympathy I seek. Sympathy would kill him.'

'I am glad to hear it.'

She held his cold gaze fearlessly. 'You are the one who has no idea. My husband did something foolish, but he has paid a thousand times over. He is a good man. If you knew—' She stopped, aware she had probably said too much already.

'He has a loyal wife.'

A loyal wife. Stratham's words cut right through everything in that moment. It was not Kit North to whom she was loyal. Or the little boy who played so happily on the lawn outside that window. In a matter of days she was going to walk away from them both and sail to the other side of the world. Nor was she even really his wife. It was all feigned, all an illusion, a marriage in name only. She swallowed hard and forced the thoughts away.

'As Emma has a loyal husband.'

Stratham said nothing, but she saw the flicker of his eyes to where his wife sat weeping by Kit on the sofa, and the way they softened for the woman and hardened with threat at her brother. Kate's gaze moved to Kit, taking in the hard line of his jaw and the way those dark eyes stared straight ahead and her heart contracted hard as if it had been punched, and a band of iron seemed to tighten around her chest, for she knew that Emma was telling him of their mother and she knew, despite all that it appeared otherwise, inside he hurt much more than his sister. He blamed himself as the cause of it all.

Kit did not tell her what his sister had revealed of the family's life following his departure. And Kate could not ask, not while Tom was present.

But that evening he went to visit his father and she read stories to Tom and played cards with the child until his bedtime. Afterwards the hours stretched on without Kit's return and her concern grew all the more.

A single candle burned on her bedside cabinet. She waited by the rain-flecked window of her bedchamber and watched for his return, worrying until at last, when she had all but given up hope, she saw the familiar dark figure upon horseback come trotting down the rain-soaked road that shimmered in the light of the gas lamps.

She heard the outside door shutting, heard the quiet tread of his booted steps on the staircase. Tensing in anticipation, she stared round at that door, willing him to open it, but he did not so much as hesitate outside her bedchamber, only walked straight on past to reach his own. Her heart wilted. She turned aside, leaning on the window sill, staring down on to that same wet, dismal, dark street, telling herself not to be such a fool, that it was better this way for them both.

A single rasp of knuckles tapped against the door connecting their chambers and her pulse leapt at the sound of it.

The door opened softly and then closed again behind him.

She turned to face him.

His face was pale, his eyes black in the candlelight. The rain had soaked his hair, making it cling dark and sleek to his head. Raindrops sat wet on his face and across the black superfine of his coat, like a scattering of crystal beads. He just stood there and said nothing, but she could sense his devastation.

She came to stand before him. He had brought with him the scent of rain and dark night and their chill. She could feel it emanating from his damp clothes without even touching him.

'You waited up for me,' he said quietly.

She nodded.

From the pocket of his coat he took a piece of white paper folded in half. It was soft with dampness. Opening it out, he looked at it.

'He would take not one farthing of it, just as Emma refused it, too.'

She stepped closer and glanced down at the paper; it was a banker's cheque made out for thirty thousand pounds.

'All that you have earned since Johor,' she said softly.

'I thought if I could give them back the money I had lost, with interest, too, that it would go some way to repairing the damage...' He shook his head as if he had been a fool.

'My father said he did not want the money, but he no longer lives the life of a gentleman. He has a house in

Whitechapel. He owns and runs a dockyard, employs men and spends his days in an office there.'

'That is a worthwhile pursuit. To provide employment. To have purpose.'

'So he says.'

He looked at her. 'How they suffered, Kate. My mother was a lady, used to a life of ease and comfort. She died of consumption in Spitalfields, penniless, seeking employment as a pieceworker!'

His pain was a living, breathing, tangible thing. It caught in her chest, sharp and painful as a blade sliding between her ribs.

'My father, a gentleman from one of the oldest genteel families in England, worked as a labourer in a dockyard. My sister, who should have been dancing at Almack's and laughing with her friends, was a serving wench in a chophouse and is married to a tough from Whitechapel. Because of me. And nothing I can do will ever change that.' The wetness on his cheeks was not just raindrops. 'I broke their world apart and I cannot fix it, Kate.'

She closed the distance between them and slid her arms around his waist, looking into his face.

'You cannot,' she said, 'because they already fixed it for themselves, Kit.'

His eyes clung to hers.

'Your sister is married to a man whom she loves and who would lay down his life to protect her. Did you not see the way they look at one another? Everything about her radiates happiness. And he seemed to me to be a very wealthy man. Your father is pursuing a life of meaning and purpose. Was he sullen, resentful, resigned to a frugal life in Whitechapel?'

No.' Kit's gaze shifted to the distance, reliving the details of the night. 'He seemed…content.'

'They do not take the money, Kit, because they do not want it.'

His eyes moved back to hers.

'And as for your mother. Trust me when I tell you she would never have stopped loving you. I am a mother, Kit, I know. And I know, too, that she would have forgiven you. As your father and sister do. As you must forgive yourself.'

'I did not come back for forgiveness.'

'I know. You came back to face them all, to face what you did, to acknowledge your mistakes and make recourse. And you have done that.'

'And it changes nothing, Kate. There is no closure. I swore I would never be Kit Northcote again. But I am. I changed my name, but I cannot escape him. I never will.'

She took him in her arms and he wept, this strong implacable man who had endured the worst of tortures, who had risked his life time and again to save hers and others. This man who was the most integral, honest man she had ever known. She held him and kissed the tears from his face and looked into his eyes.

'Kit Northcote and Kit North are the same man, Kit. They always have been. They always will be.'

She peeled off his wet clothes and her own, until they stood there naked and exposed.

'And I love him, perfectly imperfect, just as he is,' she said, and led him to her bed.

'Kate…' But she touched her fingers to his lips to silence him. Even now, when he was bleeding and hurt, all his hopes shattered, all his defences ripped aside to expose him, naked and vulnerable, he was putting her needs before his own.

'Don't,' she said. 'Just a physical need,' she whispered the excuse for both of them.

'Just a physical need,' he echoed, complicit in the lie.

Gently she pushed him back against her pillow and straddled his body, covering him with her warmth. She kissed his eyelids and his nose. She kissed his lips and his throat, and every single one of the scars that marked his body. And then she took his long hard length into her, merging their bodies as one.

Looking into his eyes, she rode him, soft and slow at first, building harder and faster, taking him in deeper. Because she needed him and he needed her. And this act of passion and love was the only thing that could drive away the ghosts and the guilt and make them forget the ache in their hearts…for this night at least.

Chapter Fifteen

Kit watched as Kate smiled her easy confident smile, and chatted and joked with Tom at the breakfast table the next morning as if nothing were wrong. But it was a play-act. She could barely meet his eyes across the table for all she was pretending otherwise. Echoes and shadows of their intense lovemaking throughout the night hung heavy and long between them. The very air vibrated with the knowledge of what they had done and its far-reaching consequences. But she was pretending for the boy's sake, feigning a happiness and normality she did not feel. Her tension was as tangible as his own, at least to him. He was no longer fooled by that smile.

When Tom finally left for his riding lesson Kit half-expected Kate to make her excuses and rush out after him, not wanting to be alone with the man who was now her husband in truth. But she just sat there, her focus all on the white tablecloth, her face pale from lack of sleep, the smile and all other pretences fallen away now that the boy was no longer with them. Kit waved the servants away, telling them to close the door behind them. Even then she could not look at him.

The small clock on the mantelpiece ticked its fast steady

rhythm. Outside the heavy wheels of a delivery cart rumbled past, with the clatter of horses' hooves. The sky was a cloudless summer blue. Clear white shafts of sunlight spilled through the window, highlighting the golden streaks within the soft brown of her hair.

'Last night…' she said. Her voice was quiet, sober, gutted. Her eyes shifted from the tablecloth to her unused cutlery. 'It was just a physical coupling…just a physical need…for us both.' Reiterating the lie she was telling herself. She ran a nervous finger along the blade of the knife, rocking it so that it flashed silver and glinted like the blade of the knife she had worn strapped to her thighs, like his cutlass, like the glitter of the ocean before the bow of a ship. 'It changes nothing.' She closed her eyes, momentarily, as if she were gathering strength. And when she opened them she swallowed and said the words again, stronger this time as if that would convince herself. 'It changes nothing.'

Her eyes finally rose to meet his so that he could see all of her guilt and confusion and split allegiance. 'You understand what I am saying, don't you?' Her brow was creased with worry, her eyes shadowed with the conflict that raged within.

'I understand, Kate,' he said softly. 'A vow is a vow.'

'Yes.' She swallowed. He could see her every breath, see the dip of her eyelashes, the way her teeth bit at her lip so hard as to make it turn white. She dropped her gaze to the table once more.

Somewhere in the distance a door slammed shut.

'You loved Wendell. And Wendell loved you.'

She nodded, but did not look at him again.

'He loved and protected you. And he wanted you and your children to be happy and healthy and safe.'

'Yes.' The word was a broken whisper.

He could walk across that room and pull her up into his arms and kiss her. He could scoop her up into his arms and take her to his bed and love all the pain away from her. He could raid her heart and claim it as his own. But that would be to use force and desire against her and it would not solve her conflict. For the resolution her soul required, she needed time. Time to make the choice herself. Time to say her farewell. Except that time was running out.

'Gunner has written to say that his business has concluded early. He will be here the day after tomorrow.' He lifted the opened letter that lay on the table before him and, rising from his chair, walked the length of the long dining table and sat the letter down before her.

She glanced up into his eyes, the look in her own shaken and haunted.

'We have accepted an invitation to Arlesfords' ball this evening, but I can send our apologies.'

'No.' She swallowed, and turned her face away. 'We must arouse no suspicions in the Admiralty's watchers, not so close to my departure.'

'As you wish.' His face felt grim, his jaw tight. His gaze lingered on her face for a moment of silence, but she would not look at him.

Three days to go, if he included this one. Was it long enough? And if not, was he really just going to let her sail out of his life as surely as she had sailed into his heart?

A curt bow of his head, then he turned and walked away.

The ballroom in the Duke of Arlesford's town house was packed to the gunnels. The French windows at the rear of the room were open, allowing the sweet dark night air to seep in and the edges of the crowd to spill out on to the stone terrace and beyond, and for the more illicit, down the stone steps into the hidden secret recesses of the garden. But the open windows and stir of the gauze curtains did little to relieve the heat and press of London's *ton* at the fashionable event.

Kate felt a bead of sweat trickle down between her breasts. She fanned herself with the black-feathered fan and was glad there was so little material in the black evening dress. The bright glow of a thousand candles set in the huge crystal-tiered chandelier above their heads brought a glitter to the beads encrusted on her low-cut bodice and a shimmer to the swell of pale décolletage exposed above its tight support.

She held her head high, met all the nosy disapproving stares with confidence and pride and amusement that belied the conflict that churned within. Standing united with her man. Her and Kit against them all, knowing the truth of what was between them, knowing that in two days she was going to have to walk away from him, just like everyone else here was doing. And the knowledge was killing her inside. She wondered how long she could keep the smile on her face.

They were feigning the truth. Neither of them able to say the words, just standing there together.

The music started for the very last dance of the evening—a waltz. She felt his fingers brush against hers and her whole body tingled and sparked from that one tiny touch and in her heart she ached all the more for him.

'We should dance.' His voice was low, his breath warm and caressing against her bare shoulder.

She did not trust herself to speak, just nodded and let him lead her out on to the dance floor. He pulled her indecently close and, unmindful of the crowd and the eyes that watched with such censure, they looked deep into one another's eyes and let their bodies move together to the music, savouring this last closeness, this last public play-act of all that was real. And she clung to it, as she clung to him, wanting these last moments to last for ever. But too soon they ended.

They stood there on that floor, their eyes locked together, even when the music had finished. Until the scandalised murmur of voices grew louder and one of the musicians cleared his throat with meaning. And they could no longer defer the end of the dance, the end of the evening, the end of Captain and Mrs North.

He led her from the dance floor, would have led them from the room, but Devlin stepped out of the crowd to block their way.

The viscount's eyes glittered from having imbibed too freely in drink. His cheeks were faintly flushed. The other three tall, dark-haired gentlemen who had been Kit's friends, looking even more foxed, flanked him.

'Leaving so soon, Captain North, or should I say young Northcote?' Devlin loomed over Kit.

'You are drunk, Devlin. And, yes, we are leaving. So step aside and let us pass.'

'You really have no shame, do you? Coming back here, with your Yankee wife and your west-country bastard. Would the tavern wench who spawned him or your darling wife have opened their legs so readily if they knew the truth of—?'

Kit reacted in an instant. Before Kate realised what was happening he grabbed Devlin by the lapels of his coat and rammed him against the wall. Kit's face was hard and focused and an inch away from the viscount's.

'You can slight me and insult me, and call me every name in the book, Devlin. You all can, for God knows I deserve it. But my wife is another matter. You will apologise to her, right here, right now, or I will—'

'Leave it, Kit!' Kate pulled at his arm. 'It does not matter. Let us just go home.'

But he never shifted that steely gaze from Devlin's. 'Oh, it matters,' he said softly. 'And Devlin will beg your forgiveness.'

'Never,' said Devlin. 'What are you going to do about it, Northcote? Run away?'

A silence was spreading over the ballroom as people began to realise what was happening and turned their eyes to the spectacle.

Kate watched the cold dispassionate focus sharpen in Kit's face and felt a tremor of fear ripple through her.

He released his grip on Devlin, smoothing down the creases he had made in the front of Devlin's tailcoat. Stepping back, he half turned, smoothing a hand through his hair, composing himself.

Devlin was still sneering as Kit's fist hit him hard, first on one cheek and then the other.

'Were I wearing gloves I would have peeled them off and slapped you across the face, but you get the idea...' said Kit, never breaking his focus from Devlin's. 'I call you out, Devlin. Name your weapon.'

Devlin wiped the blood away that trickled from the corner of his mouth. He smiled, but it was a cold smile and his eyes were narrow and filled with a chill that matched Kit's. 'Let us finish what you started, *boy*. I choose fists.'

There were gasps and whispers. She heard someone say in a stage whisper, 'Devlin is a champion pugilist. Northcote does not stand a chance.'

Devlin heard it, too, and he smiled as he glanced at the man by his side, 'Bullford will act as my second.'

'Of course I will, old man,' Bullford mumbled.

'But is there any who will act as yours, Northcote?'

The silence was resounding.

Kate made to step forward, but a dark-haired, pale-skinned man beat her to it. He was smartly dressed in the same austere dark tailcoat as the rest of the men there, the same white shirt and waistcoat, the same neatly tied white cravat. But on his finger was a ring in the shape of a silver wolf's head, and from it glinted a pair of emerald eyes as green as his own.

'I will be Northcote's second.'

Kit's eyes slid to the man's. 'Hunter.' He gave a small nod of acknowledgement to the man.

Kit glanced at Devlin one more time, before offering Kate his arm.

She placed her hand upon its crook.

A path opened up through the crowd before them.

Together they walked that gauntlet, out and along the road lined with stationary carriages until they found their own.

Only once they were safe inside, the door closed and the wheels rumbling along the roads that would take them back to the house in Grosvenor Street did she speak.

'Do not do this, Kit, please,' she pleaded, reaching her hands to his.

'You think I will just let him insult you?'

'It means nothing.'

'Your honour means everything.' He would fight all of London to defend it. To the death. He hoped she understood why.

She raised his knuckles to her lips and kissed them. 'We could go away...' She looked into his eyes.

'Run away together?' he said softly and, raising her left hand to his lips, pressed a kiss to the centre of her palm. 'Only for you am I tempted. And only for you do I refuse.'

She looked at him and the tears leaked from her eyes. But she made no more pleas. She understood, at last.

He moved across the carriage to sit by her side and wrapped an arm around her.

There was only silence and their entwined hands for the rest of the journey.

There was no time to talk to Kit. No time to tell him that she loved him and knew what he was doing for her, for them both. No time to share the comfort of their bodies one last time. They had only just arrived back in the house in Grosvenor Street when Hunter's carriage drew up outside.

The butler showed him into the drawing room where she stood by Kit's side.

'Tomorrow at dawn by the burnt oak on Hounslow Heath,' Hunter said.

Kit gave a nod. 'Thank you, Hunter,' and from the way the two men looked at one another she knew that Hunter had been there that night in Whitechapel.

Hunter inclined his head in acknowledgement and then slid a narrow green gaze at her.

'You may speak freely in front of my wife. We have no secrets.'

There was a small silence before Hunter gave a nod. 'You know that Devlin is an ardent supporter of John Jackson's Academy of Pugilism in Bond Street. He is barely out of the place these days.'

'So I hear,' said Kit with a smile.

'He is angry with you, but he also blames himself for what happened that night. We all do, but Devlin more so.'

'The blame was all mine,' said Kit.

'Largely, but not all.'

'All,' said Kit firmly.

Hunter smiled.

'Will you take a drink?'

'Thank you.'

She saw Hunter raise an eyebrow when Kit poured his guest a brandy but himself a lemonade, but he said nothing.

'Kate?' Kit looked at her and she felt her heart warm that he did not just dismiss her but would have included her in this.

She shook her head with a smile, knowing that the two men had the past to talk over and understand and resolve, and that it would be done a deal easier without her presence. 'I will leave you two gentlemen to your discussions.'

She stood by the window of that bedchamber, as she had done so many times before, looking out into a darkness that mirrored all that was closing around her.

Kit's words of earlier that day seemed to whisper in her ear. *Wendell loved you...he wanted you and your children to be happy and healthy and safe.*

Wendell. She looked down at his ring on her finger, as worn and faded as his image in her memory. A vow was a vow. To stay true to him always. There was so much love in her heart for him and for Kit. How could so much love hurt so badly? She knew that she was breaking Kit's heart as surely as she was breaking her own.

'Oh, Wendell.' She whispered his name in the darkness and closed her eyes as the tears spilled to roll down her cheeks. 'What am I to do?'

In the chill of the night darkness she felt a warmth envelop her and a feeling of peace and reassurance descend upon her. And in that darkness she thought she caught the fleeting scent of Wendell, so strong and real that she opened her eyes without a single doubt that he would be standing before her.

But the room was empty and the scent was gone.

'Wendell?' she whispered his name and, closing her eyes, tried to sense his presence as she had done so often in the early days of losing him. But there was nothing left any more. He was gone. And she was alone.

She looked up at the star-scattered sky, like diamond angels in the deep dark blue of the heavens, and as she watched one of the stars shot across the sky to disappear elsewhere.

And she understood in that moment. She knew she had her answer.

Wendell loved you...he wanted you and your children to be happy and healthy and safe.

She had stayed true to him. She always would. By being happy, by living, by loving.

Kit was right, it was what Wendell would have wanted, for her and their children.

Wendell had stayed by her side long enough to weather the grief and deliver her the right man. The vow had stopped her being forced into marriage. It had made her test Kit and herself, in every way that was possible. And it had proved that their love was real and true.

She eased the worn gold band from her finger and placed a tender kiss upon it before stowing it safely in her sea chest. Then she took Kit's ring from her pocket and slipped it on to her finger.

She stripped off her black dress of mourning and donned the white nightdress.

The connecting door between their bedchambers was not locked. She closed it quietly behind her and climbed beneath the covers of her husband's bed to wait for him in the darkness.

There were things she had to tell him before he left to face Devlin. Important things, before Gunner came the day after tomorrow.

Kate opened her eyes and realised that she had must have fallen asleep for a few minutes. But the blackness of the night was beginning to fade. Across the room the window showed that the inky hue of the sky had lightened to a deep blue. In the far corner of the heavens the first hint of day bleached it lighter still. A chill ran over her scalp. Her heart gave a stutter.

She glanced at the other side of the bed where Kit should be and saw the smooth undisturbed sheets. Her heart raced off at a hard frenzied gallop. The bedcovers were thrown aside and she was off running down the stairs, barefoot, her hair and white nightdress flowing long behind her.

'Kit!' she shouted his name. 'Kit!' so loud that it echoed all the way down the stairs and around the hallway. But the drawing room was empty just as she had known it would be. Two empty glasses sat there, one still containing some lemonade, the other drained of brandy.

Her heart was hammering so hard she felt sick.

She glanced up to find Matthews, the butler, standing there. 'Where is he?' she demanded.

'Captain North and Mr Hunter left some fifteen minutes ago on horseback.'

'Have the carriage made ready immediately.'

'Yes, madam.'

Even if she left right now, just as she was, she would not catch him. By the time she got there he would already be bare-knuckle fighting with Devlin. For her and her honour. Fighting for a woman who had refused him as her husband, who he believed was going to sail away and leave him.

She had seen the look in Devlin's eyes when he looked at Kit. And she knew that he was a man trained in using his fists. Her blood ran cold with fear for her husband, for all that she had not told him, for all that he still believed.

She stared at the two glasses, so like another two glasses aboard a ship on a night that now seemed a lifetime ago.

And then she smiled and went upstairs to ready herself for the journey to Hounslow Heath.

Dawn was only just creeping across the sky above the burnt oak on Hounslow Heath, but Devlin was already waiting there, along with half the crowd from Arlesford's ballroom.

Kit smiled grimly to himself at the sight of all those expectant faces. They were about to see a whole lot more than they had bargained for.

No matter who Devlin was, no matter what Kit had done, no matter humiliation and shame, and dishonour that could never be undone, there was one thing he knew with absolute certainty—he was not getting out of that ring, he was not going to stop fighting, he was never going to walk away until Devlin had withdrawn his insult to Kate. He had no honour left to fight for. But for her honour he would give his life.

With Hunter by his side he walked right up to Devlin and Bullford until he stood close enough that none of the crowd could hear the words exchanged.

'You are not alone, Hunter? My, my, I thought young Northcote here would have been halfway across England by now,' sneered Devlin.

'Enough,' snapped Hunter. 'You insulted his wife, damn it!'

'And he insulted every damn one of us!'

'This is not about that.'

'Is it not?' said Devlin softly, then spoke to Kit. 'You have had this coming to you for over three years, Northcote.'

'I have,' Kit said. 'But you will apologise to Kate or I will punch the life out of you until you do.'

Devlin laughed. 'You think because you have built yourself a few muscles you are a match for me?'

'No. I am a match for you because Kate is my wife and I am not going to walk away until you apologise to her.'

Devlin did not laugh at that. His old friend just looked at him as if he did not believe the words. But he would believe them soon enough.

'Ready yourself, gentlemen.' Gentleman Jackson, the man who had built his wealth and position out of bare-knuckle fighting and was the acclaimed authority on it, came to stand between them.

Devlin walked to one corner of the makeshift ring, Kit to the opposite.

Devlin removed his hat and gloves and passed them to Fallingham, before Bullford helped him to remove his coat and the subsequent layers beneath.

Kit, like Devlin and most of the others present, was still wearing last night's clothes. He began to strip off his guise as a gentleman—the black tailcoat, the white waistcoat, the white neckcloth, passing each item to Hunter. Without pausing he pulled his shirt off over his head.

The gasps sounded all around. Fingers pointed. A woman screamed. Another fainted. Voices whispered.

Kit ignored it all and walked into the ring to face Devlin.

Devlin's gaze dropped lower, wandering over the scars that marred Kit's body. Dawn was here in truth, leaving nothing of the night to obscure them.

'Apologise,' said Kit grimly.

Devlin just looked at him. 'Make me.'

Kit put his fists up and went for him.

Kate squeezed her way through the crowd that seemed out of place here in the remote spot on a wind-blown heath at the break of day. They did not step aside for her; they barely noticed her. All their attention was riveted ahead with a macabre fascination and excitement that disgusted her. She could hear the sickening punches—the thuds and crunches and grunts that made her stomach drop and quiver with dread. Part of her knew that the backs of too many tall, dark-coated gentlemen and black-caped ladies that blocked her view were a mercy, but she had to get to the front.

'Excuse me.' She pushed her way through until she caught sight of the men in a fighting ring. And the sight stopped her dead.

They were both stripped to the waist and knocking hell out of each other. Despite the chill in the air their bodies glistened with sweat and with smears of blood, neither fluid obscuring Kit's tattoo of scars with the fresh one on his shoulder, a warrior pattern more magical and meaningful than any ink could ever be, exposing him for what he was—strong, fearless, honourable. His expression was all cold, relaxed, relentless focus, just as it had been that first day on *Raven*. North and Northcote, one and the same. Tragedy and suffering had burnished away the weakness and the boy to leave only the strength and the man.

The blows were relentless and delivered with a violence that shocked even her, who had been a pirate captain. Grinding a man down with fists was so much closer and more personal than a bullet or a blade. It took something extra to use yourself as the weapon to deliver the punishment.

Devlin was taller with a longer reach and he had the finesse of training, but finesse and training and height counted for nothing against full-hearted, rock-solid determination. Kit did not even attempt to avoid Devlin's fists. It looked as though he stepped right up to them, into them, almost as if Devlin was not punching him, as if he were not a man but a training sandbag that felt nothing, was nothing, but an automaton coming in close to deliver deadly punch after punch to Devlin's body.

Devlin's right fist landed again hard against Kit's mouth, the splatter of blood from it spraying those who were ahead of her in the crowd, making some of the women shriek with a terror and delight that repulsed Kate. Devlin followed fast with a left hook that drove her husband down on to his knees before walking to his own corner of the ring as if he had won.

But Kit got back on his feet and wiped the blood from his eyes. 'Apologise,' he said to Devlin.

Devlin glanced behind him and saw Kit standing there.

A strange expression crossed the viscount's face. He looked at Kit for a moment longer, holding his gaze as if really seeing him for the first time. Then he gave a nod of acknowledgement and came again at him with his fists.

Devlin held nothing back. But Kit was relentless, soaking up punch after punch as if they were nothing, and driving his own fists hard against Devlin's body and face as if his arms would never tire.

Devlin knocked him down again.

Kit got back up. Came back at Devlin, swinging his left hook up into the viscount's nose. Punching and being punched.

The blood was everywhere.

Bone-crunching thuds—each one Devlin landed on Kit's body was as if it had struck Kate's heart. It was intolerable, unbearable. But still it went on.

She pushed her way through the remaining bodies to get to the front. Wanting to be there for him. Needing to support him. But Kit's focus was complete, honed, sharp upon Devlin.

'Apologise,' he demanded, his breaths ragged as Devlin's. And the fight continued.

* * *

Devlin leaned against him as much as Kit leaned on Devlin. The two of them supporting one another in that fist-against-ribs hold, like two dogs with jaws locked together.

Their gazes fused, neither backing down.

But something was different in the way that Devlin was looking at him.

'North, after all,' said Devlin with grudging respect.

Kit smiled. 'Northcote,' he said.

Gentleman Jackson pulled them apart, warning them to keep the punches clear.

Devlin got his fists up.

Kit went in again until this time it was Devlin down on his knees.

Kit walked up to the man who had been his friend and, reaching down to him, helped him up.

The two men looked at one another in silence, before Devlin gave a nod and Kit hit him again, the effort almost costing him his balance.

Devlin staggered.

The two of them were still on their feet, just, but bent over, panting with exhaustion, leaning their hands on their knees, their eyes still fixed on the other.

'I was wrong about you,' said Devlin.

Kit said nothing. Just waited for Devlin to recover enough to hit him again.

Devlin stood upright.

Kit stepped forward, fists at the ready.

But Devlin raised a hand to stop him, his eyes holding Kit's as he spoke the words loud and clear between his ragged breaths. 'I take back my words of last night and apologise for any insult dealt.'

'It is not me you have to apologise to, Devlin,' he said

and let himself look at Kate for the first time since her arrival on the heath.

She was standing at the edge of the ring. There was blood in his eyes but nothing would have obscured her. For she stood there in that crowd of dark coats and capes in a dress of bright yellow silk, a ray of Caribbean sunshine in the gloom of a London day. The dress he had bought for her from the Antiguan dressmaker. The dress that was nothing of mourning and all of celebration.

Devlin staggered over to stand before her. He bowed. 'Mrs North.'

'Mrs Northcote,' she corrected him, saying Kit's name with pride.

Devlin gave a nod. 'Mrs Northcote,' he said. 'I most humbly beg your forgiveness, madam.'

'I accept your apology, Lord Devlin.'

Devlin bowed again and came back to Kit, offering a handshake.

Kit accepted.

Devlin gave him a gruff clasp. 'Welcome back, Kit, in truth.'

Kit gave a nod.

Bullford hurried in and, putting a shoulder beneath Devlin's armpit, helped him away.

'A moment, please,' said Kit quietly to Hunter who stood ready by his side to offer the same service.

And then he walked to stand before his wife.

Their eyes held and hers were wet with love and pride and tenderness.

He let his gaze move down over the bright yellow dress, where the wind moulded it to her body, before coming back up to her eyes once more.

She reached out her left hand and he accepted it, taking her slender fingers in his swollen-knuckled, bloodstained ones, touching the wedding band there as she had done so many times. His eyes caressed the thick, heavy, new band and how it gleamed upon her skin. And he smiled as he raised his eyes to hers again.

She was smiling, too. 'You should get dressed, Mr Northcote,' she said. 'At least until we get home.'

He laughed and, relinquishing her hand with some reluctance, turned away to where Hunter was waiting, to do as his wife bid.

In the privacy of Kit's bedchamber, Kate stripped off her husband's clothes and washed away the blood and bathed the cuts and the discoloured bruises that were already beginning to show.

'Kit Northcote...' she whispered as she gently held a cold damp cloth against the swelling of a cut on his eyebrow, her eyes holding his.

'Kate Northcote.' He took the cloth from her and set it aside, pulling her gently into his arms.

Neither of them offered another word of explanation. They did not need to.

He just kissed her and undressed her so that they stood naked and exposed in the full glare of the daylight, not a single barrier remaining between them.

She reached out and, taking hold of his bruised hand within hers, placed it over her naked breast. 'My heart is all yours...if you want it.'

He smiled and slid his hand up in a gentle caress to capture her to him.

'I want it,' he murmured and kissed her again. 'You have no idea how I want it.' And then he lifted her up and laid her down gently on top of his bed, and there, in the bright sunlight of the London morning, he loved her, filling her body with his, taking them both to a place of sweet union, looking into each other's eyes as she softly cried out his name, as he spilled his seed within her, as their souls became joined in truth.

Afterwards, as they lay in each other's arms, skin to skin, he took her hand in his, looking at his ring upon it again in wonder and happiness.

'It was time to let him go,' she said softly.

He nodded, his eyes holding hers.

'I think he would have liked you, Kit Northcote—pirate hunter, Englishman and all.'

'I think I would have liked him, pirate, American and all.'

She smiled. 'My heart was hurting with loss, now it is full of love for you.'

He kissed her with such love and tenderness. 'You do know that I am never going to let you go.'

The tears prickled in her eyes. 'Gunner is coming tomorrow and we both know I cannot stay here. My children…my home…the war between our countries…' She stared into his eyes. 'What are we going to do, Kit?'

He smiled and kissed her fingers. 'There is nothing here in London for me anymore, Kate. I have done what I came back to do. I am stripped bare of armour and pretence. I am Kit Northcote and everything I am, flawed and damaged as it is, I offer to you. To be your husband and father to your children and Tom, and any others that come along. To be yours wholly and in all ways, for ever, and live out our lives in Louisiana…if you will have me.'

The tears were spilling from her eyes in earnest now, for this man whom she loved so much. 'But an Englishman in Louisiana at this time of war…it would not be easy for you.'

'Nothing worthwhile ever is,' he said with a smile. 'So, will you have me, Kate Northcote?' he asked softly.

'I will have you a thousand times over.' She kissed him with all the love that was in her heart.

'I had better tell Gunner he is not needed, after all, unless he wants a one-way trip with us on *Raven*.'

She smiled and so did he.

And then they made love all over again, merging their bodies and their hearts, merging their souls and their futures. Knowing the preciousness of life and love, and that whatever challenges lay ahead they would face them together. Pirate and pirate hunter, American and English, a union forged in steel and blood and a love that surpassed all.

* * * * *

MILLS & BOON®

Why shop at millsandboon.co.uk?

Each year, thousands of romance readers find their perfect read at millsandboon.co.uk. That's because we're passionate about bringing you the very best romantic fiction. Here are some of the advantages of shopping at www.millsandboon.co.uk:

* **Get new books first**—you'll be able to buy your favourite books one month before they hit the shops

* **Get exclusive discounts**—you'll also be able to buy our specially created monthly collections, with up to 50% off the RRP

* **Find your favourite authors**—latest news, interviews and new releases for all your favourite authors and series on our website, plus ideas for what to try next

* **Join in**—once you've bought your favourite books, don't forget to register with us to rate, review and join in the discussions

Visit **www.millsandboon.co.uk**
for all this and more today!